Other books by Thomas Williams:

Seas of Courage
America's First Flag Officer
Dependency, Denial of Realty
Chronicles of a Traveling Aficionado
Assassin, Denial of Reality II

William Philip
Bainbridge

The American Spirit

Historical fiction

By: **Thomas Williams**

authorHOUSE®

AuthorHouse™
1663 Liberty Drive
Bloomington, IN 47403
www.authorhouse.com
Phone: 1-800-839-8640

First published by AuthorHouse   10/05/2010

ISBN: 978-1-4490-9564-2 (sc)
ISBN: 978-1-4520-7267-8 (e)

Printed in the United States of America

This book is printed on acid-free paper.

To my love:
My wonderful wife, Toss

Contents

Commodore William Phillip
Bainbridge
by: Thomas Williams

Battle

"The chiefs who our freedom
Sustained on the land.
Fame's far-spreading voice
Has eternized in story;
By the roar of our cannon now called to the strand,
She beholds on the ocean
Their rivals in glory.
Her sons there she owns,
And her clarion bold tones
Tell of Hull and Decatur, of Bainbridge and Jones;
For the tars of Columbia are lords of the wave,
And have sworn that old
Ocean's their throne or their grave."

PROLOGUE

PIRACY
1801

The Barbary corsairs were silently shimming across the moderate seas in their galley towards their target. The thirty large oars were being powered by sixty oarsmen pulling with all their might, slowly shrinking the distance between them and the merchant frigate in front of them. The merchant ship they were chasing was not as big as an East Indiaman but it had twenty cannons mounted so it was a force to deal with. The pirates wanted the men for ransom, and the cargo for survival and trade. The ship would be an important addition to their pirate fleet for gaining more dominance on the seas.

The lateen sail on the galley was stowed and only a few of the one hundred and twenty pirates were visible on the upper deck.

There was no moon light to illuminate them, as the galley quietly approached the three masted merchant vessel sailing in the Malacca Straits on the east side of the Indian Ocean. They were in the five hundred-mile passage that is the commercial umbilical connecting Europe, the Middle East, and the Indian subcontinent to Asia and the Pacific.

The only piece of clothing each man wore was a black loin cloth hanging on their dark bodies making them nearly invisible to anyone casually looking down at the water. The galley closed in on the stern of the merchant vessel. They had lines ready to attach to the stern as well as climbing ropes to access the upper deck. Each man executed his assigned responsibility with flawless precision. They knew exactly where to attach their boat to the merchant vessel for storming the ship.

With a smooth demonstration of agility the men tossed ropes with grapple hooks to the top deck and ascended up the stern of the ship to the poop-deck and spar-deck in a matter of seconds. Those on the deck heard the clanking of the grapple hooks hit but their reaction time was too slow from preventing the invaders reaching the upper deck and dispatching them.

The pirates were each armed with a simple straight sword with 28 inch blades and iron grips. The swords were mainly a thrusting weapon and were used in dueling and general fighting but they made a wonderful weapon for the pirates. Most of the invading pirates were also carrying daggers to use in cramped quarters.

The pirates had observed on approaching the vessel that on the upper decks there were men on the rail apparently as look outs. What they didn't realize the men they were looking at were mostly dummies. The Captain had ordered ten dummies be made up and lashed to the rail. The dummies were dressed like Marines. The dummies were nothing but straw filled uniforms with head covers to make faces. Up close the dummies were obvious fakes but from a distance in the dark it was impossible to tell they were not real.

Some of the men on watch were busy with repairing lines, cleaning and painting rust areas, polishing the cannons, and doing general repairs that could be done without much noise.

The six dozen men had climbed to the poop deck and divided into prearrange groups. Two Marines on watch duty were quickly dispatched. Their timing had been calculated to arrive during the middle watch when the Idlers and Larboard watch crew would be asleep. The starboard watch crew would be the only ones on the main deck. The middle watch started at midnight and lasted for four hours giving the pirates a large window of time to capture the vessel.

Four men were assigned to dispatch the midshipman at the wheel. Midshipman, William Taylor, was on duty and did not hear the intruders until they had overtaken him. Three men went into the captain's quarters and rousted him from bed, tied his hands and feet.

"What the hell... who are you? Take your hands off of me."

"*Non aver di te paura.*"("I am not afraid of you.")

"Take him out on the quarter deck and string up to a post. I want all the crew to be able to see him," the apparent leader of the pirates ordered.

"Hay, these guys on the rail are not real, look at this," as the pirate wacked off the head of one of the dummies.

The pirates were not bent on injuring any of the men because the captured men would be held for ransom and some of the lower ranking sailors sold off into slavery.

The pirates exercise their plunder rights by gathering all the belongings of the officers and crew.

The topmen and sailors on middle watch duty were not prepared for a fight; they did not have their weapons with them. The invaders rounded the ship's crew up and placed them under guard. Two of the sailors attempted to fend off their invaders but they were over powered and knocked to the deck.

The invaders had brought with them smoke bombs that produced a voluminous amount of smoke. The smoke bombs were dispersed through all the hatchways off the main deck. They knew that many men would die from smoke inhalation but most of the men would seek fresh air and scramble up the hatches. The crew was easily subdued as they surfaced from down below; all wondering what the hell was going on.

The invaders had the captain out on the quarter deck, tied to a post, with a knife at his throat. The crew was herded into a tight group on the forecastle. The invaders took over the sails and the duties of controlling the ship. They had turned the vessel around, taking the prize to their home port. They would use the ship in the future to capture even larger vessels unless they would be offered a large amount of money for it. The pirates preferred small, fast vessels such as sloops with shallow drafts that could operate in shallow waters.

The leader of the invasion raised his arms quieting the men down so he could address them.

"We do not wish to harm you but if you resist our commands you will be killed. We are taking your ship and you are our prisoners."

"Where are we and where are we going?"

"*Ala saber donde estar tu.*"

Book One

Commodore William Phillip Bainbridge
May 7, 1774 - July 27, 1833

TWO

Jumping ahead to the future:
1793
SOUTHWAKK, Jan. 6, 1793.
ROBERT MORRIS, ESQ.:

Sir, from the present appearance of affairs I believe it is time this country was possessed of a navy; but as that is yet to be raised, I have ventured a few remarks on the subject.

Ships that compose the European navy's are generally distinguished by their rates; but as the situation and depth of water of our coasts and harbors are different in some degrees from those in Europe, and as our navy for a considerable time will be inferior in numbers, we are to consider what size ships will be most formidable, and be an overmatch for those of an enemy; such frigates as in blowing weather would be an overmatch for double-deck ships, and in light winds to evade coming to action ; or double-deck ships that would be an overmatch for common double-deck ships, and in blowing weather superior to ships of three decks, or in calm weather or light winds to out sail them. Ships built on these principles will render those of an enemy in a degree useless, or require a greater number before they dare attack our ships. Frigates,

I suppose, will be the first object, and none ought to be built less than 150 feet keel, to carry twenty-eight 32-pounders or thirty 24-pounders on the gun deck, and 12-pounders on the quarter-deck.

These ships should have scantlings equal to 74 s, and I believe may be built of red cedar and live oak for about twenty-four pounds per ton, carpenters tonnage, including carpenters , smiths bill, including anchors, joiners, block makers, mast makers, riggers and rigging, sail makers and sail cloths, suits and chandlers bill.

As such ships will cost a large sum of money; they should be built of the best materials that could possibly be procured. The beams for their decks should be of the best Carolina pine, and the lower futtocks and knees, if possible, of live oak.

The greatest care should be taken in the construction of such ships, and particularly all her timbers should be framed and bolted together before they are raised.

Frigates built to carry 12 and 18-pounders, in my opinion, will not answer the expectation contemplated from them ; for if we should be obliged to take a part in the present European war, or at a future day we should be dragged into a war with any powers of the Old Continent, especially Great Britain, they having such a number of ships of that size, that it would be an equal chance by equal combat that we lose our ships, and more particularly from the Algerians, who have ships, and some of much greater force. Several questions will arise, whether one large or two small frigates contribute most to the protection of our trade, or which will cost the least sum of money, or whether two small ones are as able to engage a double-deck ship as one large one. For my part I am decidedly of opinion the large ones will answer best.

(Signed) JOSHUA HUMPHREYS.

THREE

William Phillip Bainbridge
1774

Absalom Bainbridge, a Tory physician, assisted in the delivery of their fourth child, William Phillip Bainbridge on May 7, 1774.

Mary had difficulty with the delivery but with her husband's gentle hand and skills as a physician assured her that she was fine. She did not have any unusual bleeding; her breathing and pulse were normal. Mary was in a semi reclined position near the edge of a cloth covered bed with her left foot on a step stool and her night gown pulled up over her naval. Absalom assistant was behind Mary supporting her while another assistant prepared water to soak clean fabric in. The baby cleared the birthing channel and Absalom was as gentle as possible so Mary would not suffer any more then she had too with the delivery.

The birth took place in their home in the dedicated medical office at the front of the house of Dr. Bainbridge in Princeton, New Jersey. There was a hospital in Princeton, but Dr. Bainbridge did not think much about it as a place to have his patients go except if they had no one at home to care for them. The hospitals were not sanitary; they smelled of urine, feces and body odor; they were mainly a place to go and die.

William had two older brothers, John, almost four, and Edmund had just turned two. He also had a sister who was just one years old, Phoebe (named after Mary's mother).

There had been other children conceived over the years but they had been born dead or died shortly after birth.

William was healthy baby. In his early youth he was distinguished for his adventurous disposition. William received a good education as he grew up. His parents were bright individuals and assisted in the education of all of their children. Mrs. Bainbridge taught the children manners, proper speech, and how to read.

William grew up under British influence, his father being a good Tory was known to favor patients who were British. William never thought much about those in Princeton who were not British as he grew up. He actually liked the regimentation of the British, but most of all he liked the fact the British had large ships with tall masts and graceful sheets that were beautiful when filled with the wind.

William Bainbridge ancestor Sir Arthur Bainbridge settled in New Jersey in 1600. Sir Arthur Bainbridge was from Durham County, England. Captain Bainbridge's father was a prominent physician, descendant of the fifth generation from Sir Arthur Bainbridge. William's parent resided in their home on Nassau Street, one lot east of Van Deventer Avenue on the south side of the street.

The Bainbridge's were members of the Society of Friends. William benefited from his religious teaching as he grew up. Religion had instilled in him life's lessons in simplicity, service, and common sense. The Bainbridge's were considered a family of substance; they circulated in the upper crust of Princeton society.

Early in William's childhood the family moved from Princeton to New York. The move was instrumental in the development of William's maritime skills and knowledge. Young William continued to be infatuated with the water and he would seek out ways to go to the Hudson River to see the boats and ships. Sometimes he would luck out and see a tall ship coming into or leaving New York.

When William was twelve in 1786; political events were taking place that would have a direct bearing on his life. The United States was paying tribute payments to North African pirates. A number of men in Congress felt they could "negotiate" a peace treaty with the Barbary pirates and they would leave American merchant ships alone.

The leading politicians in the United States Congress where having long and heated debates over how to deal with radical Islamist doctrine that permitted and practiced brazen extortion on non-Muslims merchants. Some American politicians wanted to talk with them to convince them that their actions were wrong. Some of our citizens and politicians wanted to continue paying ransom, thinking the problem would eventually go away.

Thomas Jefferson, Benjamin Franklin and John Adams went to Europe to negotiate tribute payments to the Barbary pirates in North Africa. At their first meeting they were told by the Ambassador from Tripoli why they preyed upon the American merchants. They were to learn that the North African nations felt justified to war against all non-Muslim nations based on the Islamic Koran. The money was good so why change their ways.

"Are you not concerned about the loss of life of your people?" Jefferson asked.

"No we are not," The Ambassador replied.

The men were quite taken back when they were advised all Muslims who died during a siege were assured to go to paradise. Jefferson reported the Algerian Ambassador's reply to Congress:

"Founded on the laws of their prophet, and written in the Quran, all nations who did not acknowledge their (King's) authority were sinners, and it was their right and duty to make war upon them wherever they could be found, and to make slaves of all they could take as prisoners, and that every 'Mussulman' (Muslim) who should be slain in Battle was sure to go to Paradise."

It was William's grandfather, John Taylor Esq. of Monmouth County, New Jersey, that allowed William's love of the sea to flourish. John Taylor more than anyone in William's life influenced his education and then assisted him in his future career at sea.

William's father had written his father-in-law, John Taylor:

"I trust, my dear sir, that you will find our son tractable in disposition, willing and eager to meet your views, and obedient to your behests. Although he is so young, his mother and myself have discovered in him evidences of a lofty temperament, and I am sure that no lad could wish for a better promise for the future than the chance of spending his early life near one so able to teach the importance of high moral sentiments and proper rules of conduct as yourself. I shall bring William to you in the course of the next fortnight.

Believe me, I am, most honored sir, your very devoted son-in-law, Absalom Bainbridge."

John Taylor lived in a large white house on a large estate in Monmouth County near the town of Long Branch. Monmouth County had a population of 19,872 according to the 1800 census. John Taylor's house had been built by his parents, in stages without giving credence to any particular style of architecture. The house was surrounded by large shade trees which accentuated the grandeur that the house commanded. From the large porch on the front of the house the Atlantic Ocean was in full view; only a few trees interrupted the memorizing movement of the water only a few blocks from the house.

John Taylor was getting up in years; he didn't move as easily as in previous years. His wife, Phoebe Heard Taylor died in 1791. He was now using a gold-headed stick as he walked which enhanced his air of dignity. He also had the appearance of wealth and respectability that conveyed an image of significance importance.

John was looking forward to having his grandson there in his lonely grand house. John Taylor was a wonderful instructor with a natural gift of charm when imparting instructive information to others.

Several weeks passed before young William Bainbridge arrived at the Taylor residence. He arrived in a clumsy looking coach that delivered him to the large gates guarding the entrance to the Taylor estate. William was just thirteen years old and this was his first venture on his own. The trip from New York City was not far but because of the lack of bridges, they took a barge across the river extending the trip out to an entire day.

William's travel box with all his belongings was handed down to him by the coach driver. He managed to accept the box with some effort and to thank the driver. He set the box with all his worldly possessions on the ground wondering what to do next. He was eagerly anticipating seeing his grandfather but was not sure he could carry the box to the house.

Then he saw them, two figures appear on the veranda of the great white house. William removed his hat and waved since verbal communication was not audible at that distance.

William's grandfather along with his confidant, Fenwick, hurried as best they could to meet up with William and to assist him with his chest. Fenwick had been working for the Taylor's for years and was also John's intimate friend as well as his confidant.

William gave his maternal grandfather a hug. He liked his grandfather and he had been looking forward to his visit with him.

"Thank you for having me, grandfather. Mother regrets not being able to accompany me. She made me promise to make sure I told you that she misses and loves you. Father is awful busy with his practice and made it impossible to get away."

"I am sorry they could not also come and visit. I hope they are all well?" John Taylor said with genuine sincerity.

"Oh they are fine, very well, as are my other brothers and sister."

William was taken to the room that had been prepared for him. It was a large room on the second story with large windows looking out over the trees and meadows that surrounded the house extending out to the water. William freshened up after his carriage trip. He was dusty and sweaty and needed to wash his face and hands before going back to the living room to see his grandfather.

"Hi grandfather, my room is wonderful, thank you for allowing me to come and visit."

"Think nothing of it William, the pleasure is all mine. I do nothing but mope around this big house all day so having a young visitor is a ray of sun shine in my otherwise dull life."

"Your father has mentioned you desire to study to become skilled in a field of endeavor that he failed to mention what it was. So do you want to study to become a merchant, or perhaps a lawyer, William?"

"Well no sir, I want to become a sailor, sir," William was feeling somewhat uncomfortable in this revelation.

"Well, that is interesting," looking at William with some expression of surprise on his face. "How did that idea come into your head?"

"I have thought about it a great deal, grandfather; I want to be a sailor and go to sea."

"Has your father said anything about your becoming a sailor to you?"

"Well he thinks I am too young to decide what I want to do," William was now making a full examination of the floor in front of him.

"Being a sailor is not easy William, there are many hardships in a life at sea. Hardships that being a merchant do not have to experience and besides having both feet on dry ground is safe and you can live in peace and comfort."

"Yes sir, I think I would rather be at sea."

"Well, well, we don't need to decide this very minute, perhaps you might change your mind after being here awhile."

"I don't mean to be ungrateful, grandfather, but I believe I have made up my mind."

"Tell me about your studies," John wanted to change the subject.

William told him of his progress in the classics and languages and John was pleasantly surprised to how responsive William was. They talked for over an hour. John Taylor was beginning to feel a great affection for the son of his only daughter.

The next two years William spent in studying with his grandfather in the peacefulness of the New Jersey estate. William did attend school in nearby Long Branch. William got along well with the Long Branch schoolmaster and he made great strides in his studies.

William made a good impression and was liked by all those he came in contact with. The one thing that William never lost was the vision of ships and a life at sea.

John Taylor was a wise man and an excellent judge of character. He was pleased with his grandson and his progress in his studies and leadership qualities. He finally had decided that William should fulfill his desires to go to sea; only then would William know if he wanted to be a sailor.

John Taylor was able to involve William in a mercantile pursuit through his friend Captain Waldron in Philadelphia. Taylor felt William had a natural affinitive for the sea. Taylor perhaps had the desire to be a sea and was living his dream through his grandson, William Bainbridge.

John Taylor wrote his son-in-law that he was convinced that William should be placed under the charge and patronage of a 'respectable and intelligent commander' that John knew. The ship was the merchantman *Ariel* under the command of Captain Waldron and it was about to sail from Philadelphia."

William's father was not pleased with this turn of events and only with reluctance, Dr. Bainbridge agreed to the plan. William was on his way to the start of a career that would elevate him to a prominent place in American history.

FOUR

Ariel
1789

William Bainbridge was a vigorous person with an athletic frame, adventurous disposition, and a dauntless spirit. He was already an impressive looking man even though he was only fifteen years old. He was six feet tall, lean, muscular, and dark. He was "dashing" in the old fashioned sense, handsome and adventurous, with a commanding presence. He could be kind and charmingly polite. William Bainbridge was also dignified, quite manner, gentlemanly bearing, and a low modulated voice with a controlling character.

John Taylor had paved William's way with a letter of introduction for William to give to Captain Waldron. Fenwick, John Taylor's confidant and employee, accompanied William to Philadelphia and to the ship. Fenwick was like an old mother hen and lectured William the entire trip to Philadelphia on why he should not become a sailor.

Philadelphia was a large city and the seat of the new United States government until the capital was moved to it permanent home, Washington D.C. just before the turn of the century.

The population in Philadelphia in 1800 was 41,220 and the population of the United States was 5,308,483. Philadelphia was considered a large city and a major sea port for merchant trade.

When they reached Philadelphia they had breakfast down at the docks at the Exchange Coffee-house. Fenwick chattered during the entire time they ate about what a mistake he was making and that it was not too late to change his mind. William just wanted to go to the ship. Finally William was able to break away from Fenwick and go down the dock to the *Ariel*.

"Permission to come aboard, Sir?" William called up to the person standing on the deck of the *Ariel*.

"Permission granted," a loud voice called back.

William made his way up the ramp to the top deck. He was nervous about his being on a ship for his first time with strangers all around.

"Well young man you must be Bainbridge," Captain Waldron stepped forward to welcome William aboard.

"I am William Bainbridge; my grandfather instructed me to give you this letter," William assumed he was addressing the captain.

"How is your grandfather? I have always admired him," Captain Waldron commented as he accepted the letter from William.

"He is doing fine."

"Well according to this letter from him he thinks very highly of you. I am going to have to attend to the loading of the cargo so I am going to have Mr. Wish show you around the vessel and where to store your gear. I do want to talk to you more, once the ship is prepared for sailing."

"Mr. Wish this is young Bainbridge, please show him around, and where his hammock is so he can stow his gear."

"Hi, my name is John Wish, I am a midshipman under Captain Waldron," John had his hand extended.

"Nice to meet you, I am William Bainbridge," as he took John's hand.

William was given a berth of a common sailor before the mast. This was beginning of an unusual and distinguished record; William knew the moment he stepped foot on the ship that he would love the sea.

"William," John said, "if you want to be a sailor you need to start with the basics, tying knots. You need to learn how to be proficient in tying all the knots before doing anything else. The first thing is to remember the knot you tie might make the difference between survival and death in a crisis," said Midshipmen John Wish.

William was listening intently, hoping not to miss any information he might benefit from.

"The next important thing to know about knots is that some knots need to hold fast while others need to be tied for quick release. You have to do these things automatically; sometimes you don't have time to think."

John would give William a new knot every few days to master. The first knot he showed William how to make was the Sailor's Knot. It's a very easy-to-tie knot that holds strong and comes unfastened quickly if pulled correctly.

William practiced by making a loop with the first piece of line and then ran the second piece of line over the loop, around the back of one end of the first line, through the trunk of the line, over the second end of the first line, and then through the first loop.

This really amounts to making a bend with one line and then it mirrors that bend with the second line while weaving the two lines together.

At the end of the first month on the vessel, William had mastered the Sailor's Knot, Figure-Eight Knot, the Fisherman's Knot, and the Bowline. He was also becoming useful on deck with the lines.

Under the watchful eye of the Captain and following the instructions of John Wish, William graduated to the stature of sailor. He learned how to work the rigging, the anchors, and how to attend to other deck duties. William then advanced to Bosun's Mate and his first leadership responsibility. It wasn't long until William was promoted to midshipmen and learned navigation, astronomy, and trigonometry.

William was strong and agile with a natural aptitude and an inborn courage. After his fourth voyage he was promoted to the rank of first mate on board the trading vessel, the *Ariel*, trading between colonies and Holland.

It was on William's fourth voyage on the *Ariel* a mutiny arose shortly after the start of the midday watch.

"Captain, look out! William cried out."

Seven tough looking ordinary sailors had made their way to the Quarter Deck with a mission of over powering Captain Waldron and gaining control of the ship.

William was strong and an excellent boxer. Fighting two or three men at a time was not a problem for him; the receiving foe of his brute force was lucky to survive, and in this instant, one didn't.

William leaped into action and grabbed the hair of two men closest to him and slammed them together. They fell to the deck like lumps of laundry. William placed his strong left hand on the neck of another mutineer and nailed another with his right hand in the kidneys. The man he had with his left hand he also used his right hand and broke his neck. The captain also put two men down and William finished off the seventh man with an elbow to the solar plexus and a vicious upper cut to the head that put him out cold.

"Are you alright Captain Waldron?"

"I am, thanks to your coming to my assistance. Thank you young Mr. Bainbridge, you no doubt saved my life" The Captain was shaken up and he was not quite sure of the gravity of the whole situation.

"Were you damaged Mr. Bainbridge?"

"No sir, I am still whole."

"I am in your debt young Mr. Bainbridge. You will come to my cabin for dinner this evening; I want to properly thank you for saving my life and my ship."

"Thank you Captain, I will be there but right now can I help you to your cabin?"

"No, I'll be alright, a little shaken, but I think I need to deal with these ruffian's. Those men committed a hanging offence and I intend to follow through with the punishment."

FIVE

Cantor
1792

In 1792, William was eighteen years old. He was asked to be First Mate on the ship, *Cantor* sailing in the Holland trade under Captain Stebbins. The *Cantor* was a sister ship to the *Ariel*.

The *Cantor* was to provide William with a good many learning experiences while at sea. William was to learn about the skills necessary to captain the ship and more importantly the problems of dealing with a ship's crew.

The *Cantor* was battered about during the first two weeks in the extremely rough seas. The crew was so busy handling the vessel that when they were on watch the physical exertion was so demanding that they could nothing but go to sleep immediately when their duty was finished. Because the crew was also so wearied from the long watches on the turbulent seas that little time was found for grumbling about the treatment received from the captain.

The *Cantor* was being tossed around on the turbulent seas without regard for the human toll it inflicted on the men. They were very few of the crew who had not 'pump ship' (vomit) over the upper deck rail. This was also William's first experience of dealing with sea sickness.

It had not taken William very long to perceive one reason at least why it had been so difficult for the *Cantor* to secure a better crew. The vessel was small, scarcely more than three hundred tons burden that did not provide any amenities of comfort for the crew. The ship's Captain Stebbins had also received a rather bad name from all those that knew him. He was a tyrant and not much of a leader. He was considered as a "nagger". Actually he had a cowardly disposition. He was great on bluster, threats, and profanity which did not bring the best out of the men and boy's he led.

When good weather finally returned Captain Stebbins was not smart enough to ease off on the men. He drove the men as hard as they had experienced in the terrible weather. The men needed relaxation and leisure time to rejuvenate their bodies. Captain Stebbins didn't believe that was necessary and kept the men hard at it. He would find them first one thing and then another thing for them to do. He was hyper critical rating them severely on the slightest provocation. It almost appeared as if he did this to retrieve what he thought he might have lost by his timid behavior when in port.

The ship was successful in crossing the Atlantic to the English Channel, and finally dropping anchor in the roadstead of Rotterdam.

On the second day of their arrival they had passed the local customs and were going to begin the unloading the vessels cargo. The men were tired and to make things worst they had gotten a hold of a large quantity of liquor which they consumed and now some of the crew were very drunk.

"I am going to get that bastard!" one ruffian of a sailor boasted.

"I am all for that, I think I will kill him!"

"The asshole deserves to die."

"Well what the hell are you waiting for? There he is standing near the quarter-deck looking like the prick he is."

Seven drunken sailors made their way to the quarter-deck.

The crew had not been allowed to leave the *Cantor* so it was a mystery as to where the liquor had come from. There were small boats rowing around the vessel so an enterprising landsman had apparently provided the liquor for a fee.

The Captain had gone to shore earlier in the day to take care of business and he had just returned to the ship. It was late in the evening and it was dark outside. Bainbridge had been below in his berth writing a letters to his grandfather and his parents in order to send them back by a vessel nearly ready to set sail, when suddenly there came from the deck above a sound of scuffling feet.

The first thought that came to William's head was something bad was about to happen. He instinctively reached up to the rack above his head and drew forth a brace of heavy pistols and hurried out of his small cabin. At the door of the cabin he ran into Monson, almost knocking him full length against the ladder, in his haste to reach the quarter-deck.

"What are you doing here, you rascal?" Bainbridge yelled, helping Whisky Jack to his feet. Whisky Jack was very drunk.

"Hurry, sir," he said thickly. "I ain't no talebearer, but there'll be dirty work up there in a minute."

William could hear a muffled cry for help just as he reached the quarter-deck. The night was almost totally dark, but there was light enough to see a confused struggle off to the port side against the rail.

"I am coming to help Captain Stebbins."

William could see that Captain Stebbins was being held by two of the strongest members of the crew. One crew member had his arm around Captain Stebbins's neck, choking him and the other was pounding his fists into Captain Stebbins's body. The captain was no match for the two younger men and he would have died if Bainbridge had not appeared when he did.

William grasped one of his heavy pistols by the barrel and brought the butt down upon the nearest sailor's head. At this same instant he caught the other by the back of his collar and gave him a twist that set him off his feet; the man tripped and disappeared backward down the hatchway. Bainbridge's eyes had become better accustomed to the darkness by this time, and he saw that another struggling group was centered about the prostrate figure of the first officer on the deck.

"Don't use your knife, you fool," grunted someone thickly; "just heave him overboard."

Bainbridge was on top of them so suddenly that they were caught off guard. There were five of them and no other help coming to his assistance, Captain Stebbins was not in any shape to fight anymore.

William took two bone breaking strokes with his heavy pistol and two men fell to the deck.

The other three men were too drunk to do much fighting. William was not bother by the odds since he felt he could take care of these three even if they were not drunk.

William made a quick turn after landing his fist on the face of one of the mutineers and slipped, falling forward on to one knee.

One of the two remaining mutineers was above William with an open sheath knife in his hand. William quickly raised the other pistol and pulled the trigger; the powder only flashed in the pan, and the knife descended at him viciously. The point of the knife struck one of the buttons of his coat, and was deflected, entered the cloth and ripping it open the full length.

Whisky Jack had recovered from his collision with Bainbridge and had made his way on deck. He grabbed a heavy bucket and slammed it on the head of the would-be-assassin. The man's skull was crushed and he fell to the deck.

Captain Stebbins had gathered himself together, and, armed with a belaying pin, laid one of the two remaining seamen on the deck with a blow that opened his head and nearly was the end of him. The last man, who was the soberest, cried for mercy.

Captain Stebbins managed stay on his feet. He had been atrociously batter and was trembling so he could hardly stand; but the mutiny was over, and in five minutes the three ringleaders, who were the least hurt, were taken below in irons waiting to be punished. Two of the mutineers died and the other two were seriously injured but that was little consequence since they were going to be hanged.

This was an end of the trouble for some time, but when the *Cantor* was ready for her return voyage from Holland, Captain Stebbins refused to sail and resigned his command of her to William Bainbridge.

Young man," as Captain Stebbins would address William, "you are as good a navigator and practical seaman as I have seen."

"Thank you Captain, you're teaching me the skills have been appreciated."

"Young man, I talked to the owners of the *Cantor* about your capabilities before we left on this sailing. My main reason for talking to them was my retirement from the sea. They wanted to know who could take my place and I highly recommended you."

"Thank you Sir."

"Well the owners were hesitant at first but after much consideration they agreed to give you command of the *Cantor*."

William shook the Captain's hand. "I am indeed indebted to you. You can be sure I will not let you down."

Although the *Cantor* was exceedingly short-handed from the loss of the seven mutineers, Bainbridge agreed to bring her back to America, which he successfully accomplished, landing in Philadelphia in the latter part of June.

The *Cantor* had arrived safely back at port in Philadelphia. William was now nineteen years old, and something of a hero.

Bainbridge did not mention anything to anyone about his voyage except of course the owners of the *Cantor*. The story of his manly conduct and his display of nautical skill on the return voyage also reached the ears of the owners of the ship from others on the docks.

The talk about William Bainbridge as an up and coming leader was known to the owners of the *Cantor* long before he had been suggested for command. The owners of the *Cantor* had been impressed with William's acting with Captain Waldron on the *Ariel* in stopping the mutiny along with his leadership skills and his taking over command of the *Cantor*.

The senior partner offered him command of the vessel on her next voyage if he wished to accept the position.

William graciously accepted the position of command and he couldn't wait to tell his Grandfather. William was going to take a few days off and visit with his family that was gathering in New York.

When William returned home, he found that his younger brother Joseph had also decided to take up the sea as a vocation, and was then absent on his first cruise to South America.

SIX

Cantor and Hope
1796

William Bainbridge was officially named as commander of the merchant ship, the *Cantor*. The *Cantor* was a trading schooner active in the West Indies trade. William's first of three trips took him to Haarlem in the Netherlands, the Mediterranean, and south to Brazil.

William did make adjustments to the *Cantor's* rigging so as to improve her sailing speed. Bainbridge felt that being able to out run others was a good way to keep from being high jacked at sea.

Mr. Monson (Whiskey Jack) was of the first of the old crew to make application with William to sail with him. He had made a great effort to appear before William clean and sober to apply for a position.

The years went by without incident. The owners of the *Cantor* were more than satisfied with Bainbridge's operating of the merchant vessel. The loss of a merchant ship could mean disaster to an owner so returning from each voyage was a special event in their lives and their prosperity.

The owners of the *Cantor* also owned the *Hope* a larger merchant ship. The commander of the *Hope* had left the company. It did not take long for the owners to ask Bainbridge to take command of the *Hope*. They felt

Bainbridge was more than qualified to command the larger vessel and it would be easier to find a captain for the smaller vessel.

William was twenty-two years of age, when he was given the command of the *Hope* in the spring of 1796, a vessel of 140 tons burdened. She had four mounted- nine pounders and a crew of eleven men. *Hope* was new vessel owned by the same firm that owned the *Cantor*.

The ship was caring tobacco, cotton, and indigo and was bringing back silks and wine on the return trip.

Bainbridge had never had any trouble with the crews under his command. Bainbridge was a good teacher and captain. He gained the respect of his crews and had always found them willing and eager. Some of the men from the *Cantor* had requested to serve on the *Hope* and Bainbridge was grateful for their loyalty since he was not looking forward to training an entire green crew from scratch.

William had a good deal of pride in the new vessel. The *Hope* was one of the neatest looking vessels in the harbor. All the metal shone, the decks were white and clean; the crew continued to keep the paint fresh.

William had attracted a good crew to work with him. The crew of the little ship was composed of a fine lot of sailormen. They were, without exception, full-blooded Yankees, although the cook was a black, and hailed from the island of Barbados and actually possessed some culinary skills.

"Mr. Seth, I firmly believe to make a sailor content he must be well fed and kept busy."

Mr. Seth was the first officer whom he sailed with on the *Ariel*. His second was a young Yankee named Beebe. William liked Beebe; he was a few years older than William from Portsmouth, New Hampshire and a good sailor.

Just before the sailing of the *Hope* an American vessel had come into port and dropped anchor close to hand. She reported that ten days previously she had been boarded by an English cruiser, and no less than three of her crew had been taken from her by main force; deliberately kidnapped! Bainbridge's blood boiled when he heard the story, and a firm determination was formed in his mind to resist to the very last any attempt that the English might make to force such treatment upon him.

There were a number of American ships in port. William introduced himself to the other captains. Richard Samuelson was captain of the *Lafayette* out of Boston. William knew the name and that he was a friend of Captain John Barry during the Revolutionary War.

The Lafayette was half again the size of the *Hope*.

William arrived on the *Lafayette* at noon with a number of other American officers as guests for dinner.

Richard Samuelson was a gracious host. He served wine that William thought was excellent, though his experience with wine was very limited.

The talk around the table was mainly about one subject, the high-handed behavior of Great Britain on the seas.

Each of the officers had a story to tell about being stopped and good seamen taken from them. The British were displaying their superior force, flaunting it their face. The stolen seamen were made slaves on board one of the great floating fortresses of King George.

"What are we going to do, gentlemen, may I ask?" said one of the younger captains from the foot of the table. "Remonstrance is worse than useless to the deaf ears of the English. Our representatives at St. James's Court can accomplish nothing. We have no vessels of the regular navy to enforce respect."

"We are completely at the mercy of these sea robbers, confusion to them! And so far as I can see there is no ending to it."

"It is the solemn truth," put in another. "I've lost five men in the last two voyages, and would probably have lost two more if my little brig couldn't leg it pretty well; I can tell you. They took my third mate, a man who went to school with me in Roxbury. Sad news did I have to write to his wife, and he but just married."

"What would the English think," exclaimed the first speaker, "if a ship of any other nation dared trifle with their merchantmen in this fashion? There'd be a fine hullabaloo, wouldn't there?"

"Oh, just another war!" remarked Captain Samuelson. "I wish that we had a few fine live-oak frigates afloat with men like my old friends, John Paul Jones, Nicholson, John Barry, and Biddle, to command them. But no, the Government expects us to look out for ourselves. Bainbridge, tell us what experiences you have had with the John Bullies?"

"I've been most fortunate, sir," responded Bainbridge, who was by far the youngest of the five men seated in the cabin;" but I think that we have been rather too submissive, perhaps; though I say it who should not, I might feel inclined to make a show of resistance. We might even persuade the country at large that it is worthwhile to take up cudgels in defense of their citizens abroad, as well as to fight for their interests at home."

"Well said, Captain Bainbridge," put in Captain Steele, of the brig *Bangor*. "But the only trouble is that we would probably be blown out of the water for our pains. It is well to have a locker full of foreign flags at one's disposal; I find it helpful to also know a few words of foreign lingo."

Bainbridge said nothing, but he had long ago made up his mind to one thing: He would permit no one to search his vessel or to rob him without a show of the strongest remonstrance. He was afraid that if he spoke his full mind upon this occasion he might be regarded as blustering, a thing absolutely impossible to his nature, as he had never made a threat or a promise in his life that he did not intend at the time to carry out.

William realized he had not been confronted with the British stealing men off his vessel. He thanked his good fortune that he had not experienced the misfortunes of his dinner companions.

William knew that sooner or later their experience would be his. Proud of his country and jealous of the rights of her citizens, it rankled deeply to think that he would have to submit to the indignities of which he had heard the others tell.

The *Hope* was anchored some fifteen hundred yards out in the harbor. Another vessel hailing from Charleston, South Carolina was alongside the *Hope.*

Bainbridge was in his gig near the side of the *Hope,* when he suddenly perceived a commotion on the deck of the vessel from Charleston. There was a great deal of victorious talk.

William directed his attention to the commotion and just as he did he heard a hail.

"Ho, on board the ship there! Help! Mutiny!"

Bainbridge quickly boarded the *Hope* and he hastened below, and opening a chest, he drew out the two big pistols that had served him in such good stead on board the *Cantor.* He hastened up again and jumped into the gig. In three minutes he was alongside the other vessel, and followed by half his crew, he climbed on deck.

Without a shot being fired or blood spilled, the rioters were made prisoners and placed in irons. Then, after receiving the thanks of the captain, Bainbridge rowed back to the *Hope.*

As he was lifting the lid of the chest to stow the pistols away, the vessel lurched a little and the lid fell down upon his forearm, but unfortunately in such a way as to touch the hammer of one of the pistols, which was discharged, the flame igniting a bag of powder which lay in a compartment of the chest. Instantly there was an explosion, and Bainbridge was hurled across the cabin, badly wounded in his legs and the upper portion of his body.

The black powder burns are nasty. The powder consists of a mixture of Saltpeter (potassium nitrate) 75 percent, sulfur 11 percent, and charcoal, 14 percent. The black powder burns rapidly and very hot.

The crew, who were hoisting the gig out of the water, rushed down to see what had happened. A few buckets of water extinguished the flames, and a doctor came off shore at once.

The doctor pronounced Bainbridge dangerously hurt, but stated that he had a fair chance of recovery. The doctor was hoping recovery was possible if infection did not set in.

William was in a great amount of pain. The epidermal tissue was badly burned on the legs and abdominal area. There was profound injury to nerves. Bainbridge was facing potentially fatal complications that included electrolyte imbalance and respiratory distress.

No one could have been nursed more carefully than he was by his officers and crew, each vying with the other to see what he could do for the injured commander.

The doctor had felt that strips of bed sheets soaked in five percent of aqueous solution of tannic acid be applied to the wounds. The doctor instructed the officers on the ship that the wounds must be kept wet until satisfactory coagulum had been formed. The doctor suggested that a few grams of Opium be added to the mixture to help deaden the pain.

In five weeks Bainbridge was able to be about the deck again, and in healthy condition. William was lucky that his wounds had healed almost immediately. In a fortnight the Hope was loaded with a cargo, and weighed anchor for the island of St. Thomas.

The second day at sea he called the crew to the waist and made a short speech something he had never found occasion to do before.

" Men;" he said quietly, " I do not intend to allow this vessel to be robbed, and I know that you will understand my meaning when I say that if any press officer boards us and takes one of you away he will have to take the rest of us also, and probably the ship into the bargain."

With that the Hope's crew was divided into divisions and a gun captain was appointed for each one of the four nine-pounders on the vessel.

Each of the four cannons had a gun captain and each gun captain had one sailor to assist him. The Hope had only eight seamen and three officers.

Bainbridge trained the crew in the firing of the guns over the next few days. He had a limited amount of powder but he was willing to use a portion of it to make his crew proficient gunners.

They would tow a target out from the side of the *Hope* and practice using cannon balls. The practice included how to elevate and aim the guns. The men became reasonably proficient at hitting the target. There was a renewed pride in being part of a ship that had clout.

Scarborough, Tobago. 26 February 1796
Messrs. Jones and Clarke
Gentlemen
I arrived here yesterday. After a pleasant passage of 10 days I spotted no vessel on my passage, but a few days after I left Charleston, was chased by a Brig who showed Danish Colours but the Hopes legs were too long for her. The markets here are very dull, for the particulars of which I refer you to [worn away] Otis's Letter, if we should dispose of any of the cargo here it will be attended with slow dispatch owing to the ill convenient places of landing. But you may rely of my making the utmost of dispatched in my power. The English are now in Martinique the land accounts from there to this Port was that they had taken Fort St. Pier[r]e's by storm and expected in a short time to be in full possession of the Island, a number American vessels are embargoed at Barbados, and great many carried into Dominica and several condemn, etc. There [sic] behavior to the Americans - is most infamous There is an American Brig of Boston from the Island St. Vincent bound to Dominica fell in with an English Frigate Quebec, took the Captain and 500 Thannes out of her, sent the Brig back to St. Vincent, the captain to Barbados, and was so kind to themselves as to keep the money - and there is many instances of such behavior and worse. All the English Ports are open for Provisions and Lumber, Tobacco is prohibited, Slaves sell here for sixty four dollars and thousands and are in demand. It is reported here that the country of Russia has come into allies with the combined Armies against France.
I am Gentlemen
Your most obedient servant
Wm Bainbridge

SEVEN

British gall
1796

Bainbridge was making passage from Bordeaux to the island of St. Thomas.

"Sails off the port bow," one of the young sailors called down from the center mast.

Bainbridge used his glass to see what the ship might be. He determined it was a British schooner of eight guns.

"All hands to their stations," Bainbridge ordered.

Some of the crew had been sleeping and they were not happy about having to go back on duty.

It was late in the afternoon and they were off the island of St. John. The British schooner appeared to making every effort to catch up with the *Hope*. The vessel was carrying all her sails and was gaining on them rapidly.

Bainbridge orders the American flag to be raised at his peak.

The gap between the *Hope* and the British schooner closed and the Captain of the schooner hailed the *Hope*, demanding the *Hope* be stopped.

Bainbridge was not about to stop and be boarded. The captain of the British schooner ordered that their guns open fire on the *Hope*.

The captain of the schooner apparently was an arrogant individual and assumed the *Hope* would strike their colors and the challenge would be over and he would have a prize.

Bainbridge held his course. The nine-pounders loaded with as much powder as he thought they could possibly stand, and double-shotted, (two balls in one gun), and for good measure a handful of musket balls was added to each charge.

Each man also had two loaded muskets that were placed along the bulwarks. Everything was made handy in case resistance should become necessary.

Bainbridge was sure that the schooner was one of the small English cruisers whose commanders took it upon them to stop American ships at every opportunity, and, trusting to the prestige of the royal service, insist upon the right of search.

Very soon the British schooner was pacing the *Hope* alongside. She had not displayed her flag, but an officer in a cocked hat and a brilliant uniform was seen standing near the rail on the quarter-deck, trumpet in hand. Although the latter instrument was not needed, he placed it to his lip, and, disdaining the usual formalities, he bellowed at top voice:

"On board the ship there! Heave to! I'm going to send a boat off to you."

"I advise you not, sir," was Bainbridge's return to this false request.

"Heave to!" shouted the Englishman, disdaining to use his trumpet this time. "Heave to, or I'll fire a shot into you."

"I'm sorry I can't stop," Bainbridge shouted in answer to the Britishers hail. "We are in a great hurry today."

"Perhaps they're in some distress, Captain Bainbridge," suggested Mr. Beebe.

"They may be in a minute," suggested one of the gun captains. The gun captain who had overheard the remark was slapping the breech of his gun with a chuckle.

Captains Bainbridge caused the Englishmen to be surprised that this smaller American foe would not heed to their demands.

The two vessels were now so close that everything could be observed clearly and there was no mistake as to what was being said.

Bainbridge noticed that the men employed in casting the lashings off the small quarter boat stopped their work. The sailors made a deliberate display of loading the forward gun and running it in. Bainbridge had his gun crew at their stations with their guns loaded, just waiting for the command to fire.

The men on the schooner stood apparently inactive along the bulwarks. They thought the sight of the *Hope* was a joke.

"Ready there!" said Bainbridge quietly; "if a shot touches us, let them have it."

Grimly he waited for the Englishman to take the initiative.

"Roar!" The cannon reported the first gun shot from the British schooner. The ball plashed harmlessly across the bows.

"Steady!" ordered Bainbridge. "Don't fire until she hits us."

The commander of the British schooner did not know what to make of the unexpected behavior of the Yankee vessel. He was used to intimidating his foes, especially Americans. He was being ignored but he was aware the men standing by the meager display of guns were intending on using them.

The *Hope* was sailing along as if nothing was occurring. Captain Bainbridge stood at the rail with his arms folded giving the British his best 'I am not concerned' look.

The Englishman's next order was heard by every one of the *Hope's* crew as well as by those for whose ears it was intended.

"Fire into her!" he roared.

Bainbridge stepped to the side of the *Hope*. He could see that the schooner had double the guns but they were of no heavier metal than his own.

The men had all come to the port side, and the nine pounders had been cast loose. Everything was in readiness.

The commander of the British schooner did not discharge a full broadside at the *Hope*. Whatever the reason was he didn't but he did fire a second time.

The British cannon roared a second time. The round cannon ball whirred across the deck of the *Hope* hitting the deck house. Splinters were being sprayed as the ball travel through to the other side of the deck house making a great crash among the "doctor's" pans and kettles.

The smoke on the British vessel was thick so they failed to see immediately the results of their marksmanship.

Captain Bainbridge yelled "fire" just as the smoke of the British cannon was escaping the mussel. The gun crews were well trained and they returned a second broadside in one and one-half minutes.

As the smoked cleared Bainbridge could see they had successfully blown away the schooner's gaff, main-topmast, the flying jib boom, and the foretopmast stay.

The British were scurrying around attending to the wounded and the dead. The British captain seemed confused as to the carnage that had occurred on his ship. The individual at the helm had lost his sense of direction and almost rammed into the *Hope*.

Bainbridge came about to avoid the British access to the *Hope* in case the British had some idea that they would board the *Hope*. The British schooner did cross the bows of the Hope that the latter's jib boom struck her side, carrying away all her starboard shrouds and braces. She fell off rapidly to leeward, and as she did so found time to discharge a gun of her port battery, the ball lodging in the *Hope's* mainmast.

But Bainbridge's starboard guns were double-shotted also, and the answer they gave to this was almost as disastrous to the schooner as the first reply had been. One ball entered near the fore chains, and another, coming through the port, dismounted one of the guns, killing or wounding three or four of the crew. The second gun had put two balls into the schooner's side, ripping a gash but a foot or so above the water line.

The British were in great confusion. Bainbridge could see her crew running hither and thither as if they had lost their heads completely? Bainbridge was much surprise when he saw the English ensign run a short way up on the color halyards, which flapped from the wounded peak, and then hauled it down again.

Bainbridge immediately took offensive action and with the *Hope's* armament of four nine-pounder's guns. The guns delivered a deadly broadside to the schooner. Bainbridge ordered additional fire until the schooner struck her colors.

The commander of the schooner had been forced to surrender. The English schooner was a much superior vessel of eight guns and thirty men to the *Hope's* four guns and eleven men. Bainbridge had killed several of the schooner's crew with the broadside and had done tremendous damage to the schooners rigging.

America and England were no longer at war in 1796, but animosities ran high between England and the Americans. English ships felt it was their job to intimidate American ships.

"We've surrendered! We've surrendered! The English Captain was hollering at the top of his voice and waving his arms.

This was somewhat comical seeing this pompous ass that only a few minutes prior to that was so full of importance and bravado.

Bainbridge was pissed that he had to deal with the jerk he had just encountered. He was concerned as to the ramification of dealing with the English.

Bainbridge called over to the Schooner.

"What schooner is that?"

"Her Majesty's schooner *Linnet,* commanded by Captain Sir Philip Townes. What ship is that?"

Before Bainbridge could reply to this the action of his own crew drew his attention. They had given three cheers when they saw the English flag come down, and now, much excited, they were gathered in a body, evidently waiting for further orders.

"Shall we board and take possession of her, sir?" asked Mr. Beebe eagerly.

"Not for the world," replied Bainbridge." Those guns were put on board of us for our defense, and we have used them for that purpose, but we have no right to put a foot on board that vessel. Our lives would pay the forfeit, and justly too, sir."

The crew looked a little disappointed, and some were quite angered that they should not be allowed to take advantage of their victory and claim their prize. Bainbridge was well aware that if he had dared to treat the *Linnet* as a prize, he would have been guilty of piracy, or something akin to it.

Bainbridge could see that the Englishman was yet waiting for an answer. Bainbridge was displaying no indication of a desire either to escape or to renew the action; he called across the water to him:

"*Linnet,* you have just met Captain William Bainbridge of the vessel *Hope.*"

When the commander of the Schooner called to Bainbridge as to what he purposed doing with him Bainbridge responded.

"Schooner there! Please advise Captain Sir Philip Townes I have no use for him! Go about your business, and report to your masters if they want my ship they must either send a greater force or a more skillful commander."

Captain Bainbridge ordered the crew to set their sails and head for St. Thomas. He had no feelings as to offering assistance to his foe.

The news of the fight was soon traveling about Philadelphia within a few days of his arrival. This performance and victory gave Bainbridge an elevated reputation for boldness as a ship's captain in the naval circles in Philadelphia. Bainbridge was assured he could and would have command of any ship sailing from that, port.

Bainbridge did not mention the affair except in a short report to the owners of the *Hope*.

EIGHT

Stolen Sailor
1797

Captain Sir Philip Townes of the *Linnet* was never heard from on a professional level of diplomacy. Some thought that Townes was so personally disgraced that he did not report the affair.

There was no complaint made to the United States Government, and it is doubtful whether Sir Philip's masters ever received the message Bainbridge sent to them.

Bainbridge took some time off to go and visit his parents and his grandfather. He felt that he had let them down by going to sea but he also felt they should be proud of his accomplishments in his short naval career. Before Bainbridge had left Philadelphia on his trip he was surprised when a messenger delivered a dispatch addressed to him from the Secretary of the Navy. The Secretary of the Navy had been following William's young career and felt he would be available as a naval captain. The secretary offered Bainbridge the pick of the finest vessels then lying in the port of Philadelphia if he would go to work for him.

Bainbridge was flattered that the Secretary of the Navy was making him an offer. He was tempted but instead wrote back that he was going to visit relatives and he would give the matter consideration and let him know his decision on his return.

When Bainbridge returned to Philadelphia after his visit to his parents he decided not to desert the owners of the *Hope* for a more ambitious command. Bainbridge contacted the Secretary of the Navy to let him know that he would make at least one more voyage in the *Hope* before he turned her over to other hands. Bainbridge felt he owed the owners of the *Hope* notice of his leaving and not just quit; beside Bainbridge like sailing the *Hope*. He knew her tricks and her manners, and he found that the large proportion of the crew were anxious to ship out with him once again.

Mr. Seth, Bainbridge's first officer, had obtained a vessel of his own. Beebe was promoted to be first mate, and just previous to sailing, Bainbridge was fortunate enough to fill the latter's place with a young Philadelphian, Allen M'Kinsey, who, although he was but thirty-three years of age, had been eighteen years at sea, a tall water sailor and a good officer, although his lack of education had for a long time told against his securing a berth aft. His parents were respectable townsfolk; his father kept a small ship chandlery near the wharf.

The *Hope's* cargo was delivered successfully at Bordeaux, and after a short stay, Bainbridge by a most lucky chance was able to load his vessel with silks and wine and set sail, almost retracing his former course.

The sailing back to America went well until they were within five hundred miles of the American coast. It was sunrise when Bainbridge was alerted that a large vessel was descried to windward drifting leisurely down upon the *Hope* before the light morning breeze.

At nine o'clock the vessel was near enough so Bainbridge could identify it as a British line-of-battle ship The vessel was a converted three-decker cut down to two decks and referred to as a 'raze.'

The British vessel was a fine sight to behold. She had every stitch of canvas set, catching the gleams of the sun. The shadows shifting on her sails were mesmerizing as she rolled lazily from side to side on the bosom of the long, easy swell.

When within speaking distance she hauled her wind a little, and without a hail dropped a boat cleverly from her quarter, and soon a young officer in a lieutenant's uniform hailed the little Yankee ship and requested " someone there on board " to heave a line to him. As no one apparently replied to that title, which was certainly as indefinite as it was insulting, the young officer scrambled on board over the low bulwarks, assisted by no one but the members of his crew.

Bainbridge was standing near the wheel with his hands folded in front of him; calmly waiting for the interview that he knew was soon forthcoming.

"What ship's this?" questioned the Englishman, straightening his cocked hat. "Is any one in command here?"

"I suppose you wish to inquire," Responded Bainbridge, "the name of this vessel. It is the American ship *Hope* from Philadelphia, and if you are looking for the commanding officer, sir, you have the honor of addressing him."

"Very distinguished, I am sure. Have you your papers handy, my young Yankee? "

Bainbridge looked over the taffrail at the great shape of the battle ship, in whose shadow his own little vessel was then swallowed up completely. His brows knitted.

It was odious that he had to stand and bear this insult, that he felt was more leveled at his country than at him, without doing anything to resist the imposition.

"Just wait a moment, please," he said politely. And going to the head of the companion ladder, he called the steward and told him to bring up the large tin box that stood in the corner of the cabin.

His leisurely movements angered the lieutenant, who exclaimed in irritation:

"Come, come, my man, make haste. You are squandering time."

"Not altogether," Bainbridge replied. "I am giving you a few minutes to think, so that you may act with care and discretion and regain your composure."

He looked the other squarely in the eye with his fearless glance as he spoke. And, as there was no reply made, he extended the papers to his unwelcome visitor, adding only:

"Read here for yourself. I have no one shipped with me who is not an American seaman; but I assure you, sir, that were it not for the fact that we are under the muzzles of yonder guns, you would not receive the satisfaction even of my assurance, or the pleasure of glancing over the paper that you now hold. There are my men; their appearance speaks for itself."

The boarding officer, who had been followed by five or six of the boat's crew, commenced to read the names in the order of their enlistment, but everything was as plainly as Bainbridge had stated it that it scarcely needed a glance to confirm his words. The men were passed and everything appeared to be over with, when suddenly the name of M'Kinsey caught the lieutenant's eye.

"This man here, M'Kinsey, where is he? " he asked as if with a ray of hope.

"He's my second officer," Bainbridge replied," and is standing here beside me."

"You are a Scotchman," stated the officer positively, glancing from the paper in his hand to the face of the honest seaman.

"Anyone who says that is a liar!" returned the young Philadelphian hotly.

"I'll make you eat that word," replied the Britisher, stepping forward quickly. "Here, you two," he said, speaking to his own men, "lay hold of him and toss him into the boat. I'll break his heart for him."

Bainbridge quietly pushed his second mate to one side and, stepping between the two angry men, said quietly:

"Patience, sir, a moment; I know this man. He was born in Philadelphia. I know his parents. He is an American. I state this to you upon my honor. His reply to you was hasty, that I admit, but he had provocation/'

"Provocation or no provocation," was the return, "he'll come with me, or I'll know the reason why."

"Just a moment," Bainbridge responded. "May I ask your name and that of your vessel?"

"I am Lieutenant Norton, of his Majesty's ship the *Indefatigable*, Sir Edward Pellew."

"Ah, so! Then does Lieutenant Norton mean to tell Captain Bainbridge that he lies? "

There was such a dangerous light in the young American's eyes that for an instant Lieutenant Norton hesitated.

"He may have deceived you," he half faltered. "He's Scotch."

"He has not deceived me. Do you intend to take him by force? "

"Do you intend to resist?"

"I am not so foolish; but I have no objections to his doing so. Mr. M'Kinsey, in the corner of my cabin you will find two loaded pistols lying on the bunk. A sharpened cutlass hangs from the bulkhead close to hand. See if it is not as I say."

Suddenly turning, the mate jumped down the ladder, and as all this conversation had been heard by the crew grouped in the waist, an audible titter ran through the company.

"One's as good as another," the lieutenant growled, trying to affect amusement to hide his discomfiture. "I'll take this man instead."

Reaching forward his hand, he seized one of the *Hope's* crew, a lad scarcely more than eighteen years of age but well-grown and hardy. Two of his henchmen caught the young fellow about the waist, and he was unceremoniously tossed over the side almost on the heads of those sitting below on the thwarts. But the officer did not wish to make his own exit with any degree of haste, although he perceived that there was a long pull ahead of him before he would again reach his ship, as she had edged off and now lay a couple of miles distant waiting for him. He turned to Bainbridge as if to make some parting sally, but Bainbridge spoke first: "Will you convey my compliments to your superior officer and congratulate him upon having so efficient a bailiff; and also inform him that for the young man you have robbed me of I shall take one of his Majesty's citizens serving in the first ship I meet, if her force does not preclude my attempting to do so. You know as well as I do that you have taken an American citizen to lead him into a life of slavery and bondage."

"You talk well," responded the lieutenant, "but no Yankee merchant captain would dare to impress one of his Majesty's subjects. A fig for your threatening, and good-day to you."

With that he dropped down into the boat and pulled away to the battle ship.

NINE

Back at you
1797

O ne of the *Hope*'s seamen was impressed by the British man of war
Indefatigable under the command of Sir Edward Pellew.

Two days after the encounter with the British war ship the lookout
forward reported that there was a sail dead ahead holding the same
course.

"Spread all sails," Bainbridge was determined to give chase.

The *Hope* proved to be much the faster vessel and gained on the
merchant brig within minutes. The brig was about the same size as the
Hope, but not in as good of condition. Bainbridge sailed by the starboard
side of the merchant brig with his port guns trained on her.

The *Hope* raced down past her quarter firing a shot across her bow.
The *Hope* suddenly tacks in front of the brig slowing the *Hope* in such a
way that the brig, in great consternation, let go all standings, suddenly
slowing its forward motion. The sails were making a tremendous fluttering
and clattering of canvas was deafening. The brig swung about and heaved
up and down in the swells of the seas. The vessel appeared to be helplessly
confused.

The brig was within easy hail, so Bainbridge called to her stating that he was going to board, and that if she attempted resistance he would blow her out of the water.

Bainbridge was going to get his retaliation against the British. He was going to take their best seaman. Bainbridge knew that this was not going to help the sailor taken earlier from the *Hope* but he wanted to send a message to the British.

"Captain, I am sending my men over to your vessel. We are going to take one of your crew. You may report that William Bainbridge had taken one of his majesty's subjects in retaliation for a seaman taken from the American ship *"Hope,"* by Lieutenant Norton, of the *"Indefatigable."*

Bainbridge was outraged that someone under his immediate protection had been forcibly kidnapped. Bainbridge was more outrage that he was compelled to witness that kidnapping of a citizen of the United States and placed into slavery. The young man might never see his country and family again. Bainbridge felt sorry for the young man they were about to take with no apparent justification but he would be treat the same as the rest of the crew. The taking of the young man did not rectify the British act of taking an American sailor. The act did show the naval officers of Great Britain that the rights of American citizens, so far as they are committed to the protection of Captain Bainbridge, are not to be violated with impunity."

"Mr. Beebe" he said, "board that brig; take nine men with you, and bring back a healthy John Bull single and sober, and presumably industrious. Don't return without him!"

If Mr. Beebe had not returned at all, he would have left the *Hope* in a very precarious condition, for there were then on board of her no one but the captain and second mate, and an old seaman on the forecastle! Sailing the *Hope* would have been a challenge under those conditions.

When Beebe came on board the Englishman he saw to his consternation that she was much larger and more heavily armed than it was at first supposed, for she carried eight guns, and there were in the neighborhood of twenty seamen huddled on deck near the mainmast. For this reason he did not stop long to parley, but running up to a tall, tow-headed young fellow, he addressed the following question to him, roaring the words in his ear as he grasped him by the shoulder: " Young man, are you married? "

"No sir," faltered the seaman, taken all aback with the suddenness of the question.

'Then come with me," answered Beebe; and taking the sailor at a disadvantage, he grasped him from behind and hustled him across the deck through the gangway into the waiting boat before anyone could lift a hand to prevent him. There was a rush made to the side, but the boat was almost an oar's length distant from the brig. In a few strokes Beebe and the sailors from the *Hope* had placed the prisoner, who was too frightened to resist, on board the *Hope*.

"Better get out of this," panted the first mate, running aft." She's armed like a man-of-war, sir."

"Well, not before she takes a message that I have been longing to send, and wouldn't lose the chance of sending for the gain of a few minutes."

"On board the brig there! I will repeat; please report that Captain William Bainbridge has taken one of his Majesty's subjects in retaliation for a seaman taken from the American ship *Hope* by Lieutenant Norton, of the *Indefatigable* raze, and commanded by Sir Edward Pellew?"

Then sheeting was all razed and they immediately responded to the favorable winds that would take them home. The *Hope* was off before the brig managed "to get out of her own way," as M'Kinsey put it. Before night she was moving through the water at ten knots distancing them from the English brig. The English merchant brig did not make a pursuit of the *Hope*.

Bainbridge sent for the new hand.

"Young man," he said, "I am sorry for you; but now let's make the best of it. You'll be paid your wages from now on to the end of the cruise, and will be discharged at Philadelphia with money in your pocket, if," and he paused, "if you do your duty. Otherwise your position may not be quite so comfortable. Step forward."

William Bainbridge felt he had made his point with the young British seaman. Bainbridge felt bad that his actions certainly did not to make up for the hardships the poor lad had to undergo who was taken by Lieutenant Norton.

The seaman was paid in full, and as someone said at the time, he did not appear to be at all dissatisfied with either the service or the country into which he had been forced.

"We have to settle the question of the assumed right of search on the high seas," William commented to the office of the Navy. The English felt it was their right to search any ship it felt like stopping. The English loved to intimidate Americans using their superior war-ships to bring Americans to their knees.

Nothing about the searches at seas was settled until the war between Great Britain and the United States ended. It was then noted that William

Bainbridge had been in the proper arena for the display of his judgment, coolness and good seamanship.

Philadelphia was once again in a buzz about William Bainbridge and his dealings with the British.

Bainbridge was offered to take command of a larger ship of some six hundred tons about to sail for the South. Bainbridge was pleased with the work and the challenges associated with a new command, the training of the crew, and the possibility of prizes.

After landing a cargo from New Orleans in an English port, he took another shipload for the West Indies.

TEN

St. Bartholomew
1798

Part of Bainbridge's consignment was for the island of St. Bartholomew, a mere dot on the map, just north of the island of St. Christopher in the Caribbean Sea.

The island of St. Bartholomew (St Bart's) was under Swedish rule since 1784 and was Sweden's only Caribbean colony. The main trading town was Gustavia. The Sweden's monarch made Gustavia a duty-free port and its waterfront capital.

St. Bartholomew was a beautiful island but perhaps not the most delightful place in the world for a protracted stay in late 18th century. The island was rich and fertile and produced large quantities of tobacco, cotton, and indigo which it exported. One drawback of the island was it contains no permanent springs. William always had to stop at a neighboring island for water since it was impossible for a vessel fully to replenish her water supply there. The inhabitants of the island were dependent almost entirely upon the rainfall for drinking water purposes.

St. Bartholomew was a frequent stop for Bainbridge. St. Martin was to the northwest, Saba to the southwest, and St. Eustatius and St. Kitts to the south.

The harbour at Gustavia was beautiful. The harbour was protected on three sides with a narrow and treacherous channel into the harbour. The beaches were brilliant white sand with the green hills sloping up from the beaches. William was always alert when sailing a vessel into the harbor. The entrance from the sea into the harbour required flawless seamanship to avoid ripping out the hull of the ship. The tortuous channel was guarded by an abundant number of shoals and the water dept was shallow.

St. Bartholomew supported less than twenty-five hundred white people and about eight thousand blacks on the island. The blacks lived in huts scattered about the plantations, or in a little settlement of their own at the southern end of the harbor. There was a European colony on the top of one of the sloping hills on the opposite side. The low white house's stood well back from the roads, surrounded by gardens of tropical luxuriance.

Just before he was ready to sail a period of calm weather began during which scarcely enough wind blew to lift a flag, let alone to waft a big vessel through a difficult passage. William was stuck on the island at the mercy of the lack of wind.

However, calm was not unusual in the harbour and one had to wait for the winds to pick up. Bainbridge was annoyed by the delays but as it turned out, as Bainbridge often asserted when thinking back, the most fortunate happening of his life; William met his future wife, Susan.

Without much to do on the Island, William did a lot of walking. He enjoyed walking up the hill at the opposite end of the harbour and looking out at the sea. Most of the town was located there with a white church directly opposite the mouth of the harbour.

On one of his walks, Bainbridge was walking up the palm-shaded walk with Monsieur Le Vidocq, a descendant of one of the earlier French settlers. He looked down upon the harbor, where his own vessel and one or two others were lying at anchor; it was a beautiful site. William turned and spoke to the gentleman at his side, addressing him in French, for the Bainbridge was quite as familiar with that language as he was with his own native tongue. The French had owned the island up until 1784.

"Monsieur, I do not know what we will do if we do not get some wind very soon. Have you ever known a calm to last for so long a time?"

"Well, hardly, Captain Bainbridge," replied the Frenchman." That is, not within my recollection. But probably in the course of the next few hours we will see a difference with the changing of the moon."

"Indeed, I hope so, "Bainbridge replied," or I may have to resort to kedging, (use of the anchor to pull the ship) a difficult process amid such tides and currents."

He turned again and looked at the still unruffled surface of the harbor, but just as he was about to resume his walk something arrested his attention; he stood there without moving. It was the sound of a woman's voice singing to the accompaniment of a harp.

Monsieur Le Vidocq noticed the effect of the music upon his companion. "Ah, monsieur," he said," you are listening to the voice of the Rose of St. Bartholomew, Miss Hyleger, the granddaughter of a distinguished Holland gentleman who has business interests here. Yes, it is most entrancing," he added, for Bainbridge had not moved.

Miss Susan Hyleger was the daughter of a respectable and prosperous merchant, and granddaughter of John Hyleger, of Holland, for many years governor of St. Eustatia.

"Indeed you are right, monsieur," he answered at last; "form and feature to accompany such a voice would be well-nigh perfection."

"And so it is," replied the other. "Monsieur le Capitaine, I have an idea. You must meet her and determine for yourself if, in my enthusiasm, I have overestimated the talents of this lovely person."

"Thank you indeed, my kind friend," Bainbridge replied so earnestly that the other could not but smile.

"I accept your offer, and I pray you that, if it is your convenience, the meeting shall be soon."

He turned again to listen more to the low music when his eye happened to sweep out upon the harbor. A breeze had rippled the surface, and a little Swedish brig, lying far out, dropped all her sails as if to take advantage of it. For an instant duty drove all thoughts of the charmer from Bainbridge's mind.

When the breeze was evident Bainbridge forgot all about his friends and the music. He excused himself and apologized for the sudden change in plans. William took off running back to where his small boat was waiting having been drawn up into the sand.

"Off to the ship!" He shouted to the three men at the oars; and in ten minutes the capstan falls were clicking merrily as the ship crawled up to her anchor.

"Damn," he thought to himself. I did want to meet the young lady with the beautiful voice. He had not felt disappointment like that before.

He had been lonely and the thought of a young lady as a companion was appealing. He really did want to meet her.

Bainbridge was ready to sail out of the harbour but the topsails had scarcely begun to draw when the breeze died away and the ship again lay entirely motionless upon the smooth surface. The little brig farther out held it but a little longer, and then dropped anchor with a hasty plash, as if angered at the failure of the elements to help her in her escape.

"Drop the 'mud hook," Bainbridge called out. Now William was disappointed that he was unable to leave port, once again.

The first mate knocked on the Captain's door early in the afternoon. "I believe we have company Sir."

Bainbridge rose up from his small desk where he was making entries into the ship's log and went out on the quarter-deck.

"Why Monsieur Le Vidocq, what a pleasant surprise; come aboard and join me in a glass of port."

"I wish I could, thank you. What I wanted to tell you was that you are invited to my house for dinner this evening. I have also invited Mademoiselle Hyleger to attend the dinner to be given in honor of you Captain Bainbridge."

"Thank you Monsieur, I will be there."

William's heart was racing with the anticipation of meeting this young woman with the voice from heaven. He had to look his best. He felt he better bath first and the best place to do that was off the side of the vessel.

The crew was aware that their Captain was unusually happy and attentive to getting ready for the evening.

Three of the crew volunteered to row him to shore and to wait for him.

Bainbridge was dressed in his best uniform that had been rigorously brushed and all spots attended too. He struck an imposing figure as be made his way up to the little Frenchman's house.

"Good evening Captain Bainbridge, do come in."

William was taken to a large, low-ceiling drawing room to where others had gathered.

"God," thought William, "There she is." There were other women in the room but his eye went right to a tall, slender girl seated on a divan in the corner of the room. She was beautiful with her mass of shining brown hair gently gracing her shoulders; her sparkling light-grey eyes were looking directly at him.

"Captain Bainbridge I would like you to meet Miss Susan Hyleger, the girl with the voice you were so taken with."

William was blushing at the introduction.

"It is an honor to make your acquaintance," and William took her hand and put his lips to the top of it.

"When was it you heard me singing?" asked Miss Hyleger, roguishly glancing at Monsieur Le Vidocq.

"This morning, mademoiselle, and I was hoping to have the opportunity to meet you before we have to sail again; I than had to leave in a hurry when I detected the wind stirring."

"I thought you were running from me. About the time you were hastily escaping down the hill I walked out upon the veranda and observed you."

"I am afraid I have been frustrated with the delays caused by the lack of a breeze to fill my sails."

"I was happy when you were not successful. That may sound awful but here you are."

"Thank you, I am also glad that the unfavorable winds were kindly," William said. He was looking into her eyes and observing Miss Hyleger's features. His heart continued to flutter as they exchanged small talk.

"A very paradoxical statement, sir," smiled the young lady, arising as she took his arm to go into the dining room.

Susan sat next to William at the dining room table. William chatted with her about where he came from, his family, and career.

"I have lived here most of my life. My music is my salvation since activates on the island are few. I am active in the Catholic Church and play and sing every Sunday."

Dinner went well and William bid his host good-by and thanked him profusely.

"Miss Hyleger, may I have the honor of your company tomorrow?"

"I believe I would like that very much."

Bainbridge erased leaving the island from his mind. The wind accommodated his desire not to leave and it did not blow. Susan and William was an item enjoying the other's companionship every minute of the days that followed. William had not experienced a love affair but he was now living one. He was falling in love for the first time in his life.

A week later the winds picked up and they were blowing sufficiently hard so the ship could be carried out past the headland and beyond the rocky reefs.

Susan had walked with William back to his small row boat.

"When will you be back?" Susan was hoping she wouldn't cry.

"I am hoping to be back before another month passes. May I kiss you?"

"Yes, please." Their bodies were almost fused together. Susan could feel the swelling in William's pants causing a stirring sensation in her groin.

When William left the shore in his small boat Susan stayed there until he reached his ship. She then hurried back to the house and went out on the veranda.

William took his glass and he could see the tall young girl in a white dress leaning against one of the portico pillars of the white house on the hillside. Her eyes had a suspicion of tears, but she did not move from her position until she had seen the big ship break out into a cloud of swelling, gleaming sails. She was silently praying that he would have a safe voyage as the vessel reached the safe waters outside the shoals.

Captain Bainbridge, as he looked back at the hillside, realized that this little island, scarcely twenty-five square miles in extent, contained all in the world for him. As he was looking back at the island he once imagined that he saw the flash of a signal as if a white kerchief was waved from the garden-shrouded porch of the house on the hilltop.

He would return again, cargo or no cargo; to that he made up his mind: but he did not know how soon this event was going to occur. However, to his delight, when he reached his destination, one of the islands of the western archipelago, he found a letter from the owners instructing him to pick up a cargo of indigo and dyestuffs, and then set sail for Philadelphia.

ELEVEN

Building a Navy
1798

William Bainbridge was one of the fathers of the United States Navy. Bainbridge picked up where John Barry left off. Barry was the commander of the American Navy and was considered the actual Father of the American Navy; John Barry was America's First Flag Officer.

Bainbridge helped lay the groundwork by which the Navy would become a professional force. He is so esteemed that four ships in America's naval service have borne his name. Bainbridge also experienced some of the worst experiences any naval officer to ever wear the United States Naval uniform had been subject too.

On March 27, 1794, President George Washington had signed "An Act to Provide Naval Armament" authorizing the construction of six frigates (that would create the first U.S. Navy after the Revolution.) The frigates were necessary to protect American merchants at sea.

Construction of the First Six U.S. Frigates

Site:	Frigate	Guns	Superintendent;	Naval Constructor
Portsmouth:	*Congress*-36		James Sever,	James Hackett
Boston:	*Constitution*-44		Samuel Nicholson,	Geo.Claghorn
New York:	*President*-44		Silas Talbot,	Forman Cheeseman
Philadelphia:	*United States*-44		John Barry,	Joshua Humphreys
Baltimore:	*Constellation*-36		Thomas Truxtun,	David Stodder
Gosport:	*Chesapeake*-36		Richard Dale,	Josiah Fox

Four of the ships were frigates with forty-four guns and two smaller ships of thirty-six guns each. The cost for the six ships was way under estimated at $688,000.00 with an annual operating cost of $250,000.00.

American sailors were being captured at sea and held for ransom, or sold as slaves. The capture of American seamen became very frequent and was very expensive for the young American nation to pay the ransoms. Americans were sharply divided as whether to continue paying ransoms or use force.

TWELVE

Marriage
1798

J oy and sorrow were part of 1798 for William Bainbridge. Sorrow came later in the year with the news that his grandfather had died quietly at his home.

William Bainbridge was in love with the girl he met on St Bartholomew. He had written Susan almost daily. Bainbridge doubted that any of his letters ever reached Susan expressing his devotion and love for her. He felt he would see her before the letters were ever delivered.

Bainbridge arrived back in Philadelphia without incident. He was anxious to have the cargo he was carrying unloaded so his ship would be available for a return trip. The crew was cooperative and the ship was quickly unloaded.

The *Hope* needed to be re provisioned and crew adjustments made. The settling up of the pay being owed to the crew had to be made. The cargo to be delivered on a return trip had to be secured and loaded on the ship. Bainbridge confided his desire to go back to St. Bart to his employer.

"Captain Bainbridge, we could not be more delighted that you have found a girl that you want to marry," The owners were genuine in their interest in the best sea captain they had ever had in their employment.

"We certainly encourage you to return as soon as you are ready to sail."

"Thank you for your support, I hope to return to Philadelphia with her as my bride."

Bainbridge sailed out of Philadelphia almost one month to the day from the time he had left the harbor of Gustavia. His vessel reached the island without any major events in relative calm seas. Before they attempted to enter the harbour a native pilot rowed out to the ship to guide them in. The skill of the pilot was a must in safely threading the vessel through the narrow passage in the reefs into the beautiful harbour of Gustavia.

Bainbridge was busy in bringing the vessel to anchor and he was unaware of the small boat that left the little white jetty on the island.

"Company coming," hollered one of the sailors on the topmast.

The small boat was approaching rapidly under the sturdy strokes of her black crew. Bainbridge was scurrying around to prepare the ship to receive the visitors.

"Ahoy, Captain Bainbridge?"

William look over the rail and saw it was his friend the Frenchman and the other was John Hyleger, who had been for many years Governor of St. Eustatius, one of the nearby islands belonging to the Dutch Government.

"Welcome aboard," Bainbridge was hard put to hide his eagerness.

They greeted each other with warm feelings.

William was immediately asking about the health of the Honorable John's granddaughter.

"She is well and looking forward to your visit."

William was to learn later that Susan had been the first to sight the ship. She also was displaying her eagerness in informing her grandfather and his friend of the American captain's approach.

"We have come to not only extend our welcome but to offer you a lift to shore."

"Thank you; I appreciate that since the crew has more pressing duties then to wait on me."

Susan was waiting on the verandah when William reached the house. The Frenchman and John Hyleger discreetly suggested that they had other business to attend too and suggested William go to the house ahead of them.

When William saw Susan he ran to her and embraced her with such vigor that she was having trouble breathing.

"Susan, I must tell you that I am in love with you and I can't stand to leave you again," William was nearly out of breath from talking so fast.

"Oh, I have been praying that you would come back to me."

The two love birds sat on the verandah and talked about the future.

The men arrived back at the house and William enjoyed getting to know them better. They had dinner and after dinner Susan entertained them playing the harp and singing.

The Frenchman invited William to stay at his house. That was agreeable to William since he wanted to spend every minute possible with Susan.

The following day, William and Susan went on a picnic down by the beach.

Susan was an exceptional cook and she had made baked chicken and the trimmings. The picnic food was delicious, in fact William delighted in it since the food he ate on the ship left quite a bit to be desired.

Susan was just finishing packing up the picnic dishes in the wicker basket when she caught William rising on one knee.

"Susan, this maybe sudden but I would like your hand in marriage." I have a ring that I would like to place on your finger."

Susan immediately wrapped her arms around William's neck and hugged him. "Yes, Yes, Yes, I will marry you!"

The newly engaged couple went back to the house. William needed to officially ask John Hyleger for the hand of his granddaughter in marriage.

Mr. Hyleger was on the verandah when they arrived back to the house.

"Mr. Hyleger I have asked your granddaughter to marry me. I know I probably should have come to you first."

"Well, what did she say?" Mr. Hyleger had a large smile on his face.

"She said yes, making me the happiest man on earth."

"Well there you have it, welcome to the family, Captain Bainbridge"

A wedding was planned in the Catholic Church for the following Wednesday. The crew of the ship was advised as to the pending wedding and they were offering their help. The ship needed to be cleaned and made ready for a lady to come aboard for the return trip to Philadelphia.

Invitations to the wedding were hand delivered to friends and neighbors. Susan had the wedding dress from her mother though the dress needed some alterations.

A reception in the church court yard needed to be arranged; food procured and wine made available. The crew on the ship became indispensable in their efforts to make the reception a banquet.

The wedding took place at eleven o'clock in the Catholic Church. The presiding priest was an old friend of the Hyleger's. The priest made sure that the wedding was a special mass of celebration; it was also a special ceremony for him since he was losing the person that provided the music every Sunday.

All of the crew of the ship was dressed in clean dress clothes. They had all bathed and shaved and generally looked civilize. Whiskey Jack was even sober and served in the wedding party as William's best man.

John Hyleger proudly gave his daughter away. He was fighting the pangs in his heart that his granddaughter was leaving him. He knew that day would come, but not so soon.

The bride looked radiant in her mother's white wedding gown with a long train. William was dressed in a new blue coat with silver buttons as large as half dollars. Susan and William made a story book couple. The church was filled to capacity to witness the joining of these two special and talented people.

The reception was well attended by all those in witness of the wedding. The wine flowed freely. A string group provided the music for those wanting to dance. The food was good due to the efforts of crew of the vessel. The crew also took charge of serving drinks as well as serving the food. The wine and food was devoured by the ravenous well wishers before the evening ended.

The newly married couple was going to stay at the house for a few days before leaving the island for the return trip to Philadelphia.

William did not want to spend his first nights in bed with Susan on his bed on the ship. The ship at best was not too private. He wanted to enjoy his love making with Susan in as ideal conditions as possible.

They left the wedding party and went to Susan's room. Susan had a dressing room where she put on a new night gown. William had a long night shirt that he slipped into. He was standing next to the bed as Susan entered from the dressing room.

William took her in his arms, lifted up on the bed and kissed her on the lips. He lay down next to her and took her in his arms and kissed her again.

"I am so happy William, I do love you."

"I love you with all my heart. I want you in my arms forever."

"I have never coupled before William. I do not know what to do."

"I haven't either. All I know that my member is throbbing," as William place her hand on his throbbing organ."

"Oh my, said Susan, it is bigger than I ever thought and it is much ridged. It also slippery; what do you have on it?"

"Nothing added; that is just the natural fluid leaking out from the end of my member to make it slippery."

"Can I put it inside of you? If I don't I am going to burst."

William made an awkward adjustment of his body so that he was straddling Susan. He had raised her night gown and his member was entering her moist mound.

"Oh William… gently. Oh what a feeling… I have never had anything like that before."

"I can't believe the sensation." He slowly eased his member in until he met some resistance. Susan gave a slight jerk and he passed the resistance and buried his member to its entire length.

"Ah, I am sorry I can't hold it," as William jerked violently to a climax of the likes he had never experienced before.

"William, are you okay?"

"Yes, that was wonderful, I am sorry I released so quickly."

The love birds were on the island one more week before everything was ready for departure.

The island winds were blowing strong and steady. The cargo was stowed, and the sails were loosened ready to be dropped at the word. Susan's harp had been loaded on board and carefully enclosed in a wooden crate so that it would not become damaged in case of rough seas.

The newly married couple rowed off to his ship. There was a large crowd on shore cheering them on. William was extremely proud of the slender figure that sat beside him in the stern sheets; she turned from a half-tearful gaze at the little island and especially two figures standing on the shore. She glanced up into her husband's face, smiling bravely and confidently. Never was such a precious cargo carried by any ship that sailed under any flag for any port.

THIRTEEN

France
1798

The sailing back to Philadelphia was an awkward, uncomfortable, and sometimes embarrassing experience for a young lady that had led a sheltered and pampered life.

William's cabin was small. The crew had enlarged the Captain's bed so they could be relatively comfortable in the same bed.

"Where do we go to the bathroom," Susan was looking around.

"I forgot to tell you, the commode is that chair like unit with a seat on it in the corner over there; a crew member will come in and empty it every day and dose it with vinegar."

"How lovely, this might take some getting used to."

"What do you mean? William was naive when it came to women and their habits.

"I need to have time in the morning to use the toilet and to bath before getting dressed."

"No problem, I will make sure that you are not disturbed," William smiled at her with love and respect.

"If you really want to know, I use a clyster every morning so I don't go through the embarrassment of having to practically undress to use a chamber pot after I have dressed." Beside men don't know the embarrassment of having to use a friend chamber pot for anything more than relieving the bladder and here is even more embarrassing. Men just do not have any idea of the indignities a woman has to suffer through."

"My First Officer, who is my medical aid officer on the ship, sometimes insists that he give me a clyster when I complain of stomach problems. I don't mind, I just do it rather than argue with him and generally I feel better."

"When we are home I will give them to you; you should do them on a regular basis to maintain good health and prevent autointoxication," Susan seemed serious about what she was saying.

"You might also be asked to assist in treating the crew; they seem to be constipated frequently, more than anything else. Since we are a small vessel I am considered the ships chief medical person and my First Officer my aid. I have men coming to me suffering with anything from abscesses, agues, anemia, to whooping cough, wind and worms. I get wounds of various kinds, fractures and dislocations, accidents, ulcers, boils, fistulae, infected swelling, sores and skin rashes. I also get internal problems such as agues, stomach pains, and as I said, constipation.

"William you are like the general practitioner we had back on the island. Maybe I can help."

"You can observe and then decide. The men are crude, rude, and nothing embarrasses them."

"Are there men who a currently ill?"

"Nothing really, I am sure in a few days some of the men will be complaining of complications caused by the pox."

"What is the pox?"

"It is syphilis that the men develop from having sexual intercourse with whores."

"Oh."

"Well, enough of that; let me show you around you new home for the next month."

Susan adjusted quite well to the ship's life. She also found herself busy with assisting with the crew ailments. The crew was also taking advantage of the fact Susan was a beautiful young lady so William suspected many of the complaints from the crew were bogus.

William's father and mother were eagerly awaiting the arrival of William and his new bride, Susan, at a family gathering in Middleton. John Taylor was hosting the reunion and he was particularly impressed by

Susan's charm and brightness. Little did they know this would be the last time they would see John Taylor alive.

William Bainbridge was in his twenty-fourth year. He had more experience and wisdom of a much older person. He had already dealt with situations in a short span of time that seasoned sailors never experienced in the life time.

William looked young but that was certainly forgotten when older piers engaged him in conversation. He had a dignified and calm manner and most of all he was in control of his temper. His blue eyes seem to twinkle when you looked into them.

The United States was experiencing difficulties with France which led to the quasi war with that country. France felt the new United States was a push over and merchant shipping was fair game for them. They had now opened a new field for enterprising and chivalrous exertion.

The Congress had found it necessary to organize a small navy for the protection of United States commerce from the encroachments of the French privateers. William was being used to go to various navy yards to rehabilitate the service, which had dwindled almost into nothing since the close of the war of the Revolution. To Bainbridge it was inconceivable how the new government had dismissed the idea it did not have an obligation to protect its citizens that was so clearly stated in the Constitution, Article 1, section eight, paragraph thirteen, "to provide and maintain a Navy." The government was now attempting to show concern but it faced many problems.

Article one, section eight of the Constitution: Powers of Congress stipulated in paragraph eleven:

- To declare War, grant Letters of Marque and Reprisal, and make Rules concerning Captures on Land and Water;
- To provide and maintain a Navy;
- To make Rules for the Government and Regulation of the land and naval Forces;
- To make all Laws which shall be necessary and proper for carrying into Execution the foregoing Powers, and all other Powers vested by this Constitution in the Government of the United States, or in any Department or Officer thereof.

One looming problem was there were not sufficient officers to man the projected vessels that were being made ready to put to sea. The merchant marine was there main source for capable seamen. The down side of using merchant seamen was that they had not received any military instruction; they lacked knowledge in naval regulation, naval duties, and maneuvers. The past officers of the Revolution were getting old but they could be depended on to assist in training. Commodore John Barry, deceased, had single handedly trained most of the existing navel officers that were available for immediate duty.

The Secretary of the Navy felt that a judicious selection from among the commanders of the American merchant vessels was going to be necessary. Among the first names inscribed on the list of the Secretary of War, who was then acting as Secretary of the Navy, was that of William Bainbridge. Bainbridge already had an enviable reputation as a leader, for bravery, diplomacy, and also as a successful naval captain.

Captain Decatur (whose son, Stephen Decatur, was so soon to distinguish himself) sailed back to Philadelphia in the sloop-of-war the *Delaware*. He also brought back with him the schooner *L'Incroyable,* a French vessel he had recently taken as a prize.

William was accepted into the newly reorganized United States Navy with the rank of Lieutenant- Commander and given command of the schooner *Retaliation* on August 3, 1798. The schooner, then known as *L'Incroyable* had been captured from the French by the elder Stephen Decatur.

The Navy Secretary hosted a large dinner party at Carpenter Hall for the new navy officers, towards the end of August.

The Bainbridge's were among the honored guests. William was decked out in his new uniform and he looking like what the ideal man in uniform should look like. Susan had a new gown that was the envy of the ladies. She was somewhat self conscience of the fact that she was the most looked at person at the festive event.

"You are the most beautiful women here," William whispered in Susan's ear. "Everyone wants to get a look at you."

"Well, you certainly the most handsome man here," Susan came right back.

The two made a grand entrance and they were greeted by those in the Navy department.

The string orchestra was providing the music for those inclined to dance.

Susan and William danced with much grace. Their floating over the floor was much admired by those watching.

The sit down dinner was a long affair. Wine was served and toasts were made. Dinner was finally served and it was fair. There was ample amount of food but the kitchen in Carpenter Hall was perhaps stretched a bit when it came to food preparation.

The Bainbridge's did not arrive home until after midnight. William unhooked the buggy and placed the horse in the small horse barn out back. Susan went into the house to get ready for bed.

When William came in he went to their bedroom and undressed. He was hot and sweaty so he went into the bathroom and washed. He came back into the bedroom naked.

"Ho my, William, you have no clothes on," Susan was trying not to look. She did not realize William was scared as badly as he was. His upper legs were particularly scarred and parts of his abdomen.

"You have seen me naked before, any way you are my wife."

"That is true; I just haven't seen you fully naked like this. I am not acquainted with seeing a man body entirely naked except yours. I have to say I like what I see."

"Come to bed and let me caress your body and bring you pleasure."

The time passed all too fast and it was September 10th and William was scheduled to ship out the following morning.

"I am going to miss you terribly William," Susan had tears in her eyes.

"I am also going to miss you. You are the love of my life and my reason for living."

"When will you be back?"

"I will try with paramount effort to be back for Christmas. I will write to you and attempt to get letters on to ships coming back to the States."

FOURTEEN

Retaliation
1799

In a few months the vessel was outfitted, under a new name, the *Retaliation*. With William Bainbridge at the helm she set sail in September 11, 1799, in company with the brig *USS Norfolk, 18 6-pounders* under the command of Captain Williams.

Bainbridge's orders were to cruise in the West Indies to protect American commerce against French cruisers. They were to join up with the *USS Montezuma, 20 9-pounders* under the flag of Commodore Murray.

The islands of the West Indies were dangerous sailing grounds for peaceable and unarmed merchantmen. Pirates teemed in the Gulf, and the French privateers, who fell but little short of being freebooters, rendezvoused at various ports and preyed rather indiscriminately upon all vessels weaker than themselves.

Open war between France and the United States was not official but at sea that was not true, hostilities against Americans were plenteous. Americans were thought to be weak and easily intimidated.

William chased two small French vessels back to the protection of their harbors in October. Bainbridge was a new breed of captain that was not going to be easy takings for those who threaten to harm them.

Nothing else occurred until November 20rd giving William the opportunity to take advantage of the lack of activity on the seas to train the crew to function as a military unit. The men that had come on board were merchant seamen but through untiring efforts of Bainbridge they became proficient in the handling of the cannons and the ship, and how to fight. The *Retaliation* was now as good as any United States naval vessel afloat.

Bainbridge demanded that strict discipline was maintained. He used strong measures to enforce compliance of his orders. Bainbridge was a strict disciplinarian who was not particularly liked by the men under his command who were disruptive sailors; and he was none too fond of them either.

The result was the officers knew their ship and knew their men, and the latter had begun to show respect for their commander, William Bainbridge. Commodore Murray had taken occasion to compliment him on the wonderful improvement accomplished under his direction.

The *Retaliation* was off the island of Guadeloupe on November 20th. The sun was just peering over the horizon when one of the crew up on the main topsail spotted three sails bearing east-south-east and only about two leagues in the distant. At about the same time two other vessels appeared to the westward side of the *Retaliation*.

Commodore Murray in his vessel, *Montezuma equipped with twenty 9-pounders,* signaled to Bainbridge to hold his course, while the *Montezuma* and Captain Williams in the *USS Norfolk,* 18 6-pounders bore away in chase of the strangers to the west.

Bainbridge thought that the three sails they had first sighted were British. Bainbridge kept the schooner, *Retaliation with 14 4-pounders,* on his way and was not surprised when he saw the English colors go up to the peak of the leading frigate. As the ships drew within one hundred feet of each other they witness the lowering of the English flag and the rising of the France flag. The two French frigates were the *Volontaire-44 guns* and *L'Insurgent-36 guns.*

Captain Barro of the *L'Insurgent* fired a broadside at *Retaliation* that brought a few spars to deck and smashed into the bulwarks. The *Volontaire* had tacked to the other side of the *Retaliation*. The Captain on the *L'Insurgent* ordered Bainbridge to lower his flag and repair on board immediately.

Bainbridge was totally unprepared for making any resistance, and as the ship on his port hand carried forty-four guns, and the one on the other carried thirty-six, there was nothing else to do but give in.

The flag on the *Retaliation* was lowered. Bainbridge could only think that this was the lowest point in his life. He ordered the small boat to be lowered and he rowed off to the larger vessel, *Volontaire,* in obedience to the order.

The *Volontaire* was a fine craft, but as soon William step on the deck he could see that things existed on board of her that would not be tolerated on board English or an American vessel of the regular service. The men appeared slovenly and the decks were littered about with various odds and ends, and untidy to a degree. As he walked up to the quarterdeck, a handsome, middle-aged man with a great deal of gold lace on the wide lapels of his long-tailed coat approached him.

Bainbridge drew his sword and extended the hilt toward the resplendent stranger, balancing the blade across his forearm.

"May I ask to whom I have the honor of surrendering?" Bainbridge said in his best French.

"To Commodore St. Lawrence, of the navy of the French Republic; but as you had no opportunity to defend yourself; I beg you, sir, pray retain your sword."

Commodore St. Lawrence very politely then asked the name of Bainbridge's vessel, and, learning of her former career, made some remark that might be translated into "turn-about is fair play."

The *Volontaire,* crew had drawn the *Retaliation* near them so they now had complete control of the vessel. The *Retaliation* was now their prize and the French placed their crew on board.

L'Insurgent, and *Volontaire,* was making plans to go after the *Norfolk* and the *Montezuma.* Bainbridge could hear them discussing in French that the two ships had apparently run out of wind. *L'Insurgent* and a small vessel in their group had set sail to chase the *Norfolk* and the *Montezuma.* The *Volontaire* was only one mile from them, a distance they could close easily provided they had a breeze. The *Norfolk and Montezuma* were out gunned by the French ships so they would also be also taken as prizes if they caught by them.

On the deck of the *Volontaire* Bainbridge had joined the group of officers that had made their way forward to the forecastle. Bainbridge was feeling great deal of distress he watched the *L'Insurgent* near the American ships, which had little chance of escape left too them. Suddenly the French commodore turned to him.

"Monsieur," he said, " what is the size and armament of your two consorts yonder?"

Without hesitation Bainbridge made reply:

"The ship, sir, mounts twenty-eight long twelve-pounders and the brig twenty nine-pounders."

And if he breathed an inward prayer for thus doubling his friends' armaments, he must have smiled also to see the result of his ruse de guerre. Commodore St. Lawrence, displaying a great deal of excitement in his manner and gestures, hustled his officers to right and left, loudly calling upon them to signal L'Insurgent and the smaller vessel to return.

Soon it was seen that the former had perceived her recall, for she came about and waited until the *Volontaire* bore down within speaking distance. In the mean time the *Norfolk* and the *Montezuma,* having caught a new squall of air, were making off, carrying all their sail and growing smaller and smaller every minute of the time.

An amusing conversation now took place between the flagship *Volontaire* and smaller frigate, *L'Insurgent*, amusing to Bainbridge anyway.

Captain Barro, the commander of *L'Insurgent*, was livid to a point of almost jumping up and down in his anger. He was less than officer like as he demanded the reason for his being called off just as he was about to capture both vessels.

Commodore St. Lawrence called back to Captain Barro. "The two vessels were of superior force," he went on to state, shrieking his words over the taffrail, for the two ships were now near together:

"I could have taken them both, monsieur. There was not a gun on board either heavier than a six-pounder." He hammered angrily upon the rail with his heavy cocked hat, almost weeping in his wrath and irritation.

The commodore, who had spoken hitherto in fairly good English, turned to Bainbridge, who was standing by, with difficulty repressing the smile that would rise to his lip.

"Did you not say, sir that the force of these vessels was such as I have stated?"

"I did," respond Bainbridge sternly; "but if I could save two ships of my Government simply by misrepresenting their strength, I think I was justified in doing so. The circumstances warranted my hazarding the assertion, sir."

Perhaps St. Lawrence recognized the logic and made allowance for the temptation, for he said no more.

Commodore St. Lawrence requested Captain Bainbridge's presence at his table that evening, as if nothing had occurred.

During the course of his stay on board the *Volontaire* Commodore St. Lawrence he treated William Bainbridge with the greatest kindness and consideration, and presented him to General Desfourneaux, who was being sent out from France to Guadeloupe to supersede the famous Governor, Victor Hughes.

The French took the *Retaliation* into Guadeloupe, arriving the following day. The three French vessels of war and their new prize anchored in the harbour about six miles from Basse-Terre, the capital of the Island. Bainbridge and his crew were imprisoned the same morning they landed.

This inauspicious start to Bainbridge's naval career was marked by the fact that his command was the first American ship lost in the Quasi-War with France.

The officers and crew of the *Retaliation* were ordered into close confinement in a loathsome prison. The place was full of filth, bugs and rats were everywhere. Commodore St. Lawrence for some reason felt that Bainbridge and his commissioned officers should be brought back to his ship. They were transported back to the *Volontaire* and allowed to remain on board the frigate, where they were given full liberty and treated with kindness.

Ten days pasted before Bainbridge was permitted to visit the shore on his parole of honor. Bainbridge wanted to meet with General Desfoureaux whom he had met on that faithful day of their capture. They had had very few words in that meeting but Bainbridge was encouraged he could do business with him. Bainbridge felt he could arrange with General Desfourneaux, an exchange of prisoners, in accordance with instructions transmitted to him by Commodore Murray, who had sent a letter in to him by a Danish brig.

It was just at this time that the French people had begun that system of the affectation of extreme equality. Ceremony was dispensed with and a strange attitude of comradeship, simplicity, and make-believe frankness took its place.

Bainbridge dressed in civilian dress clothes for his meeting with General Desfourneaux. Bainbridge was shown into a small room with three chairs and nothing else to wait for General Desfoureaux to see him. William only had to wait for a few minutes before he was admitted, and the General asked him to seat himself at the table with him. The table was set for dinner, table cloth and matching napkins so the General could have his lunch.

The General started by declaring that: "sea fare does not agree with me, it makes my bowels lock up."

Bainbridge looked directly at him but didn't feel he needed to comment.

"Please join me in my meal; there is ample food for two of us." The General had apparently planned on the young American to join him in the meal of a "blunt old soldier."

"Captain, please feel free to talk openly and frankly to me just like any two citizens' would talk over their wine."

Bainbridge was on his guard with this crafty, wily old diplomat. He could tell the General was used to intrigue, and able to blow hot and cold with the same breath, despite his air of sincerity and camaraderie.

Bainbridge was well aware it would pay him well to be upon his guard.

"Now, captain," commenced the hoary old villain.

"Lieutenant, sir," put in Bainbridge, anxious to appear on even terms at the outset.

The general did not notice the interruption, except that he corrected himself in the next sentence, continuing:

"I do not wish you to consider yourself as a prisoner, Lieutenant, nor do I desire that your comrades shall be treated as such. I pray you look upon your stopping here as if you were visitors detained merely from political motives. We intend to treat you as both friends and allies, I assure you."

In view of the fact that his crew were now lingering in a filthy dungeon, this assertion appeared to be something remarkable, but it did not trouble the "blunt old soldier" in the slightest degree.

"Of course, it may seem strange, but I have long thought how great an advantage would accrue from the establishment of commercial relations between this beautiful island and your great country of the United States."

Bainbridge remained silent, waiting to hear what all this would lead up to, for he did not doubt that there was much more behind it.

"If you would but consider yourself the representative of your nation which you are, for there are no others that rank on the island, we could accomplish a great deal to the mutual advantage of our respective countries," went on Desfourneaux, who had lost all interest in his soldier's fare.

"I promise that I will liberate your men and officers, and restore your ship to you, if you will agree to consider, as the representative of your country, of course, the island of Guadeloupe as neutral during the passage d'armes between the French Republic and the United States."

Bainbridge saw the pit into which the other would draw him, and he replied calmly, after a moment's thought, choosing his words in order that he might not be misunderstood.

"You must know, general," William said," that my authority extends no farther than to enter into an arrangement for an exchange of prisoners. If I took upon myself to enter into such negotiations as you mention, and they were disclaimed, you would place the United States in the position of an aggressor, which probably would please you. And whatever may be your views in regard to the condition of my men I speak not for myself I consider the crew of the Retaliation as not only being held in captivity, but as being treated with great barbarity."

The general then adopted a confidential tone in his reply: "I admit that it appears so, yes," he said; "but you see Monsieur Hughes has not yet left the island. I cannot revoke his orders until his departure. This, allow me to say, is the explanation."

"General Desfourneaux," returned Bainbridge, "while your proposition seems very liberal, I cannot see my way clear to assume this responsibility; but if you wish to make a cartel of my vessel, I will vouch that my country will exchange prisoners, man for man."

"I intend to include," put in the wily Governor, as if offering special inducements, "all of the political hostages now on the island."

Bainbridge, however, was not to be entrapped, and the curious interview was terminated without any agreement.

"Thank you for lunch and wine. I do hope that your words have promise of a closer relationship."

Bainbridge was allowed to visit the prison where the "political hostages" were confined in a dungeon much too small for them. Most of the prisoners were almost naked and in a state of starvation. Many of them were masters of various commercial vessels.

The jailer of the prison was a drunken, unfeeling brute, not caring if the prisoners lived or died. The news had been circulated among the prisoners that they were about to secure their liberty. For at least a day they had hope. Their rejoicing was premature and disappointment set in as their condition grew worse and worse. It seemed to Bainbridge that the new Governor was taking revenge on them and in no way was going to help. All the assurances from General Desfoureaux the prisoners would be placed better prisons and receive better treatment were not happening.

"At least the prisoners could be treated like human beings," Bainbridge commented to no one. Bainbridge was feeling powerless is assisting his countrymen; although he boldly remonstrated against conduct so averse to the modern usages of war. Nothing but the fact that he had gained some powerful friends through his own personality prevented the Governor from placing him in close confinement.

FIFTEEN

Guadeloupe
1799

Near the end of December the *Ponsea,* frigate, from Point Petre, arrived at Guadeloupe, and on board of her were twenty or thirty Americans who had been captured by French privateers. In consequence of the diminution of the French force, as alleged by the captain of the frigate, these men had been compelled to do duty as part of the crew. Hearing of this occurrence, Bainbridge waited upon Desfourneaux, and alleged that as these men were prisoners of war they should not be kept in confinement where they might be compelled at any time to take up arms against their countrymen.

The *Ponsea* when it anchored in the harbor was under the jurisdiction of the Governor. The Governor had promised William that there was no reason to detain the men on a public ship.

But the next day Bainbridge, to his anger and indignation, saw the *Ponsea* sailing for France without one of the Americans being released from their bondage. Angry at being thus trifled with, he again sought an interview, and a heated discussion followed, which ended in the Governor's renewing his offer to liberate all citizens of the United States, provided that Bainbridge would assume the responsibility he had hitherto refused. He also insisted that Bainbridge should use his best influence to open trade with Guadeloupe, although he knew what a nest of pirates the harbor was.

Bainbridge wrote a letter to General Desfoureaux a few days later:

"To His Excellency, the Governor of Guadeloupe:

"*Sir: As you are well aware that the prisons of Basse-Terre are crowded with my fellow-citizens, many of whom have been brought into port since my arrival, and as I know from my own observation that American merchant vessels have been here condemned as lawful prizes, your Excellency will excuse me if I express doubt of your good will toward either the Government or the citizens of the United States. You offer to restore the Retaliation to my command. I cannot accept unless I am permitted to follow the instructions of my Government, viz., to capture all armed vessels sailing under the flag of the French Republic. The Retaliation is now a French prize, being captured by two of your national frigates. I cannot take command of a vessel belonging to an enemy and give a pledge to be governed by an enemy's orders without disgracing myself as an officer and rendering myself liable to deserved punishment by a court martial. If I return in the Retaliation, she must be a cartel and commanded by a French officer.*"

"*I have the honor to be yours, etc.*

"*W. Bainbridge.*"

The letter was delivered to the Governor. When the Governor was finished reading the letter he threw it on the floor and went into a rage over Bainbridge's refusal to accept his proposition. He sent for the lieutenant and informed him of his intention to place him in close imprisonment.

"Governor, I wish to assure you that no fear of punishment could induce him to abandon the principles which would always govern him as an officer of the American navy."

General Desfoureaux wanted to conciliate the United States, even if he could obtain no pledge in advance. Desfourneaux fitted out a cartel, under the command of a French captain. The orders to the French Captain were too safely transport a ship load of prisoners to Philadelphia on the *Retaliation.* The United States was to return prisoners amounting to nearly three hundred back to Guadeloupe.

In a final interview with Bainbridge he declared that he had resolved to compel the immediate departure of the *Retaliation,* and in the event of any act of hostility being committed previous to her arrival in the United States, he would put to death every American prisoner who might be hereafter captured or brought to the island.

Bainbridge was successful in his dealings with the General who was now the new governor of Guadeloupe. The General felt that Bainbridge was a man that made a better ally then enemy. Arrangements were made to have the *Retaliation* returned to the United States with as many American prisoners that he was able to negotiate for. Bainbridge had demonstrated that his tact to obtain their liberty was greatly appreciated especially by the men held prisoner.

The cartel bore prepared dispatches to the President of the United States, in which General Desfourneaux made assurances of the neutral position of the island, and pointed to his release of the prisoners as a pledge of his sincerity. What he really feared was a blockade of his ports!

SIXTEEN

Master and Commander Bainbridge, Norfolk
1799

When Bainbridge arrived back to Philadelphia he was in the Secretary of the Navy's office to receive his new assignment. The Secretary of the Navy was requesting that Bainbridge be sent to New York to oversee the ship yards. This was arduous service in the icy New York January weather.

Bainbridge learned on that visit that while he was in New York, freezing his ass off, that five lieutenants had been promoted over him to the rank of captain.

"What is this all about, these five men being promoted over me?" William was red in the face, about to explode. He remonstrated in vain against this act of injustice, but received no reparation, except an assurance that it would not occur again. Nothing but his pride and attachment to the service, and the earnest solicitation of his friends, prevented his pursuing a course which would have deprived the navy of an efficient and capable officer.

Bainbridge's conduct was highly approved of by the Government upon investigation of the Guadeloupe incident. He was immediately promoted to the rank of master and commander on March 29, 1799.

Bainbridge was given the command of the 18-gun brig-of-war the USS *Norfolk* (the vessel he had saved), then lying in the Delaware River. He was given directions to fit her for active service as quickly as possible.

The Congress passed the "Retaliation Act" against French citizens captured on the ocean in 1798. The "Retaliation Act" had passed after Bainbridge had reported to Congress the outrages committed on American prisoners. The quasi war with France, still exited without an end in sight.

The *USS Norfolk* under the command of Bainbridge was sent to the West Indies to report to Commodore Christopher R. Perry. His orders were to capture the French luger *Republican* and the destroying of any other French vessels he might encounter.

Bainbridge made a number of captures of French privateers and sinking several smaller vessels during the years 1799-1800. His main objective was capturing the *Republican.*

Bainbridge finally tracked the *Republican* off the coast of Cape Nicola Mole on November 8th.

The *Republican* was sighted and Bainbridge using the old 'line-ahead' approach over took the *Republican*. Bainbridge was able to get on the windward side of the *Republican* and rack the deck with a broadside. The *Norfolk* continued firing until the *Republican* submitted to their strength and superior seamanship of the *Norfolk,*

The crew of the *Norfolk* was elated to being able to take a prize that in some sense was an important part of their mission.

They had been set to cruise to the West Indies and even though he had his prize they captured a number of piratical craft. By the time they arrived on the island of Hispaniola, they were happy to unload their prisoners.

Bainbridge had created his own small squadron. The *Norfolk* was the flagship, the brig *Warren* 18-guns, the sloop *Pinckney* 18-guns On November 14th Bainbridge and his small squadron arrived at the mouth of the harbor of Havana, Cuba. He anchored his small force so they could blockade the harbor of Havana to prevent the escape of a large French privateer that was in the harbour. Bainbridge did the blockade so effactually that the French privateer was dismantled rather than enter into a fire fight. This singular act assured that ample protection was afforded to American merchant vessels cruising in Cuban waters. Havana was one of the largest cities of the Americas and trade with Cuba was paramount to the growth of the United States.

The French cruisers they had trapped in Havana had for years preyed on the commerce of the United States. The United States had been split as to the use of military action; in fact they had no military (navy) at the time to take any action. The damage done to American merchantmen was ruinous and could not continue; the cost was too great.

What Bainbridge brought to the trading waters was his untiring and ever vigilance dedication to seek out and control the French war-ships. Bainbridge kept continually at sea during the following six months, with the exception of ten days when he was forced to go into port for water and provisions.

The American merchants of Havana, upon his departure for the United States, presented him with the following letter, dated March I, 1800:

"Having witnessed the ample protection which you have extended to American commerce trading to this island, it would be doing injustice to our feelings were we to suppress our acknowledgments of the vigilance, perseverance, and urbanity which have marked your conduct during your arduous command on this station."

"It must afford peculiar pleasure to the citizens of the United States to know that a trade which was so recently exposed to frequent depredations now passes in almost certain security; and we doubt not that they, with us, will do you the justice to acknowledge the essential services which you have rendered your country."

Sailing from Havana in March, Bainbridge arrived in Philadelphia early in April. Susan was at the dock as the *Norfolk* sailed in. She was just part of a large crowd of Philadelphian's wanting to welcome home the *Norfolk*.

William found Susan in the crowd and waved a large handkerchief. She too was waving a handkerchief. It was an emotional event for both of them having been separated for so long. Susan was probably crying because she was so happy that her husband had arrived home alive.

William was off the *Norfolk* first having turned the helm over to his first lieutenant. He had a large package under his arm. Susan ran to him and threw her arms around his neck and planted a large kiss on his eager lips.

"Damn I missed you, kiss me again," William didn't care who was looking.

They immediately proceeded for their home in the Society Hills area. All of his family was well and anxiously awaiting him. His parents had come from New York to celebrate their son's success.

On his arriving home he learned that he had been promoted to Captain. This was to the delight of all his family and friends. To his own satisfaction, he heard that his conduct had been viewed favorably by the President, and that he had been the one who promoted him to the rank of captain; his commission was dated May 1, 1800.

Even though William was tired they had a large welcome party with music included. Susan sang William's favorite musical pieces and played the harp. William thought her voice was more beautiful then he remembered.

The guests ate and drank well. It was late when the last guests left.

"That was some party son," as William's father placed his hand on William's shoulder.

"Thank you for being here dad, it means a lot to me."

They all decided it was time to retire.

"Thank God you are here William. I have missed you so and worried."

"I missed you too. You will never know how I missed you."

"I bought you a small gift," William pulled a neatly wrapped package with a gold bow from his coat pocket.

"Thank you, the package is so pretty I hate to unwrap it," she did but she was carefully not to damage the wrapping paper.

"It is perfume, I have never had perfume before, oh how exciting! The flask is beautiful."

"That is a Napoleon III opaque glass bottle and it is hand painted. Open the flask and smell!"

"Oh it is like a piece of heaven, I have never smelled anything like that before," Susan was indeed pleased.

"The perfume is special, it come from the town of Grasses and I am told is the finest in the whole world. I learned that they make the perfume from fresh roses and jasmine."

William embraced Susan and they fell on the bed. They both were tearing at each other clothes. Finally they succeeded in pressing their naked bodies against each other. They made love with intense passion.

"Thank you for being my husband, Susan kissed William again before going to sleep.

Book Two

Captain William Bainbridge paying tribute to the Dey of
Algiers, May 20, 1800.

SEVENTEEN

Algeria
1800

Bainbridge was promoted to captain at the age of twenty-six on May 1, 1800. Bainbridge had gained the highest rank in the United States navy as captain. Only a few days later he was ordered to the command of the frigate *USS George Washington*, a fine vessel, and one of the largest in the United States navy. The frigate was designed for a complement of 220 officers and enlisted men. The ship's armament comprised of 24 9-pounders and eight 6-pounders.

The rank of captain was the highest military rank obtainable in the United States Navy. A captain might be called a commodore when more than two ships were in his command but the rank of commodore was not an official rank in the navy until the Civil War.

The United States was suffering through ignorance of infancy as a nation. Some of those in Congress felt the United States did not need to engage in conflicts with those who were doing harm to our shipping trade. A majority in Congress felt that if we were nice to everybody they would be nice to us. Many of the politicians in Congress had never met an enemy that they didn't like.

Libya was supportive of pirates but it was Algeria that was aggressive as pirates on the seas in capturing vessels. Algeria had learned that merchant vessels were easy prey and countries like the United States would pay ransom for the prisoners they would capture and best of all, Americans would pay them large sums of money to not pursue American trade vessels. The Congress caved into the Algerians demands for tribute money like a child being bullied by an older thug.

Bainbridge's new orders were to deliver tribute money to the Algerian enemy of the United States. Bainbridge found this assignment distasteful as well as objectionable to his personal values. He was not the least bit pleased that he was chosen to deliver tribute to the Dey of Algiers so that American merchant ships would be protected from Algerian pirates. There was no guarantee all the American vessels would be protected from pirates. The United States had no naval presents in that part of the world to enforce the promise.

Bainbridge was a principled individual, with high moral values; he expected others to also act in the same matter. He did not believe in paying protection money, he believed the United States had to present a show of might to include the roar of their cannons to protect their rights.

President John Adams ordered Bainbridge to delivered treaty tribute "gifts" (jizya) for safe travel in the Mediterranean to the Dey of Algiers. The Congress felt that the delivering of tribute to the Dey of Algiers would keep the Barbary pirates from raiding American shipping vessels. The Congress apparently lacked the backbone as a voting group to defend the freedom from seizer on the high seas. Some even were naive enough to suggest the problem would gradually go away.

The Muslim terrorists in Northern Africa, with the approval of the Dey of Algiers, were sworn to carry out jihad against all Western powers. The American Congress said they favored a peaceful solution of paying them tribute even though they were strapped for money as a new nation.

The President felt Bainbridge was best qualified naval representative in a position of command to affect success in delivering the blood money and affecting political stability. Bainbridge was considered by his peers as high-spirited in nature and somebody that could handle the Dey of Algiers with success. The Dey was reported to hate the Americans, but he liked the money they were foolish enough to send him.

William's father was seated in an armchair in the warm spring sunshine, and beside him sat the wife of his favorite son. Her head was leaning against his aging knee, and one of her hands was clasped in both of his.

" Indeed, my dear, it is hard to have him leave us again so soon; but

I can tell you that it is an honor, of course, that he should accept the command of such a fine vessel; perhaps he may not be sent on the foreign service for some time, and we may have him here much longer with us."

"Hello! Who is coming up the road?" he added, breaking off suddenly and raising one hand to shade his eyes.

"Someone on horseback," answered Mrs. Bainbridge, rising to her feet.

A man, on a strong brown horse, reined in at the steps and, leaping from the saddle, leaving the nag to nibble at the short spring turf announced:

"Dispatches for Captain Bainbridge, sir," he said, saluting.

"I'll bring them to him," said Mrs. Bainbridge, extending her hand. But she was saved the trouble of accepting the package; William was standing in the doorway. He had seen the rider approaching from their upstairs bedroom window.

"I'll take that my dear. It is from the naval offices and probably my orders," William could see Susan was very troubled.

"Sailing orders, William?" she asked, her under lip trembling suspiciously.

"Yes, dear, I fear so." Without breaking the seal he turned and went into the house. Mrs. Bainbridge again slipped her hand into her father-in-laws outstretched palm. A tear that she endeavored to hide stole down her cheek, but the older man had noticed it.

"A sailor's wife" he began.

"Should be brave, I know," concluded his daughter-in-law, anticipating his remark; "but sometimes it does seem hard, I must confess."

A silence followed that was broken by the footsteps of Captain Bainbridge approaching down the hallway. It was evident that he was suffering from some irritation.

"Well, William," asked his father," what's the news? Welcome, I hope."

"Quite the reverse, sir," replied the Captain. "I am ordered to take that infamous tribute to Algiers! A pretty commission for a gentleman and an officer to execute!"

"It is a disgrace to the country," exclaimed Dr. Bainbridge, thumping down both fists on the arms of his chair.

"There is one kind of tribute I would like to give them," continued William," and that is from the mouth of my guns. The idea that we, a Christian nation, and bound to be one of the most powerful, should permit

83

such a scandal as buying immunity from a lot of Barbary pirates is almost as bad as submitting to the English right of search."

"If anything, it's worse," put in Dr. Bainbridge. "Think of the contempt that they must hold us in! Dogs of Christians they call us."

"Well, there are others in the same position," Captain Bainbridge answered, sitting down on the lower step beside his wife. "Almost all of Europe pays tribute in one way or another."

"Except England," suggested Dr. Bainbridge.

"Ay, there's the rub!" was the answer. "It is my opinion that she supports these brigands and buccaneers in order to gain the supreme control of the commercial Mediterranean. Proof is not lacking to show that in this I am correct. They could suppress every pirate from Gibraltar to the Bosphorus (Turkey) in three months, but they would not have it otherwise than as it is."

"We need to look to our own government and why they continue to face intimidation from a bunch of ruffians. We sent money to them for nothing, money we can ill afford to send."

"I totally agree; we need to take physical control of the situation and open the trade routes so as merchants are not at risk."

In common with many of the officers and a large proportion of American citizens, Bainbridge held strong prejudices against Great Britain, and grumbled about her influence. William was careful not to press the issue with his father. His father was coming around to the benefits of the new country but he still was a Tory at heart.

Dr. Bainbridge during the war of the Revolution, had been an opponent of rebellion, and his own father, Absalom Bainbridge, had been an out-and-out Tory and had moved to New York during the war in order that his children should be among the adherents of the Crown, who held the city. Nevertheless all of the younger generation had grown up stout patriots, and it had not taken the honest doctor very long to change his opinions, although he would never discuss the question under any provocation.

EIGHTTEEN

Dey of Algiers
May 20, 1800

Before he left on the *USS George Washington* he said to Susan, "My orders are disgusting but duty is paramount, and my orders are to be obeyed."

"You must realize William that they want you to do this diplomatic mission because you are a good leader and officer. Beside that you are a wonderful husband," and she gave him a kiss.

Bainbridge labored industriously to ready the *George Washington* for sea. William always saw to the training of the crew as part of their readiness and the crew seemed to respond by showing greater respect for him.

When the war-ship was ready to his satisfaction there was a large congregation of people on the dock to wish them well on their voyage. Susan was there looking troubled with tears in her eyes. Each sailing was more difficult for her, but she knew that it was expected as the years passed by.

Bainbridge gave the order to cast off the lines, raise the sails and push off the dock.

He searched for Susan in the crowd and found her. He took off his hat and waved it for two minutes.

The sailing to Algiers was a productive training period on the ship because the seas were flat most of the time and the men had more time for training. The crew was attentive in the proper maintenance of the vessel but also in their personal education.

The *USS George Washington* arrived at Algiers with the annual tribute from the United States. The amount was a staggering twenty thousand dollars. Bainbridge had been uneasy about transporting this huge sum of money in his vessel. Twenty thousand dollars would be equivalent to one million six-hundred thousand dollars in early twenty-first century dollars.

William with four body guards personally delivered the money into the hands of the United States consul, Mr. Richard O'Brien.

"Captain Bainbridge, it is my pleasure to make your acquaintance,"

"Mr. O'Brien, my orders are to deliver this money to you but I must confide in you that I find the whole matter distasteful."

"It is just business," Captain Bainbridge.

"No it is not, it is extortion that weak minded Congressmen finely caved into."

"Well you have made the delivery. We are going to schedule a ceremony for the presentation to the Dey of Algiers. The Dey likes to be honored so I will make it a ceremony in his honor. I trust you and your officers will be in attendance?"

"No we will not, I am sorry that we must decline assisting in any ceremony that involves the presentation of blood money to the Dey," William was quite agitated by now.

The *USS George Washington* was the strongest American frigate that the Algerian people had ever seen, and in fact it was one of the largest ships that ever dropped anchor in the Algerian harbor.

The harbour was well fortified with two powerful batteries with more than sixty guns trained on anything in the harbour.

The Dey of Algiers was a man of no principals. He was a ruthless villain with little or no diplomatic niceties.

"Lieutenant, sitting here in this harbour makes me nervous. Look at those guns trained on us, we are sitting ducks," Bainbridge was thinking about moving the ship to anchor outside of the harbour.

The ceremony for transfer of the tribute from the United States to the Dey of Algiers was held the following day.

"Where is the Captain of the big ship?" the Dey addressed O'Brien.

"Oh, the Captain sends his regrets for not being able to attend," O'Brien lied.

"That is not acceptable! Does the American think he does not have to honor me?" The Dey was expressing angered that the Captain from American would ignore him. The Dey, wanted the Americans to know he was in charge, he was the difference between life and death in this part of the world. The Dey was jealous of the large ship in his harbour and how his fellow Algerians were impressed by it. They viewed the tall spars and finely modeled hull with envy.

The Deg of Algiers spent the next day pondering how he humble this country called the United States; a county so far away and so totally controllable.

The Deg called for O'Brien to report to him.

"O'Brien I want you to deliver a message for me."

"If it is in the possibly of my duties, I will," Richard O'Brien said. Richard O'Brien was a sagacious and intelligent man who had been a former prisoner in this very county.

Richard like the north of Africa, he was single, being the American consul he was the pipe line to the United States for money.

"The message is...I hereby command the American vessel to sail to the seat of the Grand Seignior at Constantinople," the Deg had a grin on his face. "I might add if the Captain refuses I will blow his vessel out of the water."

O'Brien went directly from his audience with the regent at the palace to the shore of the harbour. When he arrived at the shore he was fortunate enough to find a cutter of the *USS George Washington* waiting at the dock.

"Young man, I am the American Consul Richard O'Brien and it is of the upmost urgency that I see Captain Bainbridge."

"Captain Bainbridge is on the ship, Sir," the Coxswain said.

"I am in luck since the urgency of my seeing him is imperative."

The young Coxswain had well developed arm muscles and a few minutes later O'Brien was on board the *USS George Washington*.

Explaining to the Coxswain the urgency of his desire to see Captain Bainbridge, he was placed on board at once.

"Mr. O'Brien, why this is a pleasant surprise," Bainbridge was feeling more cheerful then at their last visit.

William requested the cabin boy to bring them a bottle of his best wine to his cabin. William had some wine on board that his father had imported and given to him.

"You look worried Mr. O'Brien," William could detect that O'Brien was evidently in some distress.

"Here, come relax and sit down at the table. These other officers have just finish dinner with me and they just were leaving."

"Thank you gentlemen, but I think I need to converse with our American Consul, Mr. Richard O'Brien in private."

"Well, sir," he said, " what is amiss? What can I do for you? "

"I do not know what is to be done," responded the consul, "but I must speak quickly and to the point. Your life and those of the crew are in danger."

"Pray tell me."

"I intend too, but first I must regress and give you some back ground. As you are well aware of that all the Barbary States are under the direct control and obey the commands of the Grand Seignior at Constantinople. They are practically hirelings and dependents upon the Turk and the Ottoman power."

"I was not that familiar with the politics, but go on," William encouraged Richard O'Brien.

"Well according to my informants the Dey of Algiers has got himself into a mess with the Porte. The Dey has accomplished to enter into a treaty of peace with France just at this time when Turkey, and England, her ally, are carrying on the war in Egypt against the young General Bonaparte," O'Brien let out a sigh. "There is the situation in a nutshell."

"But does the Dey have the authority to enter into anything with France?"

"Well he did and the Turks and British are not taking kindly to this unauthorized political maneuver."

"What does this have to do with me?"

"Well the old unscrupulous fart thinks if he sends the heathen Turk presents of money and various things that of course are stolen he will appease him. He wanted these items accompanied by a special ambassador to Constantinople."

"Well, I can see no objection," returned Bainbridge.

"Yes; but my friend, excuse me Captain; he wants to send them in your ship, in the *USS George Washington*, that bears the flag of the United States, by all the powers!"

Bainbridge threw back his head and laughed heartily.

"Do you suppose for one minute that I intend to allow him to carry out his intentions?" he asked. "He wants to use my ship like it is his?"

"The Dey of Algiers, is not asking you he is demanding that the United States ship *George Washington* should carry an Algerian ambassador to Constantinople, with presents to the amount of five or six hundred thousand dollars, and upward of two hundred Turkish passengers.

The light in which the chief of this regency looks upon the people of the United States may be inferred from his style of expression. He remarked to me: "You pay me tribute, by which you become my slaves; I have therefore a right to order you as I may think proper."

"But, my dear Captain, make note of this: he is a murdering old devil that will stop at nothing. Can't you sail out this very instant? "

"Not without some wind to sail with," responded Bainbridge, looking out of one of the after ports. "Can't you secure an audience for me with the regent? I should like to politely express my opinions to him."

"You will find that once he has made up his mind to do something he like talking to a rock," replied Mr. O'Brien. "Could you warp the vessel to the mouth of the harbor?"

"It would be a hard job," Bainbridge answered. "But for that matter, if they wanted to prevent my leaving, they could dismantle me before I had sailed a cable's length. Just look up there."

"This is a mess," Richard O'Brien lamented.

"I can see that I am being boxed into a corner. If I refuse this pompous ass his wish I could lose my ship and the men on it."

"That only part of it," Captain. "You have to anticipate that refusal could accelerate piracy by the Algerians on American Commerce."

"I agree with you Mr. O'Brien, the American government does not realize the humiliation that has been self inflicted by paying tribute so its merchant ships might pursue their trade without being boarded by pirates. Our politicians are in total denial; they are functioning with their heads up their ass."

"Mr. O'Brien, will you convey to the Dey that I will go to Constantinople, and deliver his ambassador to the Ottoman Porte?"

"Thank you Captain, I appreciate your candor and cooperation in a difficult situation. I will relay your message."

"Please inquire as to when we are instructed to leave to do his dirty work?"

Bainbridge called a council of his officers that night in his cabin.

"Gentlemen, the Dey is making overtures of all out war against the

United States. He is a crazy old man but he possesses the power; our ship and lives are in immediate danger."

They discussed the escaping the harbour but determined it was impossible if the wind did not favor them.

The next morning Bainbridge wrote the following letter, which he placed on board a small vessel bound for Spain, with instructions to put it on board the first home-bound American ship that might be met with. The epistle was addressed to the Secretary of the Navy, and after the introductory form, it read as follows:

"The unpleasant situation in which I am placed must convince you that I have no alternative left but compliance, or a renewal of hostilities against our commerce."

"The loss of the frigate and the fear of slavery for me and crew were the least circumstance to be apprehended; but I knew our valuable commerce in these seas would fall a sacrifice to the corsairs of this power, as we have here no cruisers to protect it. Enclosed is the correspondence between Richard O'Brien, the American consul general, and myself on the subject of the embassy, by which you will see that I had no choice in acting, but was governed by the tyrant in whose power I had fallen."

"I hope I may never again be sent to Algiers with tribute, unless I am authorized to deliver it from the mouth of our cannons. I trust that my conduct will be approved of by the President, for, with every desire to act rightly, it has caused me many unpleasant moments."

WB

NINETEEN

Constantinople
May 20, 1800

Bainbridge, having been forced to submit to this indignity, made up his mind to do it as gracefully as he could; but a crowning affront was to be offered him before he cleared the mouth of the harbor. An Algerian rowboat, manned by twenty oarsmen, came alongside the vessel with orders from the Dey that the *USS George Washington* should proceed to Constantinople flying the flag of Algiers! An Algerian flag was handed up to him for the purpose.

Bainbridge called away his gig at once and, thoroughly angry, rowed ashore, and made his way to the palace.

The Dey would not see him, but he carried on a conversation with him through one of his head men.

The American captain remonstrated in vain, and was forced at last to row back to the ship and hoist the hated flag at his peak while he flew the Stars and Stripes at his main and fore. Once outside of the harbor and beyond range of the guns that the Dey could bring to bear upon him, the green and yellow rag was lowered. The flag of the United States arose in its place. The Algerian flag disappeared and was not accounted for ever again. Bainbridge was the last person seen with the Algerian emblem; it was presumed lost overboard.

William Bainbridge set sail on the *USS George Washington* from Algiers for Constantinople on October 19, 1800.

Head winds and bad weather were encountered from the outset, and the crowded condition of the ship made everyone just that much more uncomfortable.

Bainbridge was looking over the mass of Turks he had been ordered to accompany him on the voyage. He was not happy about them being on his ship.

Bainbridge was learning about the religion of the Mussulman. He was learning that they were compelled by their religion to pray frequently at various stated intervals during the day. That was not the problem the problem was how. They all prayed sine qua non facing toward Mecca in this instance toward the east. It was a remarkable sight to see the ambassador and the others prostrating upon the deck, and then, as the ship swung off upon another tack, rushing to the binnacle to be sure that their prayers were directed properly. With the sailors hauling and bawling about them, and not any too careful how they stepped among the worshiping Turks.

Bainbridge found that the Algerians were difficult to manage. He was in favor of taking severe measure to restrain them but reconsidered feeling it would have been hardly proper under the circumstances, as they were supposed to be distinguished guests.

After twenty days of severe tossing about in the *USS George Washington*, the entrance to the Dardanelles was sighted, with the two large forts guarding the channel to Constantinople.

The *USS George Washington*, 24-guns, was the first vessel to fly the flag of the United States under the walls of Constantinople. People were lining up along the shores as the three masted vessel made it way up the harbour. The stars and stripes were proudly flying and the fact they were never seen before they were a strange sight to all those who noticed.

Bainbridge took on board a pilot when they were still some distance from the harbour entrance. As they approached the narrow gateway the officer of the deck was told that it was always necessary for foreign ships to come to anchor under the guns of the great fortress to the east and await there the permission from the Grand Seignior. Bainbridge was informed by the pilot that they must drop anchor immediately. Bainbridge could see no reason for doing that so his ship would be a target. He was also disturbed at the prospect of having to remain detained any longer than was absolutely necessary. Bainbridge was distressed by these events.

"Lieutenant, instruct the men to keep the sails full and to proceed. Call the guns crews to their station," Bainbridge was going to overcome this obstacle and move on. The guns of the forward battery were loaded with a double saluting charge. The frigate was under favorable winds, swept up the narrow channel, while clewing up her topsails and hauling down the jib as if it was her intention to anchor.

It was a warm, hazy day. The ramparts of the fort were seen to be lined with soldiers watching the strange frigate as she approached with the odd striped flag displayed. The *George Washington* was about midway in the passage when Bainbridge ordered the guns to fire a twenty-one guns salute. The gun crews preformed with precision firing as rapidly as their guns could be loaded and primed.

At once both forts began to answer. The air clouded up with the white, opaque smoke, and when it cleared away the Turks must have been astonished to perceive the vessel they supposed they would find anchored near to them was a full mile or more up the straits, sailing along with studding sails and royals set and drawing.

The pilot was an elderly man proved to be the captain of the port, and he bore instructions to conduct the frigate into the inner harbor. The anchor was tripped as she entered into the mole, passing close to the castle and firing another salute of twenty-one guns, which apparently afforded much satisfaction and was returned promptly.

Bainbridge brought the *USS George Washington* to anchor shortly after midday near the populace center of Constantinople on November 9th. *USS George Washington was* the first ship to sail into the Constantinople harbour not having first secured the permission of the Turkish Sultan.

The frigate lay in the lower part of the harbor. The many minarets and slender spires and domes of the city gleamed in the sun. The gray castle and the fortifications that lined the water's edge were crowded, as the forts had been below, with troops of curious soldiery and citizens.

The *USS George Washington* had come to anchor near the castle. It was late in the afternoon and the light was beginning to fade. The midshipmen on watch sighted a boat pull out from the castle. The rowers were pulling long oars with handles that were weighted at the end, and they made her dance through the water at a lively pace towards the ship. Un-be-known to Bainbridge they were delivering an invitation from the Grand Seignior for the American commander to appear before his august presence. The

Algerian ambassador was not mentioned, although word had been sent of his arrival.

A voice called up from the small boat in Arabic. Bainbridge anticipated the language bearer. Captain Bainbridge went to the rail and replied in French.

"We are here with the Ambassador from the Dey of Algiers bringing tribute to his Porte."

There was an extended silence before a voice came back in French. "We welcome you. May I have permission to board?"

Bainbridge could see a man with a large turban on his head sat in the stern sheets, and seeing that it was his intention to board. "Yes, please come aboard." The ladder was hastily dropped, and in another instant the man with a turban was standing the gangway.

"What vessel is this?" he asked, speaking very good French.

"The *USS George Washington* from the United States," Bainbridge replied, lifting his hat.

To every one's surprise, this answer was sufficient, for without coming down upon the deck, the visitor hastened down to his waiting boat, and at the same racing pace rowed back to the castle.

Before the sailors had finished rigging the starboard gangway the man in the turban had again returned. He was allowed to board the ship; he approached Captain Bainbridge and made a low obeisance.

"The Turkish Government sends greetings," he said.

"But no one here has ever heard of such a Government as the United States, it signified nothing to the governor of the Ottoman Porte. Will the captain please explicitly describe what country he hails from and what government he represents?"

Bainbridge thought for a minute, and then made his answer.

"Will you say to those who sent you," he said, discovering that the gravely of the confused visitor that he was merely a messenger, "that this frigate comes from the country to the westward, the New World discovered by Columbus?"

This seemed entirely satisfactory, and the turbaned one took his departure for the second time in great haste. A few hours past and darkness had settled in. The lights on a larger boat were seen approaching with the same messenger, accompanied by an elderly man; Bainbridge ordered that they come on board at once.

The entourage boarded with gifts.

"We bring this lamb as an emblem of peace and the flowers as our jester of welcome," The tall man with a turban expressed to Bainbridge in French. "His Highness the Ottoman Porte wishes to extend an invitation for you to meet with him tomorrow morning at eleven a.m."

"Thank you very much. I would be honored to accept the Ottoman Porte's invitation."

Bainbridge was received very kindly the following morning by the Ottoman Porte at the castle. The Porte was the opposite of the Dey. The Porte did not seem to have an aggressive agenda or any hidden animosities.

Bainbridge allowed the Ambassador from The Dey of Algiers to present the gifts for the Sultan of Turkey. A strange assortment of presents they were, and only such as one barbaric power could send to another, and especially if that power had at some time had free access to the contents of various vessels of all nations. Silks and satins from French looms, cloth and handsome embroideries, plate and chinaware from various places, three handsome Arabian steeds, and two tame lion cubs were stored on board, and the entourage of the ambassador, numbering some two hundred Mohammedans, thronged the decks.

The Grand Seignior's first remark was about the new United States flag that he had particularly noticed and apparently liked.

"It is, like my own," he said," decorated with one of the heavenly bodies, and I consider this coincidence a good omen of the future friendly intercourse between our respective nations. It is most probable that we have many affinities of laws, religion, and manners."

Bainbridge tried to explain in a few words a little about his country, and the Sultan displayed great interest but great ignorance.

The next morning the Algerian ambassador reported himself at the palace but was denied an audience, word being sent to him to wait until the return of the Capudan Pasha, or High Admiral, then absent on a cruise. As the ambassador refused to leave the ship, Bainbridge was compelled to put up with him as a guest for some time longer; but he hoped the Capudan Pasha would not delay long, for he was anxious to get rid of his mission and proceed homeward.

The eighth day after the arrival of the *USS George Washington* a very resplendent dragoman came offshore, and by means of an interpreter, who spoke French, he inquired of Captain Bainbridge if the latter did not know that there was such an officer as the Reis Effendi in the city of Constantinople. (Reis Effendi was the title of an officer of state in the Ottoman Empire.)

"You have reached this port," added the dragoman," without either the consent or the acknowledgement of the Turkish Government something without precedent and you have neglected to report yourself to the proper officer, and thereby you have offered him an indignity which requires a reparation. His Supreme Royal Highness, the Reis Effendi, hereby orders you to report and appear before him tomorrow morning at ten o'clock."

Bainbridge was not impressed at first, but he concluded that it would be best to put on a bold front, although he did not know against whom he had offended.

"Although I command this ship, tell your master," he said," I carry an ambassador with presents to the Sultan, and I feel under no obligations to hold intercourse with members of the Government other than an interchange of civilities."

"No matter what your own personal feelings may be," responded the dragoman, nodding significantly," I advise you not to disobey the commands which I have delivered."

"I do not regard them as commands," Bainbridge said rather hotly, for the understrapper's insolence was calculated to disturb one's peace of mind. "And as for his threats, tell him they amount to nothing. This is all I have to say."

Upon thinking matters over later in the day, it seemed to him that it would be prudent to find out from some of the resident ministers of one of the countries friendly to the United States exactly what position the Effendi held, and what it would be best for him to do under the circumstances. As the United States had no representative at all at the Sultan's court, Bainbridge accordingly waited on Lord Elgin, the British ambassador, and told him the whole story, informing him of the message he had received from the Reis Effendi, and expressing a hope that the amicable relations then existing between their respective governments would justify his calling upon him for such aid as he might find necessary in case any trouble should arise.

Lord Elgin responded promptly by offering his friendly services, and stating that the object of the Reis Effendi was merely to obtain a bribe. He promised to send a message by his dragoman to the demanding gentleman that would prevent all further annoyance.

"You see, Captain Bainbridge," Lord Elgin said, "the Grand Vizier, or Reis Effendi, as he calls himself, is actually next in rank to the Sultan. But he and the latter are comparative strangers for the simple reason that the Ottoman potentate has no private correspondence or interviews with any high official of his Government unless it happens that the officer has some near relationship through blood or marriage a most singular regulation but in this case one that works to your favor, for the Effendi and the Sultan scarcely speak to one another, and only meet at public functions."

After expressions of gratitude for his lordship's kindness, Bainbridge went back to his ship, much reassured. He knew he was placed in a worse position in Constantinople than he was in the harbor of Algiers. There was no one at all to represent the United States Government, and being under the guns of the fort, attempting to escape was beyond question.

Two weeks went by, and on the fourteenth day a man working up aloft shouted down to the deck of the *George Washington* that a large fleet of thirty or forty sails was approaching, distant about six or eight miles.

Before sunset the Capudan Pasha, the Lord High Admiral, sailed into the harbour. The squadron was returning home from Egypt, with fifteen sail vessels of the line and thirty smaller vessels. As the leading battle ship entered the harbor the *USS George Washington* fired a salute. But no answer was given, for at that moment a heavy squall blew across the Bosporus, and many of the vessels were taken all aback, the largest, the flagship, only being saved from going ashore by dexterous handling. Bainbridge was disappointed and hurt that no attention had been paid to his twenty-one guns salute.

Bainbridge, early the next morning, was advised that the admiral's private secretary, Mr. Zacbe, was waiting to see him on the ship. Upon being ushered into the captain's presence he advanced, and, omitting the low obeisance of the Ottoman, he extended his hand in European fashion, at the same time saying in good English:

"The admiral's compliments to Captain Bainbridge, and he regrets that an accident alone prevented his replying to the captain's courteous salute. He desires me to state that he will return it at noon today, gun for gun."

Bainbridge could not help expressing his delight at meeting one who was close to those high in authority, who could speak his language, and who was knowledgeable his country.

"Ah, indeed, I know of it well," returned the admiral's secretary. "I was educated in Paris and London, and while in the former place I had the great pleasure of meeting the illustrious Benjamin Franklin. Indeed, although I was a very young man, I might say that we became good friends."

Bainbridge was much taken with Mr. Zacbe's engaging manner, his demeanor, and intelligence and he held quite a long conversation, in which the secretary expressed himself as a great admirer of the structure of our institutions, and displayed no little knowledge of United States history.

A friendship was thus commenced that lasted through many years; until Mr. Zacbe's death; regular correspondence was exchanged, although Bainbridge and he were so many thousands of miles apart.

TWENTY

Turkey
1801

President Jefferson had taken office on January 20, 1801 and one of his first items on the agenda was Tripoli's demands. Tripoli was demanding the United States to pay a onetime $225,000 payment to be followed by annuals payments of $25,000. The $225,000 would be at least $18,000,000 in today's dollars.

In the Presidents first message to Congress as President Jefferson said. *"To this state of general peace with which we have been blessed, one only exception exists, Tripoli, the least considerable of the Barbary States, had come forward with demands unfounded wither in right or in compact, and has permitted itself to denounce war, on our failure to comply before a given day. The style of the demand admitted but one answer. I sent a small squadron of frigates into the Mediterranean."*

On May 10, 1801 the Pascha of Tripoli declared war on the United States by having the flagpole on the consulate chopped down. The flag pole was the highest thing surrounding the consulate; the land was devoid of trees so the flag pole was symbolic of toppling the last tall pole, the pole belonging to the United States.

Commodore John Barry sent a letter to Congress:

Gentlemen of Congress, I wish to address the issue of having adequate naval protection. We may have ended the war with the English but our ability to freely trade in other parts of the world is being hampered by the aggressions upon United States commerce. Pirates are more plentiful then ever and cause commerce in the Caribbean to become restricted. The monetary loss of ships' cargos has made the prices of rum, for instance, higher. American merchant ships are being captured and sailors tortured and killed. It is well known the Algerians have taken an aggressive action on American commerce. They are aware that our new country has no defenses at sea. I would strongly encourage the Congress to consider commissioning five ships of the line and ten frigates.
Your humble servant, John Barry

Promptly at twelve o'clock the Turkish flagship was good to their word and fired a twenty-one gun salute with the broadside guns. Shortly after the salute a messenger delivered to Captain Bainbridge an invitation to visit the admiral at his palace, which was near to that of the Sultan and not far from the water. Capudan Pasha received the American officer with the greatest hospitality and many protestations of delight.

When Lord Elgin was informed by Bainbridge that the Capudan Pasha had taken the *George Washington* under his immediate protection, he was profuse in his congratulations, stating that it was an honor that had been extended to few vessels, and was full of promise for any negotiations that he might seek to bring about, or any favors he might desire to ask.

"Your way is now paved," he said, "and no better opportunity could present itself for extending an entente cordiality between the Ottoman Government and your own."

Bainbridge saw this, and after his reception by the Turkish admiral he invited the latter on board the frigate *George Washington* and made every preparation to make a favorable impression. Although the admiral declined the honor of dining, owing to the fact that he would have to meet the ambassador from Algiers, who had not been accredited, he came on board with a large entourage in great splendor late in the afternoon.

"John will you assist me in entertaining these despicable people on board the ship. I feel we are going to have a tough time of it." John Ridgely was the ship's surgeon and they had become good friends during their short time aboard.

"I would be delighted to assist you; I just hope we can communicate successfully."

"It seems that most of the people in the palace speak French so we can converse."

Captain Bainbridge arranged to entertain the Ministers of the Sublime Porte on board the ship on the quarter deck. William Bainbridge had to do some instruction as to how the men should set the tables, pour water and to serve the guests.

Since the Muslim does not profess to drinking wine, Bainbridge ordered that decanters of water be placed on the table.

When Bainbridge was address the delegation at the dinner on the vessel he told them: "The water, said Bainbridge, comes from four quarters of the globe; water from America, Africa, Europe and Asia."

The guests were impressed with this display. Even the wife of the British ambassador borrowed the four decanters to grace her own table the following day at a formal event she was hosting for Bainbridge and his officers.

The ship had been covered with bunting, the yardarms were manned, and the crew was dressed in clean white uniforms. The Capudan Pasha was delighted with everything he saw.

"Captain Bainbridge I must congratulate you with great approbation on the correct deportment of your officers, and praised highly the discipline and subordination of the crew," the Capudan Pasha said with great sincerity.

The Capudan Pasha was amazed at the structure of the *George Washington*, the heaviness of her bulwarks, and the strength of her timbers. The Capudan Pasha marveled at the cleanliness and neatness that prevailed throughout the ship. He regretted frankly that such a state of things would never be found on board a Turkish vessel, and humorously expressed it that he was afraid his junior officers would see no use in such carefulness and attention to detail. Bainbridge was thinking that he bet his officers would hear about it.

Before he left he invited Bainbridge and his first lieutenant to dine with him at his palace on the next day.

Although this was not a state function, and there were but seven seated at the table, the dinner was of great importance, as Bainbridge learned. The British embassy helped pave the way but it was the Capudan Pasha that he needed to certify the meeting.

The Capudan Pasha informed Bainbridge that he was animate that the presents of silks and satins, the lion cubs, and the Arabian steeds that Bainbridge had brought were all to be returned back to the Dey.

"What message the Grand Seignior intends to send to the Dey of Algiers has not yet been determined upon, but the Sultan has expressed the greatest displeasure at the conduct of Algiers, and will probably demand of him immediate reparation for the depredations he has committed on the commerce of Austria and other friendly nations, and also for his disobedience in making peace with France, our enemy."

Bainbridge then told of the insolent demand of the Dey that he should fly the Algerian flag. When he heard of this, the Pasha frowned.

"While in Ottoman waters," he said at last," pray fly no flag but that of your own country, and as upon your return voyage you will still be under my protection, I respectfully request that you do not fly any other but that which is now at the peak of your vessel."

Altogether the dinner was a great success. Much to Bainbridge's delight one of the guests was the great English traveler, Edward Daniel Clarke, who had traveled by land to Constantinople from St. Petersburg in Russia. He was the first foreigner to make this long and hazardous journey.

This was by no means the last of the meetings between the admiral and the American captain. Visits were exchanged on many occasions, and several long excursions were made into the surrounding country and up the Thracian Bosporus, Bainbridge penetrating in his long boat even as far as the Black Sea, where he wished to hoist the American flag for the first time.

The Thracian Bosporus was the strait that separated the European and the Asian portion of Turkey, connecting the Sea of Marmara with the Black Sea. The strait was 19 miles (31km) long and 2.3 miles (3.7km) at the widest point.

Bainbridge was also fortunate enough to secure a closer view of the private and social life of the Turkish ruler. William Bainbridge was a delightful person and he had brought to the Turks a personality and mannerism that instantly made him their new best friend.

Mr. Clarke one day presented Captain Bainbridge to Count Browlaski, a Pole in the service of the Sultan, a high officer in the court circle, and one who had immediate supervision of the gardens and the policing of the palace grounds.

Bainbridge had expressed a desire to see the inside of the seraglio and the harem, which's many grated windows' looked down upon the blue waters of the bay from above the palace walls. The Englishman at once laughed and shrugged his shoulders.

"That speech shows your innocence, Captain Bainbridge," he said. "No one, not even our friend the count here, has had that privilege."

At this Count Browlaski looked over his shoulder, and observing that no one was near; he confided to them that if they wished to run a certain amount of risk he thought the adventure might be carried out. Accordingly plans were arranged, and the visit was successfully accomplished. Mr. Clarke wrote in his book of travels that he met Captain Bainbridge during his visit in Constantinople. Mr. Clarke comments on going with Captain Bainbridge into the inner recesses of the palace in disguise.

"I have to advise you Captain Bainbridge that it is forbidden to enter the inner recesses of the place. We would be placed in grave danger with our transgression," Mr. Clark was emphatic with his warning.

Later, in a letter to a friend of his, Bainbridge made light of them in describing the same event. But he added generously, upon reading Mr. Clarke's account: "One gentleman may honestly apprehend great peril where it cannot be perceived by another."

In return for all the courtesies that had been shown him, Bainbridge gave a party on the quarter deck of the *George Washington*. Although the admiral again declined the honor of being present, he was represented unofficially by Mr. Zacbe, his secretary. The disgruntled Algerian ambassador was also present. He was a man of grave deportment and good manners, and Bainbridge had begun to feel really sorry for him, owing to the failure of his mission, and the consequences that it might entail upon him and his family, for eastern vengeance does not stop at the principles involved in trouble or disgrace.

It was a remarkable entertainment in more ways than one. Upon the four corners of the table were so many decanters containing fresh water from the four quarters of the globe. The natives of Europe, Asia, Africa, and America sat down together at one board. Fruits, preserved dishes and viands were passed about a sample of four different continents. In writing of this affair, Mr. Clarke explains it thus: *The means of accomplishing this extraordinary entertainment is easily understood by his (Bainbridge's) having touched at Algiers in his passage from America, and his being at anchor so near the shores of both Europe and of Asia.*

Two more very important interviews Bainbridge held with the Capudan Pasha.

"Sir, may I inquire as to how much longer we might expect to be detained in port?

"Is the Captain getting anxious to leave our hospitality?"

"I have been away too long and I need to return to the United States following my stop in Algeria to return the ambassador and his suite," William thought he was feeling sorry for the ambassador since he had not been permitted to leave the ship since their arrival.

"We will be sorry to see you go Captain Bainbridge but you should plan on leaving in four or five days."

The trip had exceeded Captain Bainbridge's expectation in what had been accomplished. Bainbridge had had many conversations with the Pasha on the subject of a treaty of commerce with the Ottoman Government. They also discussed many other topics that would be of mutual benefit in the future.

The Turkish Admiral had apparently just learned of the *George Washington's* coming into port without the usual restraints of the Dardanelles.

"I assure you, Monsieur le Capitaine, that it is the first time a foreign armored vessel has reached this port without our express permission and recognition from the Grand Seignior. Oh, do not apologize," he added, seeing that Bainbridge was about to speak. "I attach no blame whatever to your honorable conduct. You are a stranger to the laws and customs of this country and could not be expected to know our rules and regulations. But," he added, frowning, "it was, nevertheless, the governor of the castle's duty to stop you at the Dardanelles, even if, alas! He had to sink the fine vessel which you have the honor to command. He is not to escape punishment for this obvious breach of duty, for he is at present under sentence of death for his dereliction. It requires but my signature, and that, I promise you, shall not be withheld. He dies the day after tomorrow at sundown."

Bainbridge drew back in revulsion. The idea of allowing an innocent man to suffer for something he initiated was beyond Bainbridge's comprehension. The people in this strange land had customs that made no sense to a reasonable thinking person. No matter what the consequences might be, he would make a statement.

"I assure your highness that the governor of the castle at the straits is not even censurable for his conduct. Believe me; it was through no fault of his that my vessel came by him."

The Capudan Pasha smiled and shrugged his shoulders.

"He should have stopped you at all hazards, Monsieur," he said." Pray explain how any vessel could pass those powerful batteries upon which the safety of this city depends without gross neglect on the part of the commander of the castle."

"But he was not neglectful." Bainbridge spoke almost loudly now in his eagerness to convince the admiral of his sincerity. "He was not neglectful. He imagined that I was coming to anchor. I frankly confess to you that I did everything in my power to deceive him into thinking that I was going to comply with the requirements of the port, for I knew well of the custom, and determined to evade it, if I could, to avoid delay. If anyone should be punished it should be myself. But I trust that you will consider the circumstances and my haste to perform the mission that I had so unwillingly undertaken."

Bainbridge had no idea what would be the effect of this remarkable statement. The surprise of the admiral was plain at the outset, but as Bainbridge proceeded, the frown gradually left his face to be replaced by one of friendly amazement, and when the captain had finished speaking, the Pasha extended his hand.

"Thanks, a thousand times, for your brave words, my friend," he said. "The Governor was an old and trusted friend of mine. I now believe him to have been a faithful officer. I thank you from my heart again for saving me much pain, and preserving to the service of the Sultan a loyal servant. Do not fear that the words you have said shall cause you to suffer in any way. Tonight one of my swiftest sailing boats will leave bearing the message that the governor is pardoned and restored to his former authority."

An English ship was about to sail for the port of Gibraltar out of the Turkish port. Bainbridge was able to send the following letter, with a request to the captain to place it on board the first vessel bound for the United States. The dispatch was addressed to his Excellency the Secretary of the Navy of the United States, and read as follows:

"SIR: On the 23d of December, 1801, I was requested by the Capudan Pasha to wait upon him at his palace. I was received in a very friendly manner, and had some conversation respecting the formation of a treaty with the Ottoman Porte, and he expressed a very great desire that a minister should be sent from the United States to effect it. I informed him that there was one already named, who at present was in Lisbon, and probably would be here in six months. He said he would write to the ambassador, which letter would be a protection for him while in the Turkish Empire, and gave me liberty to recommend any merchant vessel to his protection which might wish to come here previously to the arrival of the ambassador. I thanked him in the name of the United States for the protection he had been pleased to give the frigate

under my command, and for his friendly attentions to myself and officers. I conceive it to be a very fortunate moment to negotiate an advantageous treaty with this Government. . . . The Capudan Pasha requested me to take two messengers and land them at Malta, being destined for Tripoli and Tunis, which I have consented to do, conceiving it to be good policy. I think it very probable that the States of Barbary will shortly receive chastisement from the Turks."

WB

The ambassador of the Dey requested the honor of an interview with Bainbridge the next morning. The ambassador was in a towering rage, and was almost unintelligible, as he tried to explain that at last the Grand Seignior had condescended to answer him. He said he was directed to return at once to Algiers, which country was ordered to immediately declare war against France; his master, the Dey, was to be compelled to pay the large sum of one million of piasters, (Piaster was the unit of currency in the Ottoman Empire and was equal to one silver dollar), and that only sixty days were to be allowed for the transmitting of this dispatch to Algiers and for an answer to be returned to Constantinople. If this time was exceeded, war would be at once declared on Algiers.

The ambassador begged and implored Bainbridge to make haste and leave the shores of Turkey behind him. All his airs of superiority and importance disappeared. He was a frightened, cringing, and well-nigh hopeless creature whose ruin stared him in the face.

Bainbridge had been requested to wait upon the Capudan Pasha the next morning, it was impossible for him to leave until this was complied with; but yielding to the importunities of the frightened ambassador, he sent a messenger to the palace, asking that he should be allowed to see the admiral in the afternoon in order that he might sail at daybreak the next morning. Word came back that the Pasha would be glad to see him.

After presenting Bainbridge with a letter addressed to the Honorable William Smith, minister plenipotentiary of the United States at the port of Lisbon, the admiral turned with a great deal of courtesy and said the following words in parting:

"As your ship has been under my protection, she shall receive the honors that are reserved exclusively for my flag. In passing the fortress of Tanana it will salute you, which, of course, you will return."

By regulation the fortress of Tanana saluted no one but the Capudan Pasha. The compliment of the salute had never before been extended to any foreign vessel of war, nor even to Turkish vessels commanded by a less personage than an admiral. Bainbridge had left the port with the Capudan Pasha giving him passports for the *USS George Washington* which entitled that vessel and her commander at all times to receive the greatest respect in all Turkish ports, and from all Turkish ships.

The officer at the Dardanelles, who had been restored to his command, as a result of the gallant conduct of Bainbridge, invited him to his castle.

The Governor greeted Bainbridge with sincere gratitude and thanked him for having saved his life.

"I must tell you with all humility that I had given up all hope that my life might be saved. I had made my last will, excepting surely to perish."

"Sir, I am deeply troubled that I have caused you the trauma you have suffered."

"Captain it was not your fault. You were not familiar with our regulation."

"I would like to deliver to your frigate a cargo of fresh provisions and fruit as a small token of my endless gratitude for your honor and honesty."

"Thank you Governor, I do hope that I have the opportunity to find myself in your company again."

Captain Bainbridge was instrumental in securing an order from the Sultan to the Dey of Algiers obliging him to release 400 prisoners; Maltese, Venetians, and Sicilians prisoners.

Bainbridge realized the Dey was not going to be happy with the turn of events.

TWENTY-ONE

Algiers, Dey
January 21, 1802

Bainbridge returned to Algiers from Constantinople on January 21, 1802. It had been 85 days since he had departed from Algiers. He was not looking forward to his returned visit and dealing with crazy Dey.

Bainbridge also lamented the fact he had been away from his wife and home for a greater time than originally anticipated. He had not planned on being away for such a lengthy time but that had not been in his control. He had sent letters to Susan whenever he was lucky enough to find ships traveling away from the Algerian thugs.

The *USS George Washington* reached the Algerian harbour and Bainbridge anchored well away from the channel into the harbour. Bainbridge wanted his ship to be well beyond the reach of the guns mounted on the hill tops.

As soon as he had appeared, two large sailboats put out to meet him; one contained Mr. O'Brien and the other a representative from the Dey, and it was a race to see which one would arrive first. O'Brien's sailboat, however, caught a bad current by keeping too close to the shore, and the regent's boat was the first alongside. Bainbridge received the court officer without much ceremony, and was rather amused to notice that the effect of seeing the returned embassy still on the ship. Bainbridge could see the messenger was processing the negative effect of telling the Dey the bad news and his violent reaction to the rejection of his gifts.

Before the court officer had asked any questions of his countryman, he hastened to deliver a message for his master, in the following words: "His High Mightiness the Dey has noticed at what distance the honorable captain has dropped anchor, and he expresses great solicitude that immediately the frigate should be moved nearer the city. It surely must be inconvenient, his High Mightiness fears, for the officers to have communication with the shore."

Bainbridge wanted no part of this. He had the USS *George Washington* anchored well beyond the reach of the guns of the fort. He stayed anchored in the bay out of range of the shore guns until the Dey had given his solemn promise (after Moslem fashion) that he would not require Bainbridge to return to Constantinople.

O'Brien finally reached the ship to greet Bainbridge. The court officer was finishing his instructions from the Dey just as O'Brien came on board. Bainbridge thanked the court officer and indicated he would get back to the Dey.

"Welcome aboard Mr. O'Brien, come join me in a glass of wine in my cabin. This gentlemen was just leaving, he has delivered his message from the Dey.

"Yes I could do with a glass of wine after having to deal with that old fart. I had to listen to the blackguard blame me for your cautiousness! He is nothing more than a nattering old scamp!" he exclaimed, after greeting Bainbridge.

"Indeed I am sorry for your having to put up with the villain but will not allow my ship to be under the guns of his fortress again." Bainbridge said, half smiling."He is going to have to give in to our position, meaning he won't get me there so easily this time."

"I see you've returned the menagerie," commented O'Brien.

"Yes, and I'll be glad to be rid of them," said Bainbridge, watching the preparations that were being made for the Moslems to leave the ship.

Bainbridge was greatly relieved when the last one had gone over the side, and were it not for one thing, Bainbridge would have sailed away.

William brought O'Brien up to date on the Turkey political front. He advised O'Brien on the possibility of a treaty between the two countries.

O'Brien arranged a meeting between the Captain and the Dey for the following afternoon. The arrangement required him to make several trips back and forth between shore and the ship.

Previous to sailing to Turkey, Bainbridge had taken aboard as ballast a large number of old iron cannons, which he promised to return, and he felt himself in duty bound to do so.

Bainbridge ordered his gig be lowered so O'Brien could join him to be rowed into the harbor. They intended to obtain an interview with the Dey that very afternoon. The Dey was not going to accommodate them and they failed in securing a direct audience. The best they could do was to be content carrying on a species of verbal correspondence through the medium of one of the court officials.

The next day Bainbridge had allowed Mr. O'Brien to begin the negotiations, but the Dey's reply to the usual formal greetings showed his position clearly.

Point-blank he made the request to the consul general to order Bainbridge to return at once with his messenger to Constantinople. Bainbridge, upon hearing this, could not contain his indignation. Whirling suddenly, he advanced upon the astonished minister and in loud tones delivered himself of the following speech, while poor Mr. O'Brien almost collapsed in a state of fright, fearing the result of his friend's temerity:

"Tell your master," Bainbridge said fiercely to the interpreter, "that he has forgotten the oath he swore not to make any further demands upon me after the first voyage was performed. Now, in the face of such a solemn declaration, he makes another insolent request. Anyone who thus proves his unworthiness should be denied all credence. Tell him I do not doubt his disposition to capture my frigate and enslave my officers and crew. To preserve peace I complied with his first demand. I have done everything which the commander of a ship would be justified in doing to prevent hostilities; but, mark you, if the Dey is determined to have war, if he is so mad as to make the Americans his enemy, he soon will have caused to regret it."

With these words Bainbridge beckoned for the consul to follow him, and stalked out of the palace. Bainbridge had written another letter to the Secretary of the Navy saying that he anticipated a demand of this character, but giving assurance that he intended to resist it," believing that the Government of the United States would never sanction an act so humiliating."

The following morning he requested from Mr. O'Brien that he send laborers off to the ship to receive the old cannons; but the Dey, hearing of this, not only forbade the consul making use of local laborers, but declared that in the event of the guns not being returned at once, war would immediately be made upon the United States.

Mr. O'Brien was very fearful at the Dey's threats and asked Bainbridge to soften the matters by running his ship into the mole and unload the cannons. Bainbridge refused to do this until he had received a positive promise from the Dey that he should not be approached upon the subject of a second voyage.

Reluctantly the Dey gave his word, not that his word could be trusted but Bainbridge did not want to get into a battle with the rouge. When Bainbridge came ashore after seeing that the cannons were hoisted over the side on to the dock, he was met by a court official accompanied by some thirty or forty armed janizaries, (Elite army corps) and word was given him that the Dey requested his presence on a matter of the utmost importance.

The meeting with the Dey was in his palace. The Dey greeted Bainbridge coldly.

Leaving orders with his first lieutenant to begin at once to warp the ship out into the harbor and set sail if he did not return within two hours, taking with him only a midshipman, Bainbridge waited upon "his High Mightiness" at the palace and found him in a towering rage.

"Dog of a Christian, down on your knees!" shrieked the Dey, pointing to the floor at his feet. " Down, I say!" he continued, jumping up as he noticed that Bainbridge's only reply was a calm folding of his arms and a more erect carriage to his figure, in every motion of which the little midshipman accompanied him.

The Dey was absolutely foaming and spluttering in his wrath. He drew his long curved scimitar, and at the motion the crowd of armed men drew theirs also. The minutes that Bainbridge and his midshipman companion had to live seem numbered. Bainbridge suddenly thought of the firman (manuscript) that he had thrust in his pocket a minute before he had left shipboard. Not having the least idea of what the result would be he drew it forth.

At sight of the document, with its two ponderous seals, the Dey's jaw dropped, and sheathing his weapon, he fell back timorously before Bainbridge, who, backed up by the unflinching little middy, advanced upon him, unrolling the document and displaying it triumphantly for the Dey's inspection. It was a mandate from the Capudan Pasha at Constantinople (a great friend of Bainbridge).

The Dey immediately had a change of attitude towards Bainbridge. The Dey seemed to react as if God had appeared before him and he needed to get his act together. Bainbridge was astonished that such transformations could take place before eyes.

It was as if he had pronounced some magic words, some open sesame whose power was resistless. With a weak motion to his astonished court the Dey bade the janizaries to withdraw. Bainbridge was amazed at the immediate change in the Dey. Standing front of him was not an arrogant, bloodthirsty tyrant, but a cringing, humble dependent, alone but for a single dragoman who had prostrated himself upon the floor.

"Oh, Captain Bainbridge I want to apologize for any previous misunderstandings," said the Dey showing his true colors.

The Dey from that moment on treated Bainbridge with a great deal of consideration.

O'Brien smiled at Bainbridge's one-up-man-ship.

Almost abjectly he requested the honor of having the American captain sit down beside him on the divan. As Bainbridge wrote, " his bearing became less lofty, his words honeyed, and his offers of service most liberal."

The Dey did all he could to entice Bainbridge into his power and force him to return to Constantinople with more presents but Bainbridge told him he would not.

The Dey cut down the flagstaff before the French consulate, declared war against France, and made preparations to send an installment of the money demanded by the Sultan, amounting to one million five hundred thousand piaster's, and humble apology thrown in, to Turkey.

By orders of the Sultan also he had been compelled to liberate about four hundred Venetians, Maltese, and Sicilians, whom he had taken prisoners when they were traveling under the protection of British passports. All these people hailed Bainbridge as their generous deliverer.

Just before Bainbridge was ready to sail, it was rumored that the citizens of the French Republic, fifty-six in number, consisting of men, women, and children, had been by the Dey's orders thrown into chains and treated as slaves.

Bainbridge and Mr. O'Brien waited upon the Dey, and expressed to him their ideas about such treatment.

Apparently Monsieur Dubois de Trainville had been in the background and he stepped forward so Bainbridge could see him.

"I am Monsieur Dubois de Trainville and my men and I have had the misfortune of being His High Mightiness the Dey guests for the past two years. I realize that our countries are now at war but I beseech you for the cause of humanity to take me and the other French prisoners aboard of your ship."

"Where would we take you?" Bainbridge was somewhat astonished at the new revelation. He thought about the situation and the fact the United States was at war with France.

"I must beeches you," addressing the Dey, "that you cannot continue to hold these people prisoner," Bainbridge could not believe the continued revelations being brought to light. "You must release the French prisoners also," Bainbridge said to the Dey. Bainbridge did not want them but felt they were being treated inhumanly and he needed to save them from this unjust cruelty.

The Dey than said to Bainbridge, "If you want prisoners released than you must carry the French dogs on your ship."

"That is most interesting," Bainbridge said to the Dey. "You must know that the United States is in a war against France."

"There are no vessels ready to convey us;" Monsieur Dubois de Trainville lamented, but yours Captain Bainbridge."

"All right, you will all leave on my ship," Bainbridge pronounced.

"There is one condition," the Dey broke in.

"What is that," Bainbridge looked quizzical at the Dey.

"The French can go but I will only allow forty-eight hours for them to be placed on board your ship or they stay my prisoners."

At this moment Richard O'Brien spoke up. He endeavored to explain the position in which Captain Bainbridge was placed. He informed the Dey that such procedure was contrary to all national law, and he said that the whole of Europe would revolt at such an arbitrary mode of procedure. But nothing moved the obstinate old Mussulman, and when Mr. O'Brien had finished speaking the Dey intimated that the audience was at an end.

Once out in the open air, O'Brien expressed his feelings in no measured terms. Bainbridge was too angry to speak, but he was going over everything calmly and dispassionately in his mind. He knew that the Dey would make good his threats, and he thought of the unprotected commerce that would be at the mercy of the ruthless barbarian if the Algerians were turned loose to seek their prey.

"It is a good deal like having a man put a pistol to your head and order you to dance," remarked O'Brien.

"Yes, somewhat similar," Bainbridge returned, "What would you do in such a case?"

"By the saints, I suppose I'd foot it," answered the little Irish-American with a shrug of his shoulders. "Couldn't you slip your cable and get out under cover of darkness?

"No, I will honor the deal with the Dey and I will take the French prisoners with me and take them to France."

The French prisoners rushed from their prison the next day to board the ship with great hope of leaving their living hell they had been subjected too. This was a major inconvenience for Bainbridge and his officers. Bainbridge gave up his cabin for the use of the ladies, and supplying them all with what necessities he could for the voyage. The poor French prisoners left in such a hurry to board the *USS George Washington* that they brought nothing but the clothes they wore. They were dirty, hungry, and some in need of medical attention but they were grateful to Bainbridge and his crew.

Bainbridge managed to sail out of the harbor and set sail for the France without further incident. He would disembark his passengers and then head for the United States. His greatest hope that he would not be ordered to return Algiers; little did he know.

TWENTY-TWO

Alicante, France
1802

The *USS George Washington* sailed away from Algiers with its human cargo. Bainbridge was feeling his need to thank God that he was finally leaving this barbaric country. The crew also felt the need to be thankful that this was their farewell to Algiers. They had set their course for France with renewed hope of soon being home themselves.

The voyage to France was smooth and after a short passage they arrived safely at Alicante, France. The gratitude of the people whom he had saved was unbounded. Napoleon, at that time was the first Alicante consul, tendered his "acknowledgments and thanks to Captain Bainbridge for the important services he had rendered the republic, with assurances that such kind offices would always be remembered, and reciprocated with pleasure whenever the occasion occurred."

From Alicante, Bainbridge set sail for America. The trip back to the United States was uneventful. Bainbridge was anxious to go home and be with his wife. He had to make one stop at Washington to see the President before going home to Philadelphia.

William Bainbridge went immediately to see the President when they reached Washington.

The President was delighted to see Bainbridge, he had been fearful that Bainbridge had been made a prisoner or worst. Bainbridge greeted the President and gave him as brief of a report that he could and not leave out any salient points.

The President expressed his approbation, and even commended him for the judicious and skillful manner in which he had discharged his duty while under the pressure of such extraordinary circumstances. The President requested that Bainbridge stay over a day and address a joint session of Congress. Bainbridge was not happy about extending his stay in Washington but he also welcomed the opportunity to hopefully change a few minds as to the policies regarding tributes.

Bainbridge was given the opportunity the following day to address Congress. In his speech he suggested that a continuous policy of burying ones head in the sand was going to shut the merchant trade down off the North African coast. Bainbridge talked in positive terms about Turkey and encouraged Congress to start talks with the Sublime Porte.

Bainbridge then sailed to Philadelphia. Spring was in the air as the USS George Washington sailed up the Delaware River to Philadelphia. The crew was all on deck mostly to see the sites. The crew of the George Washington was anxious to come home; the tour of duty in Northern Africa had confined them to the ship most of the time. The men were looking forward to female entertainment and some of the luxuries available from being on land.

Susan was as always over joy to hear that the sails of the ship her husband was on had been sited coming up the Delaware River.

She took the horse and buggy to the port to meet them. William would have his large sea chest and they needed the buggy to transport it.

The USS George Washington docked without incident and to the delight of all the well wishers. The docking of a large ship was a novelty to even those who had seen hundreds of docking.

Bainbridge had his hat off waving it over his head. Susan found him easily and thanked God that he appeared to be in one piece.

Susan's and William's reunion was joyous. Susan had one hundred and one things to tell him. They embraced for a long while before Susan suggested they get the buggy before people took notice of their behavior.

"Everybody is well and anxious to see you. They all want to hear about your adventures and places you have been," Susan was holding on tight to William's hand.

They want us to come to Middletown immediately and stay for a while.

"That sounds wonderful but I need to check with the Secretary of the Navy and see what he has in mind. I also need to deliver my written impressions of future developments and hostilities in the Mediterranean."

"That won't take long will it?"

"I hope not since they probably do not want to hear what I have to say."

Captain Bainbridge was so successful in his diplomatic endeavor in this first encounter with the Porte he was able to pave the way to the first treaty between the United States and the Sublime Porte.

A historian, writing contemporaneously of these times, says as follows: *"This humiliating condition in which Captain Bainbridge was placed arose out of the feeble policy of our Government in stipulating to purchase immunity from insult to our citizens, and spoliations on our commerce by paying an annual tribute to barbarians whom it could have readily controlled by force. There is other way of giving complete protection to our citizens and to our property afloat than by ' the cannon's mouth.' Dearly-bought experience has proved the utter fallacy of Mr. Jefferson's scheme of preserving peace by pursuing a pacific and upright policy toward all nations."*

"The point is now settled, however, that nothing less than an exhibition of force and willingness to exercise it can maintain unimpaired our national rights and dignity."

The United States had been guilty of caving into intimidation and paying ransom. This was not a sustainable position for the new government to be in. Bainbridge was an advocate of a very different line of action. The President was impressed with display of knowledge and the use of good judgment that William had displayed. The Congress was all addressed on the tinder box waiting to explode in Northern Africa.

The President was convinced that Bainbridge could answer for himself in the event of troublous times and was an advocate for his returning to Algiers.

President Thomas Jefferson had decided that war against the Barbary pirates was a better course than continued tributes. The First Barbary War began (1801-1805); the United States was in need of a larger navy to defend the rights of the new nation. Merchant ships were going to North Africa to trade for carpets, olive oil, textiles and precious metals. The pirates were bothering all those vessels that failed to pay a tribute.

TWENTY-THREE

Essex
1802

The Bainbridge's managed to escape to Middletown for two weeks. It was a gorgeous time of year with the cherry blossoms coming out and the new greenery on the trees and bushes. The woods were coming alive for another summer season.

Towards the end of May, the Bainbridge's were back in their Philadelphia home. Susan was in the yard when sighted a lone horseman came towards the house. Susan saw him coming in the distance and her heart sunk, she knew it meant William was being called to duty.

The rider arrived at the house and delivered a long envelope. The rider was hot and tired and he was invited to spend the night and par-take in their evening meal.

William did not open the envelope until the family was gathered at the dining room table for dinner. He read the directive from the Secretary of the Navy and couched in the following terms: *"Appreciating highly your character as an officer, the President has selected you to command the frigate Essex, and has placed the whole squadron under the command of Commodore Richard Dale, to whose orders he enjoins you to pay strict attention and due obedience."*

"When do you have to report," asked Susan.

"It would appear that I have to be on board June 5th."

"Will you be gone long?"

"I doubt it, since there are not enough ships to make up a squadron."

As Bainbridge predicted not much came of this cruise since U. S. naval strength was not sufficient. Much to Susan delight William was back in Philadelphia to help rectify this problem of the Navy not having sufficient ships of war. William was placed in charge of the construction of several new ships.

On May 2, 1802, William Bainbridge sailed out of Philadelphia as the captain of the *USS Essex*. The squadron had grown in size because of the new construction was completed on a number of war ships. They now had five U.S. Navy frigates in the squadron and they were being sent to protect American shipping in the Mediterranean. The five Navy frigates were under the command of Commodore Richard Dale fighting the North African Barbary pirates.

The pirates had accelerated their jihad against Christian seafarers, Europeans and Americans. The pirates were in control of the powerful trade routes in the Mediterranean disrupting merchant trade. Somebody was going to have to travel there, with tribute, to quite the situation down.

As the *Essex* was then in New York, Bainbridge joined her at once, and found that the squadron preparing for sea consisted of the *USS President*, flagship of Commodore Dale; the *USS Philadelphia*, under command of Captain Barron; his own vessel the *Essex*; and the schooner *Enterprise*, under command of Commandant Sterrett.

The *USS Essex* was a 36-gun sailing frigate and was launched on September 30, 1799 at a cost of $139,362. The name was chosen because the lion share of the money came from the residence of Essex County in Massachusetts. On December 17, 1799 the frigate was presented to the United States and accepted by Captain Edwards Preble.

The squadron had orders to proceed to the Mediterranean to protect American commerce, with whose interests the Bashaw of Tripoli had seen fit to interfere.

"I have to tell you Susan that I feel honored to have been named to command of the *Essex*. The ship is one of the best we have," William was much more excited about the ship then his wife Susan was.

"I am happy that you like your new assignment, but I am sad that you are leaving again."

"You know I am too, but it is my duty and beside I will be home soon."

Bainbridge was looking forward to this expedition. He had handpicked his officers, all of them being fine young officers and seamen. He was particularly pleased that Stephen Decatur would be his first lieutenant. Stephen, like his father, was a man of character and determination; there was not much difference in their ages.

After a pleasant voyage, the squadron arrived at Gibraltar, their first stop. There were also two large Tripolitan vessels at anchor in the harbour. The *USS Philadelphia* was detailed to watch the movements of the Tripolitans. The *USS Essex* was dispatched to Marseilles, Barcelona, Alicante, and other ports on the coast, for the purpose of collecting the American merchant fleet, preparatory to escorting it through the Strait of Gibraltar.

Barcelona was the *USS Essex's* first port visited on this leg of the cruise. The Yankee frigate was received with a great deal of courtesy especially from other crews on adjoining vessels. The first two days in port went well. On the third day the officers of a Spanish guard ship, became angered and jealous because of the comments of their countrymen in comparing their own craft with that of the Americans. The Spaniards decided to make it disagreeable for officers going on shore or passing off the vessel.

The Spanish officers took it upon themselves to stop at four boats and insulted the officers. The morning after this occurrence Decatur rowed to the Spaniard's vessel, and demanded to see the officer in command with the intensions of challenging him to a duel. The officer in charge told him that the lieutenant he was after had gone ashore. Decatur left the following message for him, to be given to him on his return:

"Tell the man who threatened to fire into an unarmed boat's crew that Lieutenant Decatur, of the *Essex,* denounces him as a cowardly scoundrel, and when they meet on shore he will cut his ears off."

No meeting ever took place. Lieutenant Decatur was an excellent shot and would have no doubt killed the man he challenged. He did receive a written apologize from the insolent Spanish officer before they departed the Harbour.

The *Essex* escorted a large fleet of merchantmen out of the Barcelona harbour that had been collected in the various harbors of the Mediterranean.

The *Essex* saw them safely outside of the strait before returning to Gibraltar.

Bainbridge received news when they arrived in Gibraltar that the Tripolitan corsairs had been successfully cooped up and dismantled by the *USS Philadelphia*. Their crews were sent over to Africa in small boats by night, to make their way to Tripoli across the desert, while the Tripolitan admiral had taken passage in an English vessel bound for Malta.

Captain Bainbridge received new orders from the Squadron Commander to sail to Algiers. The *USS Essex* was made ready with water and supplies. William made sure he purchased ample wine for the voyage and stay in Northern Africa.

Bainbridge by now was familiar with the sailing route and the waters going to North Africa. He enjoyed cruising in the warm waters and relatively flat waters of the Mediterranean.

Captain Bainbridge sailed the *Essex* to the mouth of the harbor where the Dey of Algiers held control, but he did not take the *USS Essex* into the well fortified harbor. He instead anchored outside of the bay, out of range of the cannons on shore.

Lieutenant Parker commented to Captain Bainbridge that he had counted over two hundred pieces of ordnance aimed on the harbor. There were also innumerable loopholes in the castle; a fire of musketry could have swept her decks and tops.

Near the entrance to the harbor two crescent-shaped batteries stood close to the water's edge, and at the inner bend of the anchorage another small fort looked out over the roadstead.

"I do believe the Dey is serious about war. He has increased his ordnance considerably; this is not an encouraging sign."

"Gentlemen," Bainbridge was addressing his officers, "the calculating old scamp would have the *Essex* under the guns of his fortress again if he could," Bainbridge said half smiling. "He won't get me there so easily this time and we need to wary of any tricks he may attempt."

Richard O'Brien witnessed the arrival of the American frigate. He was not aware that Bainbridge was on board, but that made little difference since he felt it was his obligation to personally greet all American vessels.

O'Brien took his row boat and made his way to the *USS Essex* to welcome and confer with the ship's captain.

"Permission to come aboard?"

"Permission granted."

"Captain Bainbridge, what a pleasant surprise!"

"Richard, I was just thinking about you and if you were still posted here in the god for shaken place."

Captain Bainbridge was genuine in his greeting of the American Consul Richard O'Brien.

"It is good to see you Richard, you are looking well."

"Good to see you Captain but I wish it was not always in Algeria."

"Come lets go to my cabin and talk, you need to catch me up on what had transpired these many months."

The two men chatted over a glass of wine about the state of affairs in Northern Africa.

"I had a reason to come so early to your ship. I am double glad it is you that is also in command of the ship. You see, William, The Dey of Algiers is on a rant. Actually I think the man get crazier as the days go by."

"What is his beef now, he gets his blood money and I have been authorized to pay more if necessary."

"He wants you for some reason and perhaps he wants your ship."

"He would have no idea that I would be back here."

"Somehow he guessed you would be sent back and he would control you this time to do his bidding."

"Tell the His High Mightiness the Dey that Captain Bainbridge has not forgotten the oath he swore not to make any further demands upon me after the first voyage was performed."

"You know as well as I do the Dey is not mentally balanced."

"I do know that but still in the face of such a solemn declaration he makes another insolent request."

"He has the power and the people on his side."

"I realize that but still anyone who thus proves his unworthiness should be denied all credence," William was infuriated.

"You know William, I don't owe the Dey anything, I only deliver messages and hope he doesn't shoot the messenger."

"Tell him I do not doubt his disposition to capture my frigate and enslave my officers and crew. He needs to realize in order to preserve peace I complied with his first demand I have done everything which the commander of a ship would be justified in doing to prevent hostilities. But mark you, if the Dey is determined to have war if he is so mad as to make the Americans his enemy he soon will have caused to regret it."

But the next morning Bainbridge found that Mr. O'Brien had been successful, and that the Dey would grant him an audience soon after his morning meal, which took place at noonday.

"Mr. O'Brien, tell the Dey I will be coming ashore in the early afternoon to meet with him."

"Lieutenant Parker prepared the small launch for going to shore at one bell."

Captain Bainbridge, Lieutenant Parker, two midshipmen and two able sailors rowed to shore. Waiting at the dock was an advance party to greet them and escort the captain and lieutenant to the Dey's palace. The four crew members were left with their weapons to guard the boat until they returned.

Bainbridge and Parker were shown into the receiving room where the Dey was seated in his throne. The Dey did not make any effort to welcome them.

The Algerian Potentate was sitting cross-legged on a luxurious divan, being fanned by two large slaves, while his ministers sat at some distance against the walls. No chairs were provided for the guests, the guests were required to stand. A translator was available to translate from Algerian to French. Bainbridge stood in his most erect stance, with folded arms, and indulged in none of the genuflections that characterize court etiquette in Algeria.

His High Mightiness the Dey was not a pleasant mood and Bainbridge was not about to let his bad manners become an issue. Bainbridge was not going lower himself to kissing up to the Dey; all those in the room were aware of the mounting tension.

"You don't seem happy to see me," Bainbridge was yanking the Dey's chain.

The Dey snapped back, "Down on your knees you dog of a Christian!" shrieking the words out and pointing to the floor at his feet. You must know that it is written in the Koran, that all nations which have not acknowledged the Prophet are sinners. You are a sinner. It is my right and duty being one of the faithful to plunder and enslave. Every Muslim is willing to die to eliminate Christen dogs. It is also an honor to die in battle with Christians since every Muslim who is slain in this warfare will go to paradise."

"Down I say," the Dey continued jumping up as he noticed that Bainbridge's only reply was a calm folding of his arms across his chest. The Lieutenant followed Bainbridge's actions and they stood there with towering erect carriage looking down on the Dey.

The Dey looked at the American consul, Richard O'Brien and said;

"Has the consul expressed my desires to the American captain?" was the first question the Dey asked.

"He has, and the American captain regrets that he cannot comply with the distinguished request, as it would be contrary to the orders of the United States Government that he received before leaving home."

"That is all right on the other side of the water," the Dey responded," but here my wishes are of more importance."

"That I deny," returned Bainbridge speaking French through the interpreter.

The Dey did not allow it to be seen how these words nettled him, but the retort that he made showed the position he intended to take in the matter.

"For what your country says," he sneered," I care no more than for a handful of dried dates. You are in my power. It makes no matter to me whether you declare war or not. It would only make me richer and more powerful; but this much must be understood: either you take my ambassador and my presents to Constantinople or you sink where you are."

Bainbridge was not going to stand for any more brow beating from this unreasonable jerk. Without saying another word to the Dey Bainbridge turned on his heels and left with the others following.

"We need to go back to the ship immediately and leave this area," Bainbridge was concerned that the Dey might attempt to imprison them and take the ship.

They made it back to the ship and set sail before Bainbridge had time to inform his officers of what had transpired.

When the *Essex* was well away from Algiers, Bainbridge briefed his officers in his cabin. He said they were in transit back to the United States where he would take up the Algerian matter with the Secretary of the Navy.

"Please inform all the men as to what our plans are and then come back for a glass of wine," Bainbridge was happy to be in route for home.

TWENTY-FOUR

Home
1802

The Bainbridge's were living in Philadelphia in cramped quarters provided by Captain Waldron in his home. The arrangement was satisfactory while William was at sea but it was agreed that it was only to be temporary until they found a home. Susan wanted to become pregnant so larger quarters were going to be necessary sooner than later. William was finally home on leave. The young couple now had time to find their own house before William had to ship out again.

Philadelphia was growing; the population in 1800 was 41,220 and population of the United States was 5,308,483.

From Philadelphia's founding through the early 1800's the City was considered the area between the Delaware and Schuylkill Rivers between Vine and South Streets.

William Bainbridge wanted to live in Philadelphia because it was the temporary capital of the United States but Susan was attracted to the city being the publishing, artistic, literary, and social center. As Henry Adams put it, Boston was our Bristol, New York our Liverpool, and Philadelphia our London."

William and Susan had been looking for a home in Philadelphia for a number of months. Captain Waldron was gracious enough to let the Bainbridge's stay with them until they were settled in their own home. Susan was enjoying living in Philadelphia and the Waldron's had been taking good care of her while William was gone.

Susan had become involved with singing at the Catholic Church. Philadelphia was one of the few eastern cities that had a large Catholic congregation. Susan was thankful for the support of the Catholic Church with William being gone so much of the time.

"William Bainbridge, this is large, wonderful city; why this must be the largest city in the world! I have never been to a city that even came close to being this big, and I love it here." Susan was as happy as she had ever been.

"No," said William laughing, "Philadelphia is a large city and perhaps the largest in the United States, but cities like Havana in Cuba are much larger."

"Whatever, all I know is that I want to live here and raise a family with you. Can we start looking for a home tomorrow?"

"Sure, I'll do some inquiry with the Navy Department if they are aware of any homes for sale that we might consider."

William had to check in with the Secretary of the Navy the following morning so he could find out who might have a property for sale. William also reported his confrontation with the Dey.

William was able to find out that a couple had a nice home in Society Hill's for sale. William felt they needed to go see the house so he rented a buggy and horse for a few days. He felt that Susan would also like to see more of Philadelphia and what better way than in a buggy.

Susan was excited that they might find a real home of their own. They went 186 South Front Street address on Society Hill and found the house he had been told was for sale.

"William, the house is beautiful but it is huge and probably will cost a fortune."

"We will find out, let's go knock on the door and see if by chance the owners are at home."

The owners were at home and they were most hospitable, inviting the Bainbridge's inside and giving them a tour of the house. The house had a large foyer, with a large living room to the right and a dining room directly behind the living room. Across from the living room through the foyer were a library and a separate music room. The kitchen and smaller eating area were at the back of the house. The second story was the bedrooms and bath for the family in the house. The servant quarters were on the third floor.

"It is so beautiful inside, William. Look at the chair rails, the molded cornice and I love the round-arched cupboards with carved pilasters and keystone."

The master bedroom had a bathing room. "You will like the bathing room, the owner said, the water comes from the cistern from the kitchen range's water reservoir and the water is piped to the bathtub. After you have bathed the water is emptied into a pipe that dumps the water in the yard. We have found this most convenient, especially in the winter."

Susan was almost falling over her feet looking at everything.

"The house is lovely, and the music room is something I have always dreamed about; can we purchase it?"

"We better find out what they are asking for it to see if we can raise the money."

The owner took William into the den and they hammered out a price of $2,200 for the price of the house and one acre of surrounding property.

John Taylor had left William $5,000 dollars in his will so William felt that investing half in the house was a wise investment.

The Bainbridge's were able to move in two weeks later. The house came furnished which was another blessing since they had no furniture.

It was some time before Bainbridge went to sea again. Susan was elated to have William at home. They were invited to parties and government functions. She would sometimes be persuaded to sing for those in attendance at the parties.

William was home; home was becoming a strange occurrence for William but he enjoyed the puttering and fixing of things. It was during this time that William and Susan conceived Susan Parker Bainbridge.

TWENTY-FIVE

Preble
March 7, 1803

Bainbridge was being attached to the squadron of Commodore Edward Preble. He was now considered a one of Preble's Boy's. The squadron consisted of:

Flagship:	*Constitution,*	44 guns, Edward Preble
Brig:	*Siren,*	12 guns, Captain Stewart
Schooner:	*Vixen,*	14 guns, Lt-Cdr. J. Smith
Constellation,		16 guns, Lt-Cdr. Isaac Hull.
Nautilus,		12-guns, Lt-Cdr. R. Somers
Enterprise,		12-g, Lt-Cdr. Stephen Decatur.
Philadelphia,		36-gun, Capt. Bainbridge

On March 7, 1803 Bainbridge was ordered by the Ordnance Department of the US Navy to superintendent the building of the *Siren* a12-Gun Ship at Philadelphia. Captain Bainbridge was also ordered to superintendent the building of a schooner at Baltimore, the *Vixen* with 14-guns. Both these vessels were going to be under ommodore Edward Preble.

Bainbridge was not particularly happy with having to commute 102 miles between the two cities. Going by horseback took him two days of hard riding. He much preferred taking a small sail boat down the Intracoastal Waterway.

On May 21, 1803, Bainbridge age twenty-nine, was given command of the brand new frigate the *USS Philadelphia*, 1,240-tons, and boasted thirty-six 18-pounders guns. She was the pride of a new squadron, under Commodore Preble, being fitted out to fight the Barbary corsairs. His orders were to cruise against Tripolitan cruisers in the Mediterranean.

The whole expedition was fitted out with the intention of cruising in the Mediterranean, but as it would be some time before they would all be ready.

Bainbridge first task was to find a complement of men for the new ship. He was gratified with being able to find four lieutenants to assist him putting together the balance of the 303 men needed to sail the ship.

First Lieutenant: David Porter
Second Lieutenant: Jacob Jones
Third Lieutenant: Theodore Hunt
Fourth Lieutenant: Benjamin Smith

His pick of midshipmen included James Biddle, Robert Gamble, James Renshaw, Benard Henry, B.F. Reed, James Gibbon, Wallace Wormly, William Cutbush, Richard R. Jones, Simon Smith, and D.T. Patterson.

John Ridgely was the ships surgeon and his mates were Jonathan Cowdery, and Nicholas Hanwood.

Keith Spence was the Purser; William Knight was the Master, and his mate was Minor Fountaine; William Godley was the ship's Carpenter. George Hadger was the Boatswain; Richard Stevenson the ship's Gunner; Joseph Douglas, Sail-maker; and William Osborne, Lieutenant Marines. Bainbridge's clerk was Williams Adams.

William had been on leave since April. Susan was feeling like they were a family living a normal life that a family is supposed to live. They were invited to parties, events and generally sought after to attend Philadelphia social event. Susan was feeling in her element and certainly proud of her husband's achievements.

At on very special party in Carpenters Hall Susan was requested to sing and play the harp that someone had thought ahead of the moment to make sure her harp had been transported to the hall.

Susan selected to sing *Cantatas for Female Voice* by Hasse. The selection had originally been scored for orchestra but adapted for the harp. Other favorites that Susan sang bits from included; *The Marriage of Figaro, The Abduction from Seraglio, and Cosl fan tutte.*

The vocal selections that Susan sang were originally for the unique vocal talents of famous Italian and French divas. Susan's voice was not as strong but her range was equal to the task; her voice was light and agile.

Her harp was a Louis XVI with seven pedals. The harp had been made by Jean Louvet in Paris at the request of her father.

The harp was beautifully painted with floral ornaments and fantasy landscape. When Susan played, the bright, brilliant and transparent sounds that filled the room with an air of magical music were hypnotic. She was a good Harper as well as an excellent singer.

Susan received a standing ovation for her concert. She was pleased they enjoyed her efforts and William was swelling with pride for his wife's gift to sing. The beauty of Susan's voice had been mesmerizing to the appreciative gathering of friends.

"I didn't realize what it would be like to be away from you. I love my work but I love you more." William whispered in Susan's ear.

The two were lying on top of the bed with the spring breeze gently stirring the air in the bedroom through the slightly opened windows. The smell of fresh cut grass added to the ambiance of the moment.

William had learned to be more attentive to the stroking and feeling of Susan's erogenous zones. He was more delicate and aware of her ability to build to a climax.

"I love you William, my hero. Come to me and do your magic. I do love it when you are inside me."

William straddled her and slowly let his member work its way into her moist and eager space of heaven. With slow and short strokes he gradually went deeper until he could go no further. With a circular movement of his lower body the sensitive contact of his being inside her was exciting her to a powerful and uncontrolled release. He used some of the spillover of the body's lubrication to moisten his index finger so he could commence doing rings around her anus. Susan was mourning with that sound of her coming to a climax that was becoming more urgent with each thrust.

William did a few more deep thrusts and let his finger enter her anus and Susan went into spasms of exotic pleasure. William let her enjoy the full bodily experience that comes with a perfect organism before withdrawing his finger. His member went limp from also exploding immediately when the virginal muscles pulsated on his penis sending it into uncontrolled contractions.

William rolled off. "That was wonderful by love and how I miss it."

"I also miss it my love. Our time together is precious and I cherish every moment."

William gently kissed her and drew her next to him while again penetrating her moist and slippery virginal opening. He was slow and deliberate in his motions. Susan was also participating making them move a one in the motion of exotic pleasure. They kissed and creased each of their bodies until the pressure built up to another uncontrollable mutual release.

Commodore Edward Preble personally delivered William Bainbridge's orders on July 13, 1803. Preble wanted Bainbridge to sail before the rest of the fleet for the Mediterranean.

Bainbridge was under the authority of an act of Congress, to subdue, seize, and make prizes of all vessels, goods, and effects belonging to the Bashaw of Tripoli or his subjects, who had declared war against the United States.

His complex of 307 men was on board and the ship was ready to sail. William had even made sure five cases of wine were also stowed in his cabin for safe keeping.

The trip across the Atlantic was uneventful, the weather had been good, no tropical storms that are always possible to encounter in the summer. The *Philadelphia* passed from the Atlantic Ocean into the Mediterranean which was always a marvel to Bainbridge. Bainbridge was calling to the attention of the crew the fact they were able to see two continents, Africa on the starboard side and Europe on the larboard side of the ship.

"That is the country of Morocco and that is the city of Tangiers off our starboard bow and off the Larboard bow is Spain and the city of Gibraltar," Lieutenant Porter was going around the ship and make sure the crew understand what they are looking at. Bainbridge was always aw struck by the marvel of seeing two continents from one location.

Few days after entering the Mediterranean on August 21, 1803 one of the topmen spotted ship on the horizon.

"Land Ho!"

On August 26 the *Philadelphia,* 36-guns, was off Cabo de Gata a promontory on the coast of Spain in the Mediterranean.

"I believe that is the vessel *Mesh-Boha,* a Moorish warship with 22-

guns, 120 men, belonging to the Emperor of Morocco and commanded by Ibrahim Lubarez. Just astern of her was a little brig, evidently in her company. It was so dark that it was impossible to determine the character of either vessel

As the new day commenced the early daylight provide sufficient light to determine their speculation of what vessel it was proved correct. There was no doubt that the ship was heavily armed, although all of her guns were housed. Her appearance was suspicious, as her decks swarmed with swarthy men, and she displayed no flag.

The gun ship attempted to out run Bainbridge but without success. Bainbridge ordered a shot across the warship bow and then he delivered a full broadside causing the ship's captain to strike his colors.

Captain Bainbridge had reason to believe that the captured the 22-gun Moorish warship *Mesh-Boha* had been molesting American vessels. He also recaptured the America brig *Cecilia* that had been taken by the vessel *Mesh-Boha*.

Bainbridge was pleased that they had eliminated this Moorish warship from further depredations upon American commerce.

Without stating who he was, Bainbridge hailed her, and ordered her to send a boat and one of her officers on board to him at once. The fact that the brig was so close to the other almost confirmed him in his suspicions that she was a prize. An officer from the *Mesh-Boha* came aboard the *USS Philadelphia* in obedience to Bainbridge's command. The officer was dressed in a European costume and spoke both French and Spanish, so Bainbridge had no problem with communicating with him.

The officer in the Moorish costume denied that the brig was a prize, but confessed that she was an American. He claimed they had been sailing with them four or five days, but was not in any way detained.

Lieutenant Porter rowed off to the ship in order to see if there were any American prisoners on board, but Captain Lubarez prevented his boarding.

Lieutenant Porter came back to the Philadelphia. "Lieutenant, take twenty armed men and go search the vessel."

"Captain Lubarez, the men coming across to you are to be allowed to search your vessel. If you show any resistance to their ability to search the ship I will fire on you," Bainbridge was not going to let his original request go unenforced.

The officers in the funny costume stated that his own ship was a Moorish cruiser of twenty-two guns and carrying one hundred and twenty men; that she belonged to the Emperor of Morocco; that her name was the *Mesh-Boha*; and that she was commanded by Captain Ibrahim Lubarez.

Captain Bainbridge's wrote later in his journal:

"No opposition was offered to this force; they (the boat's crew) found Captain Richard Rowen, of the American brig Cecilia, owned by Amasa Thayer, of Boston, and seven of his crew, who were taken on the 17th of August, twenty-five miles eastward of Malaga, whither they were bound. The Moors confined them under deck, which they always do when speaking a vessel the character of which is not known. The Moorish captain displayed a passport that had been obtained from the United States consul at Tangiers, and, on seeing this, I had no hesitation in making all on board prisoners because of the violation of faith."

The Americans were taken off the *Mesh-Boha* taken to the *Philadelphia* so John Ridgely the ships surgeon could examine them.

Bainbridge ordered two groups of the *Philadelphia's* crew to board both vessels take the Moorish crew prisoners. They also had to take control the *Mesh-Boha* and the *Cecilia*.

When John was finished looking at the crew from the *Cecilia* they were taken back to their vessel. They were anxious to be on their way and sail to Malaga.

The officers of the *Mesh-Boha* were brought over to the *Philadelphia*. The officers were treated well.

"Gentlemen, you will be treated with courteous as long as you cooperate with us. I will not put up with any attempts to do something foolish," Bainbridge was stern in his warning.

The morning after the capture, Bainbridge held a conversation at some length with Commander Ibrahim Lubarez.

"Commander, why have you violated all rules of honor by capturing a vessel of a friendly nation while sailing under her passport?"

Lubarez was acting cocky. "Why not take the ship. We will soon to be at war with the United States. So perhaps I was starting a little early."

"Is that the truth?" questioned Bainbridge, upon hearing this.

The Moor signified assent.

"Then, sir," returned Bainbridge sternly," I must consider you a pirate, and will be obliged to treat you as such. If in one quarter of an hour your authority for preying upon the commerce of the United States is not forthcoming, I'll hang you to yonder main yardarm as a malefactor."

Bainbridge dismissed Lubarez with an armed guard to his cabin. The Lubarez was visibly shaken by the idea he may be hanged.

In a quarter of an hour he had Lubarez brought on deck.

"Now Mr. Lubarez you can see that we have a freshly woven noose just for you," Bainbridge dangled the noose in front of him.

"Here, here is a document for you to consider," said Lubarez as he drew out a document from an inside pocket of his waistcoat.

Bainbridge accepted the document and read it.

"According to this document the Emperor of Morocco has authorized all vessels under his command the right to capture American vessels."

"Well Captain Lubarez it would appear you were not acting on your own but under orders of your government. I am going to have to confiscate this document."

Bainbridge had the document to give to Commodore Preble when he eventually would rendezvous with the *Constitution;* it was a discovery of great importance.

After discovering that the captain of the *Mesh-Boha* was not acting on his own responsibility, but really under orders of his Government, Bainbridge treated him with great courtesy. Bainbridge also gave orders to treat the other prisoners not as pirates but as prisoners of war. Bainbridge was strict about treating the prisoners well. When one of the *Philadelphia's* seamen struck a Moorish sailor he was punished.

Commodore Edward Preble

TWENTY-SIX

USS Philadelphia
1803

Bainbridge had learned from conversation with the Moorish Captain that a Moorish thirty-gun ship was cruising in the area of Cape St. Vincent.

The *Philadelphia* sailed to the area around Cape St. Vincent but they were unable to locate the vessel. After several days, Bainbridge ordered the *Philadelphia* back to the Mediterranean to cruise off Tripoli and wait for the arrival of Preble.

Commodore Preble arrived a few days later.

Bainbridge reported to him on the *Constitution*. He gave his commanding officer the document he had taken from the Captain of the prize they had taken.

"William, this is nonsense, I am going to leave you at first light and sail for Tangiers."

"Yes sir, should we continue on to Tripoli?"

"That would be good. While you are there I am going to demanded instant reparation from the Emperor of Morocco."

Commodore Preble thanked Bainbridge officially for his vigilance and foresight.

Bainbridge learned later that Commodore Preble met with the Emperor of Morocco and the Emperor said that the Moorish cruisers had not sailed under his orders but under those of the Governor of Tangiers. The Emperor was attempting to make a scapegoat out of the Governor of Tangiers. Preble's was not fooled, he knew the Emperor was his foe and had written the document.

Commodore Preble also assured Bainbridge that Congress would vote the approval of prize money to the value of the Moorish vessel to be divided among the crew.

Bainbridge was sitting in his cabin late one morning looking over some maps when Lieutenant Porter stopped at the cabin door.

"Well, Mr. Porter," said Captain Bainbridge, looking up and smiling, "come in. Did you wish to speak to me?"

"Yes, sir," replied Porter, entering. "You remember the news that the captain of the Neapolitan merchant brig gave us this last week, saying that a Tripolitan brig had just sailed out for a cruise."

"Indeed I do," cried the captain eagerly. "Did the *Vixen* capture her? She could not have been far behind us."

"No," Porter answered;" but there is a strange sail, evidently a Tripolitan, standing close inshore."

"Let's up and have a look at her," Bainbridge laughed, jamming his heavy hat down upon his brows. "I think a little excitement would do us good. How's the wind? "

"About due east, sir."

The *Philadelphia* arrived off the shore of Tripoli on October 31, 1803. Tripoli was in full sight for all the crew to see. Their mission was to blockade pirate corsairs belonging to the North African nation-state of Tripoli.

Bashaw Yusuf Karamanli, regent of Tripoli, had declared war on America two years earlier in order to prey on American commercial shipping in the Mediterranean.

Tripoli was a Turkish vilayet (regency) of North Africa. Tripoli was bounded on the north, by the Mediterranean (between 11° 40' and 25° 12' E.) with a coast-line of over 1,100 miles.

Tripoli comprises of at least five distinct regions - Tripoli proper, the Barca plateau (*Cyrenaica*), the Aujila oases, Fezzan and the oases of Ghadames and Ghat - which with the intervening sandy and stony wastes occupy the space between Tunisia and Egypt, extend from the Mediterranean southwards to the Tropic of Cancer. The country has a collective area of about 400,000 sq. m., with a population estimated at from 800,000 to 1,300,000.

TWENTY-SEVEN

Bad Choice
October 31, 1803

It was nine o'clock, for two bells were struck just as the captain and the lieutenant returned on deck. The former took a squint through the telescope at the white sail inshore and then turned hurriedly.

"It is the cruiser; I'd almost swear to it," he exclaimed." Make all sail, and take after her. We are but six or seven leagues to the east of Tripoli, and, by George! We'll head her off. We've got all the water we wish under our keel; let's put our best foot forward."

As they neared land they spotted a Tripolitan raider. Bainbridge made a note of the time, half-past ten, when he cited a ship near the shore off his port bow. The excitement of spotting the Tripolitan raider motivated Bainbridge to have the crew piped to battle stations. The call went out with the crew scrambling to their pre-assigned stations. The crew welcomed the diversion after the long crossing on the Atlantic.

Bainbridge gave chase but soon realized that he could not over take the ship and perhaps force the ship to shore. Bainbridge was caught up the moment of the chase and failed to use prudent judgment and went too close to shore.

There was much bustle and bawling as the *Philadelphia* broke out her studding sails and spread her royals, and slowly she began to creep up upon the chase. The cruiser was more than aware of the *Philadelphia* and was making all efforts to escape. The cruiser had spread a great lanteen sail forward that stretched almost to the water's edge over her bulwarks. (The lateen sail is a triangular sail set on a long yard mounted at an angle on the mast running in a fore-and-aft direction.)

Bainbridge called for more sail and with the strong winds narrowed the distance between them in one hour. The *Philadelphia* was in within long range cannon fire. Bainbridge assumed she was armed and was not going to risk being fired on. Bainbridge began to fire at her with his forward division; most of the balls fell short, but the firing did not interfere in the least with the other's attempt to get away.

The 'would be prize' seemed to increase her speed, and did not make a response, although the long range practice was kept up for forty-five minutes. By this time the entrance to the harbor was in full view, and it became apparent that to reach there in advance of the other vessel was an impossibility.

Bainbridge and Porter had charts of the area and they were making frequent observation since the water appear to be shallow. One midshipman was doing depth testing with a hand-lead on a line. The soundings ran from seven fathoms to ten, and the chart showed clear water up to the harbor's mouth. Reluctantly Bainbridge gave orders to take in sails and abandon the chase. The foresail was dropped, the helm was ordered hard aport, and the *Philadelphia* began to haul offshore. There was a strong current setting in toward the mouth of the harbor, but the wind was fresh, and soon the frigate had good headway on her.

"It is a shame to give up after getting so close up," grumbled Lieutenant Porter, noticing that the corsair had taken in her sails, evidently satisfied that she had shown the big ship a clean pair of heels.

Bainbridge had picked up a glass and was squinting over the taffrail at the low-lying coast and the clustering white-walled houses and spires that marked the city of Tripoli. "By George, sir, look at that fleet of small craft lying alongside the wall just inside the harbor!" he exclaimed, handing the glass to Porter.

"Not so very small," the lieutenant replied; "I should judge those vessels ranged from thirty to ninety tons or more. They are the craft which do the most damage to our shipping; pirates every last man of them!"

No sooner had he finished speaking than Bainbridge made a quick spring forward. He had been listening to the monotonous voice of the man heaving the lead, and the last sounding had filled him with a sudden consternation. Eight fathoms and the next heave seven! It was impossible, but he was not the only one who was listening.

"Plash!" went the lead.

"By the mark, six! " roared the man in the fore chains, changing his sing-song to a shrill, frightened tone.

Such an abrupt shoaling meant nothing less than immediate danger. The maps had shown safe water, but there was no gainsaying the testimony of the lead.

"Port your helm!" roared Bainbridge, twirling, and letting go the words at the quartermaster as if he was firing off a pistol.

The yards were braced about sharply as the vessel answered to her helm, but the *Philadelphia* had been running at the rate of five or six knots. It was not possible to stop such headway quickly.

Bainbridge ordered the helm a port so he could seek deeper water. Midshipman Robert Gamble was casting the lead weighted line calling out the depth of the water. "Eight fathoms, seven fathoms, six and a half fathoms"…and just then the *Philadelphia* rammed hard into the reef tossing the men on to the deck. The ship's bow was elevated about five to six feet.

The *Philadelphia* was sailing at about eight knots when then hit the reef. The effect of the impact was that of running into a brick wall.

The moment impact was felt by all the crew; the men did not say a word. Most of the men were being slammed to the deck from the sudden shock of running up on the reef. To make matters worse all of the objects on the deck were tumbling toward the stern. The crew was hanging on to whatever was near them. They were all experiencing the raising motion created by the upward lifting motion of the bow. Then there were the loud sounds cause by grinding, crunching sound of the frigates timbers in the bowels of the ship crying out as if they were undergoing some frightful strain.

Bainbridge uttered no exclamation; he was dazed by the impact of hitting his head on the ships wheel. He exchanged a glance with Porter that telegraphed his immediate feelings of astonishment and distress. But no fear showed in the face of either, although it was a moment to frighten the stoutest of hearts.

"Lieutenant Jones, where did that reef come from? It was as if some enemy of the deep had suddenly risen up to crush the vessel in its spiteful jaws.

"I don't know Captain, but I believe we are in trouble."

The watch below had come pouring up on deck; but seeing their commander calmly giving orders from the quarter-deck, and their companions scrambling aloft to lay the sails aback in obedience to his commands, without the least confusion they followed suit, going to their stations as quietly as if it were fire drill instead of a sudden danger they had to face.

Lieutenant Jones, who had gone forward to the forecastle, sent Midshipman Biddle hurrying aft.

"There's not fourteen feet below us at the fore channels, sir!" he said breathlessly, saluting Bainbridge, who saw to his dismay that the sails were not working the vessel off the reef.

The next order was to run aft all the guns of the forward division in the hope of raising the bow until she should be clear of the rocks. The trunnions (the cylindrical projections on the side of the cannon barrel) allowed the cannon barrels to bang on the deck as the sailors wrestled the heavy, clumsy guns down the sloping deck until they were all huddled well behind the mainmast.

"Has she lifted, sir?" asked Bainbridge of Lieutenant Jones.

"Not an inch, sir," Jones said with apprehension.

Matters indeed looked bad.

"Cut away both those anchors, Mr. Biddle," Bainbridge thundered.

A few blows with an axe and the four tons of iron plashed from either side of the bows. Still she did not move. The sails aloft were drawing well. The *Philadelphia* was grounded and it was not going to give way.

The ship was in a cross-current but the sea was flat so no expected rocking of the sea was going to help them.

The slight breeze was not sufficient to fill the mainsail and left it romping and flapping. The deck was not moving; the ship had never been as still as it was wedged on the reef. The men were not use to the vessel being stationary and that along made everyone uneasy. They must have appeared like a sitting target to the enemy that was now aware that the *Philadelphia* was in trouble. Nobody on the ship was idle; they were all aware their lives were becoming more in danger by the minute; they could see the approaching enemy vessels.

"Where's the carpenter? Send the carpenter aft to me," said Bainbridge quietly to Midshipman Robert Gamble. The middy ran below. "Godley, you're wanted on the quarter-deck," he cried to a tall seaman into whose arms he almost fell. "Captain wants to speak to you. Lively there! Don't stop."

The carpenter went up the ladder in three jumps; in two more he was at the break of the poop.

"Get ten men and stave in those forward water casks every one of them."

Off went the carpenter, plunging down the companion way.

"Bosun," roared Bainbridge, catching sight of Boatswain George Hadger hurrying across the deck, "is there any water in the well?"

"No, sir," the old seaman cried, saluting;" and it's just been sounded. She's tight and dry, sir."

"Rig the pumps, then, and get this fresh water overboard."

In three minutes the steady "slish, slosh, click, clack" of the big pumps sounded throughout the ship, and the water from the springs of Pennsylvania poured out into the scuppers. Below, the carpenter and his crew could be heard assailing the stout ribs of the water casks.

The *USS Philadelphia* was stuck to a point that her nose did not rise a single inch, and now a new danger appeared. Bainbridge, following the pointing arm of a man on the forecastle, turned around, but it was only for an instant. He had seen enough, however. Out from the mouth of the harbor was pouring the Tripolitan fleet; their pointed, white sails scores of them gleamed in the sunlight. If the *Philadelphia* could not be wore off before they arrived within gunshot her chances of not being taken as a prize were slim.

The majority of the crew on deck, hidden by the bulwarks, was ignorant of the new terror.

"Ask Mr. Porter to step here quickly," said Bainbridge to one of the midshipmen; and at the same time he gave an order that to an inexperienced ear might have seemed a strange one under the circumstances. It was a desperate resort nothing less than to cast overboard all the guns that could be loosened; and soon almost the entire starboard battery had been put over the side.

The forward division on the port hand followed suit. "Look there, Mr. Porter," said Bainbridge, nodding his head backward at the approaching fleet. "Cast loose and provide the stern chasers here, and run two of those heavy guns into my cabin. Break out the stern gallery."

"There's where they will take position. Has she moved? "

"Not an inch, sir," replied Porter firmly. "We'll have to fight for it."

Suddenly the boom of a gun sounded the leading Tripolitan had commenced firing! Before five minutes had passed four large gunboats had taken their station under the larboard quarter. The splinters began to fly, the enemy cannon shot was ripping and tearing aloft, crippling the yards and spars. Already three or four men, red and gory, had been carried below. The quarter-deck, on which Bainbridge was standing, was quivering from the discharge of the carronades that had been trundled into the cabin. Sulphur smoke was in the air, but the men were not cheering. They were fighting with a sullen determination to keep their freedom.

A big boatswain's mate, serving one of the after guns, was standing upright, motioning the men with the handspikes how to adjust the piece. (Handspike was four foot long stout hardwood pole.)

With the one hand he was trying to stop the flow of blood from a great splinter wound in his breast. But before the piece could be fired the frigate gave a lurch, her bow rose a few feet higher on the sunken reef, and the brave sailor pitched headlong to the deck.

"Help me to my pins!" he cried weakly, making frantic efforts to rise; but it was useless. Another pitch and the deck was at such an angle that even the able-bodied could scarcely keep their feet. Only three guns now could be brought to bear, and the crushing sound of the Tripolitan broadsides became an uninterrupted roar. The balls were entering the hull from all directions. One came in the stern port, and, being deflected, crossed to the other side and back again, as a billiard ball would bound from the angles of a table. The balls were tearing into the wood sending deadly splinters scattered in its wake. Not a sign of fear, however, was to be observed among the crew, although three fourths of them could do nothing but stand idly by.

"Cut away the foremast!" cried Bainbridge, making a trumpet of his hands.

With a crash the great pine timbers yielded to the strokes of the axes, and down tumbled the towering sails, hampering the forward deck and covering the forecastle in a mass of billowing, fluttering canvas.

The hull was almost on her broadside now, and the main-topgallant mast was cut away, but no relief was afforded. The proud vessel was a wreck. The enemy was unrelenting in their firing on the *Philadelphia*. The immobile ship was not any threat to the enemy since most of their guns were either over board or pointed towards the water. The enemy seemed to enjoy inflicting as much damage as they could on the crippled ship.

The *Philadelphia* held out for almost another hour using the limited fire power that remained on board.

"No white feathers here," said Midshipman Biddle to his friend Gamble. And it was a fact. Not a single skulked attitude was displayed among the *Philadelphia's* crew; the men were fighting for their lives.

"Word's been passed for the officers," said Gamble, pointing.

There, under the shelter of the poop, for the quarterdeck was now swept by a murderous fire, Bainbridge, with his three lieutenants, and William Knight, the master, were in consultation.

"I cannot sacrifice the lives of my brave men longer," the captain said. "Gentlemen, I've done my best; for the cause of humanity we will have to strike."

The ship had been rendered defenseless since the larboard guns were pointed at the water and the starboard gun up into the air. Bainbridge could not bring his cannons to bear since his ship sat at an angle, and he was forced to surrender.

The Tripolitan gunboats ran alongside of the *Philadelphia* and took possession. Captain Bainbridge ordered the crew not to resist being taken prisoners. He was fearful of the men being randomly killed. Bainbridge knew that the Muslim terrorists were sworn to carry out jihad against all Western powers.

It was a cruel fate. To strike his country's flag to a civilized foe after a hard-fought battle would have been gall and vinegar to the commander's high-strung nature; but to yield to this uncivilized and barbarous enemy was humiliating.

"Sir," said Porter, extending his hand," we've all done our best, and we appreciate your feelings; but there is nothing for it."

The silence of the other officers made known their acquiescence.

"Tell the carpenter to scuttle the ship," Bainbridge said calmly, "Overboard with the small arms, Mr. Porter. See that the magazine is flooded Mr. Jones, I am sorry, sir; haul down the flag!"

The proud emblem came slowly to the deck; the carronades ceased their useless replying to the enemy's well directed fire. An unearthly, discordant yell broke from the line of the barbarians. A few of the smaller craft, that had just sailed into range, discharged their guns with screams of triumph, much as cowardly savages would fling their darts into the helpless body of some great beast that the real hunters had dispatched at their peril.

TWENTY-EIGHT

Captured
1803

Bainbridge ordered the men to collect their personal belongings.
Bainbridge was fearful the barbarians would kill for the joy of
experiencing the carnage; he wanted to prevent a massacre. The helpless
feeling of not being able to affect the outcome would dishearten even the
strongest of men. The men had to hope the victors of this one sided fight
would treat them with respect.

The officers searched everywhere for small arms, heaving them out
of ports and over the bulwarks; this last operation was hardly completed
before the first boat of the Tripolitan fleet gained the side. With shrill cries
the dusky, turbaned Muslims swarmed aboard through the ports, and in
an instant the ship was surrounded by the clamoring, screaming horde.

The crew was well aware that they were serious danger. The sailors
had retreated to the forecastle, where they were gathered in a compact
body, held only in check by the calm words of the officers scattered among
them.

The crew of the *Philadelphia* was ordered to strip off all their clothes
and stand together. They had no idea what was happening except they
were totally defenseless. The men were wondering if they were about to

be killed? The men were only being placated by smoothing words from Bainbridge and the other officers.

Communications with the pirates was difficult. The pirates had no understanding of English but they had developed over the years their own language. They had been preying on Europeans for years and had leaned a slang belonging to them alone called *Lingua Franca*. The language was a mixture of Italian, Spanish and African all in infinitives and without prepositions. The language was not used beyond the tightly knit urban context of pirates and traders confined to the North Africa port vicinity. The rest of the county only understood Arabic or Berber dialects.

"Steady, now, men," said Midshipman Biddle in an undertone;" make no resistance if you wish to save our lives."

As he spoke the midshipman gazed with calm eyes into the face of a bearded, swarthy pirate, who flourished a sharp scimitar within an inch of his throat. The men in the front rank, following their officer's example, folded their arms and stood erect. Not a sound broke from them, except a few curses as they perceived that the Tripolitans were not going to respect the laws of private property. Ditty-boxes and bags were broken into, and their contents scattered about and scrambled for on deck.

Suddenly the frigate settled a little at the stern, and it was remembered that the carpenter had been ordered to let the water into her. Obeying the commands of one or two who seemed to be in authority, and kept in order by their own officers, the men clambered over the side on to the deck of one of the large gunboats that lay grinding against the rail.

"Quelqu'un satisferait me disent qui est responsible?" Bainbridge was saying in French slowly in hopes he would get some response. The pirates were not paying any attention to their captives they were only interested in the loot they finding and carrying off the ship.

Bainbridge continued addressing in French and Italian the dangerous looking pirates that were looting the vessel, asking repeatedly for their leader for someone to whom he could surrender his sword and from whom he could claim protection. But no one paid attention to him so intent were the fiends upon bringing everything of value up from below, for they feared that the ship might sink at any moment. The setting sun threw a red light across the scene. To leeward hung the white cloud of battle smoke, almost a mile distant by this time, and in the sharply defining rays the varied colors worn by the Tripolitans, shuffling and scampering on the main deck, stood out brightly, like the shifting tones of a kaleidoscope.

All at once the hubbub ceased for an instant as if they had just caught a glimpse of the tall, broad-shouldered figure looking down upon them from the quarter-deck.

His three lieutenants stood but a few paces behind him, with set faces and firmly compressed lips. A great, heavily turbaned pirate shouted something, and climbed up the steps of the quarter-deck followed by a half-score of others, bearing their plunder underneath their arms, as if fearful of dropping it. Bainbridge advanced to meet the leader, extending the hilt of his sword as he did so. The cut throat took it.

"Dog of a Christian!" he cried, making a vicious thrust at the middle of the captain's body. The point struck the heavy belt plate and glanced harmlessly, and the man drew back. Bainbridge was standing there with his arms folded and a smile upon his lips. The corsair lowered his arm; then he pointed with his finger at the heavy pistol in Bainbridge's belt. Bainbridge removed the pistol, slowly so as not alarm the pirate, and handed it to the pirate by the barrel. The pirate grasped the pistol handle and jerked the gun from Bainbridge's hand and pointed the pistol directly at Bainbridge's head.

Bainbridge gazed unflinchingly into the pirates eyes. The pirate smiled at Bainbridge and then lowered the pistol seeing that his captive was not afraid of him.

Porter, who was standing but a few feet away, was about to spring, but his commander caught the movement.

"Steady, gentlemen!" he said; "your lives depend upon it; we must submit," Bainbridge thought he would never have to say those words.

The pirate then said "Se taire," as his right hand grab one of the heavy gold epaulets from Bainbridge's shoulder. He then took the other gold epaulet before withdrawing the jeweled pin from Bainbridge's neck cloth.

The Tripolitan corsairs stopped their plundering for a few minutes to watch the intimidation being conducted on Bainbridge. Others then followed the example of their apparent leader and removed the coats and waistcoats of the other officers of the *Philadelphia*. They found the heavy fobs and watches the men had in their possession. The men all remained calm, not offering any resistance to the roughens violating them.

Bainbridge's eyes were following every movement of the man who was submitting him to this indignity. Bainbridge was remaining calm in his outward appearance but his mind was whirling as he observed the demise of their dignity. He was also thinking about the gold chain around his neck that suspended the miniature of his wife, Susan. He was hoping the chain had not been noticed. In any event he was not about to let any of these pirate thugs that smelled from a lack of bathing take it from him.

Bainbridge was standing calmly. All at once the gleam of the gold chain caught the eye of one of the robbers with dirty blood stained hands. With a swift motion the robber tore the soft linen shirt of Bainbridge's open at the throat. There lay the miniature, the calmly smiling face of a woman, in a white, high-waist gown. With a greedy cry he reached for it, but his eager fingers never touched the shining gold chain. With a roar like a cornered beast that counts no odds, Bainbridge seized him by the throat. As he stood there no one could have failed to notice the tremendous muscles strength Bainbridge displayed. Bainbridge had cut off the pirates air way and he had become unconscious as he was being held up with his toes barely touching the deck. Bainbridge then brought the pirate down making sure his skull hit the rail, cracking it open. Bainbridge then lifted the pirate over the rail to watch the body limply fall on the heads of other pirates below. There was for brief seconds dead quiet on the ship as the pirates looked at this display of super human strength.

Porter, Jones and Lieutenant Hunt sprang for ward, but before they could gain their captain's side they were pinioned hard and fast. Bainbridge stood there panting. Someone fired a pistol at him at point-blank range, but, owing probably to the jostling of the crowd, the ball missed its mark. With a cry of rage five or six of the corsairs made at him. He felled the first one with a blow from his great fist, but they swarmed upon him almost too closely intertwined to draw their daggers. Again he struggled to his feet. With a mighty effort he grasped one of his assailants by his heavy cloth belt and whirled him overboard into the sea. Again they closed upon him. Their object now was to gain possession of the gleaming miniature. They had him down more than once, but could not force it from his grasp, although his fingers were torn and cut. It seemed to be ages that he struggled as if gifted with the strength of more than a dozen men. Time and again he rose to his knees only to be hauled down, like a fighting bull, by a pack of hungry wolves. For the fourth time he managed to stand erect and get his back against the rail. Bainbridge was unarmed, except for his magnificent strength; he stood there like a warrior of the Stone Age. The corsairs were almost awed at the sight of this man and the fight they had witnessed.

But a commotion suddenly began among those who had stood aloof as if waiting to see what the result would be. A handsomely dressed figure, in a brilliant red tunic and silk scarf, was calling out to the others to make way for him. He gained the deck, and thrusting back the ill at ease villains, he approached Bainbridge. The latter gathered himself as if for an onslaught, but the Moor bowed low before him, and turning so as to confront the others, he drew a long jewel-hilted pistol. He held both arms in the air to silence the crowd of pirates that had gathered to see the confrontation. There were no challenges to his authority. The officers of the *Philadelphia* were feeling a great full relief, at least for a short while, that their lives maybe spared. The frustration of the past few minutes had played havoc on their individual emotions, watching their captain being brutally attacked. They, perhaps, for the first time in their young lives, had experienced the inability to act when they were needed.

The well dressed man made use of his commanding position and directed the ragged pirates to clear a passageway and motioned to his prisoners to follow him.

Bainbridge had recovered enough so that he could stand up. He still had the miniature of his wife tightly grasped in his bleeding hand. He was breathing hard from the one man battle against a hoard of pirates, but he was still able to motion the other officers to precede him. The officers were also made to strip off all their clothes. Bainbridge was now stripped of everything but his glory and the bruises he had just acquired. Bainbridge was the last of the *Philadelphia's* crew to leave his ship.

All the men were transported on the gunboats to shore. It took three hours to transport all three hundred and fifteen captives.

It was ten o'clock at night, some six hours after the surrender of the *Philadelphia* that the officers and the crew members were landed near the Bashaw's castle. The officers were now all naked since the pirates also wanted their clothes.

The fancy dressed Tripolitan officer, who had saved Bainbridge from being killed, secured for him a makeshift suit of clothes. Bainbridge and his twenty-two quarter-deck officer's, who were still naked, were taken into the Bashaw's castle to appear before him. They were taken to the audience hall to await an audience with the Bashaw. When they were finally shown into the room with the Bashaw, he was sitting casually on his divan, surrounded by his richly uniformed guards.

The balance of the *Philadelphia's* crew was marched though crowds of shouting and spitting Muslims to the Kasbah Fortress that had built in 1535 by Charles I of Spain. The fortress was very large, the largest of the Tripoli's fortifications, a castle that overlooked the harbor. The fortification was nothing more than a rundown warehouse, not fit for human occupation.

The Bashaw subjected the officer's of the *Philadelphia* to a rigid cross-examination while they stood in front of him naked. The women in the room were eying the naked men and giggling as they pointed to the obvious focus of their attention. The men kept their composure while answering numerous questions about their mission. When the Bashaw decided they were done, the party of officer's were conducted to another apartment where supper was served to them. At midnight they were taken back to the hall again and found that they had been placed in charge of the Minister of State, Sidi Mohammed Dgheis. This official proved to be a fine, dignified man of commanding presence, who was well acquainted with European manners and customs, and from the outset he not only enlisted the respect of his prisoners, but appeared anxious to do anything he could to serve them.

Sidi Mohammed Dgheis spoke excellent French, and informed them in the first words he spoke that he hoped to make their stay as little of a hardship as possible.

"I will be your advocate as long as you give me your trusted word not to escape while under my immediate charge." Scarcely waiting for an answer, Dgheis dismissed the guards and bade them to follow him. As he conducted them through the town, he told them that they were bound for the late American consul's house, which had been assigned to the officers as a temporary prison. The American Consulate had been abandoned since the war with Tripoli had begun.

Upon their arrival they found that the kind Tripolitan had also secured for them the clothing of which they had been despoiled all but the epaulets and some of the ornamentation. He bade' them good night after doing all he could for their comfort.

William Bainbridge was as depressed in spirit as he had ever been. He grieved at the loss of the new and beautiful frigate, and was apprehensive that his countrymen might censure him before the true cause of the disaster could be explained. Most of all he was disturbed that he might not ever see his wife again.

There was one thing, however, that gave him comfort it was the locket which he still wore upon his breast, and for which he would have laid down his life.

The Bashaw of Tripoli had shown some compassion for the officers by arranging for better quarters and proving some creature comforts for them. Tripoli's Pasha Yusuf Qaramanli and Pasha Yusuf Karamanli could care less how the captive American's were treated.

The Minister of State, Sidi Mohammed Dgheis made sure the American Consul's house had enough bedding for the twenty-two new occupants. The living conditions in the house were perhaps better then on the ship, they had more space. They had a good view of the harbour so they could see the *USS Philadelphia* at anchor. Food was provided to them daily so they did have some comforts while the rest of the crew suffered deprivation in dungeon like conditions.

The enlisted crew was treated as slaves, they were provided nothing. On one occasion, four men were mustered to carry loads of supplies through the streets, to Yusef's harem. The women there, naked to the waist, giggled at the Americans and offered them dates, olives, oranges and milk until the guards hustled the men away. The guards would talk and jester in a way that crew could understand they were to be ransomed off.

A few days afterwards on November 2, 1803 the *Philadelphia* the pirate's largest prize ever taken was floated off the reef. The pirates were partly assisted by the aid of a high wind. The *Philadelphia* was taken in triumph to the city, the leaks being stopped. The guns, anchors, and other articles which had been thrown upon the reef were raised, and the ship was partly repaired, and moored near the town, about a quarter of a mile from the Bashaw's castle, her guns being remounted.

TWENTY-NINE

Koran
1803

It was written in their Koran, that all nations which had not acknowledged the Prophet were sinners, whom it was the right and duty of the faithful to plunder and enslave; and that every Mussulman who was slain in this warfare was sure to go to paradise. He said, also, that the man who was the first to board a vessel had one slave over and above his share, and that when they sprang to the deck of an enemy's ship, every sailor held a dagger in each hand and a third in his mouth; which usually struck such terror into the foe that they cried out for quarter at once.

Many of the enlisted crew were put to work in galleys, others hauling rocks at construction sites, working in mines or cutting timber. The prisoners were living in horrendous conditions. They were subject to disease, unabated hunger, all manner of cruelty inflicted upon them by their guards. The mental state of the prisoners was deteriorating with the general despair of captivity. Bainbridge was not allowed to see them but he continued to request that he be allowed to visit his men.

The prisons in North Africa were called 'bagnos.' These hell holes were un-ventilated, overcrowded and dangerous. Besides the squalor living conditions the prisoners they were also going to find out that they were always in danger from cannon fire from the American fleet.

Over the past centuries conditions had improved in the 'bagnos' over the original 17th century sure death sentence. The 18th century 'bagnos' allowed the "salves" to have chapels, hospitals (meaning a separate area for the dying), run small businesses, and bars all run by the slaves. They were allowed to keep whatever profit they might make but they had no money. The prisoners were robbed when captured so any money they had would have to have been stolen.

The names of the American held prisoners were sent to the United States in hopes that ransom money would be raised for the release of a few prisoners. The church pulpit was the main source of information as to the names of the prisoners being held. Church attendance on Sunday was probably augmented with hopeful relatives and friends looking to find their love ones.

The roll of all the names provided to them was read out in the churches of Salem, Newport, and Boston. The listing noted all the men and boys on the *Philadelphia*.

Ransom rates were officially set for those Americans already in Barbary prisons at $4,000 for each crew member; and $1,400 for each cabin boy. It is estimated that the pirates, over the years, had captured 800,000 to 1.25 million Europeans as prisoners forced into slavery. The North Africans had found a lucrative business in ransoming off all their captives.

Congress would only pay $200 of the ransom which was considered by those in Congress very generous amount. The pirates could always count on the United States to cough up money for their illegal activities. The relative or friend would have to raise the balance of the ransom. Four thousand dollars was a very large amount of money in the early 19th century and in 2008 dollars would be roughly $320,000. Raising this much money privately was impossible for the majority of the victim's relatives.

The United States eventually had to come up with the ransom for the American prisoners that served on the *Philadelphia*. They even had to pay a ransom for thirty-seven prisoners that had died while guests of the Bashaw of Tripoli.

Most of the crew from the *Philadelphia* had been put to work building fortifications and ships. They worked from dawn until dusk, with a lunch of bread dipped in olive oil. At first, they were fed salt pork and beef from their frigate. When that ran out, dinner was bread and couscous. Many of the men from the *Philadelphia* got sick, and six died during the first six months of captivity.

The following morning after captivity at the officer's prison, Lieutenant Porter appeared at the Captain Bainbridge's door in the former American consul.

"The compliments of the *Philadelphia's* officers to Captain Bainbridge," he said. "They beg that he will accept this paper which was prepared for his perusal."

Bainbridge opened it and read as follows:

TRIPOLI November 1, 1803
We late officers of the United States under your command wish to express approbation of your conduct concerning the unfortunate event of yesterday and do conceive that and soundings justified as near an approach to as we made and that after she struck every expedient was tried to get her off and to defend her which courage or abilities could have dictated. We wish to add that in this instance as well as in other since we have had the honor of being under command the officers and seamen have always appreciated your distinguished conduct. Believe us sir that misfortunes and sorrows are entirely absorbed in our for you. We are sir with sentiments of the highest and most sincere respect your friends and sufferers.

This paper was signed by all the lieutenants, midshipmen, officers, and petty officers from William Godley, the carpenter, to William Adams, the captain's clerk twenty-seven signatures being appended.

But shortly after Bainbridge had received this letter, which caused him almost to break down, because of its kindness and honest feeling, the Minister of State was announced. With him was Mr. Neil C. Nissen, whom he introduced to Bainbridge as his particular friend. Mr. Nissen was the Danish consul, and Sidi Mohammed Dgheis took the opportunity to say he was the only consul in Tripoli for whom he had the least respect.

The Dane expressed great sympathy for Bainbridge in his misfortunes, and the American captain saw at a glance that he was a friend worth keeping. Mr. Nissen's manner satisfied all of the American officers that he was well entitled to the esteem that had been expressed for him by the Tripolitan minister. As soon as he had departed, Bainbridge asked for pen, ink, and paper, and, sitting down at the little table, the only bit of furniture the room possessed, he wrote the following letter to his wife, even before he inedited the official notice he intended sending to Commodore Preble and to the Secretary of the Navy.

Captain Bainbridge was able to secure primitive writing materials so that he could communicate with his wife, Susan. He was not concerned that his personal message to his wife would probably be read by many.

TRIPOLI November 1, *1803*

MY DEAR SUSAN,

With feelings of distress which I cap not describe I have to inform you that I have lost the beautiful frigate which was placed under my command by running her afoul of rocks a few miles to the east of this harbor which are not marked on the charts. After defending her as long as a ray of hope remained I was obliged to surrender and am now with my officers and crew confined in a prison in this place. I enclose to you a copy of my official letter to the secretary of the Navy from which you will learn all the circumstances connected with our capture.

My anxiety and affliction does not arise from my confinement in prison these indeed I could bear if ten times but is caused by my absence which may be a protracted one from dearly beloved Susan and an apprehension which constantly that I may be censured by my countrymen. These impressions are seldom absent from my mind act as a corroding canker at So maddened am I sometimes by the workings of my imagination that cannot refrain from exclaiming that it would have been a merciful of Providence if my head had been shot off by the enemy our vessel lay rolling on the rocks You now see my beloved wife the cause of my distress.

My situation in prison is entirely supportable I have found here kind and generous friends such as I hope the virtuous will meet in all situations but if my professional character be blotched if an attempt be made to taint my honor if I am censured if it does not kill me it will at least deprive me of the power of looking any of my race in the face always excepting however my young kind and sympathizing wife. If the world desert me I am sure to find a welcome in her affection to receive the support and condolence which none others can give I cannot tell why I am so oppressed with apprehension I am sure I acted according to my best judgment. My officers tell me that my conduct was faultless that no one indeed could have done better but this I attribute perhaps in my weakness to a generous wish on their part to sustain me in my affliction. I hope soon to hear that your health is good and that you grieved at my misfortune are yet surrounded by dear and friends who will in some measure assuage your affliction.

Perhaps you will be able to tell me that I have done injustice to my countrymen that so far from censuring they sympathize and some even applaud God grant that this may be the case why should it not. They are generous as they are brave I must stop my dear wife for I see am disclosing my weakness these are the mere reveries which pass through my heated brain. I beg you will not suppose our imprisonment is attended with on the contrary it is as I have already assured you quite a state. Your ever faithful and affectionate husband.
WILLIAM BAINBRIDGE

Through the influence of Mr. Neil Nissen, Bainbridge succeeded in getting all of his letters on board an out-bound vessel, and also sent a long communication addressed to Commodore Preble.

What William did not know that Susan had successfully given birth to a baby girl, Susan Parker Bainbridge. She was their first child.

Bainbridge had stated his position rightly when he said that his stay in captivity promised not to be so much of a hardship as might be expected; Mr. Nissen had brought bedding, furniture, and all sorts of useful household articles to the place where the officers were confined.

"My dear Captain, I have also learned that the crew of the *Philadelphia* is in a well-ventilated quarter of the castle. I have not been allowed to visit them so I personally do not know of their condition."

"I might add that although these people live by piracy, and have little or no legitimate trade, those high in authority have had intercourse with Christian and civilized nations, and have dropped many of the attributes of the barbarian. Sidi Mohammed Dgheis is a man of fine character and sterling worth. You can trust in him implicitly," Nissen looked Bainbridge directly in the eyes.

The officers were left to their own the following week. There was nothing to do but chat with each other in the officer's prison. There were no books, no writing paper or ink; they just had their wits to entertain themselves.

"I think we have company!"

Sure enough Mr. Nissen was passing through the garden entrance leading a donkey with two large crates strapped on his back.

Bainbridge went to greet his new friend. "It is good to see you Mr. Nissen. What is in the large crates?"

"You will see shortly. Another thing Captain, please drop the Mr. Politeness and call me Neil."

The other officers were now in the garden also to see what was transpiring.

"Come gentlemen give me a hand off loading these crates from this miserable creature," Nissen had a smile on his face.

Once the two crates were on the ground they took the tops off and to their surprise were their books and a great deal of their personal property from the ship.

"Neil, where in the world did you obtain our property? We thought we would never see these things again."

"Predictably, I found all these things in a shop keeper's store. I offered him a small amount of money for the entire lot and he was glad to especially get rid of the books since nobody could read them."

"We owe you Nissen, tell us what the cost was and we will reimburse you as soon as we can acquire some money from the Squadron."

"Neil, I need to send Commodore Preble a letter and for oblivious reasons it cannot be read by the enemy. I will also instruct him to pay you for the books and personal items you have brought us," Bainbridge was walking along side of Nissen as they entered the house.

"Of course it is to be expected that anything leaving your prison is going to be scrutinized. All correspondence carried on between you and Commodore Preble will be viewed by the Tripolitan minister," Nissen confided with Bainbridge.

"Do you have any suggestion?" Bainbridge was open to ideas.

"I remember hearing a long time ago, when I was in France, a very interesting thing. You know a writing fluid may be prepared which is entirely invisible until the paper has been subjected to heat. The recipe for making this fluid, if I remember rightly, is something like this; in fact, I am quite sure this is correct."

With that he detailed a simple formula which Bainbridge copied, and put it to good use afterward.

Bainbridge ran their prison like they were still on the ship. He provided direction to his officers. They had classes in French and Spanish, history, navigation, and mathematics just as they would do had they been on board ship. It was rather a remarkable fact that the majority of all those living together at the American consul's house were extremely young men, but one of the officers being above thirty years of age. The midshipmen, with one or two exceptions, were hardly more than boys.

Bainbridge felt it was his continued duty to teach the principles of honor and high sense of duty to his men. He had a contact with these young men, to make them the future captains and commodores of the navy. Bainbridge was a good instructor and he instilled good study habits in all the men which were rigidly enforced.

On the tenth day, while Bainbridge was exercising in the little courtyard surrounded by the high white wall around their prison, a messenger appeared with orders from the Bashaw for him to appear at once at the vice-regal palace, in order to talk with the regent upon a matter of vital interest.

The Bashaw was a man very different in character and personality from Sidi Mohammed Dgheis. He was evidently angry at something, for he scarcely waited for Bainbridge to be seated before beginning upon the subject.

"I have here," he said, "letters from the commander of one of my ships, the *Messurre,* complaining most bitterly of the treatment he has received from your Captain Chauncey, of the frigate *John Adams.* We have treated you kindly; we have given you of the best of the land, in order to prove that we are different from what we are held to be in the opinions of European nations. But this cannot be forgotten. Any ill treatment of my subjects shall be retaliated upon the heads of you and your officers."

Bainbridge did not reply, for he saw that this was not all of the interview, and he knew that there was some reason other than this for his having been ordered to be present. There was to be a condition.

"If," continued the Bashaw, "you will write at once, before that shadow yonder has reached that spot near my hand, a letter to your Commodore Preble, asking him to release the prisoners from Tripoli, I will allow you to stay in your present place of confinement. If you do not, it will go hard with you. What have you to say?"

"Only this," Bainbridge replied: "I cannot believe that the information you received is correct. It is the practice of Americans to treat prisoners with kindness and magnanimity and never with cruelty. In regard to the subjects of your Royal Highness, when our squadron lay in the Bay of Gibraltar I saw with my own eyes one of your captains visiting on familiar terms the officers of the various ships in company with the officers of the vessel in which he was supposed to be confined."

"You will not, then, write the letter?" asked the Bashaw threateningly.

"I cannot write what you demand, for the reason that Commodore Preble is my senior," answered Bainbridge;" and besides this, my advice is useless, because by becoming your prisoner I have lost my rank and power."

"Have you any objections to stating the substance of our conversation in a report to the commander of the squadron?"

"None in the least," Bainbridge answered. And taking up pen and paper, he wrote for a few minutes and read aloud what he had written. This ended the meeting, and under guard he was sent back to join the officers, who were anxiously waiting to hear what had resulted.

In regard to what the Bashaw intended to do, Bainbridge could say nothing; but they were not long kept in ignorance. The Bashaw within an hour sent soldiers to their prison. Some of the prisoners heard a loud commotion out in front of the little building that served as their prison that normally had only three armed men, two on the doorstep and one at the gate leading into the courtyard, guarding them.

One of the midshipmen came running down the stairway and knocked on the door of the room in which the officers were holding their conference. Porter arose hastily and opened it.

"The courtyard is full of soldiers heavily armed and bearing torches," said the middy.

"Surely they can not intend to turn us out at such short notice," grumbled Lieutenant Hunt.

"I suspect strongly, gentlemen," put in Bainbridge, "that such is their intention. At all events, the Bashaw has decided that we have been altogether too comfortable, and now intends to move us."

A noise in the hallway brought everyone to his feet. The heavy door was unlocked, and a number of Tripolitan officers were seen standing there in consultation. Beyond them the startled Americans could see the courtyard filled with the swarthy-faced soldiery, and against the blackness of the night the torches flickered weirdly. Towering shadows wavered to and fro on the walls of the courtyard.

"What is the meaning of this?" Bainbridge inquired.

"We have come," answered the officer, " to escort you and your companions to a different place of confinement; but we have just received another order countermanding the first, and stating that your quarters will not be moved until tomorrow morning at nine o'clock, so I bid you prepare for departure."

Plainly this last message had been delivered just in time to prevent the discomfort of a hasty change of base. As it turned out afterward, it was the result of the intercession of Sidi Mohammed Dgheis, who objected bravely to the Bashaw's sudden determination.

By nine o'clock the next morning the courtyard was again filled with soldiers under the command of the same officer who had reported the night before. The officers of the *Philadelphia* were ready, each with his belongings done up in a bag or basket, and it was with a great deal of sorrow that they bade farewell to their comfortable quarters. They were marched through the narrow, dirty streets, bound for what they knew not.

They were not taken on the most direct route, but marched and countermarched through the lower portion of the town, much to the delight of the crowds through which their guards had difficulty in forcing their way. At last their prison dawned in sight, a low whitewashed building made of heavy stones and mortar. The interior of the building was filthy; the building had been used by generations for smoking hides and for confining refractory or runaway slaves.

The officers were crowded into three rooms on the north side of the courtyard that had small grated windows opening on the well-guarded sea wall. On the opposite side of the open space were the large cells in which the crew of the *USS Philadelphia* was imprisoned. When the crew of the *Philadelphia* saw that their officers had come to join them, broke out into a cheer as the party marched through the yard.

The quarters that Bainbridge and the rest found unprepared for them possessed no accommodations fit to make life bearable. The heavy doors were shut upon them and they sat down upon the damp stone floor.

Hours went by. No one came to see them. Not a drop of water or a bit of food had passed their lips. About five o'clock in the afternoon they managed to communicate their distress to the crew confined across the way, and the loyal Jack tars bribed one of their own keepers to bring over a portion of their scant evening meal black bread and water with a small cruse of olive oil, which was the food of the lower order of Algerian slaves and laborers.

Before it was dusk there came a clanging at the door, bolts from the outside were dropped, and a strange-looking figure entered. It was a man clad in the loose-flowing garments of the Tripolitan sailor, with turban and turned up slippers, but his face had none of the darkness of skin; it was red and mottled, and the chin was overgrown with a thin beard of wiry red. His first words created more of a sensation than did his remarkable appearance.

"Weel, weel, and here's where ye are noo! Is Captain Bainbridge here?
"

"I am Captain Bainbridge," he said as he raised his hand; "and may I ask whom I have the honor of addressing?"

"Admiral Lisle, of the Tripolitan navy, is my name. Hoot, mon, but this is nae place for the confinement of officers and gentlemen!"

"We are not here by our own choice," answered Bainbridge, " and we are very willing to exchange it for anything better, for in fact we could not be treated to a worse fate than be left here where we are."

"It may be summat of your ain fault," the odd-looking admiral replied, winking his little Scotch eyes knowingly.

"May I ask you to explain yourself, sir?"

"Wha don't you accede to the wishes of the Bashaw?" Tis naught he demands but a little scribbling on a bit of paper that will do ye no harm to write for him. You're daft, mon, not to do it."

"You'll pardon me," interposed Bainbridge." I have not the least idea how great is your knowledge upon the subject of which you speak; but mark you this: the Bashaw can torture me; he can lop off my head; but there is one thing that he cannot do: he cannot force me to commit an act that is incompatible with the honor of an American officer. If this is the object of your visit to us, I can only say that you will obtain neither satisfaction nor promises. If it is an answer you demand, you have it."

The admiral appeared to be somewhat confused at the force with which Bainbridge had uttered the last words, and he mumbled something inarticulate as he backed out of the doorway. No sooner had he disappeared than Porter, Jones, and Hunt grasped Bainbridge's hand in turn. Without a word he understood that these men felt as he did; no explanation was necessary and none was offered.

Darkness came on. Just before midnight the door to their prison was again opened, and there stood the same guard that had escorted them thither in the morning.

"Follow us," said one of the officers. And forming a column of two's, the prisoners marched out into the night, taking their personal belongings with them.

This time they were not marched through the backstreets, and in less than a quarter of an hour they found themselves back once more at the house that had belonged to the American consul before the outbreak of hostilities.

A few days later Bainbridge, to his delight, found that his first missive had reached Commodore Preble when Mr. Nissen stopped by the house.

Bainbridge invited Neil inside while he by means of the sympathetic ink wrote another letter.

"Thank you for establishing this line of communication, it means a great deal to us. I am also going to give you this ink written letter. The letter contains nothing in it that cannot be read by anyone. The letter is a decoy so to satisfy the snooping Muslims."

The Danish consul was also sending the epistle to his confrere at Malta, and by this latter gentleman they were forwarded to the commander of the American squadron.

It had been found necessary to resort to this means, as the Bashaw subjected all communications to a rigid inspection and kept copies of all the correspondence.

A month went by; school was resumed, but the confinement was beginning to tell upon the spirits of the officers, although they were well fed and comfortably housed.

The crew of the *Philadelphia* who were confined in the same loathsome dungeon that they had been at first thrown into; daily living was challenge to stay alive. They were not used to the food, and sickness had spread among them. Bainbridge and his officers had not been permitted to hold intercourse with them, and knew nothing of their condition. The officers had only been informed that they were kept employed at their trades. The men that had no trade skills were placed to work on the fortifications of the town.

From an upper window of their prison house, which was near the water front, a glimpse of the harbor could be obtained; and occasionally Bainbridge or one of his lieutenants had been allowed to stroll along the ramparts under the watchful eye of two guards. Bainbridge had looked many times with deep sorrow at the *Philadelphia*, his fine old ship, as she lay there well protected by the guns of the castle, herself a great adjunct to the protection of the town, for her guns had been fished up and replaced on her decks.

He regretted more than once that he had not proceeded to extreme measures and, instead of scuttling her, set her on fire when he had seen that her defense was useless.

He returned from one of these walks that he had taken on the December 5th, elated with an idea that had entered his mind. It was one that would require immediate co-operation of Preble and the squadron, and demanded great intrepidity and daring for its successful accomplishment; but brave and adventurous spirits he knew were not lacking. He could have called the names of a half dozen young men now with the commodore to whom he would entrust the leadership.

He had noticed that all of the enemy's gunboats were hauled up on shore, and that, owing to the transfer of guns, the small crescent-shaped battery was almost in a dismantled condition. Dipping his pen into the invisible ink, he wrote the following letter, sending it to Preble through the usual channels.

Bainbridge wrote on December 5th.

"Charter a small merchant schooner, fill her with men, and have her commanded by fearless and determined officers. Let the vessel enter the harbor at night, with her men secreted below decks. Steer her directly on board the frigate, and then the officers and men board, sword in hand, and there is not a doubt of their success and without very heavy loss. It would be necessary to take several good rowboats in order to facilitate the retreat after the enterprise had been accomplished. The frigate in her present condition is a powerful auxiliary battery for the defense of the harbor. Though it will be impossible to remove her from her anchorage, and thus restore this beautiful vessel to our navy, yet, as she may, and no doubt will be repaired, an important end will be gained by her destruction."

Mr. Nielsen delivered the above message from Captain Bainbridge to his squadron commander, Commodore Preble. Preble after reading the communication sent one of his lieutenants in a small boat to the other vessels to advise them of a meeting on his ship on the following morning.

Preble convened their meeting with his officers in the squadron the following morning at ten a.m.

"Gentlemen, thank you for being here. I have a communication from Captain Bainbridge that was covertly brought to me." Preble read the message and the group discussed it. They were well aware they were not making any progress against the much superior forces of the Dey.

The officers all agreed with the concept.

"I would like to suggest that Lieutenant Stephen Decatur be placed in charge of the planning and execution of a plan to destroy the *Philadelphia*."

The council of officers all agreed to the plan and to the appointment of Decatur to head it up since Decatur was a personal friend of Bainbridge's.

Commodore Preble replied to Captain Bainbridge's suggestion as to the destruction of the *Philadelphia*.

Dear Captain Bainbridge:

Your idea has been reviewed and discussed. Your friend, SD, has volunteered to head up the project you have suggested. I will keep you informed.

P

"Gentlemen," Bainbridge was addressing anyone in the room, "Commodore Preble has reviewed the suggestion to burn the *Philadelphia* with the other officers in the Squadron and they have agreed to proceed. Lieutenant Stephen Decatur is to head up scheme and to proceed immediately with making plans."

"Hurrah!" a few of the men cheered.

"That is good news and we have a front row seat when the event happens," Porter commented.

The euphoria of anticipation that the *Philadelphia* would be destroyed, soon worn off as the weeks passed by and nothing transpired as to the implementation of the plan. The New Year came and all the information they had received was that several schemes had been suggested but nothing that seem practical had yet been settled on. The men were becoming weary of keeping watch on the harbour waiting for some sign of action from the squadron.

Bainbridge had even suggested in another letter to Commodore Preble that landing four or five thousand troops would result in the capturing the town.

Commodore Preble wrote back that he agreed with Bainbridge that the landing of or five thousand troops would certainly result in the taking of town. The problem was he did not have five thousand men in his command.

Bainbridge was most concerned for the survival of his men especially the crew that was being mistreated. He urged Preble's to act in whatever manner he could. He informed Preble that he had petitioned the offices of Mohammed Dgheis to allow him to do something for his men. The men, he had been told, are in unbearable conditions and not expected to survive if something isn't done. He requested that the crew be given more clothes and sustaining food that was eatable.

Bainbridge was not aware that his first child had been born, Susan Parker Bainbridge. If Susan had written any letters to William they were never received. Bainbridge suspected the Bashaw would confiscate the letters and destroy them.

Bainbridge would live to see his new born daughter marry Thomas Hayes on March 24, 1825. Thomas Hayes was the son of Patrick Hayes the nephew of Commodore John Barry. John Barry and his wife Sally (Sarah Austin) had raised Patrick from the age of two when John's sister Eleanor passed away in 1780. John Barry never saw baby Susan; John Barry died September 12, 1803.

THIRTY

USS Philadelphia burned
February 16, 1804

Preble finally wrote to Bainbridge in February that preparations were being made to carry out the plans as he suggested to burn the *Philadelphia*. He advised Bainbridge that his friend, Lieutenant Stephen Decatur, had volunteered to command the expedition and he had formulated a doable scheme. Mr. Nissen on his next visit to the flagship was given the message to take to Bainbridge.

Bainbridge was hopeful that his plan would be carried out soon. Nothing happened and the winter passed into spring and then they entered into another year without anything happening. Bainbridge was advised about a number of schemes suggested for the destruction of Tripoli. The prisoners were losing hope of gaining their freedom.

Bainbridge was very discouraged; he was helpless being in captivity. He was missing his wife and family, he had not heard from them. Susan had written many letters to William but he received none of them.

To make matter worst for Bainbridge was the information he was receiving about the squalor conditions his crew was enduring and the abuse to their personal selves.

Bainbridge was able to send a message to Bashaw through Mr. Nissen.

He was requesting that Bashaw intervene to do something to make the existence of his crew more bearable. Bainbridge made the same request he did to Mohammed Dgheis requesting the men be given clothing, and more sustaining food that could be provided by the men on the squadron ships.

Bashaw reacted positively to Bainbridge plea and through the kind offices of Sidi Mohammed Dgheis clothing and food was allowed to be passed from the squadron to the prison.

Mr. Nissen continued to come and see Bainbridge on a regular basis. The two men had formed a friendship that assisted Bainbridge with enduring the terrible situation he was in. Neil was able to roam freely and his frequent trips to the squadron ships also provided news that Bainbridge was interested in.

The Mohammedans are a peculiarly religious people or at least they pretended to be religious or risk fearing for their lives.

Every year for thirty days the Muslim world celebrates Ramadan. Actually Ramadan is the ninth month of the Muslim calendar. The Feast of Ramadan is a time of worship and community.

Ramadan is a period of religious abstinence, during which the good Mohammedan imposes upon himself moral and physical restraint to an extreme degree. He is compelled by his creed to harbor only kindly thoughts and deeds, such as hospitality to strangers and charity to the bitterest enemies.

During Ramadan the fighting was stopped with the American squadron. The men on the ship were always perplexed as to how you interrupt a war and then resume it after the month long holiday.

The tradition of Ramadan dictated that little or no food is partaken of between sunrise and sunset. After sunset it was time for feasting and the evening meal could be a lengthily affair with volumes of food.

At the end of Ramadan after a month of daily fasting and nightly feasting the Biarian festival takes place. The Biarian festival can be from three to six days long and amounts to a period of gorging and rejoicing.

Neil had explained to Bainbridge that the Muslim calendar was based on the moon. He explained that each month in the Muslim calendar begins when the crescent moon is sighted in the night sky. This method makes each month approximately 28 days long.

"This year William, Ramadan will start around November 27th," Neil informed William.

From the lowest household in its mud-wall hut to the Bashaw in his palace all Muslims were instructed to pray and then enjoy themselves. It is also a day of forgetting old grudges and ill feelings towards other fellow men.

On this occasion Bainbridge and Lieutenant Porter were invited to the Bashaw's residence, where they were treated as guests of honor and received with Eastern civilities. The Bashaw made sure his guests were allowed to bath and have clean uniforms supplied by the squadron to wear for the event.

They also attended a feast of the Prime Minister, who was a Russian by birth, although he had lived for a long time in Tripoli. The largest ceremony they attended, however, and one that exceeded in point of splendor all the others, was a banquet, at the residence of their good friend, Sidi Mohammed Dgheis, Minister of State.

Through his intercession also, permission had been obtained for the officers under a small guard, and on their parole of honor, to ride a few miles back into the country. It was a great relief to them to secure these outings, but it made their confinement perhaps the harder to bear.

The officers of the *Philadelphia* were more than aware of the despicable treatment of the enlisted men. They were thankful for having the comforts they were currently enjoying knowing things could change on a moment's notice.

Lieutenant Hunt and Porter enjoyed being allowed to ride two small mules beyond the walls of the city. They were always accompanied by two armed janizaries that looked mean enough to kill them on the spot just for sport.

It was a fine warm morning, and a breeze that blew from the north rustled the branches of the trees. It was a beautiful sight. On all sides were the barley and wheat fields, with their waving grain; the groves of dates, of olive and of fig trees; the orchards of lemon, orange, apricot, and peach; the well-kept gardens that surrounded the country houses of the wealthy. They could scarcely imagine themselves prisoners, although they knew at any time they might exchange all this for close confinement and blank dungeon walls.

They were riding on a road way, further than they anticipated. They had before them the blue waters of the Mediterranean. The water could not be more than a half mile away. They stopped and observed the beautiful site of the blue waters framed by the green arching trees over the road way.

"It is almost enough to incline one to turn Turk and settle down here forever," said Lieutenant Hunt with a sigh.

"Well, it appears that we shall most probably stay here for some time to come," answered Porter. "Not a movement yet from our fleet, and Preble is not a man to hesitate or to put off action. In my opinion something will be done soon that will relieve us from our position of uncertainty at least."

"Well, I'd like to know where he is and what he's doing," Hunt remarked, loosening his long legs from the stirrups. "This is all very fine, but I'd just like to know. You see, by Jove!" he exclaimed, suddenly interrupting himself, "look down there, man, straight ahead."

Porter followed his glance. In the little space enclosed by the green frame was a fine, large ship, with all sails spread, sailing to the westward. She was less than two miles from shore.

"The *Constitution*!" exclaimed Porter. "I know her by her lofty rig."

"Aye, and here comes another," interposed Hunt.

"The *Nautilus*, I take it."

Yes, there they were, three or four now, seen all at once, and on they came until they had passed by.

Hunt and Porter were back at their prison by evening.

"What a day, they said. We saw a sight that made us feel much better. We saw the *Constitution* and the *Nautilus* along with two other ships a short distance from here. Finally something is going to happen!" Lieutenant Porter had a smile on his face.

The following morning Nissen came to visit Bainbridge.

"William I have good news, more American ships have arrived. Commodore Preble was very tight mouthed about was his plan is though."

"How is the Bashaw reacting to this new influx of war-ships?" Bainbridge was curious since it might affect their treatment toward them.

"William you know that Tripoli is defended by twenty-five thousand soldiers, 115 cannons on shore and 25 war-ships in the harbor. What will seven ships and just over a thousand men do up against that?"

As predicted nothing transpired from the American's, or at least nothing that Bainbridge was aware of.

A plan was being hatched by Decatur. Decatur was in a harbor at Syracuse (southeastern Sicily) preparing his men and vessels to go to Tripoli.

Decatur was commanding the ketch *Intrepid*, with 4-guns and a crew of sixty men. The brig, *Siren* 12-guns, was going to accompanying *Intrepid* to Tripoli.

The two vessels set sail early on February 2nd. The weather was stormy and the seas very rough. During the two weeks it took them to reach their destination, outside the Tripoli's harbor they continued to be buffeted by severe storms. They arrived on February 16th.

The beating the officers and crew took on the two vessels was damaging to their bodies. To make matters almost a total disaster the Purser discovered their supply of salted meat was rotten. The smell was gagging and off loading the rotten meat was difficult in the rough seas. Many of the men spent time leaning over the rail to 'pump ship.'

The crew was forced to exist on biscuits and water. Their strength had left them, they were sick and disillusioned.

Decatur felt the men needed a few days of good food and rest once they reached the squadron and dropped anchor. He sent one of his officer's to requisite food supplies for the crew to eat.

Stephen Decatur reported to Commodore Preble's that he was ready to proceed with his plan to destroy the *Philadelphia*.

"When do you think we should initiate our plan," Decatur was looking straight at Preble.

"Two nights from now there will be no moon and by the looks of the weather it will also be cloudy. I also want to have the men in the squadron at their battle stations just in case things get out of hand."

The few days of rest and good food revived the men on the *Intrepid*. Decatur sent his first officer to confirm with Commodore Preble that they were going into action at one a.m.

The *Intrepid* left their anchorage at one a.m. The night was a wall of black. The *Siren* was hanging back to wait for the *Intrepid* return. The *Intrepid* was drifting slowly into the harbor using the lights on the enemy ships for guides. Their destination was the dark hull of the *Philadelphia*. The *Philadelphia* was anchored directly beneath Tripoli's gun batteries high on the hill side.

Decatur had hired a pilot to take them into the harbor. This was a customary procedure of any vessel entering the Tripolitan Harbour. The pilot was a Sicilian by the name of Salvatore Catalano and he was dressed for the part he was playing.

Decatur was at the bow scouring every inch of the way. The element of surprise was their only weapon. The crew was doing their best to hide from the eyes of anyone looking down on the water. The men were laying flat on the deck hidden from view by the bulwarks.

Decatur had Mediterranean seamen costumes made for eleven men before coming to Tripoli. These men now dressed in their new garments were standing in full view acting like typical Mediterranean seamen.

As they neared the *Philadelphia*, Decatur's pilot, Salvatore Catalano, called out that they were a ship from Malta who had lost their anchor in the recent storm, and asked if they could please tie up to the *Philadelphia* for the night. Amazingly, the crew on the *Philadelphia* fell for this ruse and tossed over a hawser. As the ships touched, Decatur gave the signal, and the hidden sailors leaped up and boarded the *Philadelphia*. As one midshipman wrote about the fray, *"The Tripolitans on board of her were dreadfully alarmed when they found out who we were. Poor fellows! About twenty of them were cut to pieces and the rest jumped overboard."* Decatur's men had rehearsed and rehearsed how they would dispatch of the *Philadelphia*. The crew would go to assigned locations on the ship distributing and lighting combustibles in strategic places.

Decatur wrote in his report, *"I immediately fired her in her Store Rooms, Gun Room Cockpit and Birth [Berth] Decks, and remained on board until the flames had issued from the Hatchways and Ports."*

In only fifteen minutes, Decatur and his men had successfully turned the *Philadelphia* from a graceful frigate into a mass of flames. Now, escape remained their biggest concern. Not only were the men of the *Intrepid* under fire from sailors aboard nearby Tripolitan vessels, but the flames from the *Philadelphia* were an inferno, which created a huge vacuum that tried to suck in the *Intrepid*.

The battery cannon were coming into action. One cannon ball struck the topgallant sail and nearly destroyed it. Decatur ordered two small boats with sweeps (oars) lowered from the *Philadelphia*.

Each of the boats had seven oars on each side, fourteen rowers. The men on the oars were pulling with all of their might. Their adrenalin was running high and spurred on by the arterial fire directed at them they were quickly headed out of the harbor. To make the rowing task more difficult they were towing the unsailable *Intrepid* in route to rendezvous with the *Siren*.

The timing for burning of the *Philadelphia* turned out to have been excellent. The Bashaw had been retrofitting the *Philadelphia* for battle. The ship was so near ready to leave the harbor that it had its gun room full of powder and the cannons had been loaded. The disadvantage of having the cannon's loaded was the fire ignited the pre-loaded charges and a broadside was fired directly into the town. The damage to the town was more than any damage previously inflicted on the town by the cannons of the squadron.

Bainbridge was awakening about two a.m. to the sound of heavy cannon fire. There was no doubt about it the loud booms were reverberating in their prison confinement. He could hear the distant rattle of musketry. Then there was a loud roar all coming from the direction of the harbour.

From the little window upstairs in the room where the midshipmen slept they could get a glimpse of the waters. Occasionally they would see the *Philadelphia* as it swung on its anchor. Seeing the *Philadelphia* was a tantalizing sight to the eyes of the prisoners. The burning of the *Philadelphia* was a spectacular display of fireworks.

Bainbridge had hardly reached the door when he heard a shrill, boyish cheer from the "steerage," as the middy's called their dormitory.

" The *Philadelphia* is on fire! The *Philadelphia* is on fire!" cried young Reefer Biddle, who, in scanty attire, was leaning over the stairway.

It was in the early morning hours of February 16, 1804 when the *Philadelphia* was burned. The frigate had a short life but served an important purpose.

The midshipmen cleared the way so the officers could look out the window at the burning inferno. The ship burned for 36 hours according to witnesses who watch the affair the following day.

Bainbridge was observing with great satisfaction as the fire consumed the great ship. The fire was so intense they could feel the heat of it in their prison. The fire grew and grew until Bainbridge was able to make out the outline of the vessel and see the flames pouring from her ports.

The *Philadelphia* was swinging at her cables, and gradually she worked around until the hull was hidden by the neighboring houses. There was an eerie red and orange glow in the sky. The color was exacerbated by the clouds that would reflect various hues of red and made contortions of the glare.

Suddenly there came the roar of a tremendous explosion. Bright flying sparks like rockets were hurled into the air, and when they had fallen the glare had disappeared.

"The end!" said Bainbridge calmly, turning to the officers." Who do you suppose did that? "

Bainbridge knew himself, of course, but he wished to see what they would say.

"Stephen Decatur!" exclaimed a small midshipman involuntarily, clapping his fist to his mouth after he had spoken, as a bashful schoolgirl might.

"Perhaps it was Somers," ventured one of the lieutenants.

"Mr. Gamble was right," remarked Bainbridge; "it was Stephen Decatur, unless I am much mistaken, and God help and save him and all the brave men who assisted him."

"Amen!" said the rest in chorus.

Stephen Decatur and his men had been 100% successful. They had all come back alive. One of the crew had been struck in the butt by a musket ball but it did not do any damage to the bone. Three other men had minor injuries, mostly cuts.

Decatur reported to Commodore Preble the following morning.

"I have to commend you and your men for your bravery and success in successfully completing your mission," Preble was relieved the mission had gone well and that the safety of the men was preserved."

"I could not have accomplished the mission without the help and leadership of Lieutenants James Lawrence, Joseph Bainbridge, Midshipman Charles Morris, and seventy fine seamen."

"I will make sure that Captain Bainbridge is advised of the success. I am sure he will want to know of the safety of the men especially his brother Joseph."

"You know this was Captain Bainbridge's plan down to the last detail.

"I must say Stephen that at first I had a hard time imagining sailing a large ketch up long side of the *Philadelphia*, boarding her, cutlass in hand, dispatch the enemy on the ship, set fire to it and escape while the battery of cannons were shooting at you. Doing all that and not losing a man."

Nissen was at the door of Bainbridge's prison. He was able to identify the elation on the officer's faces as he entered into their prison.

"Neil, you look like you have seen a ghost!" Bainbridge greeted him.

"Perhaps I have. I have received bad news that has me worried about you and your men."

"The Bashaw's in a frightful rage," Neil went on," and he is determined to inflict his vengeance somewhere over the burning of the *Philadelphia*. I fear that he will vent it upon all of you. He would not have lost that ship for anything in the kingdom. I trust my dear friends that you will not suffer if I can prevent it. I am going to see Sidi Mohammed Dgheis to-day and find out how affairs now stand," Nissen assured them.

The next two weeks the presents of fruit, and fresh eatables ceased. The Bashaw was sending a message of displeasure but nothing else occurred.

It was March 1, 1804, some two weeks after the destruction of the *Philadelphia* that the wrath of Bashaw was felt.

A knock came at the front door of their prison. Bashaw goons came swarming into the prison.

"What is the meaning of this intrusion?" demanded Bainbridge.

"Shut your mouth and listen," the goon in charge bellowed out. "All of you scum are going to be moved to another prison. You have five minutes to gather you personal things and be out in front of the house ready to go."

The men scurried to gather their meager belonging together. The Americans were herded through the crowded streets of the town. The people jeered at them, spit on them and some threw things at them.

The Bashaw had found a new prison for them that were to his liking. He wanted to make sure that they would now be incarcerated in a place that was cold and damp. He wanted them in a prison without windows to look out of and strong iron bars on all openings to contain them. There was a small window well way above the height of a man's head but that was it.

They were even denied the privilege that the crew of the *Philadelphia* were given that of exercise in the open air.

The first night at the prison was a nightmare. They had only the things that they could carry. They had no bedding, no food, or water.

"Gentlemen, we are being treated badly because of the burning of the *Philadelphia*. We are going to have to make the best of it until we receive some help or figure out how to escape. Since we all need to keep active to keep alive, I suggest we all concentrate on plans for escaping.

Nissen, being the good friend that he had become, was incensed that his friends were being treated like the slaves the Muslims transported out of Africa.

It took Nissen a week of going to see the Bashaw before he was granted permission to visit Bainbridge.

"William, my god, what have they done. This is not a fit place for pigs let alone anything human."

"Apparently the Bashaw was strongly affected by the burning of his pet project the *Philadelphia*," Bainbridge exclaimed.

"I need to get word to Commodore Preble, can you deliver a letter for me."

"I figured you might want to do some correspondence so I brought you paper and pen and ink."

Bainbridge had to clean off a space on the floor for the paper so as to write his letters. Nissen spent his time waiting by talking with the other officers about conditions of the squadron and the politics of the Muslims.

"I perhaps failed to mention to you gentlemen that I was also a prisoner in Algiers. Here is something I wrote in 1790 in my journal that I have always carried with me," Nissen reached into his pocket for his wallet.

February 19, 1790:

"Picture to yourself your Brother Citizens or Unfortunate Countrymen in the Algerian State Prisons or Damned Castile, and starved 2/3rd's and Naked...The Chains of their Legs, and under the Lash...Beat in such a Manner as to Shock Humanity...No Prospects of ever being Redeemed or Restored to their Native Land & Never to See their Wives & Families...Viewing and Considering of their approaching Exit, where 6 of their Dear Country-man is buried with thousands of other Christian Slaves of all nations...Once a Citizen of the United States of America, but at present the Most Miserable Slave in Algiers."

"Things have not changed much have they? Thank you for sharing that with us," Lieutenant Porter remarked.

"My pleasure, that how I know what you men are suffering, I've been there in your shoes. That is why I decided when I was released that I would come back here somehow to help others."

"Thank you for all you have done, we appreciate your help and we are thankful beyond your wildest dreams."

"I have to go men; I think the Captain has a letter ready for me."

Nissen smuggled out a letter destined for the squadron then cruising off the mouth of the harbor, for the blockade of the port was now rigidly enforced.

All regular communication between the prisoners and the outside world was interdicted by the Bashaw's orders. The prisoners were search on a regular basis. This was more for intimidation then actual hope they would find something.

Bainbridge was able to have a letter delivered to Commodore Preble referencing a scheme for escape.

"*We are attempting to excavate an escape tunnel under the castle, and sea wall. Our desire is that we and exit into the water and be picked up by five fast rowing boats. I will update this effort as we proceed with the excavation."*

WB

The prisoners began digging through the wall. All of the prisoner's tools were crude and the disposal of the dirt was slow, one cup at a time to be scattered in the yard.

The officers soon had discovered a problem that caused them to stop. As they dug down they came to the realization that they were going to encounter water.

Bainbridge gathered the men to discuss the discouraging situation. "Gentlemen, we are going to have to abandon the tunnel idea. We need to pursue other methods of escape."

Commodore Preble had been aware from the infancy of a tunnel plan proposed by Bainbridge that it would be impossible for it to success. The Dey had sentinels placed along the sea wall and the shore for several miles on either side of the city. Preble knew that it would be impossible to send boats into the harbor with our being observed and being destroyed from gun fire.

One dreary night, as Bainbridge, Lieutenants Porter, Hunt and Smith lay talking together in low whispers; Lieutenant Jones crawled over to them.

"I've been thinking, gentlemen," he observed, making his way into the center of the group, "that it might be possible to explore the adjoining apartment here on our port hand. We may find a window unbarred, or some way by which we can reach the sea wall, and lower ourselves to the ramparts."

"It will do no harm at least to try," said Bainbridge, knowing that it would give employment if nothing else, and keep their minds from dwelling upon their unfortunate situation. The following morning the prisoners were broken up into watches so work could commence. The men with renewed enthusiasm began the systematic work of removing the window bars.

With the aid of some hoop iron and one knife, the mortar was removed from several large stones in the side of the room. Their work had to be disguised quickly if the watch group saw the enemy approaching. There prison was subject to inspection with no regularity and the times of the inspections were random and unannounced. Every day the blocks were replaced in the wall. I was difficult to make the replaced blocks look natural. The men had devised a method of turning the stone dust into a paste that was used to conceal the grout lines of the block.

Once the men had removed the face stones they discovered the space behind the stones was filled with earth that had been loosely mixed with mortar. All this earth had to be removed and disposed of. Once they had completed this task the opposing blocks were removed. They had achieved an entrance to the adjacent apartment. The pushing the blocks into the adjoining apartment had risk associated with it. They had no idea if anyone was in or around that space. To hedge their bets they broke through at night when they anticipated the number of guards to be few, if any at all.

The hole in the wall was large enough for a man to crawl through to the other side. Bainbridge selected two of his lieutenants, Porter and Jones to join him in crawling through. It was a tight fit for the heavy muscled Bainbridge but he was able to wiggle his way in, feet first and drop to the floor.

The three men stood in the large open space. They were in the extreme wing of the prison. The roof had fallen in piling mounds of debits on the floor. The walls were devoid of window at the lower levels assessable to the prisoners. Way above their heads was a small window.

"Come on Jones," said Lieutenant Porter, climb up on my shoulders and see what you can out of that window."

Lieutenant Joncs like an acrobat showed his agility and positioned himself on Porter's shoulders.

Jones was looking out the window. "We are in luck; the bars on the window are loose. I believe I can even dislodge them with my bare hands."

Lieutenant Porter was glad the bars were loose but he also was not enjoying the raining down on this head the dust and particles Jones was showering down on him. Porter's hands were holding on to the legs of Jones so he was unable to brush away any particles in his face and eyes.

The window looked down upon the top of the rampart at an angle where a few heavy guns pointed out over the harbor, but it was a drop of forty feet to the water's edge, and fully fifteen from the window to the ground outside.

As nothing could be done that night, they again returned to their companions and blocked up the passageway, before retiring.

Early the following morning Bainbridge assembled the men. "We have a new challenge in front of us," Bainbridge was recharged with a new energy in his voice.

"We need to formulate a new means of lowering ourselves to the ramparts and then continue to the water's edge."

"We need ropes," Lieutenant Porter spoke up.

"You are correct Lieutenant, any suggestions?" Bainbridge was anxious to have the men participate in a plan for escape.

One of the men suggested that they could make ropes from the blankets they were given. They even decided that next time Nissen came to see them they would ask him to request additional blankets.

"What do we do it we are lucky enough to get to the water alive?" one of the officers inquired.

"I am afraid that is where only the strongest of swimmers among us could swim to boats anchored about a quarter of a mile from shore."

Bainbridge was not a good swimmer so he elected to stay behind. Bainbridge wanted to have those attempting the feat to success and make it to the squadron. He realized that the few of them remaining behind would share the wrath of their captors.

Nissen was successful in the acquisition more blankets. They were able to sharpen splinters of stone to be used as a cutting tool. The making of ropes from the blankets was a slow process but that was no deterrent to the men who had nothing else to do.

The ropes were woven and proved to have an amazing amount of durability.

The select group to attempt the escape entered the adjacent room on a moonless night. They were dressed in only their shirts and trousers to give them the best chance of shimming down the ropes.

The man who volunteered to use his shoulders to allow the other to gain access to the window obviously was not going make the dangerous descent.

Bainbridge had instructed the men to replace the stones just in case things did not go well. "Well gentlemen, we sit and wait."

In less than an hour a scratching was heard upon the opposite wall; the stones were again withdrawn, and the men filed back again.

Lieutenant Jones was out of breath as he crawled back into their prison. "Mary, Jesus, and Joseph, we made it to the rampart and we were about to lower ourselves to the water. We made our line fast to one of the guns when a guard was spotted approaching us."

"We felt it best that we abort the plan and regroup," Lieutenant Porter said.

The next morning Bainbridge was doing an observation of the water and saw that the boat they were counting for usage had changed her anchorage. If the men had attempted to swim in the dark towards the fathom boat they would have perhaps had drowned or have been shot by the sentries.

The failure of the escape was disappointing but the attempts did occupy their time and made the time pass rapidly.

Bainbridge felt all the escape ideas the men had were worth exploring.

One escape attempt was made involving the undermining of the rampart allowing them to enter a large vault. The excavation into the vault had weakened the supports. The cannon above them were a forty-two pounder weighting 8,672 pounds. The weakening of the supports caused the cannon to fall through to the ground below.

The dust and mold that was released made the air in their prison almost un-breathable. They had terrible ventilation; very little fresh air reached them.

The prisoners were suffering from the foul and stagnant air. Their lungs hurt, and their strength was deteriorating. Bainbridge and sent many letters out with Nissen requesting the ventilation be improved. Bainbridge expressed his concerned for the health of his men. He was suffering, his breathing was shallow and his chest hurt.

The men were not receiving any satisfaction so the men took matters into their own hands. They decided to make a large hole in the outside wall eighteen inches above the floor.

The men were not concerned with their jailer confronting them. They removed the face stones and stacked them inside their prison. They then dislodged an exterior stone so then could get rid of dirt by dumping through the opening.

The fresh air flowed into the prison and the prisoner breathed a sigh of relief.

Surprisingly enough, the large hole in the wall was not notice for a week. When the not too attentive jailer, a bad tempered black man from the desert named Sossey, discovered the hole he was beside himself. He was angry that his charges had made a hole in the wall without his being aware of it and also that it would not go well for him for not being more observant.

"Someone will pay for this, there is going to be terrible punishment maybe even death," Sossey was raging with threats and cursing. "Who dared to do this act?"

Porter stepped forward and informed the jailer that he was the guilty one. Immediately he was hurried away from his companions and placed in solitary confinement in a horrible dungeon not more than eight feet square. On the second day Porter was brought before Sidi Mohammed Dgheis, who expressed his sorrow that he could do nothing to help the prisoners, as the Bashaw was implacable. But, nevertheless, Porter was returned to his companions and Sossey was removed from his position.

On July 12th and the sun was rising when the men were awaken by the roar of cannon fire coming from the mouth of the harbor.

"Preble is at it again. Hurrah!" exclaimed Porter with a laugh. "Oh, I wish we were there with him!"

"Come, let us go into the next room through our passageway," suggested Jones. "We can watch what's going on."

No sooner had he spoken than a heavy explosion sounded quite near to them.

"Hurrah!" cried Bainbridge. "Gentlemen that were a good Yankee shell."

Another one burst in the direction of the Bashaw's palace.

"I'll bet their high-cockalorum bowed his old head to that," said a middy.

The stones were removed in a matter of minutes and the men scrambled into the next apartment. The men were taking turns at the opening to see what was transpiring.

"Just look at those three boats bear down on that division of the enemy, nine of them, by George! I'll wager that we'll see some tall fighting now," cried Jones.

It was so far off that the boats looked to be mere dots. But the white smoke soon blotted out even the details, and the firing became steady. When the breeze had cleared the air a little it was seen that three of the Tripolitan gunboats had been taken and the others were in flight, making their way with splashing sweeps up the harbor. One of the big gunboats was some lengths behind the rest.

"Look there! Look there!" cried Jones, pointing.

"See that small boat chasing the whole lot of them."

"It's one of their own," suggested Smith.

"You're mistaken, sir," said Bainbridge quietly, for his eyes were like those of a hawk. "That's one of the ship's cutters, and they're some of our lads putting their backs into that steady stroke."

"They're after that last galley, then," roared Porter, "and they are going to catch her, too! I'll bet Decatur is in that cutter!"

Just as he spoke the men at the oars tossed them inboard. The men then with great athletic strength leaped for the side of the Tripolitan vessel and boarded it. The other five enemy sail boats continued on their way and did not stop to help their companion. Soon the captured enemy vessel was observed to come about into the wind and, with the cutter in tow, make for the safety of the American line. The cutter was successful in capturing Tripolitan vessel in a matter of minutes!

One of the Squadron gunboats had grounded near the crescent-shaped battery, where she was subjected to a terrible fire from the battery of shore canons. The gunboat managed to free itself while continuing to fire at the enemy with her one big gun.

"Hurrah for the man who commands that little skipjack!" shouted Lieutenant Hunt.

"Cleverly done indeed!" Bainbridge exclaimed, rubbing his hands together with delight. "Did you mark, gentlemen, how he crept out of range of that big gun on the point without receiving his fire? He is brave and clever."

The Bainbridge did not know that it was his own brother, Lieutenant Joseph Bainbridge, whom he was eulogizing. He certainly would have proud of his brother and he was when he later learned that it was him.

Nissen, sometime later, told the officers that the little Tripolitan boat that had been captured by the Americans was commanded by Stephen Decatur. Decatur had captured the Tripolitan vessels and taken the corsairs prisoner. The Tripolitan vessel apparently had attacked the *Siren* to gain revenge for the fire she was inflicting on the hill side batteries. The Tripolitans were showing no fear of the Americans either by large egos or stupidity.

Decatur was watching another enemy vessel make an additional attempt on the destruction of the *Siren*. The *Siren* was so busy directing fire on the hillside batteries she did not consider them a threat. Decatur sailed towards the Tripolitan vessel and he was about to annihilate the vessel when the corsairs captain struck its flag.

"Look over there," Bainbridge pointed his finger. The Nautilus was engaged in a fight with five Muslim enemies at close range. They were using muskets and pistols in the attempt to take the Nautilus. Somers was in command of the Nautilus that was defending the ship against the five enemy vessels. The men were well trained in rapid cannon fire and the Muslims were getting the worst of the fire fight. Somers was a natural born strategist and a fire fight was right up his alley.

Bainbridge commented, "That must be Somers, he does not know defeat."

The men were cheering as the anxiously watched from their prison confines. The men than all cheered again when they witnessed the retreat of the five corsairs vessels.

Three Squadron boats pursued the enemy into the Harbor in hopes of capturing one more vessel. The Tripolitan suddenly rallied in force. From where the prisoners were it appeared that the few American vessels were in great jeopardy, for they were almost surrounded. Then they saw the coming into the mouth of the harbor the great frigate *Constitution* to the rescue!

The *Constitution* came well into the harbor and she was well in range of the guns of the Tripolitan hillside batteries. The *Constitution* was rapidly blazing away with her broadside cannons that were spurting flame and smoke. The effect on the Bashaw's hillside guns was to quite them, the Tripolitan gunner were not accustom to having their fire returned. The small American squadron made their retreat as the *Constitutions* powerful guns made the enemy take cover under the hillside.

The *Constitution* came about within three cable lengths of the flanking fortress, and as she pointed her nose once more toward the entrance of the harbor. She silenced the hillside guns with the discharge of her port battery, while with the starboard guns she sent shot and shells flying over the walls of the city causing much damage to the houses and the palace gardens.

The Bashaw had promised the people of the city rare sport if the American fleet should ever venture within the harbor. The *Constitution* was making a significant showing, inflicting damage way beyond the promises the Bashaw to his people.

Prisoner's continued to watch even though they were in danger of being struck by one of the *Constitution* balls. The *Constitution* did fire and the prison was hit causing damage to the roof.

Mr. Nissen was the only one of the foreign consuls who had stayed in town after the beginning of the bombardment. Nissen had become so devoted to the interests of his American friends that he remained at the risk of his life in order to be near them should his services be required.

Several shells fell in and about Nissen's house, but fortunately none of them had exploded.

The prisoners had hoped that the bombing would lead to their release. The withdrawal of the squadron the hopes of the prisoners diminished and their spirits were noticeably lower.

The prisoners were at least encouraged by the new American determination to bring the fight into the harbour.

The summery of the events was recorded by Commodore Preble and a copy sent to Bainbridge. *"The three captured boats contained one hundred and three men, of whom forty-seven were killed and twenty-six wounded. Three of the enemy's vessels were sunk with all their crews, and a number of guns in the batteries along the shore had been dismounted."*

On the fifth day of August Nissen brought the news that Preble had returned all the wounded Tripolitan prisoners. Nissen also reported that he overheard one of the captured officers say to the Prime Minister that the Americans in battle were fiercer than lions, yet in their treatment of prisoners they were even kinder than Mussulman. The result of this humane treatment on the part of Commodore Preble was that the Bashaw, in thanking him, stated that if any injured Americans fell into his hands he would treat them with equal kindness.

Commodore Preble entered into negotiations in regard to the establishment of peace were now begun, but they were soon discontinued owing to the extravagant demands of the Bashaw, who was yet very proud and haughty.

A second attack upon the city followed two weeks later by the Americans. There was much injury that was done by round shot and shells. Most devastating result of the skirmish was a small American vessel was blown up by a red hot shot, losing ten of her crew killed and six wounded.

On August 27th a third attack was begun by the Americans. Bainbridge had been unwell for some three days and was lying on his pallet of straw suffering. When the American bombardment commenced the balance of the officers went to their vantage point in the adjoining apartment. The *Constitution* had opened fire at long range, and it was by one of her shots that Bainbridge nearly lost his life.

A thirty-two pound cannon ball struck squarely on the outside of the wall, almost above Bainbridge's head. The masonry gave way under the impact, and the captain was literally covered with almost a ton of stone and mortar. His officers, who were at the end of the narrow cell, hastened to him and they were able to extricated him. William's ankle had been badly crushed, but not broken, by the falling of a part of the embattlement, and he was covered with cuts and bruises.

Commodore Preble had ordered the cannon's on the American ships to be fired as rapidly as possible. This means they had to make sure the cannons were cooled off properly so as to not have an accidental cannon discharge.

The affect of the fire from the American squadron forced the Tripolitan guards to flee from their places on the terrace ramparts and hid behind the walls of the prison.

Their cowardice excited the merriment of the Yankee midshipmen, and they were jeered unmercifully. Angry at this, the poltroons threw stones in at the prisoners through the windows that opened upon the yard. The midshipmen armed themselves with bits of the debris scattered about their apartment and returned the fire, a most riotous proceeding in the eyes of the head jailer, for he threatened to shoot down the offenders if they did not desist. This stopped the miniature battle; but Bainbridge wrote a note to Sidi Mohammed Dgheis, complaining that the guards had been the first offenders and he had the satisfaction of being informed that the villain who began all the trouble had been severely reprimanded and dismissed.

A few days later news was brought that the squadron was again entering the harbor, and soon the guns of the forts encircling the shore had begun to roar defiance. The Americans were delivering one broadside after another. The enemy guns were not wishing to be aggressive as in the past. The American squadron entered the harbor with continual gun fire. The Tripolitan admiral was congregating all of his fleet close under the walls. The Yankee squadron separated as it entered into the harbor. One half of the ships sailed boldly in upon the mass of Tripolitan shipping, while the rest bravely engaged the forts. Two bomb ketches kept on until quite close to shore and began throwing shells into the town with great effect. But from their exposed position it was seen that they had no chance to survive the furious fire directed at them. They both seemed doomed, when all at once Preble, in the *Constitution*, came down as he had done before to help them out. So close was he to the terraces that the figures of the men upon the spar deck could be distinguished. Seventy guns were playing down upon him, but so rapidly and effectually did the Squadron serve their broadsides that the Tripolitan slackened their fire, and under cover of the frigate the bomb ketches retreated safely.

The efforts and aggressiveness of the Americans had caused the Bashaw some severe damage. He had lost two more of his fleet, and suffered a great deal of damage by the shells that fell in the heart of the city. But, although the Americans had been subjected to a cross fire, not a man from the squadron was killed in the whole affair. The physical damage to the squadron consisted mainly of wrecked spars and injured rigging.

Under the orders of the Scotch-Turkish admiral it was concluded not to use the galleys except as an assistant force to the land batteries. They remained moored stem and stern in a compact mass at the upper bend. Nothing could tempt them from their safe retreat.

No other demonstration was made by the squadron during the following week, and despair and gloom settled upon the *Philadelphia's* officers confined behind the gray stone walls. The American squadron was not doing the damage it needed too against the powerful batteries of the enemy. The American guns had been successful in destroying considerable property within the city itself.

Bainbridge and his officers had a long period of captivity staring them in the face. They could see no end to it, and it was no easy matter to stir up the courage of the sick and despairing.

Between nine and ten o'clock on the evening of the of September 4th, while they were preparing themselves to pass through the long hot night, there came a terrific explosion that jarred the air and sent particles of plaster falling in all directions. A midshipman, awakened from his sleep, cried aloud in fright. The report had been preceded by a red flash, as if a great thunderbolt had exploded just outside their grated window.

"What do you suppose that was," exclaimed Lieutenant Jones, starting up and rushing to the small ventilating window that, owing to the kindness of their friend Sidi, had not been filled in.

Everyone had crowded about him, but there was nothing to be seen except the darkness of the night.

"Stop talking! Listen!" ordered Bainbridge.

From the direction of the harbor came cries and distant murmurings. A long wail, like a chorus of many voices, rose in the air and died away; then all was silence.

"A magazine has exploded," said Porter.

"It sounded to me," replied Jones," as if it came from out on the bay."

In an attempt to duplicate the success of Decatur's raid, Lt. Richard Somers and twelve men sailed the *USS Intrepid* back into Tripoli harbor as a fire ship, intending to destroy the anchored pirate fleet, but the ship exploded in the harbor without doing the damage to the enemy that they had anticipated on.

When the remains of the men of the *USS Intrepid* washed ashore on September 5, 1804, the surgeon of the *Constitution,* Dr. Jonathan Cowdery oversaw the identification of the bodies and their burial near the old castle fort. During both battles of Tripoli Harbor (August, 1804), Lieutenants Stephen Decatur and Richard Somers had led flotillas of ships and cannon barges into the harbor and were met by pirate ships that came out to fight them. The Americans won both engagements.

In the morning they all learned what it meant. That explosion sounded the death knell of the gallant young Somers, the popular and well-beloved young officer who was known to all of them. Lieutenant Wadsworth, Midshipman Israel, and ten brave seamen shared his fate.

Also in the explosion over two hundred Tripolitan lost their lives.

Commodore Preble wrote to Bainbridge. "*Somers sailed in the ketch Intrepid, laden with one hundred barrels of gunpowder, for the purpose of destroying the Tripolitan vessels huddled within the mole. The Intrepid had been boarded by the enemy just before she reached her destination, and the terrible result of the explosion. In what manner the trains of powder had been ignited has never been found out. It may have been from accident, or it may have been done in a moment of desperation by the heroic Somers himself.*"

RP

Two days later Bainbridge and his four lieutenants were permitted to view the bodies that had washed ashore.

So mutilated and disfigured were they by the explosion that it was impossible to identify any of them. But over their graves Bainbridge read a funeral service, and they were placed to rest with all the small honors that could be given them.

All of these attacks made the Bashaw more inclined to negotiation for peace, but yet his demands were considered exorbitant, and the United States sent out a larger squadron, under the command of Commodore Barren, who superseded Preble, the latter returning to America, leaving the *Constitution* under the command of his young friend, Stephen Decatur. The new commodore retired with his ships to Syracuse, and began making plans for active operations in the spring. It was now decided to attempt the reduction of Tripoli by means of a land force.

Their intelligence was good since they had the assistance of the deposed ruler of the country' The Bashaw presently on the throne usurped the power that had rightfully belonged to his uncle. Plans were made in secret for an invasion both on land and by sea. The new sea attack was to position the ships so the maximum number of gun could be fired at the same time.

The prisoners were becoming more despaired then ever at the thought that their county had forgotten about them.

They had not heard from Barren; there was no news from their country since the squadron had departed; the unhappy prisoners deemed themselves deserted. The prisoners indulged in the most desperate plans and projects for escape, one of which was to break jail and storm the castle of the Bashaw.

The prisoners came up with some excellent escape plans but owing to the watchfulness of the guards, nothing was accomplished. The feeling of despair settled heavily upon them.

Weeks pasted before Nissen was granted permission to see Bainbridge and his officers.

"God it is good to see you Neil," Bainbridge proclaimed. "We had all but given up that anyone would ever see us again."

"It has been difficult getting approval from the Bashaw to come and see you. He still has not recovered from the pounding the squadron did on his city. I am afraid he has deepened his hatred towards Americans and your survival no longer concerns him."

"We have felt the attitude of the guards has turned sour towards us."

"I do have some news that you may like. General Eaton, an officer of the American army, had joined forces with those of the deposed Bashaw's. They are currently marching through the deserts of Libya with the intention of taking Tripoli from the rear."

"That is encouraging news to say the least. The plan may work."

"Well there is a hitch. The Tripolitan potentate has learned of this plan and is making and redoubled his efforts to increase the fortifications in and about the city."

"How about the American Squadron?" Bainbridge was now feeling like there was hope for a future.

"The best information I have is that in two days time you will see them approaching the harbour," Nissen could see the eyes of the prisoners have more glimmer in them.

The men began to take turns acting as look outs for the squadron.

"There they are!" a joyful holler, echoed through the prison.

The sight of the American flag flying was a glorious reassurance that salvation for them was again real.

The troops did attack Tripoli from the rear and they were successful in gaining entrance to the city and disposing of the military that was used to fighting with cannons, not face to face.

Commodore Barren sent a message to the Bashaw that he was here to negotiate with them but if necessary he would unleash all their fire power on the city and talk later.

The Bashaw was now for the first time fearful of his continued existence and sent word back to Commodore Barren that he was ready to negotiate.

The Commodore was insistent that all the negotiations take place on the *Constitution*. The Bashaw had appointed the Spanish consul to represent him at the conference.

Nissen came to the prison to deliver the news to Bainbridge that the Spanish consul was representing the Bashaw in the initial talks.

"Neil, I feel you must immediately advise Commodore Barren, and Colonel Lear (United States Consul General to the Barbary powers) of the Spaniards' enmity towards the United States. The Spaniards have a great amount of antagonism towards us and they will not go well in any talks to bring peace."

"You are correct in your assessment of the situation. I have talked with Sidi Mohammed Dgheis, and as much as he has done to you he is still wise and far-seeing, much more so then the Bashaw. He has confided in me that he is in doubt of the good will of the Bashaw's emissary. He did feel that the Bashaw was genuine in his desire to come to some terms of settlement so perhaps the Spanish will be dropped from the talks. I will deliver your message."

"Would you also see if I may be granted permission to attend the negotiations?" Bainbridge knew how the Muslims thought and what their wants and desire were and felt he could be helpful in the talks.

Nissen said he would talk to Sidi Mohammed Dgheis about getting Bainbridge paroled on his honor to return. Nissen had gained another interview with Sidi Mohammed Dgheis to present his plan of letting Bainbridge attend the talks.

"I have the pledge of Bainbridge's officer's that they would forfeit their lives if Bainbridge fails to return." Nissen realized the men lives would be in jeopardy whether they pledged them or not but he knew Minister of State like that kind of negotiation.

"Mr. Nissen I find only one fault with your suggestion and that is the Bashaw going along with it. Bainbridge is in much disfavor with the Bashaw. As far as I am concerned Captain Bainbridge's own word of honor is good enough for me."

After some deliberation he agreed to ask the Bashaw to consider it, and to use his best offices in gaining a favorable answer to the request. Thinking it might be a good plan to have something to show, he asked that the officers could draw up and sign a paper in order that he might show it to his High Mightiness. It was also thought best for the captain to accompany him to represent his cause.

This Bainbridge agreed to, and he was witness to a remarkable scene. He had learned enough of the language to understand what was going forward, and his respect and admiration for Sidi Mohammed Dgheis rose mightily, although he had always considered him most friendly.

"Are you so mad as to believe that Captain Bainbridge will return after getting on board a vessel of his own nation, simply because he has made a declaration to that effect?" asked the Bashaw with a sneer.

The minister made a low bow.

"You have the pledge of his officers," he answered.

"True enough," the Bashaw put in," but I value Captain Bainbridge as a prisoner more than all of his officers put together, and I place no reliance on their pledge."

"Pray listen to me," answered the minister. "Your servant has lived long in Christian countries and has seen much of their officers, and he knows that the pledge of a parole of honor is not to be broken."

The Bashaw shrugged his shoulders.

"I have contracted a friendship for this American," went on Sidi Mohammed. "I have full confidence in his honor. You know that I am a Tripolitan by birth, that all my affections are for my country, and that I would propose no measure by which it would be injured. Grant Bainbridge's request, and I will leave my son in your castle, and in the event of his not returning according to my promise, you can take the head off him whose life I value more than my own."

Although the privilege was absolutely unprecedented, the Bashaw could not but yield to these circumstances. But no one about the court believed that the Christian would return, and they considered Sidi Mohammed Dgheis a ruined man indeed.

On June 1, 1805, Bainbridge left the shelter of the castle in a small boat and was rowed off to the fleet. He spent the day in consultation with the officers, and returned late at night to the palace, where he waited upon Sidi Mohammed, who had not displayed the slightest anxiety, although the Bashaw had begun to rebuke him for inducing him to place the least reliance on the word of a "Christian dog." His surprise at seeing Bainbridge was ill concealed. When he heard the terms upon which the United States was disposed to treat he became furiously angry and declined to enter into further negotiations, but the next day a special meeting was held, and in place of the Spaniard, Mr. Nissen, the Danish consul, was selected to renew the negotiations, and went on board the *Constitution* to confer with the American officers. Without trouble they came to an agreement upon which to form the basis of a treaty.

On June 3 the Bashaw stated that he was ready to listen to propositions and to consider whether peace should be rejected or concluded. Captain Bainbridge and Mr. Nissen were invited to be present at the council.

The meeting was held in the large trial chamber of the palace. The members of the Bashaw's cabinet and the invited guests and representatives sat about arranged in the form of a crescent, the regent being in the center, his Prime Minister being on the right, and the Minister for State and Foreign Affairs on the left hand. The strangers were invited to be seated, and the Bashaw turned to Captain Bainbridge.

"In order that everything shall be perfectly fair," he said, "the debates on the subject of this treaty are to be carried on in French, and if you, sir, understand the language, you will be able to hear the opinions of my ministers from their own mouths. In thus admitting you to my private divan you have received an honor never before conferred on a prisoner in Barbary."

Then arising with a great deal of dignity, he submitted the question of "peace or war with the United States." The various members of the council addressed the regent in turn in well-chosen words, in short but direct speeches. After the debate had continued to the end a vote was taken, and it was seen that of the eight who had the privilege of casting a ballot, only two were for peace Sidi Mohammed Dgheis and the Rais of Marine.

Each requested the privilege of adding a few more remarks, and with a great deal of eloquence they pressed their claim, with the result that two of the members came over to their side of the question upon a second voting. The Bashaw now arose.

"Four of you are for peace, "he said," and four for war. Which party shall I satisfy? How shall I act? "

He hesitated and resumed his seat as Sidi Mohammed stepped forward.

"You are our Prince and Master," the minister said, making obeisance. "You have not called us here to dictate to you, but to hear our opinions. It now remains for you to act as you please; but let me entreat you, for your own interests and the happiness of your people, to make it peace."

Again he bowed low and returned to his seat.

The Bashaw cast his eye about the half circle, and leaning forward, took a signet from the bosom of his silken gown and pressed it down upon the treaty.

"It is peace!" he said.

It did not take long to ratify the treaty, and Mr. Nissen brought it on board the flagship, signed with the Bashaw's signature in due form.

THIRTY-ONE

Freedom
June 29, 1805

"God, I can't believe that we maybe finally leaving this rat hole," Lieutenant Parker commented to Bainbridge. "We have been here for over nineteen months and seem like ten years."

"Tomorrow, I have been told that we will be free," Bainbridge was hoping the crew would be in condition to travel.

The news traveled quickly through the great prison where the crew was then confined. Cheer after cheer arose as the Tripolitan castle fired a salute of twenty-one guns, and from out in the harbor and the Constitution answered it.

"What is the procedure of the release?" Lieutenant Parker inquired.

"The Bashaw is sending all the American prisoners out to the American squadron that is anchored in the harbor off of Tripoli. The Bashaw demands that the prisoner exchange will be man for man."

"Where are the enemy prisoners being held?" Parker did not have any idea there were Algerian prisoners.

"From what I have been told the enemy prisoners are in Syracuse and they will be delivered back here in Tripoli," Bainbridge had a concerned look on his face.

The Bashaw had about three hundred Americans and the United States squadron had eighty-nine Tripolitan they had taken in skirmishes. A man for man exchange was not going to be possible so the American commissioners negotiated with the Bashaw to accept $60,000 to compensate for the other two hundred American prisoners.

The $60,000 was really ransom that was demanded by the Dey of Algiers and Pasha of Tripoli for all American captives.

The Bashaw was finally satisfied that the Treaty of Peace was made on honorable and mutually beneficial terms.

The Americans were taken to the various American war-ships. Bainbridge was able to coordinate the release of the crew of the *Philadelphia* so they could stay together as they left the prison.

The American squadron did not waste any time in sailing out of the harbor and head back for the United States.

A jailer, a slave to the Tripolitan, had treated Bainbridge and his men so kindly that they had insisted upon purchasing his freedom, and they succeeded in so doing with the advance money from their wages to the amount of seven hundred dollars.

When a head count was finally made of the men from the *Philadelphia* there were 296 surviving Americans out of the original 307. They had been held captive in Tripoli for nineteen months until June 3, 1805.

The missing eleven (of the original 307 Americans taken as prisoners from the *USS Philadelphia*) included six who had died in captivity, and five who had converted to Islam much to the annoyance of the rest of the crew. The Bashaw of Tripoli offered the five converts the choice of staying in Tripoli and living as Muslims, or returning with the Americans. Four of the converts of the five that were going to stay in Tripoli and live as Muslims decided to renounce Islam and go home. The Bashaw of Tripoli regarded this as a gross insult to Islam. He called his guards to take those four men away…One American recalled the look of horror and despair as they passed him. Those four men did not get to go home, and they were never seen or heard from again.

THIRTY-TWO

Treaty, Home
June 3, 1805

Treaty of Peace and Amity, signed at Tripoli June 4, 1805 (6 Rabia I, A. H. 1220). Original in English and Arabic. Submitted to the Senate December 11, 1805. Resolution of advice and consent April 12, 1806. Ratified by the United States April 17, 1806. As to the ratification generally, see the notes. Proclaimed April 22, 1806.

The English tent of the copy of the treaty, signed by Tobias Lear, follows; to it is appended the receipt for the $60,000 ransom paid on June 19, 1805 (21 Rabia I, A. H. 1220), as written in the same document; then is reproduced the Arabic text of that paper, in the same order as the English. Following those texts is a comment, written in 1930, on the Arabic tent.

Treaty of Peace and Amity between the United States of America and the Bashaw, Dey and Subjects of Tripoli in Barbary.

ARTICLE 1st

There shall be, from the conclusion of this Treaty, a firm, inviolable and universal peace, and a sincere friendship between the President and Citizens of the United States of America, on the one part, and the Bashaw,

Dey and Subjects of the Regency of Tripoli in Barbary on the other, made by the free consent of both Parties, and on the terms of the most favoured Nation. And if either party shall hereafter grant to any other Nation, any particular favour or privilege in Navigation or Commerce, it shall immediately become common to the other party, freely, where it is freely granted, to such other Nation, but where the grant is conditional it shall be at the option of the contracting parties to accept, alter or reject, such conditions in such manner, as shall be most conducive to their respective Interests.

ARTICLE 2ᵈ

The Bashaw of Tripoli shall deliver up to the American Squadron now off Tripoli, all the Americans in his possession; and all the Subjects of the Bashaw of Tripoli now in the power of the United States of America shall be delivered up to him; and as the number of Americans in possession of the Bashaw of Tripoli amounts to Three Hundred Persons, more or less; and the number of Tripolino Subjects in the power of the Americans to about, One Hundred more or less; The Bashaw of Tripoli shall receive from the United States of America, the sum of Sixty Thousand Dollars, as a payment for the difference between the Prisoners herein mentioned.

ARTICLE 3ʳᵈ

All the forces of the United States which have been, or may be in hostility against the Bashaw of Tripoli, in the Province of Derne, or elsewhere within the Dominions of the said Bashaw shall be withdrawn there from, and no supplies shall be given by or in behalf of the said United States, during the continuance of this peace, to any of the Subjects of the said Bashaw, who may be in hostility against him in any part of his Dominions; And the Americans will use all means in their power to persuade the Brother of the said Bashaw, who has co-operated with them at Derne &c, to withdraw from the Territory of the said Bashaw of Tripoli; but they will not use any force or improper means to effect that object; and in case he should withdraw himself as aforesaid, the Bashaw engages to deliver up to him, his Wife and Children now in his powers

ARTICLE 4ᵗʰ

If any goods belonging to any Nation with which either of the parties are at war, should be loaded on board Vessels belonging to the other party they shall pass free and unmolested, and no attempt shall be made to take or detain them.

ARTICLE 5ᵗʰ

If any Citizens, or Subjects with or their effects belonging to either party shall be found on board a Prize Vessel taken from an Enemy by the other party, such Citizens or Subjects shall be liberated immediately and their effects so captured shall be restored to their lawful owners or their Agents.

ARTICLE 6th

Proper passports shall immediately be given to the vessels of both the contracting parties, on condition that the Vessels of War belonging to the Regency of Tripoli on meeting with merchant Vessels belonging to (citizens of the United States of America, shall not be permitted to visit them with more than two persons besides the rowers, these two only shall be permitted to go on board said Vessel, without first obtaining leave from the Commander of said Vessel, who shall compare the passport, and immediately permit said Vessel proceed on her voyage; and should any of the said Subjects of Tripoli insult or molest the Commander or any other person on board Vessel so visited; or plunder any of the property contained in the full complaint being made by the Consul of the United States America resident at Tripoli and on his producing sufficient proof substantiate the fact, The Commander or Rais of said Tripoline Ship or Vessel of War, as well as the Offenders shall be punished in the most exemplary manner.

All Vessels of War belonging to the United States of America meeting with a Cruizer belonging to the Regency of Tripoli, and having seen her passport and Certificate from the Consul of t] United States of America residing in the Regency, shall permit her to proceed on her Cruise unmolested, and without detention. No pass port shall be granted by either party to any Vessels, but such as are absolutely the property of Citizens or Subjects of said contracting parties, on any presence whatever.

ARTICLE 7th

A Citizen or Subject of either of the contracting parties having bought a Prize Vessel condemned by the other party, or by any other Nation, the Certificate of condemnation and Bill of Sale she be a sufficient passport for such Vessel for two years, which, considering the distance between the two Countries, is no more than a reason able time for her to procure proper passports.

ARTICLE 8th

Vessels of either party, putting into the ports of the other, and having need of provisions or other supplies, they shall be furnish at the Market price, and if any such Vessel should so put in from disaster at Sea, and have occasion to repair; she shall be at liberty to land and remark her Cargo, without paying any duties; but in no case shall she be compelled to land her Cargo.

ARTICLE 9th

Should a Vessel of either party be cast on the shore of the other all proper assistance shall be given to her and her Crew. No pillar shall be allowed, the property shall remain at the disposition of it owners, and the Crew protected and succored till they can be sent to their Country.

ARTICLE 10th

If a Vessel of either party, shall be attacked by an Enemy within gunshot of the Forts of the other, she shall be defended as much as possible; If she be in port, she shall not be seized or attacked when it is in the power of the other party to protect her; and when she proceeds to Sea, no Enemy shall be allowed to pursue her from the same port, within twenty four hours after her departure.

ARTICLE 11th

The Commerce between the United States of America and the Regency of Tripoli; The Protections to be given to Merchants, Masters of Vessels and Seamen; The reciprocal right of establishing Consuls in each Country; and the privileges, immunities and jurisdictions to be enjoyed by such Consuls, are declared to be on the same footing, with those of the most favoured Nations respectively.

ARTICLE 12th

The Consul of the United States of America shall not be answerable for debts contracted by Citizens of his own Nation, unless, he previously gives a written obligation so to do.

ARTICLE 13th

On a Vessel of War, belonging to the United States of America, anchoring before the City of Tripoli, the Consul is to inform the Bashaw of her arrival, and she shall be saluted with twenty one Guns, which she is to return in the same quantity or number.

ARTICLE 14th

As the Government of the United States of America, has in itself no character of enmity against the Laws, Religion or Tranquility of Mussulman, and as the said States never have entered into any voluntary war or act of hostility against any Mahometan Nation, except in the defense of their just rights to freely navigate the High Seas: It is declared by the contracting parties that no pretext arising from Religious Opinions, shall ever produce an interruption of the Harmony existing between the two Nations; And the Consuls and Agents of both Nations respectively, shall have liberty to exercise his Religion in his own house; all slaves of the same Religion shall not be Impeded in going to said Consuls house at hours of Prayer. The Consuls shall have liberty and personal security given them to travel within the Territories of each other, both by land and sea, and shall not be prevented from going on board any Vessel that they may think proper to visit; they shall have likewise the liberty to appoint their own Dragoman and Brokers.

ARTICLE 15th

In case of any dispute arising from the violation of any of the articles of this Treaty, no appeal shall be made to Arms, nor shall War be declared on any pretext whatever; but if the Consul residing at the place, where the dispute shall happen, shall not be able to settle the same; The Government of that Country shall state their grievances in writing, and transmit it to the Government of the other, and the period of twelve calendar months shall be allowed for answers to be returned; during which time no act of hostility shall be permitted by either party, and in case the grievances are not redressed, and War should be the event, the Consuls and Citizens or Subjects of both parties reciprocally shall be permitted to embark with their effects unmolested, on board of what vessel or Vessels they shall think proper.

ARTICLE 16th

If in the fluctuation of Human Events, a War should break out between the two Nations; The Prisoners captured by either party shall not be made Slaves; but shall be exchanged Rank for Rank; and if there should be a deficiency on either side, it shall be made up by the payment of Five Hundred Spanish Dollars for each Captain, Three Hundred Dollars for each Mate and Supercargo and One hundred Spanish Dollars for each Seaman so wanting. And it is agreed that Prisoners shall be exchanged in twelve months from the time of their capture, and that this Exchange may be effected by any private Individual legally authorized by either of the parties.

ARTICLE 17th

If any of the Barbary States, or other powers at War with the United States of America, shall capture any American Vessel, and send her into any of the ports of the Regency of Tripoli, they shall not be permitted to sell her, but shall be obliged to depart the Port on procuring the requisite supplies of Provisions; and no duties shall be exacted on the sale of Prizes captured by Vessels sailing under the Flag of the United States of America when brought into any Port in the Regency of Tripoli.

ARTICLE 18th

If any of the Citizens of the United States, or any persons under their protection, shall have any dispute with each other, the Consul shall decide between the parties; and whenever the Consul shall require any aid or assistance from the Government of Tripoli, to enforce his decisions, it shall immediately be granted to him. And if any dispute shall arise between any Citizen of the United States and the Citizens or Subjects of any other Nation, having a Consul or Agent in Tripoli, such dispute shall be settled by the Consuls or Agents of the respective Nations.

ARTICLE 19th

If a Citizen of the United States should kill or wound a Tripoline, or, on the contrary, if a Tripoline shall kill or wound a Citizen of the United States, the law of the Country shall take place, and equal justice shall be rendered, the Consul assisting at the trial; and if any delinquent shall make his escape, the Consul shall not be answerable for him in any manner whatever.

ARTICLE 20th

Should any Citizen of the United States of America die within the limits of the Regency of Tripoli, the Bashaw and his Subjects shall not interfere with the property of the deceased; but it shall be under the immediate direction of the Consul, unless otherwise disposed of by will. Should there be no Consul, the effects shall be deposited in the hands of some person worthy of trust, until the party shall appear who has a right to demand them, when they shall render an account of the property. Neither shall the Bashaw or his Subjects give hindrance in the execution of any will that may appear.

Whereas, the undersigned, Tobias Lear, Consul General of the United States of America for the Regency of Algiers, being duly appointed Commissioner, by letters patent under the signature of the President, and Seal of the United States of America, bearing date at the City of Washington, the 18" day of November 1803 for negotiating and concluding a Treaty of Peace, between the United States of America, and the Bashaw, Dey and Subjects of the Regency of Tripoli in Barbary-

Now Know Ye, That I, Tobias Lear, Commissioner as aforesaid, do conclude the foregoing Treaty, and every article and clause therein contained; reserving the same nevertheless for the final ratification of the President of the United States of America, by and with the advice and consent of the Senate of the said United States.

Done at Tripoli in Barbary, the fourth day of June, in the year One thousand, eight hundred and five; corresponding with the sixth day of the first month of Rabbia 1220.

[Seal] TOBIAS LEAR.

Having appeared in our presence, Colonel Tobias Lear, Consul General of the United States of America, in the Regency of Algiers, and Commissioner for negotiating and concluding a Treaty of Peace and Friendship between Us and the United States of America, bringing with him the present Treaty of Peace with the within Articles, they were by us minutely examined, and we do hereby accept, confirm and ratify them, Ordering all our Subjects to fulfill entirely their contents, without any violation and under no pretext.

In Witness whereof We, with the heads of our Regency, Subscribe it.

Given at Tripoli in Barbary the sixth day of the first month of Rabbia 1220, corresponding with the 4th day of June 1805.

(L. S.) JUSUF CARAMANLY Bashaw
(L. S.) MOHAMET CARAMANLY Bey
(L. S.) MOHAMET Kahia
(L. S.) HAMET Rais de Marino
(L. S.) MOHAMET DGHIES First AIinister
(L. S.) SARAH Aga of Divan
(L. S.) SEEIM Hasnadar
(L. S.) MURAT Dqblartile
(L. S.) MURAT RAIS Admiral
(L. S.) SOEIMAN Kehia
(L. S.) ABDAEEA Basa Aga
(L. S.) MAHOMET Scheig al Belad
(L. S.) ALEI BEN DIAB First Secretary

[Receipt]

We hereby acknowledge to have received from the hands of Colonel Tobias Lear the full sum of sixty thousand dollars, mentioned as Ransom for two hundred Americans, in the Treaty of Peace concluded between Us and the United States of America on the Sixth day of the first Month of Rabbia 1220-and of all demands against the said United States.

Done this twenty first day of the first month of Rabbia 1220.

(L. S.) Signed (JOSEPH CARMANALY) Bashaw

Source:

Treaties and Other International Acts of the United States of America. Edited by Hunter Miller, Volume 2, Documents 1-40: 1776-1818, Washington : Government Printing Office, 1931.

Liberated: Upon the establishment of a treaty of peace with Tripoli, 3 June 1805, Captain Bainbridge returned to the United States in the frigate *President*.

"Now be it known, That I John Adams, President of the United States of America, having seen and considered the said Treaty do, by and with the advice and consent of the Senate, accept, ratify, and confirm the same, and every clause and article thereof. And to the End that the said Treaty may be observed, and performed with good Faith on the part of the United States, I have ordered the premises to be made public; And I do hereby enjoin and require all persons bearing office civil or military within the United States, and all other citizens or inhabitants thereof, faithfully to observe and fulfill the said Treaty and every clause and article thereof."

The first suggestion for destroying the *"Philadelphia"* is said to have been sent to Commander Preble in a letter from Bainbridge while he was a prisoner. Bainbridge and his officers and crew remained prisoners for nineteen months during the Tripolitan war, after the court of inquiry, Bainbridge was not given another command, but was ordered to the navy yard in New York to supervise construction of new vessels.

At Syracuse a court of inquiry was held on board the *Constitution*, and an investigation was made under orders of the Secretary of the Navy in regard to the loss of the *Philadelphia*. Bainbridge was acquitted immediately and with honor; and as soon as possible he returned to the United States, landing in Hampton, Va.

He was received with every mark of approbation by the public and by the officials at Washington, and as soon as Congress had been informed of the high conduct of the Danish consul they passed resolutions of thanks to him for his benevolent actions.

The following news article appeared in the *American and Commercial Advertiser* on September 25, 1805.

"We have received the official account of the proceedings of the court of enquiry in the case of Captain Bainbridge, which shall appear at length in our next paper. The following is the result of the enquiry:- The court having deliberated on the evidence deduced from the testimony of the witnesses, heard in this case, are decidedly of opinion that Captain William Bainbridge acted with fortitude and, conduct in the loss of his ship the United States frigate *Philadelphia*, on the 31st October, 1803, and that no degree of censure should attach itself to him from that event."

THIRTY-THREE

Merchant Service
June 7, 1806

William Bainbridge returned to Philadelphia on the *USS President* on June 3, 1806. He had been away nearly two years and was worried how he would find his wife and children. As they frigate approached the dock his eyes searched the crowd of well wishers and families lined up to catch the first glimpse of their love ones or friends.

Susan was in the crowd and waving her hat at the incoming ship. William was on the rail waving his hat. It was not until they were some fifty feet from the dock did he pick Susan out of the crowd. She was as beautiful as he had remembered her. Her long hair was blowing the light June breeze and her smile was as wide as her face even as the tears rolled down her face.

The frigate docked and the lines were quickly secured to the dock. The gang way was lowered and William was the first off the ship.

They embraced in silence as their only child, Susan Parker Bainbridge, tugged at William's trouser. Susan was only one year old when he left and now she was three and only knew her daddy from her mother's telling her about him.

"William, thank you for being alive, I love you."

"I can't tell you how much I have thought of this day. You have been in my prayers every day. I love you too."

The two continued to hug until little Susan brought them back to reality. William reached down and picked her up and gave her a big kiss.

"Are you my daddy?" she asked.

"I sure am; I sure am, and we have a lot of catching up to do."

"Let's go home."

"Where are your things?"

"Everything I had has been stolen; these clothes are all I have left."

When they returned to their home William found it looking better than he had remembered.

"William I am so happy you are home safe and sound. I can't begin to tell you how I worried."

"There were times I gave up hope of ever seeing you again but that is behind us now."

"I would like to take a bath before doing anything else. I don't know how you can even kiss me looking the way I do."

"Go upstairs and take those filthy clothes off. I think we have enough hot water for you to bath in."

William shed his clothes and used the commode when Susan came into the bathing room.

"My lord, William you are nothing but skin and bones. I can see I have my work cut out for me getting you back into good health."

"I am looking forward to your loving care and making up for the last two years."

"I am so happy you still have the miniature of me around your neck."

"I fought hard to keep it, one man died because he thought he could take it. The picture of you was my hope each day that we would be back together."

Bainbridge regained his health and strength. His crushed foot had healed but he would always have a limp as a reminder of his imprisonment. The men from the *Philadelphia* were thankful to be home. The crewmen had under gone beatings, having to live in barbaric living conditions, no beds, no clothes, no water to wash with, and forced to eat food that was unfit to eat.

The Secretary of the Navy ordered a court of inquiry to look into the loss of the *Philadelphia* and the imprisonment of Bainbridge and the crew of ship.

The men serving on the court of inquiry were all known to Bainbridge and they all respected his character on honor. Bainbridge testified as well as the Lieutenants that served on the ship. The court took five minutes to come to a unanimous vote to acquit Bainbridge of any blame for the loss of the *Philadelphia,* on June 29, 1805.

There was no official censure for his conduct much to Bainbridge's relief.

When he arrived home he confessed to Susan that he was greatly relieved the inquiry was over.

"I have to confess, Susan, that even though the inquiry is over I will always live with the stigma of losing my ship."

"It was not your fault William. Accidents happen, and now it is over and you are home, safe and sound, from a horrific ordeal."

On June 5, 1806 Bainbridge met with Robert Smith, the Secretary of the Navy. They had a long talk about many topics but especially about Algiers. Bainbridge filled him in on the events as they occurred over the past two years, especially the intolerable treatment given to the crew of the *Philadelphia.*

"I need help New York making the navy yard functional. You can't believe the negative attitude some of our law makes have. Some of the law makers I swear cannot see beyond the end of their noses."

"What do you have in mind?"

"I need you to take command of the navy yard of New York."

"Robert, the last two years have been a drain on my personal resources. I do not know if I can afford to accept appointment."

"Think about it William."

Bainbridge was not pleased about this assignment but he agreed to think it over before giving his final decision to the Secretary.

When he arrived home, Susan greeted him at the door.

"How did it go?"

"Not well in my opinion. The Secretary has ordered me to take command of the naval yard in New York."

"Are you going to accept the assignment?"

"I don't think so. The last two years have been financially ruinous for us. I need to make more money than paltry sum the Navy wants to pay for land duty."

"What are you thinking of doing, William?"

"I have had an offer to Captain a merchant schooner. The pay is $128 dollars per month plus a bonus for successful voyages; that beats the $60 a month they are offering me now."

"I thought you were making more than that."

"When I am at sea I am being paid $100 per month plus the bonus when I take a prize."

On June 7, 1806 William Bainbridge was furloughed by the Secretary of the Navy for merchant service. He was granted furlough for two years, 1806-1808.

The following summer the Secretary of the Navy, Robert Smith, was dealing with pressure from the President and Congress over the anticipation of a war with England. The Secretary of the Navy was desperate for qualified war-ship's captains.

William was also saddened in 1807 by the passing away of his father in New York City on June 23rd. The Bainbridge's traveled to New York to be with his mother and to assist with his father's funeral. The service was held at Trinity Church and then he was interned in a vault at the church.

A few months later, William Bainbridge's friend, Commodore Edward Preble had died on August 25, 1807 of a gastrointestinal illness at the age of 45. Many of the qualified Navy officers from the Revolutionary war were either dead or too old to serve in the new United States Navy the Secretary was attempting to form.

President Thomas Jefferson was receiving pressure from owners of the merchant ships to do something about the continued impressments of American seamen into the service of England. Trade with Europe was becoming a problem because of the loss of vessels and men. The United States, being a young growing nation, depended on trade as its life blood of commerce.

President Jefferson addressed Congress: "Gentlemen we must change our non-defense attitude. The lack of a United States navy has placed us into accepting the domination of England over the European seas. American vessels are being captured and the crews placed into slave service of the English. American lives are being ruined, young men taken from their county and never heard from again. We need to fight back as a country, the county we fought for that very reason, individual right to freedom. I have instructed Secretary of the Navy, Robert Smith, to contact our past naval officers to assist in the forming of an offensive naval fleet to protect American shipping rights."

The Government at last concluded that it was time to order the best officers to active duty.

Dated: March 05, 1808 from Robert Smith, Secretary of the Navy to Captain William Bainbridge:

"Captain Bainbridge, it is my pleasure to notify you of your appointment to fill the vacancy of Commodore Preble. The appointment is effective immediately as Commodore of the squadron cruising the Eastern Atlantic. You are requested to take command of the USS President as the flagship. Your full pay status will be also granted immediately plus the usual 'prize' reward for vessels captured by you. Please respond by return currier as soon as possible."

Regards,

Robert Smith, Secretary of the Navy

THIRTY-FOUR

USS President
March 5, 1808

The *USS President* was a 44-gun frigate of 1,576 tons. The ship carried 32-24 pounders, 22-42 pounders (carronades), and one 18-pounder (long-gun). The frigate was launched on April 10, 1800 and was one of the larger war-ships in the United States Navy.

The *USS President* was in New York. He did not know what condition he would find the vessel in. There was a crew on the ship that was supposed to have been caring for the ship and making repairs to assure that it was sea worthy.

Captain Bainbridge found the *USS President* in the harbor of New York. He was taken back at the poor condition of the ship. The last time he had been of the ship it was relatively new and was a proud ship of the fleet.

The crew members on the ship were a sorry lot. To make matter worst the crew wanted to be discharged and paid off.

"Our time has expired; we no longer have to be here. We want our money!" they demanded of Bainbridge.

Bainbridge sensed the pending trouble that was brewing. He called the men up on deck and advised them they were going to sail the ship to Washington D.C. to make repairs.

"Gentlemen you are going to stay with the ship until we reach Washington. Once we are in Washington you will be paid as you leave the ship."

There was mumbling in the ranks of the men. Bainbridge addressed the muteness attitude of the sailors by stepping up to a number of them and telling them to obey orders or be subject to punishment.

"Aye, and who is going to enforce it?"

Bainbridge swung around and grabbed the man and slammed him against the mast causing the man to drop to the deck unconscious. "Any more questions, gentlemen?"

Bainbridge made the ship ready for sailing in the next three weeks. The ship was not ready by any means to go to sea but stable enough to sail to Washington.

They arrived in the Washington navy yard on August 7th. The men whose time had expired and wanted to depart the vessel were paid off. Some of the men he invited to leave the ship, Bainbridge wanted men who would be dependable sailors not slackers.

Over the next three months that *USS President* was dismantled and the necessary repairs were made to bring the frigate back to its pristine condition. The money for doing the repairs was difficult to obtain but Bainbridge through persistence got what he needed. Bainbridge was well like by the politicians and he had a close ear of the President.

Susan was happy that she could be with her husband during the period of retrofitting the *USS President*. The Captain's cabin of the ship was fairly large and airy. Little Susan was delighted about living on the ship. She was the queen of the ship and she made sure she knew she knew all of the crew.

Susan was busy making the Captain's cabin a livable space. She had the area between the ceiling beams smooth over with putty. She had a floor cloth added of a black and white pattern. She found curtain material that was to her liking and made curtains for all the cabin windows. She also made a curtain enclosure around the commode so as to provide some privacy. William had to admit the cabin did look homier.

December 18, 1808 William Bainbridge sailed the frigate *USS President* out of the Washington Naval yard on southward cruise in protection of American merchant ships.

The cruise lasted until March 7, 1809 when they sailed back to the Philadelphia harbor.

Susan was waiting on the dock eagerly waiting the docking of the *President*. The sailors were lining the rail and they looked like a smart looking outfit. The training of the men while they were at sea showed and those on the docks were proud to see such a fine showing of discipline.

"William, give me another kiss. I am so glad to see you."

"I am glad to see the love of my life. You are looking more beautiful every day."

The Bainbridge's waved at those that were there to express their welcome.

A young seaman from the Navy was also on the dock with an envelope for William.

"Captain Bainbridge, one moment sir. I have an envelope from the Secretary of the Navy."

Bainbridge opened the envelope and read the memo that was inside. William turned to Susan. "Secretary Smith has advised me that he leaving office on March 4th and he will be replaced by Paul Hamilton of South Carolina on May 15th, 1809. He also ordered me to available here in Philadelphia to arrange for recruiting new sailors.

"Oh that is wonderful you will be home with me. I have wonderful news, I am pregnant again."

"William picked Susan up and said, "That is the most wonderful news I could receive."

"How are you feeling?"

"Just fine William, feeling good and I am so happy to know you might be around for awhile.

John was enjoying life at home.

On October 24, 1809, William B. Bainbridge was born to Susan and William Sr. The baby was a spitting image of his father. Susan did the delivery at home with the aid of a midwife and two assistants.

The Secretary of the Navy had authorized William Bainbridge to continue on board the *President*, during 1809-1810.

The Secretary of the Navy had advised William about the increased hostilities between the United States and England. The Secretary was advising Bainbridge that war was imminent.

Bainbridge had trained the crew of the *USS President* to be the best in the Navy. He had strived to make the crew of the frigate under his command able and effective. William was a good teacher and he knew the importance of informed and skilled sailors.

The *USS President* spent a long and stormy winter at sea. They did have some warmer weather when they sailed to the southern waters of the Bahamas. Life on the frigate in the cold waters of the Atlantic was not easy. The fire of the cooks stove was a favorite hangout for the sailors.

When Bainbridge returned on May 9, 1810 the crew of the *USS President* was perhaps the best drilled and disciplined body of men that could have been found afloat.

THIRTY-FIVE

Merchant Service
1810

The Congress had been making overtures to the British in order to naturalize affairs but to no avail. The British knew they were the most superior naval force in the world and Americans were an inferior nuisance to take advantage of. The British were regularly preying on American shipping. The talk about war seemed no nearer than it had for the past five or six years, Americans were passive.

"Jesus, Mary, and Joseph, we can't continue to live on what little the United States Navy pays us and not be able to obtain an occasional prize at sea."

"What do you suggest William."

"I am not sure Susan but the pay of a captain in the service is less than a hundred dollars a month. We are not being encouraged to take prizes so something has to be done so I can support our growing family."

Bainbridge solicited another furlough from the government, which was granted, accompanied by a letter of gratitude from Paul Hamilton, Esq., then secretary of the navy.

"Your letter of the third instant, wherein you resign the command of the frigate President, for the purpose of making a voyage in the merchant service

has been received, and has very much excited my sensibility; as the ability and zeal with which for many years you have served our country, cannot fail to cause me great regret at parting with you 'even for a time.

That you have made great sacrifices to patriotism, I well know, and it is only by combining this consideration with the motives on which your request is founded, that I am enabled to comply with your wishes.

"In whatever situation you may be placed, and at all times, be assured your prosperity and honour will be extremely dear to me; and while I shall anxiously wish for your return, at the earliest moment your scheme will admit, I present you my sincere wishes for complete success in it."

"You are at liberty, on receipt of this, to quit the frigate; in which case Lieutenant Morris will proceed to Hampton-Toads, there anchoring, and wait further orders."

William Bainbridge was one of the most sought after ship's captain in the United States. The owners of merchant ships would all like to have Bainbridge running their vessels carrying their precious cargos of merchandise and commodities for trade in foreign countries. Bainbridge was also yielding to the strenuous advice of a number of his friends that he needed to go into private service.

The Bainbridge's had another big event happen back in their Philadelphia home; a daughter was born on February 1, 1811, Mary Taylor Bainbridge. Susan had neighbors assisting her and a local midwife that the ladies seemed to trust. Giving birth was never easy. Susan always knew when the time was coming so she could have an enema to empty her bowels so she would not contaminate the baby with the enviable release of feces when pushing to deliver the baby.

The neighbor took turns staying with Susan, helping with the children and assisting in the house. Susan also had a live in maid, Martha, so things were under control.

Bainbridge accepted a position once more in the merchant service and proceeded on a voyage to St. Petersburg, Russia, and India.

Captain Bainbridge proceeded on a voyage to St. Petersburg on what started as a smooth crossing over the Atlantic. Nothing of interest occurred until he passed the sound into the Baltic. When just inside the straits of the Baltic his vessel was captured by a Danish privateer and carried into Copenhagen. As luck would have it, he had not been at anchor more than a few minutes when that should come off to him in a small boat from the shore but his old friend Neil C. Nissen, of Tripoli! Nissen had been a zealous friend of the American prisoners in Tripoli. He was now calling on him to tender his services, with his characteristic kindness and sincerity.

The meeting between the two friends was cordial and their greetings more than hearty.

The first interview between Nissen at Copenhagen was rendered more interesting by a strange coincidence of circumstances. At the very juncture when Nissen heard that his old Barbary friend had been brought into port, he was engaged in unpacking the silver urn, which was presented to him by the American prisoners in Tripoli, to whose comfort he had so largely contributed. The making of the urn had been awarded to an English silversmith for manufacturing. England was continuing to be preoccupied with battling the northern powers of Europe and individuals such as the silversmith were employed with making arms for Her Majesty Service.

Mr. Nissen had been notified in Copenhagen of the delay. The urn was finally completed and sent to him as a token of the American officers' gratitude to their benefactor.

Nissen said that he had just happened to hear that the captured ship claimed to be an American, and someone who landed from the privateer had remembered Bainbridge's name. So at once he had hastened to tender his services.

"The very strangest coincidence, my dear sir," said Neil Nissen, as he seated himself beside Bainbridge in the cabin," is that this very day, aye, only an hour ago; I received the handsome urn which you and the rest of my kind friends, whom I had the pleasure in meeting when they were guests of the Bashaw, had sent me. It has only now arrived owing to the fact of our war with England."

"Yes, I remember," returned Bainbridge; "we ordered it from a London silversmith, and I trust that you will live long to possess it."

"Now, in regard to your being taken for an Englishman, and the mistake of your being brought in here," Nissen continued, "leave it all to me and do not worry."

In a few days Bainbridge parted from his old friend and went on to St. Petersburg, Nissen having completed all arrangements for his release.

Neil Nissen was never as happy as when in the exercise of disinterested benevolence. Nissen directed all his interest and energy to obtain the release of Captain Bainbridge's vessel.

"I am forever in your debt. Once again your munificent efforts have been rewarded with complete success. I have my ship back so I can proceed with my voyage to St. Petersburg."

"You have to know that it my pleasure to be of service to you."

Bainbridge completed his voyage to St. Petersburg and back to Philadelphia without any further incidents.

Captain Bainbridge made a second voyage to St. Petersburg, in the autumn of 1811. He was entrusted with an important mercantile negotiation. Bainbridge was aware winter was rapidly approaching so he had made arrangements to remain in the Russian capital until the next spring.

Shortly after Bainbridge arrived in St. Petersburg he received a letter from the Secretary of the Navy. The Secretary wanted Bainbridge to be aware of the action that had taken place between the United States frigate *President,* and his Britannic majesty's frigate *Little Belt.* The British attack on the American frigate was almost the last straw that might lead to a war. The Secretary expressed his concern that war was unavoidable. He was encouraging Bainbridge to return to the States as soon as possible. He needed Bainbridge to assist him in making the U.S. Navy a functional foe against the English.

William did not want to be absent from his naval post in the hour of danger. Leaving Russia and traveling back to the United States was going to be difficult. Bainbridge was determined to surmount all the difficulties of being stranded in St. Petersburg in the winter, and return to the United States so he could report personally at Washington for duty.

It had been a frigid winter and the Baltic was frozen over. The only route was over land through Sweden to Gothenburg, a distance of nearly eleven hundred miles. A journey of this kind during the inclemency of winter was considered so perilous, that to a mindless energetic, the enterprise would have been disaster.

Prior to his departure from St. Petersburg, Bainbridge met with the honorable John Quincy Adams, resident minister from the United States at that court, and acquainted him with his determination to return to the United States.

John Adams was aware of the pending conflict with England and provided Bainbridge with a courier's pass so he could leave immediately. Bainbridge was commissioned by Adams to carry dispatches to the United States minister at the court of St. James. From there Bainbridge intended to return across the Atlantic in a merchant vessel to the United States.

During Captain Bainbridge's residence at St. Petersburg he formed an intimate acquaintance with Doctor Jacques Wylie, the private physician, as well as the intimate and confidential friend of the Emperor Alexander; these connections assisted in giving him great influence at court.

Bainbridge was impressed by the lacquer boxes he saw in the St. Petersburg shops. He thought to himself that Susan would perhaps enjoy the artistry of the lacquer miniature paintings on the boxes.

On one of his frequent visits with Doctor Jacques Wylie, William asked about purchasing one of the beautiful gifts for his wife.

"I can tell you, William, that the nicest works come the village of Fedoskino; a small town about forty kilometers to the north of Moscow."

"The boxes seem to be very expensive, what makes them so pricey?"

"My understanding is they have a secret of making and paintings on the boxes on papier-mâché developed in Fedoskino. The art of doing this process has been passed from one generation to another for over two hundred years."

"Do you think my wife would like one of the boxes for her jewelry?" Bainbridge was not about to invest in something that might not please Susan.

"By all means she will love it. Women like things like this so they can show their friends."

The following day Bainbridge went shopping for a lacquer box.

"Sir, would you tell me something about these beautiful boxes you have on display?" William was speaking French hoping the shop keeper could converse with him.

Much to William satisfaction the shop keeper could speak passable French.

"You have a good eye; all those boxes are linked to the Russian graphic art of recent years."

"They are so shinny, how is that done?" William was getting hooked on the items before him.

"The artists do a multi-layer oil painting on the primed papier-mâché surface with special linings. Most of the Fedoskino boxes have a black background on the outside and are covered inside with scarlet or bright-red lacquer," the gentleman was proud of his offerings.

"I do like the box with the three horses."

"That is the most popular, and in Russian they are called 'troyka.' That particular box you are holding was the art work of Khomutinnikova, one of Fedoskino masters.

"Would you be able to pack the box so I could transport it back to the United States safety?"

"Why, yes I could. Your wife is a very lucky person to have a husband with such a good eye."

Bainbridge was ready to leave Russia and he was dependant on the influence of his new friends to help remove all obstacles that were in place do to the French being also at war. Count Romanoff made sure that Bainbridge was placed under the protection of the Russian government. In return for this favor Count Romanoff also gave Bainbridge dispatches to deliver to Baron Nicholn the minister plenipotentiary of his imperial majesty at the court of Sweden. He also requested Bainbridge to deliver letters to General Steingal, Governor and Captain General of Finland; and to Barclay de Tolly, adjutant general of the Russian army, and governor of the islands of Alands in the Gulf of Bothnia.

The young Barclay de Tolly, who was the pupil of Dr. Wylie, also gave Captain Bainbridge a very warm letter to his father.

Bainbridge was reasonably protected from hostilities from enemies. The Count had arranged that Bainbridge be accompanied as far as the frontiers of Sweden by a Russian commissioned officer. It was the dead of winter and traveling was tedious, mostly because of the total deterioration of the roads. To make things worst there were no public houses of entertainment on the way. The carriage they were riding in was their only shelter. There was sense in stopping since they would freeze to death. They traveled day and night only stopping to relieve their bladders and to feed the horses.

Sleeping in the carriage was impossibility; besides being cold the carriage was bouncing every which way possible. Bainbridge thought there is nothing like riding on water. The only food they had was what they were able place under the seat. To place anything in the boot would freeze not that it was much warmer inside the carriage. Bainbridge was not hungry, he knew he need to eat something, but he did not feel much like it and beside he was extremely constipated. They went to Helsinki and Bainbridge delivered the letters to General Steingal, the Governor and Captain General of Finland.

When he arrived at Abo, situated on the Gulf of Bothnia the ice prevented them from proceeding by water to Stockholm direct, which was the usual route.

Bainbridge was not one to be defeated. The Gulf of Bothnia was partially frozen so he would have to go by boat. The treacherous crossing would be somewhat safer by traveling from small island to island to the larger island of Alands.

When they arrived on the island of Alands they stopped at Mariehamn to deliver the letter from his friend Dr. Wylie. It was then he learned with great regret that Barclay de Tolly had left his station that morning by order of the emperor to repair with dispatch to St. Petersburg in order to make the necessary arrangements for opening the campaign early in the spring, against the Emperor Napoleon.

Bainbridge was fairly beat up from the trip and the Russian officers stationed there treated him with great courtesy and hospitality, and insisted on his remaining with them in order that he might recover from his fatigue. Bainbridge accepted their hospitality.

The next morning they traveled in the four-wheeled carriage the balance of the distance over Alands to the eastern coast.

The crossing of the ice to Sweden would be trickery since that is where the Baltic Sea and the Gulf of Bothnia meet. The twenty-five mile crossing was dangerous to the island Oland just off the coast of Sweden. He was advised that it was impossible to do in the inclement seas that were roaring.

Bainbridge found owners of two large boats that could carry him, the dismantle carriage, two horses, the driver, and the other two men traveling with him. Bainbridge laid in a fresh supply of food and additional blankets. One of the boat owners took pity on Bainbridge and provided him with a bed and his second hot meal he had had in over a week. Bainbridge slept like the dead and he felt renewed in the morning.

The carriage had been dismantled the previous day and loaded on to the larger of the two boats. The horses rode with Bainbridge on the other boat along with his three companions.

They left the shores of Alands early in the morning. The waters in the Strait were nearly ice cold with large floating masses of ice threatening to the safety of the boats. The horses had to be harnessed and roped to the boat sides to prevent them from being injured. The forward movement was slow, the sails on the boat were difficult to control but Bainbridge was able to demonstrate to the boat owners handling skills that they were not aware of. The wind exacerbated the intensity of the cold. Some would freeze to death if they were stranded in the ice cold waters.

Once they reached western shores of Sweden, Bainbridge goal was to go to Gothenburg on the eastern coast where he hoped to find a vessel to carry him to England.

But first he needed to travel north to Stockholm and deliver the dispatches to Baron Nicholn at the Court of Sweden. The roads to Stockholm were not a bad as those traveling out of St. Petersburg but they were not good either. The frozen ground with a fresh topping of ice smoothed out some of the pot holes.

The trip to Gothenburg was estimated at two hundred miles over ice and snow. He would need to go by sledge. He did find a sledge owner who was willing to transport him across the county. Bainbridge bid his traveling companions a farewell after buying them supper in a road house they were near. Bainbridge rented a room for the night so he would be fresh for the long trip in the morning. The driver of the sledge was waiting for Bainbridge the next morning. The dogs pulling the sledge seemed to be more anxious then William to get started.

They made it to Jonkooing, about half way to Gothenburg where they put up for the night. The driver was a pleasant fellow and he did understand some French so they were able to converse on a limited basis. The following night they were in Gothenburg.

Gothenburg was a seaport and active with merchant vessels. Bainbridge main goal was to go to London and deliver the letter from John Adams to the United States minister at the Court of St. James.

Bainbridge did locate a merchant schooner going to England. The Captain of the vessel was pleased that Bainbridge would travel with him. The trip went fairly well in spite of cold rough seas up until they were off the coast of England. The seas were twenty foot swells and battering winds. The schooner was being bounced around like a toy boat on a pond. The storm claimed the lives of three of the Englishmen. The three of them were swept over the side of the vessel and lost in the severe storm. The vessels captain was having difficulty with the control of the ship. Captain Bainbridge saw that they were in trouble and he took over command of the vessel until the danger was over. If he had not acted quickly the vessel would have been lost at sea.

They reached the mouth of the Thames and safely made their way to London. The merchant ship's captain was still telling Bainbridge how grateful he was for saving his ship. He was sad that he had to report the loss of three men.

Bainbridge completed his assigned mission and located a vessel going to the United States. Once the captain discovered that Bainbridge was a sea captain he was welcomed with open arms. He was pleased to have an experienced sea captain assist him in the crossing.

Bainbridge had been recovering from a head injury received from falling over a precipice with his carriage in Finland. He had no doubt received a concussion and he had not fully recovered.

He had traveled by sledge, rowboat, horseback, and coach in his journey back to the United States. It had been a very difficult trip but he was ready to again serve his country.

Bainbridge arrived at Philadelphia on January 31 on a merchant vessel.

William was elated to find Susan waiting for him at the dock. Susan's greatest fear was that William would get into a shooting battle and that his life would be in jeopardy. William hurried off the ship and gathered Susan in his arms and kissed her. Their action did not go unnoticed and the cheers from the ship's deck brought them back to reality. Susan waved to the men on the ship.

William and Susan headed for home where the children had been left in the care of the maid, Martha. They spent three days at home getting reacquainted and making love. Susan also was determined to get William healthy again.

William presented the present he had purchased in St. Petersburg for Susan.

"Oh my William, what is it?"

"You need to open it up and see," William had his fingers crossed hoping she would like it.

"William this is beautiful, I have never in my life seen anything as lovely as this," Susan was pleased.

"I will make a special place in the living room so I can show the box off to our friends."

Susan gives William a long passionate kiss and she could feel the hardness in William's pants.

"Come upstairs we have time to make love."

They then packed up the kids and traveled to New York to visit his mother.

BOOK THREE

USS Constitution **in battle with** *HMS Java*
December 29, 1812

THIRTY-SIX

War
January 13, 1812

On January 13, 1812, the brig was again struck by a heavy gale while passing through the channel between the Orkneys and the Shetland Islands. Bainbridge was delivering dispatches to the English as to the intensions on the part of American to be at war with them.

The waters were turbulent with large breakers on the port bow. The crew was applying reefing ties to reduce the face of the sails which was no easy task in the howling winds. The vessel was coming dangerously close of becoming sideways to the large breakers they were encountering.

The English captain who was in charge of the ship was calling out orders that would send the ship on to the rocks. Bainbridge was also at the helm and immediately countermanded the English Captains orders. Bainbridge could see the captain was close to causing the masts to submerge as they neared the rocks as the ship became out of control from the battering it was taking. Bainbridge was quick to access the situation and avoided the deadly reality of the ship being lost. The crew had previous experience with Bainbridge's averting disaster and the held on her course. If they had listened to the English Captain's orders the ship would have been lost.

The ship passed the rocks and the danger was averted and the turbulent waters subsided.

"Captain Bainbridge, thank you for saving us from a near disaster," the English Captain was appreciative of Bainbridge's quick thinking and a bit shaken from the realization of the near tragedy.

After landing in England, Captain Bainbridge made all haste to Liverpool, stopping only for a visit to the American minister in London, to whom he delivered the dispatches. On February 12, 1812 he arrived back in New York and proceeded at once to Washington, where he reported himself ready for active service.

Congress was just at that moment deliberating on the subject of declaring war against Great Britain. Bainbridge learned, to his great sorrow and chagrin, that in a Cabinet council it had been determined to lay up all the United States frigates and vessels of war. It was again those in Congress that were afraid to take naval action against England. They felt that further antagonism against England would only generate more attacks on American merchant ships. The Congress felt the few vessels the navy possessed would be lost to the larger English force. The Congress would rather lose the war without defending the United States rights. Some in the Congress were totally intimidated by the gigantic navy at the disposal of King George. They just wanted to tell the English navy it was not nice to capture American vessels.

While Captain Bainbridge was in the new nation's capital, Washington D.C. he ran into an old allied, Captain Charles Stewart. Stewart was one of the few Naval Captains he respected as a brave fighter. Most naval captains were experienced merchant captains but they did not have the military experience.

"Charles have you heard what the Congress is attempting to do? Nothing!" Bainbridge did still not believe what the Congress had done.

"William, you are absolutely correct this is a deplorable situation, we need address our concerns with Congress and the President.

"I am glad you feel the same way as I do, let us first express our remonstrating strongly against the measure to the Secretary of the Navy."

The two men drafted the following letter to the Secretary of the Navy.

"*The United States Navy is capable of defending it rights on the open seas*" *The United States Navy is equally ready with Naval officers every bit as qualified as their land counterparts are to defend our freedoms. The Navy has* war-ships that can be place in active service to meet the English in face to face battle. As officers in the United States Navy we beseech the Congress to the reconsideration of not allowing naval action against the English. The United States needs to preserve the right of freedom on the seas to preserve our counties ability and freedom to trade."

Charles and William also made a verbal plea to the President. The President had to agree and the ships the Congress wanted to place in mothballs were released for active duty.

Bainbridge was assured that he had succeeded by the Secretary of the Navy. "I owe you one William, but right now I need you back in Boston to protect the harbor against the British war-ships. Bainbridge was now ordered to command the Charlestown navy yard in Massachusetts on March 2, 1812.

Bainbridge hastened to assume his post but not until he had returned to Philadelphia to bring his family with him.

"Susan we are going to war again with the British. My orders are to go to Boston and take charge of the Charleston Naval Yard."

"When will the fighting stop?"

"I am not sure but I do know I want you and the children with me. The Navy will provide us housing in Boston," William was sounding concerned.

He found the Charleston yard in a bad condition, but he at once began to make extensive changes, and to prepare for building a large naval station.

While in the midst of these operations the expected news was brought to him of the declaration of war that had been passed on June 18, 1812, by the United States against Great Britain.

Congress was not sure that what little ability they possessed to do battle on the ocean that perhaps it was unwise to jeopardize the few frigates and sloops they had against the gigantic navy of Great Britain.

On July 28, 1812 Bainbridge applied to Secretary Paul Hamilton for the command of a frigate.

His request was granted, and, to his delight, Bainbridge found that he had been appointed to the command of a small squadron of three vessels, consisting of his own vessel the *Constitution*, the *Hornet* a sloop under the command of his old shipmate Captain James Lawrence, and the *Essex,* a frigate, under the command of Captain David Porter, who had suffered in Tripoli with him.

A land post was not the place for a man of Bainbridge's disposition and perhaps the Secretary was aware of that. The *Constitution* was in the Charlestown navy yard and needed to be fitted out. The *Constitution* was then the pride of the navy. She was a better sailor and a finer ship in every way than the *Constellation*. Bainbridge had learned that Isaac Hull intended to give the *Constitution* up.

"Susan, I have good news to tell you," William had just arrived back at his home from a meeting with the Secretary of the Navy.

"Calm down, I am right here."

Susan Hyleger and William had been married for fourteen years. They had three children, William B. age three; Mary Taylor, age one; and Susan Parker Bainbridge age nine.

"I just learned that I have been given command of the *Constitution* replacing Isaac Hull."

"Oh, that is wonderful my dear. When do you take command?" Susan always began to feel sad when William received new orders.

Captain William Bainbridge took command of America's favorite ship, the *Constitution*. Bainbridge had the embodiment of the ideal naval officer. He was more than six feet tall and he radiated an undeniable sense of authority. Bainbridge towered over most of the crew on the ship. Most of the men on the ship were less than five and one-half feet in height. The advantage of being tall made his presence as commander of the ship visually an asset as to authority. The disadvantage of being tall was that he had to duck down when going below deck because of the low ceiling heights. Captain Bainbridge was the youngest captain in the Navy; he was twenty-nine years old. He was a graduate of the Merchant Service. He also had all the personal qualifications and character that assisted in making him renowned.

The *Constitution* didn't return to Boston for three days. The *Constitution* had been on duty under the command of Isaac Hull. The *Constitution* brought news of the victory over the *HMS Guerrière on August 19, 1812. Guerrière* was taken as a prize.

The Department of the Navy commissioned Bainbridge to take over command of the frigate and cruise in the South Atlantic.

Bainbridge took the "*Constitution*" immediately after it arrived in port. Bainbridge was replacing Captain Isaac Hull on the 44-gun *Constitution* as Commodore Bainbridge.

Bainbridge was at the dock to meet with and congratulate his old friend. Captain Isaac Hull intended to remain on shore for a few months to attend to some private affairs. His timing for taking leave was not appreciated by the Secretary of the Navy but Hull certainly had earned the right. The news of Hull's sea victory over the British frigate made news that flew about the town quickly.

When the *Constitution* was built, there were three classes of ships that formed the bulk of the U.S. Navy, sloops, frigates, and line-of-battle-ships.

A frigate was always ship-rigged and carried guns on two decks. The main or gun-deck had a complete battery. The upper or spar-deck guns were only on the forward and after parts. The waists seldom mounted any guns.

The power of a frigate was correctly indicated by the number of guns, thirty-six, or forty-four gun ship. The invention of the carronade meant that ships exceeded the number of guns that they were rated at. With the addition guns being added to a ship the classification remained the same.

The size and shape of the hull precluded a heavy battery on the spar-deck in fear of making the ship top heavy and danger of capsizing.

Bainbridge had to overcome a bad reputation with the crew of the *Constitution*. The crew was aware that Captain Bainbridge had lost three ships in a row to pirates or warring navies. Captain Bainbridge inherited Captain's Isaac Hull's crew and there was grumbling amongst themselves about their new boss.

Before long the *Constellation* was almost ready to go to sea, and Bainbridge returned to Charleston to make arrangements for leaving his family before going a cruise.

The War of 1812 was fought mostly by merchant ships, because the U.S. had almost no Navy. The battle cry was; **"Free Trade and Sailors' Rights!"** During the War of 1812, the U.S. Navy and Privateers together captured 30,000 prisoners, while the American army captured 6,000 British prisoners. Privateers captured British prizes worth almost $40,000,000.

Comparison of Navy vs. Privateers during War of 1812"

	U.S. Navy	Privateers
Total ships:	23	517
Total guns on ships:	556	2,893
Enemy ships:	254	1,300

Captain Bainbridge and other captains felt that with the demand for high discipline in the United States navy, mixed with the eagerness of the officers and crews to engage the enemy, that the United States would invariably be triumphant at sea. The captains all agreed that they would certainly not ever disgrace themselves or the nation on purpose.

A rendezvous was appointed, and on the fifteenth day of September, 1812, Bainbridge flew his first blue pennant. Porter, who was then at anchor in the Delaware, was directed to set sail for the Cape Verde Islands, stop at Porto Playa, a bay in the island of Santiago, and from whence he was to proceed to the island of Fernando de Noronha. And if the *Essex* did not meet with the *Constitution* and *Hornet* at the last-named port, Porter was ordered to touch at the island of St. Catherine, and if unsuccessful, cruise to the southward, his only orders being to use judgment and to annoy the enemy's commerce.

The *USS Constitution: Launched October 21, 1797*

Mr. Humphreys design of the masts, yards, and rigging was in every way admirable. The extra beam given to all his ships afforded a better angle in staying the masts to resist rolling in a seaway, and the increased diameter of the several parts gave much greater stiffness in case the rigging was cut, or part of a mast itself was cut away by shot. The advantage here cannot be overestimated. Most of the engagements were fought with the ships rolling and a pressure of wind on the sails. Even a slight looseness of the shrouds was dangerous. It must be remembered that we are referring to the days of hemp rigging and of hemp cables for the anchors. Commodore Morris relates of the first ship in which he went to sea, the Congress, that she was dismasted in a gale. Her rigging had been fitted during the winter. She left New port in January, and in a few days ran into much warmer weather. The rigging slackened up and did not afford sufficient support to the mainmast, which fell overboard in a gale of wind. Without the rigging, ships masts one hundred years ago would probably have gone overboard in a heavy sea even though no sails were set. The masts were also in very great danger during an engagement, if the standing rigging was much cut. It is recommended with much advisability of making all the parts extra heavy. The Constitution was not exceptionally well built for an American frigate in this respect. Her sides tumbled home so much that the masts could not be stayed to the best advantage. Many complaints were made by her commanding officers of the weakness of the channels, probably that part of the side to which the lower end of the rigging was secured.

Notwithstanding the improvements made by Mr. Humphreys, the merits of the Constitution were not discovered until after she had destroyed two

British frigates. At the beginning of the century English officers had been disposed to treat our new ships contemptuously, criticizing their batteries as too heavy and their general design as too clumsy.

They had ample opportunity to examine the Constitution in the West Indies and the Mediterranean, and the general opinion seemed to be that she was too heavy for the rapid maneuvering demanded of a frigate. Some of the British news papers went even further, and referred in derision to all of Mr. Humphreys ships as "fir-built frigates." The real fact is, that the first success of the Constitution and her sister ships effected almost a revolution in the design and armament of foreign vessel. There has never been any doubt since 1812 of the superiority of these ships over everything of their class afloat during their first sixteen years. Mr. Humphreys planned them to excel in every respect and he lived to see his expectations fulfilled. In committing himself to long 24-pound guns for the main-deck batteries, he was really striking out in a new path. Only a few frigates had previously carried such heavy guns, and they were not looked upon as examples to be followed. An 18-pounder was regarded as the effective limit for good work able frigates. Perhaps this departure from the ordinary type did as much as anything else to bring our young navy into ridicule abroad.

The first battery placed on board the Constitution was bought in England, and bore the stamp G. R. It consisted of twenty-eight long 24-pounders on the gun deck and ten long 12-pounders on the quarter-deck. These were carried through the war of reprisal against France, and the main-deck battery was used against the English in 1812. In 1804 Commodore Preble obtained at Naples six 24-pounders, which he mounted on the spar-deck for use against the Tripolitans. The upper deck guns were afterwards exchanged for 42-pound carronades, but these were found too heavy for the hull, and Captain Hull replaced them with 32-round carronades. In the beginning of 1812 we find her, therefore, with a battery somewhat lighter than those of her sister ships, the President and the United States. She carried on the gun deck thirty long 24-pounders, on the quarter-deck sixteen 32-pound carronades, and on the forecastle six 32-pound carronades, one long 18-pounder, and two long 24-pounders as bow chasers. After Hull's victory two of the carronades were taken out, leaving her with fifty-three guns in all.

It was October 26, 1812 when the *Constitution* and *Hornet* sailed from Boston together. Fair weather was met with, and the two vessels reached Fernando de Noronha early in December. For some time they waited hoping that the *Essex* would join them. The island was a penal colony of

Portugal; it was not a pleasant anchorage, nor was their position exactly agreeable to Bainbridge, for he was compelled to sail under false colors, something distasteful to his nature. The Portuguese Government was then in league with Great Britain, and both the *Constitution* and the *Hornet* flew the English flag. Bainbridge was representing himself as Captain Kerr of his Majesty's ship *Acasta* of forty-four guns, and the *Hornet* pretended to be the *Morgiana* of twenty guns.

THIRTY-SEVEN

Food and Spirits
1812

B read and spirits appear with unfailing regularity, the one usually stale and the other always good. Sometimes in port the men got fresh provisions by commuting a certain number of rations to be paid in money. They were often able to lay in potatoes and onions for themselves. The crews of a ship were divided into messes with from eight to twelve men in each mess for the convenience of supplying them.

There was a ships cook for all and one boy for each mess. The ship's cook was usually a disabled seaman that had no culinary skills. The latter drew the provisions from the purser and took general care of the outfits. Their lot was not an enviable one under the best of conditions.

Although there was much sickness and many deaths at sea, it was possible, as Captain David Porter demonstrated in the *Essex* by strict regulation as to diet and cleanliness, to keep a crew in good health for long periods. A sailor required as much looking after as a child.

Cost $2.06 per week per man to feed them:

Beef	3 ½ pounds	29 cents
Bread	98 ounces	30 ½ cents
Butter	2 ounces	3 cents
Cheese	6 ounces	6 ½ cents
Flour	1 pound	4 cents
Molasses	½ pint	3 cents
Pea's	1 pint	34 ounces
Pork	3 pounds	28 ½ cents
Rice	1 pint	5 cents
Spirits	3 ½ pints	35 cents
Suet	½ pound,	6 ½ cents
Sugar	7 ounces	7 cents
Tea	4 ounces	12 cents
Vinegar	½ pint	2 cents

The only fire allowed on the vessel was in the galley on which food was prepared. Wood or coal was used as fuel. The Captain's cabin and sick bay were heated by hot shot partially buried in sand in an iron bucket.

Daily, the Purser would bring, in the evening, an allotted amount of meat for the next day. The meat would be placed in a steeping tub filled with fresh water to leach away the salt preservatives. Two petty officers would oversee the division of the meat into equal portions for each of the messes. The two petty officers would then take samples of the cooked meat to an officer for their approval before portioning it out to the crew.

The crew would eat in messes of eight. The captain had his own cook and servant. The warrant officers also had their own servants. Bainbridge was always sent off to sea with personal food items that Susan felt he needed.

THIRTY-EIGHT

Ships schedule
1812

The ship's schedule: (Each watch was marked by a series of bells at 30 minute intervals; one bell ='s the beginning of the watch and 8-bells was the end of the watch.)

Midnight to Four A.M.; **Middle Watch**:
> **Idlers:**   Sleep (actually midnight to 5 a.m.)
> **Larboard Watch:** 12-4 a.m. on watch or working
> **Starboard Watch:** 12-4 a.m. Sleep

Four a.m. to Eight a.m.; **Morning Watch:**
> **Idlers:**   Sleep to 5.a.m.; on watch 5-7:30; eat.
> **Larboard Watch:** 4-7:30 a.m. Sleep; on watch 30 minutes
> **Starboard Watch:** 4-7:30 a.m. On watch; 30 min. breakfast

Eight a.m. to Noon; **Forenoon Watch**:
> **Idlers:**   On watch or working
> **Larboard Watch:** 8-8:30 eat; Sleep; on watch or working
> **Starboard Watch:** 8-noon Drill or Exercise

Noon to Four a.m.; **Afternoon Watch:**
> **Idlers:**   Noon – 1 p.m. eat; 1-4 On Watch
> **Larboard Watch:** Noon-1 p.m. eat; 1-4 Leisure

Starboard Watch: Noon –1 p.m. eat; on watch or working
Four p.m. to Eight p.m.; **Two Dog Watch**:
   Idlers: 4-4:30 eat; 4:30-6, watch; 6-8 leisure
   Larboard Watch: 4-4:30 eat; 4:30-6, watch; 6-8 leisure
   Starboard Watch: 4-4:30 eat; 4:30-6, leisure; 6-9 watch
Eight p.m. to midnight, **First Watch:**
   Idlers: 8-9, watch; 9-5 a.m. sleep
   Larboard Watch: 8-midnight, on watch
   Starboard Watch: 8-9:00 p.m.; 9-midnight, sleep

Punishment on board a ship, 1812

There was a great difference between the American and British navies in the treatment of men on board their vessels.

"We had no imprisonment for petty offenses, and our system of punishments was more humane. Flogging was limited to a dozen lashes with plain cat-o -nine-tails," Bainbridge was instructing his officers in one of their daily classes.

"I also have a statement from Lord Dundonald regarding the British Navy," He said, "No man acquainted with the facts can wonder that interminable cruises, prohibition to land in port, constant confinement without salutary change of food and consequent disease endangering total disability, should have excited disgust and often terror of a sailor's life."

The sailors grumbled from time to time but, nevertheless, the lot of a sailor was hard. Bainbridge appreciated the sailor's life and he did all he could to have the sailors become better educated. He felt that education was not only about their job but about their personal maintenance.

The sailor was perceived as everybody's slave at sea and beneath notice on shore, as he really was too often a drunkard and a near-do-well. Every generation has its victims, men whose lives go to the service of others. In spite of all the drawbacks of service in the Old Navy, many men acquired a genuine love for the seafaring life and grew attached to their ships. There was enough change and adventure to satisfy the cravings of most sailors, especially in the large demands made upon the early sailing vessels of the nineteenth century. The sailors spirit and sense of humor are exhibited in the nicknames given to their guns, ships, and, sometimes, to their officers.

Bainbridge was a sea captain that sailors respected and served under to the best of their abilities.

THIRTY-NINE

Constitution, 1812

Captain Bainbridge was issued the following orders by the Secretary of the Navy, Paul Hamilton:

Regulations respecting the form and mode of keeping the Log-book and Journals on board of ships, or other vessels, of the United States.

For the purpose of establishing uniformity, James Madison, President of the United States ordered the following:

1. The quarter-bill, log-tables or book, and journals of the officers, must be kept conformably to the annexed models.

2. The captains or commanders will cause to be laid before them, the first and fifteenth of every month, the journals of the sea lieutenants, masters, midshipmen, and volunteers under their orders, and will examine and compare them with their own.

3. If any of the said journals contain observations or remarks which may contribute to the improvement of geography, by ascertaining the latitude and longitude, fixing or rectifying the position of places, the heights and views of land, charts, plans or descriptions of any port, anchorage ground, coasts, islands, or danger little known; remarks relative to the direction and effects of currents, tides or winds: the officers or persons appointed

to examine them, will make extracts of whatever appears to merit to be preserved; and after these extracts have been communicated to the officer or author of the journal from which they have been drawn, and that he has certified in writing to the fidelity of his journal, as well as of the charts, plans and views which he has joined to it, the same shall be signed by the officers and examiners, and transmitted with their opinion thereon to the secretary of the navy, to be preserved in the depot of charts, plans, and journals.

The *USS Constitution,* details:

The *USS Constitution* had a capacity to carry 48,600 gallons of fresh water. If there were 468 crew on board that would be 103 gallons of water per man. If the average usage was one half gallon per man they would have a 206 day's supply of water. The water was carried in wooden casks and stowed in the hold. This was actually not enough water per man but it was all they could carry.

Stopping in ports where water could be obtained was important. The men should have had at least three quarts per day. They would collect rainwater but there was always a risk of dysentery from drinking impure rainwater that had not been boiled.

The *USS Constitution* carried 7,400 cannon shot and 11,600 pounds of black power.

The most important cargo was the 79,400 gallons of rum on board, 59 gallons per day; one pint at lunch and one pint at dinner. (Grog) Each of the crew was given one gallon of beer per man per day. Bainbridge had his own stores of wine for entertaining. Bainbridge was not in favor of the drinking allotments but it was a custom the crew was not about to give up easily.

The *USS Constitution* on starting out on her last cruises had an extraordinary number of able seamen aboard, 218, with but 92 ordinary seamen, 12 boys, and 44 marines, making, with the officers, a total of 440 men.

The *Constitution,* 1,533 ton, 44-gun frigate, was ordered on March 1, 1794 and the builder was Edmund Hartt of the Edmund Hartt's Shipyard. Construction on the *Constitution* commenced on November 1, 1794 and launched and christened on October 21, 1797. This was considered a fairly good turnaround time for building a frigate of this size. The frigate was outfitted and a crew assembled over the next few months to get ready for the vessels maiden voyage on July 22, 1798.

The *Constitution* fell into the upper middle spectrum of wooden warships in size. Today, the *Constitution* would be the equivalent of a large modern cruiser, armed with heavy ordnance.

The cost of the ship was $302,718 (in 1797 dollars). Her annual expenses when in commission were estimated at $100,000. Her payroll was in the neighborhood 0f $5,000 per month. (In 1812 the value of the money to the modern equivalent could estimate by multiplying 1812 money by eighty. $5,000 then would be at least $400,000 today.)

The homeport was Charlestown Navy Yard. The nickname of the 44-gun frigate was "*Old Ironsides*." The frigate had displacement of 2,200 tons. The ship measured 204 feet (62m) in length, the beam was 43 feet six inches (13.3m); the foremast was 198 feet, and a draft of 21 feet (6.4 m) forward and 13 feet (4.0m) aft. The hold was 14 feet three inches (4.3m).

The British were opinionated about the design and construction of the *USS Constitution*. The British officers treated the new design contemptuously, criticizing their batteries as too heavy and the general design of the ship as too clumsy. The general opinion seemed to be that she was too heavy for the rapid maneuvering demanded of a frigate.

As it turned out the design of the *Constitution*, that Mr. Humphreys was responsible for designing, was excellent in every respect. The British found out the hard way by the loss of a number of their 'superior' vessels to the *Constitution*.

The British government passed an act to cut down some of their line-of-battle-ships in order to overmatch the *President* and the *Constitution* with ships of their own rating. The unusual hardness and weight of the timber and the planking of the *Constitution* gave her the name of *Old Ironsides*.

The morning watch on the *Constitution* commenced at four a.m. with the start of the sand-glass. It was the Starboard watch that was on duty from four a.m. to 7:30 a.m. The men would then have breakfast from 7:30 a.m. to eight a.m.

The Idlers were sleeping until 5 a.m. and the Larboard watch was scheduled to sleep from 4-7:30 a.m. The watches were alternating so the crew had more space to sleep in and better ventilation.

Traverse board recorded the course of the ship during a four hour watch. The traverse board consisted of a piece of wood marked out with a compass rose and eight holes bored along each point. Every half-hour (by sand-glass time) a peg was inserted into a hole marking the compass point on which the ship had run. At the end of the watch, the mean course during the watch was determined from the position of the eight pegs.

FORTY

Constitution, Routine
July 7, 1812

It was 7:55 a.m. when midshipmen James Biddle called "First Call, First Call to Colors." They were still at dock but they were preparing to sail later in the morning.

At eight a.m. the morning colors were raised. The word was passed and all those on duty stopped whatever they were doing and stood quietly while the colors were raised. The Union Jack at the jack staff and White Ensign at the ensign staff. The bugler, Frederick Baury, then played indicating it was time to "carry on" and resumed their work.

"Captain, your flag has been raised." Lieutenant Beekman saluted. "If you don't mind, what is that flag?"

"That, Mr. Beekman, is a special flag presented to the commander-in-chief of the Navy by Christopher Gadsden in 1775. I personally like the flag since it is a reminder that we had a great need to unite in defense to protect our God-given and inherited rights. I am proud of our country and of the crew who is willing to defend it."

"Very good, sir."

Captain Bainbridge's wife, Susan along with their three children,

William, Mary; and Susan all came down to the dock to wave and throw kisses at their father who was standing proudly on the quarter deck.

"God bless you and may he keep you safe," Susan was saying rather loudly.

William was not hearing her but he knew what she was saying and shouted back, "Thank you."

The *Constitution* departed Boston at 9:30 a.m. with Captain Bainbridge at the wheel of the magnificent vessel. The frigate's three masts supported 42,710 feet of sails made out of cotton and hemp. The ship had been known to have been propelled through the water at 13 knots, a feat not many ships of war could boast about.

The crew was not entirely happy about Bainbridge taking over as their Captain. It was well known that Captain Bainbridge in his past engagements been captured and certainly he did not come home with many 'prizes.' This was not just about bad feelings; the crew wanted a captain who had a reputation for taking prizes. The taking prizes, enemy vessels, at sea were important in augmenting their meager wages.

USS Constitution's spar deck, her open "weather deck," was usually the busiest part of the ship. On a portion of it astern was called the quarterdeck, where the officer of the deck and the helmsman stood their watches.

From here Captain Bainbridge directed his commands. The spar deck was also the frigate's "engine room." Above the spa deck raised the massive network of masts and rigging which propelled *Constitution* through the water. This was often a hive of activity as the hands double-timed to their stations to make or to take in sail or to man the web of lines that adjusted the spars to take advantage of the wind.

The *Constitution* was always ship-rigged and carried guns on two decks, the main or gun-deck having a complete battery, and the upper or spar-deck having guns only on the forward and after parts.

The *USS Hornet* a war-brig was accompanying the *Constitution,* in accordance to orders. The *USS Hornet* was a 20-gun, 441 ton brig-sloop under the command of Captain James Lawrence.

Captain Bainbridge's orders were, "annoy the enemy and to afford protection to our commerce, pursuing that course, which to your best judgment may…appear to be best."

Bainbridge had plotted a course to follow the broad wind patterns of the Atlantic, sweeping across to the Cape Verde Islands, then southwest below the Equator to the sea lanes of Brazil, where the British had considerable trade.

Bainbridge had ordered the 'working sails' be set; the 'working sails' could be changed rapidly in variable conditions. They were much stronger than the light sails but still considered lightweight. He made sure they had several sets of reefing ties so the area of the sail could be reduced in a stronger wind.

Bainbridge was a master of balancing the force of the sails against the drag of the underwater keel in such a way that the vessel would avoid broaching (turning edge-to-the-wind) and being beaten by breaking waves. Bainbridge was always alert to having the correct sail-plan. If the sails were not correct the wind could knock the vessel sideways and submerge the masts in the water; causing the vessel to capsize and possibly sinking. Bainbridge was well aware that in any give year over two thousand vessels were lost at sea.

The topmen were scurrying around on the rigging like ants. They did not have to attending to the 'standing rigging' since it was fixed in place supporting the masts. They were dealing with the 'running rigging' that applies to the adjustment of the sails.

As soon as the *Constitution* was out of site of land, the colors were ordered lower. The bugler, Frederick Baury, sounded the call for the occasion while the crew looked on.

Captain Bainbridge had charted the course to San Salvador. His main concern the weather especially late season tropical storms.

Course: Boston to San Salvador: (Bainbridge generally assumed that the latitude stated was more accurate than the longitude.)

PORT: Latitude Longitude   Distance Ideal   Actual

PORT	Latitude Longitude	Distance Ideal	Actual
Boston	42 17.377 N 070 45.116 W	0	
Bermuda	32 23.193 N 064 56.795 W	897 nm*39 hrs	8 days
Antigua 12 days	17 09899 N 061 57.772 W	1,138 nm	114 hrs
Waypoint 14 days	13 14.394 N 058 11.014 W	1,450 nm	145 hrs

San Salvador 13 27.304 S 038 24.491 W   1,182 nm   118 hrs
11 days
    (outside the harbour off shore)
          4,601 nm   47 days*
    •   Assuming 10 knots per hour.
    •   San Salvador is currently called Bahia, Brazil
    •   October 27 – December 13, 1812
Optical system sextant: 1 minute equals 1 nm. Each 15 degrees of longitude equals one hour of time.

Bainbridge's first stop was Bermuda at St. George's Harbour. The harbour was a difficult harbour to navigate because of the reefs that were shallow on both sides of the channel into the harbour.

November was still considered hurricane season but seldom were ships confronted with a hurricane this late in the hurricane season. When leaving Bermuda the winds generally were out of the north blowing in a westerly direction. Bainbridge was keeping the wind on his starboard quarter.

Bainbridge's navigation skills were among the best in the young American navy. He was a good teacher and demonstrated that by his making sure his lieutenants were more than proficient in the use of the sextant. The lieutenants were than responsible for making sure the midshipman's were capable of teaching the able seaman.

Navigation was taught to all hands on board. Boys were taught, with words and diagrams, the nature of sine, cosine, tangent, cotangent, secant, and cosecant, the relation between them, and their value in helping to find your position in a prodigious ocean, with no shore, and no landmarks for thousands of miles. The Robinson's Elements of Navigation along with Requisite Tables and Nautical Almanac were a part of every sailor's sea chest.

The sextant worked by holding and pointing the instrument vertically towards the celestial body. You would than sight the horizon through an unsilvered portion of the horizon mirror. You than had to adjust the index arm until the image of the sun or star, which has been reflected first by the index mirror and second by the silvered portion of the horizon mirror, appears to rest on the horizon. The altitude of the heavenly body can be read from the scale on the arc of the instrument's frame.

The finding of latitude was reasonably accurate but determining longitude was a work in progress. The astronomers had developed a method for predicting the angular distant between the moon and the sun, the planets or selected stars. Using this technique, the navigator at sea could measure the angle between the moon and a celestial body, calculate the time at which the moon and the celestial body would be precisely at that angular distant and then compare the ship's chronometer to the time back at the national observatory. Knowing the correct time was the key to the navigator knowing longitude.

The winds on the voyage were variable winds between latitudes 25o and 35o. The sailors referred to this area as "Horse Latitudes" since the vessels could be becalmed for weeks and the crew would resort to eating the livestock.

Bainbridge taught his lieutenants the three factors that influenced the formation and direction of the wind:

1. Atmosphere pressure
   (A falling barometer would indicate a depression that could last for days)
2. Air temperature
3. Rotation of the earth

It was impossible to obtain a supply of fresh water in Bermuda, and so Bainbridge determined to sail away, leaving a letter addressed to "Sir James Yeo," which was the name agreed upon that Porter would take if he stopped at the island. Bainbridge bade farewell to the Governor and made off for San Salvador.

Commandant David Porter did receive the missive left for him. He was to sail the *Essex* for San Salvador and join up with the *Constitution* and the *Hornet, 20-guns*. He failed to catch up with them he was to go to San Salvador and wait for their return.

FORTY-ONE

Captured Brig
November 9, 1812

On November 9, 1812 Bainbridge captured the brig *South Carolina*. The crew spirits were lifted with delight at the prospect they were going to be paid additional compensation.

Bainbridge was hoping to continue to the south to be able to prey on the British trade coming around the southern tip of Africa from India before these forces could catch him.

On December 12th the *HMS Java* captured the American ship *William*. The *William* was an American merchant vessel on a trade mission. The British were feeling cocky and perhaps attempted to impress their distinguish guests on board that they were delivering to the West Indies. They took the *Williams* without a fight. The captain of the merchant vessel struck her colors and they were boarded. The *HMS Java* sufficiently staffed the captive vessel with a mate and nineteen men from the *Java* personal.

The *USS Constitution* and the *USS Hornet* arrived off San Salvador, Brazil (Bahia, today) on December 13, 1812. Bainbridge was protective of the *Constitution* and he did not reveal his full strength to the pro-British

Portuguese who then ruled Brazil. The *USS Hornet* had managed to keep up with the *Constitution*.

Bainbridge was the Captain in charge and ordered Lawrence to report to the British Consul to discover what the current military and political situation was in the area.

To visit the British Consul, Master Commandant James Lawrence had to enter the San Salvador harbor with the *USS Hornet*. The *Constitution* would remain anchored at the entrance to the harbour to protect the slight chance of the *Hornet* being trapped. His instructions were to ascertain through the British consul the disposition of the Government of Brazil toward the United States.

Lawrence was to find out if there were any British cruisers on the coast.

The *USS Hornet* was brought to anchor. Lawrence had not visited the San Salvador harbour before. He was cautious about being in places not familiar to him particularly when the guns pointed at the ships in the harbour were not friendly. He was using his glass to survey not only the harbour but the small islands nearby. He saw off in the distant under the lee of a small island in the inner harbor a fine, loftily sparred sloop of war. The vessel was a few more tons burden than his own, but not large enough to frighten him.

Master Commandant James Lawrence disembarked the *Hornet*, as per Bainbridge's orders, and went to the British Consul.

Lawrence introduced himself and provided the British consul with his orders.

"It is my pleasure to meet you Master Commandant we are not visited by Americans very often. My name is Fredrick Hill, how can I be of service to you?"

Lawrence got the business out of the way regarding the Government of Brazil's attitude towards the United States. He also inquired about any British ships in the area.

"May I ask what other vessel that is in the harbour?"

"Certainly, that is his Majesty's corvette *Bonne Citoyenne*, the "Good Citizens," Mr. Hill informed him confidentially.

"What are they doing here? They are English, are they not?"

"You are correct and I understand that the English ship is laden with specie to be taken back to England."

"How long have they been here?" Lawrence was now thinking what a prize she could be.

"As far as I have been told they have been ready to sail for two or three days," Mr. Hill was happy to part with the information.

"Thank you Mr. Hill for the information, I will give Captain Bainbridge your best wishes and the information we have discussed."

Master Commandant James Lawrence wasted no time sailing back out of the harbor and bringing the *Hornet* to anchor near the *Constitution*. Lawrence had his shore boat lowered so he could visit Bainbridge in person. Lawrence wanted the opportunity to speak to Bainbridge about large 'prize.'

"Captain Bainbridge, I believe we have stumbled on to a possible prize," Lawrence hadn't so excited in a long time.

"Well, tell me before you bust."

"The British consul, Mr. Hill, told me in confidence the English war-sloop, *Bonne Citoyenne*, 18-guns, was in Bahia and I saw her. The best part is the *Bonne Citoyenne* is carrying a reported $1.6 million in specie."

"That is intriguing Mr. Lawrence. I was going to leave but if what you say is true we will linger here and see if she leaves the safety of the harbour."

Bainbridge was hoping for ten days as he lingered off the coast that the Britishers might attempt to make a break out. The prize was in an amount a ship's captain always dreams of taking. (That would be about 128 million today.)

Lawrence made another trip to see the American consul, Fredrick Hill. Bainbridge had encouraged Lawrence in seeing if an action between the *Hornet* and the *Bonne Citoyenne* could be arranged by Mr. Hill. Bainbridge also instructed him to tell Mr. Hill that he was taking the *Constitution* out further in the sea to find enemy vessels.

Mr. Hill was not over joy by the request to confront the Captain of the *Bonne Citoyenne*. Lawrence had written out the challenge he wished Mr. Hill to deliver.

"Captain Greene, my name if Hill, I am the British Consul stationed here in Bahia."

"What can I do for you Mr. Hill?"

"I have been requested by Master Commandant James Lawrence of the *USS Hornet* to issue you this challenge to fight him on one-to-one bases."

"That other ship will not interfere in our fight?" Captain Pitt Barney Greene inquired. Greene was not about to enter into a fight and jeopardize loosing the money he was carrying in anyway shape or form.

"Tell Captain Lawrence that I am not interested in his offer to fight me. I would foolish to think that other American ship would not come to the aid of Captain Lawrence."

Hill delivered a message to Lawrence that the Captain of the *Bonne Citoyenne*, Captain Pitt Barney Greene, was not interested entering an action where two ships might attack him.

Lawrence again went to anchor near the *Constitution* so he could discuss the matter with Bainbridge.

The two men talked and weight their chances of getting the English captain to leave his safe harbour.

Bainbridge finally ordered Master Commandant James Lawrence to return to the British consul and advise him that Captain Bainbridge was holding five English officers prisoners. He felt that Captain Greene might give consideration to taking his countrymen back by force.

Lawrence immediately sent the following communication to Consul Hill:

"When last I saw you I stated my wishes to meet the *Bonne Citoyenne*, and authorized you to make it known to Captain Greene. Captain Bainbridge also wants Captain Greene to be aware that he has five English officers as prisoners on his ship. He would be willing to release them to Captain Greene if he would leave the safety of the harbour and engage me. I now request you to state to him, and pledge my honor, that neither the *Constitution* nor any other American vessel will interfere with our fight."

The British consul Hill without delay transmitted the communication he had received from Master Commandant James Lawrence to Captain Greene. The English officer, Captain Greene, proved to be a very prudent man for he replied that while he did not doubt that he would be successful should a combat take place between his own vessel and the *USS Hornet*, he really doubted that Commodore Bainbridge would abstain from taking a hand, for the reason that the "Paramount duty which he (Bainbridge) owes to his country would prevent him from becoming an inactive spectator and seeing a ship belonging to the very squadron under his orders fall into the hands of the enemy."

When the British consul had read Captain Greene's reason for not wishing to meet the *USS Hornet*, he wrote immediately to his British friend, stating that Bainbridge had given assurance that he would confirm Captain Lawrence's statement, making use of the following words: "If Captain Greene wishes to try equal force, I pledge my honor to give him an opportunity by being out of the way or not interfering. I will also release the five English officers from the *Carolina* to him as my means of showing good faith."

Greene was giving consideration with this favorable opportunity to engage in battle with this inferior American Captain Lawrence. Like most English Captains he felt he was superior in every way to the Americans. He was sure that he would prevail in this meeting of an equal force and under equal circumstances. Captain Greene also was a prudent man and considerations had to given to the safe guard of the money he was trusted with.

"Dear Mr. Hill, please inform Captain Lawrence that I decline the opportunity to engage him combat and I regret not being able to bargain for the release of the five English officers."

Lawrence reported back to the *Constitution* on the 18th that Captain Greene was not going to take the bait. He was disappointed that the English were going to continue to use the safety of the harbour to avoid any confrontation.

Nevertheless, Greene was being forced to keep his ship in the harbor, and Lawrence attentively blockaded him with the *USS Hornet*. The Governor of Bahia, Count d'Arcos, had displayed a very unfriendly attitude toward the United States, and objected to the *Hornet's* anchoring in the harbor. Bainbridge, hearing of this impingement of his honor, as soon as he returned wrote a strong letter of remonstrance to the count.

The *USS Constitution* parted company with the *USS Hornet* off St. Salvador on December 23, 1812. The *Constitution* had continued to hang out near the Bahia harbour entrance but out of sight, hoping the Britishers would be foolish enough to break out.

Bainbridge then again set out alone with the *Constitution* after sending the following order to the waiting Lawrence: "I shall keep off the land to the northward of latitude 12' 20", when you will meet me there, except you have great reason to believe the *Bonne Citoyenne* is coming out. In that case watch close and join me on Saturday next. May glory and success attend you?"

WB

Commodore William Bainbridge wrote in his Journal on December 23, 1812:

"I had a singular dream in which I foresaw the Constitution going into battle with a frigate of similar tonnage. I was seeing a fierce battle and severe action with an English frigate, in which we ultimately triumphed; and

among the prisoners were several army officers, one of whom had the rank of General."

"John I have to confide in you about a dream I had last night," Bainbridge was still living the event.

"Do tell me, dreams are revealing sometimes."

"My dream was our going into a fierce battle lasting many hours with death everywhere. The only bright part of the dream was we won the battle."

"Perhaps it is a premonition of things to come William, it is not uncommon," said John.

On the morning of December 25th the ship was a scurry of activity. The day had started out in bright sun light and balmy breezes. It was Christmas day and the men were preparing to celebrate.

Captain Bainbridge held a short religious service following the call to colors. Bainbridge was accustomed to reading passages from the Bible and conducting funeral services for the crew. Today was a joyful day and Bainbridge wanted to make sure the men had the day to remember.

The men were setting up tables on the upper decks so they could all celebrate a Christmas dinner together. The crew all pitched in assisting with the food preparation, clearing the decks so table could be erected, and then finally all of them were required to bath and put on their dress uniforms.

Dinner was at one o'clock. Extra rations of grog and beer were made available. The tables for the officers were on the quarter deck and Bainbridge treated the officers from his own private food stash. Best of all Bainbridge supplied the officers with wine, not that the officers did not have their own wine, but this was good French wine.

Some of the talented crew played their string instruments while others sang Christmas carols.

Dinner was a three hour event with much laughter and good cheer.

After the feast was over the men cleaned up the decks to make room for dancing and acrobatic demonstrations for the amusement of others.

Many of the men were passed out long before the party ended. Some of the crew took pity on those who drank far too much and moved them to areas on the deck where they could throw up and not bother others.

Bainbridge was toasted and praised and he also toasted the men and returned the praise.

FORTY-TWO

Prelude to battle
9 a.m., December 26, 1812

"Lieutenant, I do have other news that the *Montague*, 74-guns, and two lesser vessels of the Royal Navy were in Rio de Janeriro or further south," Bainbridge was trying rekindle the hope that a prize was waiting for them in the near future.

Bainbridge began their cruise down the coast of Brazil keeping the land aboard. They were about sixty hours out from leaving the Island of San Salvador.

Captain Bainbridge wrote in his journal: "On my leaving the coast of Brazil, I left Captain Lawrence to watch her, and have no doubt, should he fall in with her, that the result will be honourable to his country and to himself.

WB

It was the morning of December 26, 1812, on a beautiful clear winter day with a moderate breeze from E.N.E.; Bainbridge found the chance that he had so long been waiting for. They were at latitude 13, 6, S. longitude 31, W. The *Constitution* was ten leagues from the coast of Brazil.

"Hoist our ensign and pendant," Lieutenant Ludlow bellowed out.

Able Seaman James Renshaw was on look out from the capabarre (the topmost summit, the ultimate pinnacle of a mast.) spotted the masts of a ship in the distance.

"Ship ho!" Renshaw was hollering with all the voice he could muster. "Ship ho off of larboard bow."

The morning was blessed with a fine sailing breeze blowing, and the shore of Brazil bore about ten leagues off on the port hand when two sails were sighted on the weather bow.

They were very distant, and it took over an hour's sailing to determine their character. Then Lieutenant Aylwin reported to the cabin that the strangers were evidently large ships, and as the *USS Constitution* approached they parted company; one stood on to meet her, and the other made in to the safety of the harbor.

Lieutenant Parker, of the *Constitution,* at first thought that the approaching vessel might be the *USS Essex* under the command of David Porter, but Bainbridge, after a careful look through the glass declared her to be British, and at eleven o'clock he tacked to the southward and eastward, hauling up his mainsail and taking in his royals in order to give the stranger an opportunity to draw near. In half an hour he made the private signal for the day, and perceiving that it was not answered, he immediately set his mainsails and royals again, and made preparations to get out his studding sails. Observing one of the officers cast a curious look up aloft; Bainbridge turned and spoke to him laughingly: "They do not realize our speed, we will catch them."

FORTY-THREE

Constitution/Java
December 29, 1812

The chiefs who our freedom sustained on the land,
Fame's far-spreading voice has eternized in story;
By the roar of our cannon now called to the strand,
She beholds on the ocean their rivals in glory.
Her sons there she owns,
And her clarion's bold tones
Tell of Hull and Decatur, of Bainbridge and Jones;
For the tars of Columbia are lords of the wave,
And have sworn that old Ocean's their throne or their grave."

"Come, lads, draw near, and you shall hear,
In truth as chaste as Dian, O!
How Bainbridge true, and his bold crew,
Again have tamed the lion, O!
'Twas off Brazil he got the pill
Which made him cry *peccavi*, O
But hours two, the *Java* new,

Maintained the battle bravely, O!

Officers of the USS Constitution in action with the HMS Java, 29 December 1812

From the Journal of Captain Bainbridge:

"Tuesday, December 29, 1812, at nine, a. m., discovered two strange sails on the weather bow. At ten, discovered the strange sails to be ships; one of them stood in for the land the other stood off shore, in a direction towards us. At forty-five minutes past ten a.m., we tacked ship to the northward and westward, and stood for the sail standing towards us. At eleven a.m., tacked to the southward and eastward, hauled up the mainsail, and took in the royals. At thirty minutes past eleven, made the private signal for the day, which was not answered, and then set the mainsail and royals, to draw the strange sail off from the neutral coast, and separate her from the sail in company."

WB

The Forenoon watch came on at eight a.m. The Starboard watch was on duty while the Larboard watch attended breakfast and then they were off to bed. The Idlers were also working.

The bugle called, and "First Call" was sounded and the colors were raised.

Captain Bainbridge also conducted a brief religious service for those on the upper deck at eight a.m. Bainbridge felt it was important to read passages from the Bible to the men at the start of the forenoon watch. He particularly liked the passages from Matthew. Most of the men had no other exposure to religion.

The *USS Constitution* was about ten leagues (thirty miles) southeasterly off Bahia or known as San Salvador (Coast of Brazil).

The wind was out of the northwest. The vessel they had spotted was the *HMS Java* a Pallas-class frigate of 1,083 long tons and a crew of 277 officers, seamen, marines, and 23 boys. They also had 97 passengers for a total of 397 personal on board before giving up twenty men to the *William*. When the *Java* sailed towards the *Constitution* the total number was reduced to 377.

The *Java* was a recent prize of the British. The British had captured the *Renomuree* a year earlier from the French and renamed the frigate the *HMS Java*. The vessel carried twenty-eight 18-pounders, two 12-pounders, eighteen 32-pounder carronades and one 24-pounder carronade.

"Captain, there are now, see the two strange sails appearing off the weather bow," Lieutenant John Aylwin confirmed.

"Look closely Lieutenant, they are coming towards us," Bainbridge exclaimed.

"They were apparently off the Brazil-coast; there is a smaller vessel behind them."

The *Java's* Captain was named Lambert. The smaller ship they had behind them was the *USS William,* a recent prize of the *Java.* Captain Lambert had ordered the *William* to go to St. Salvador ahead of the *Java.* Captain Lambert had seen the *USS Constitution* and he was already thinking of how he could spend the money from such a great prize.

Captain Lambert had ordered the ship's crew to catch up to the *Constitution.* He also had alerted the men to report to their battle stations.

"This won't take long gentlemen and in fact, turning to his guests on board, you all may rather enjoy the show," Captain Lambert was very sure of his aptitude.

Captain Lambert was not 100% sure the vessel they were about to encounter was the *Constitution* but at least a vessel similar to *Old Ironsides*. He was familiar with the American vessel and like others in the British navy they thought the vessel to be inferior in design to the English ships of war.

Captain Lambert turned to his guests on the quarter-deck and said, "Gentlemen, never before in the history of the world did an English frigate strike to an American."

The *HMS Java* was sailing S.S.W. at 13 6' South Latitude and 38 West Longitude towards the *Constitution*. It was not until later did Captain Bainbridge discover the name of the vessel was the *HMS Java*. The vessel was British and they had sailed from England on November 12th 1812.

"What do you make of the ship that appears to be approaching us, John?" William Bainbridge was hoping the ship might turn out to be British, he also wanted a prize.

"Well they certainly aren't bashful about making it clear that they have an interest in us," replied John Ridgely the ship's surgeon.

John Ridgely had come on to the deck to have his morning chat with the captain before attending to his duties.

"Well William, as your ships 'Crocus' (surgeon) I need to attend to sick call. I am never in want of customers, I will report back to you later when I am done administering to the best of my abilities to their ailments."

"I'll be here monitoring our-would be visitor," Bainbridge responded.

FORTY-FOUR

Pre-Battle *Constitution*
9:15 a.m. December 29, 1812

The two ships were windward (northwest) of the *Constitution*. It was a pleasant warm day; the seas were nearly flat, with a light breeze from the northwest.

Captain Bainbridge had a fleeting thought of how nice it would be to live in this climate rather than in the miserable Philadelphia weather.

"Captain, the vessel appears to be a large frigate and they have made all their sails to gain on us," Aylwin reported.

Bainbridge did not know it but for once he was going to be lucky. The *Java* carried a very raw crew, which included only a few real seamen, with cocky officers to direct them. The ship's captain had only seen fit to have one day's gunnery drill since leaving port a month earlier.

Captain Bainbridge had paid a great deal of attention to honing gunnery skills in his own crew. He had learned the importance of having a seasoned gun crew from his mentor, Commodore John Barry. Barry had trained most of the officers currently available in the current conflict with the British.

John Barry had died a few years prior at a relatively young age of 58 in 1803 from complications of Asthma. John Barry was considered as the Father of the American Navy.

The ship's surgeon, John Ridgely, was on the forecastle deck when sick call was piped at nine a.m. The men seeking remedies for their ailments were also assembled to wait their turn to see the doctor.

The binnacle list excusing men from duty by the surgeon, or for other causes, was posted each morning near the helm. The log of the *Constitutions* during the month showed a daily sick list varying from eighteen to twenty-seven men out of a crew of four hundred and sixty-eight.

Some of the men would have rather had been in their Hammock then waiting to see the ship's surgeon since it was their time to sleep.

Nineteen members of the crew were assembled on the forecastle deck to await the ship's Surgeon to appear. John also had two surgeon mates, Jonathan Cowdery and Nicholas Hanwood to assist him with his normally busy daily schedule.

Those reporting to sick call usually had rheumatism, consumption, syphilis, debility, and scurvy. Scurvy was fairly common and was characterized by excessive bleeding, especially from the mouth. The crew lacked vitamin "C" in their diet.

In larger ships, the 'orlop' deck was usually the lowest deck. The 'cockpit', surgeon's room, on the orlop deck was located between the main and the mizzenmasts. The room was thirteen by eight feet with the overhead space being four foot ten inches. Situated below the waterline, it was very dark and cramped. During battles it was often transformed into an area for surgery and medical treatment.

Surgery usually involved a sailor having his leg amputated because a large piece of wood was embedded in it. Large splinters were a common injury. The enemy cannon balls when they hit the ship's wooden structures would spray wooden splinters out like a shotgun blast. Anesthetics were not yet in use so sailors had only alcohol for pain relief and a piece of leather to bite on when the pain was at its height. A tub beside the ship's surgeon table might be filled with limbs during a gun battle.

The surgeon would treat the sailors in the order they arrived rather than by their injuries, and not prioritized according to the severity of their injuries. Infections and blood poisoning spread easily as the same equipment and sponges were used on everyone without being washed after each patient was treated.

John Ridgely was a conscience medical officer. He had selected two Surgeon mates, Jonathan Cowdery and Nicholas Hanwood to assist him because of their experience. Ridgely had confided in Bainbridge that he needed two older seamen who had experience with medical problems and could carry some of the load. He also was concerned that his assistances were clean and would be dependable in keeping the cockpit scrupulously clean, well fumigated and sprinkled with vinegar.

Some of the crew referred to the Surgeon's mates as "waister" since they spent a good deal of the day in the middle or waist of the ship.

"Mr. Cowdery, please take down the names of the men reporting to sick bay and as best you can what their ailment is."

When the weather permitted, sick call was held on the open deck.

Ridgely least favorite part of treating the crew was the fact they failed to wash their bodies, especially if they had been under the weather, lacking the personal motivation to clean up.

The overcrowded and unhygienic conditions on the ship made the situation worse so Ridgely was wise in having the men wash before seeing to them.

"Loosen up men; most of you are familiar with the routine in sick bay. You need to bath before I will attend to you. We have water in the large tub over there and cloths and soap to scrub your bodies with. So let's see nothing but bare bodies and some action over by the water tub."

"When you finished washing you come and see me before getting dressed. It you clothes are not clean you will wash them and go get clean dry ones to put on."

Ridgely preferred the open deck since the stench of the ubiquitous pus and infection could be over whelming in the cock pit. Today was a beautiful day, warm air and a light breeze. John was thankful for these beautiful days since they all could breathe the fresh air.

The men on the ship referred to the thick creamy pus from a staphylococcal infection as "laudable pus" because it tended to be local in nature. The more serious infection from streptococcal infection produced a clear watery or bloodstained discharge and was called malignant because it caused septicemia and death, hospital gangrene and osteomyelitis, (bone infection). The latter was a chronic infection in bone which was a complication of the almost inevitable infections which followed broken bones exposed to the air. The presence of osteomyelitis was a common indication for amputation and it could appear in a few weeks or in two or more months.

The causes of infection were not understood. Ridgely was not concern about washing his hands or the fact he was requiring the crew to use the water from the communal tub to wash with.

"Mr. Ongrain, what brings you here today?"

"I feel terrible, I can't anything down and I am shitting in my pants."

"How long has then been going on?"

"Since yesterdays mid day meal."

"Well it appears to me that you have a case of the 'Gripe' and we can take care of that immediately."

"Mr. Hanwood, this is Mr. Ongrain if you have not made his acquaintance. Mr. Ongrain has a case of the grip and need to have an enema to clean out his bowels."

"Mr. Evans, what can we do for you today?"

"I can't pee, and I have too."

"What do you mean you can't pee?"

"Just that, I can't pee and my stomach is killing me with pain."

"Let's see, stand closer, I am going to press on you penis, I'll try not hurt you."

Ridgely had found that most of the crew contacted venereal diseases when they had been on shore. He would treat the infected area with a mercury base ointment and sulfur was applied to treat the itching. A pewter clyster syringe would be used for flushing out the urethra and bladder.

"Mr. Evans I need to insert this catheter into your penis to see if we can relieve the suppressed urine. Don't move so I can insert the silver catheter into your bladder and not make you bleed. The catheter will bend some but still I need to have you perfectly still. Ah, there we are." The urine began to flow out of the end of the catheter into a bucket.

"That feels better, Sir, I can feel the pain going away."

"Drink lots of water and come back tomorrow morning. The good news is you don't have syphilis but something is going on. Give this note to the cook for an extra allotment of water."

John Ridgely was seeing patients the balance of the morning. He prescribed thirteen more enemas. He felt that maintaining regularity of the bowels was an important part of patient management. "Without a daily bowel movement the entire system will become deranged and corrupted," John said out loud.

The crew's diet was mainly the problem for bowel problems. The crew did not drink much water and ate large quantities of meat. Most of the fluids a sailor drank were grog and beer.

Captain Bainbridge stopped by to see how the sick bay was going and advise John about the impending action.

"John I am afraid you are going to have to tell your patients to hurry up. We need to prepare the ship for battle."

"Are being threatened by that ship we saw earlier," John inquired. "I've so busy I have not looked up. We had an active sick call this morning. Hanwood has a list of the crew and their ailments for your log."

Patients were frequently bled by their physicians in the 19th century and this was considered a panacea for numerous complaints ranging from headaches to gout. It was almost certainly ineffective in 99.9% of them. One such phlebotomy instrument used was the "spring lancet". The name is largely self explanatory. The device is primed by pulling the black lever which also moves the blade upwards and holds it in position under tension. The lower edge of the instrument is held over the area to be bled and it is fired by pressing the arm on the side which released the blade at speed into the flesh. The ensuing blood was usually collected in cups applied to the skin. I doubt that this spring lancet came with the set originally but would have been a later addition. It is the sort of instrument Dr. Ridgely might well have carried on his person or in his medical bag. Physicians also used small knives and thumb lancets to do the bleeding but because the spring lancet was able to pass the blade through the skin more quickly, they were less painful. Later automatic devices called scarificators worked on similar principles but primed multiple blades at a time.

The Loblolly Boys first appear in Navy records in the 1798 muster roll of the *USS Constitution*. The name "Loblolly" was derived from the porridge served to the sick and wounded in the British Navy. Loblolly Boy was the title given to the man or boy who was first designated to specifically assist in the care of the sick and wounded. He was originally a boy or seaman who was not able to perform the demanding duties of handling sails or similar work. The Surgeon's Mate would give the Loblolly boy all such liquors and comforts as are prescribed for the sick. The Loblolly Boy was not allowed to dress wounds or ulcers. Prior to battle he would provide the cockpit with water. Another duty of the Loblolly Boy was to provide the charcoal for heating the irons to sear the amputated stumps and heat the tar with which to stop hemorrhage.

Comparative force of the two vessels

		Java	Constitution
Broadside-metal (in pounds)	Long Guns	261 (49 guns)	384 (54 guns)
	Carr. 274	370	
Complement:	Complement: 397	440	
Size in tons:	1,073 tons	1,533 tons	

FORTY-FIVE

Battle
10 a.m. December 29, 1812

"Lieutenant Ludlow hand me my glass," Bainbridge wanted to see who his foe was.

"Thank you Lieutenant," Bainbridge looked the ship over taking in the capacity of the sails, the cannons and the number of crew on the top decks.

"Lieutenant I believe we have a British ship of war and they appear they have their sights set on us."

"Alert all the crew to 'Battle Stations' and prepare all guns."

The ship's marine drummer summoned the men to their stations. The first order of action was to stow everything that was not needed below decks. The galley fire was extinguished. The furniture in the Captain's cabin was moved below deck since the cabin housed two of the ships guns.

A detail of men mounted each of the ship's fighting tops to make emergency repairs to rigging damaged in battle.

The deck was sanded for better footing. Water was placed in tubs for drinking and for firefighting.

Captain Bainbridge had assigned a midshipman to command twenty-nine of her thirty gun-deck's 24-pounders, 15 guns on each side of the ship. These were organized into five-gun divisions, each commanded by a lieutenant. Bainbridge had personally selected each gun crew of twelve men and a powder boy for each cannon. A general rule of thumb was one man per five cwt of gun.

The original cannons were manufactured by Furnace Hope in Rhode Island. The original cannons were casted solid and bored out. These cannons were replaced in 1807 by cannon's made by the Cecil Iron Works. The new 24's were 9'6" long and heavier than their predecessors.

The *USS Constitution* was outfitted with thirty new Cecil Iron Works twenty-four pound long guns on the gun deck. Each one of the twenty-four pound guns weight 6,000 pounds and they were nine feet six-inches long from breech to muzzle with a 5.8-inch bore. The 24-pound gun could propel a 24 pound ball 1,200 yards. Each cannon cost about $225 each and weighed nearly three tons.

The one eighteen pounder long gun that had been added as a chase. The spar deck was equipped with twenty-four 12-pound Foxall carronades. Each one of the twelve pound guns weight 4,100 pounds and they were eight feet long gun but Bainbridge had it eliminated. Bainbridge did not want to be bothered with the additional powder cartridges and shot required for one gun. A mistake in the heat of battle could cost the lives of his crew from the use of a wrong powder cartridge. The *USS Constitution* had 54 guns in all and the men were well trained in the use of them.

Each gun crew acted in the following matter.

a.   First Captain: Primed & aimed the gun. Ordered the firing of the gun. (Usually an able seaman)

a.   Second Captain: Fueled the firing lock, slow match (slow burning match) & fired.

b.   Three men: 1} Sponger, 2} Rammers, 3} one to relieve the other at those strenuous tasks to keep up the rate of fire.

c.   One man to bring the flannel powder cartridge. A wire was run down the touch hole to pierce the powder cartridge and then primed with a quill of black powder.

d.   One man to bring shot from the rack. (Brass monkey)

e.   One man to place a wad in the muzzle to keep the ball from rolling out.

f.   Two men to tend the tackle & hold the gun in place while it being loaded and then run the cannon out on its carriage.

g.   One man to assist with the "quoin" (wedge) to alter the elevation to +10o to -5o using handspikes or crowbars.

h.   One man acting as a fire fighter, called boarders.

i.   One marine as sharpshooter

j.   Powder boy (Powder-Monkey)

Firing at 200 yards was ideal for 24-pound cannons. The cannons could be adjusted to a 45 degree angle to the right or left. The maximum effective range of the cannon was about 1,200 yards. Bainbridge had made sure that his crews were proficient in firing their assigned cannons. Speed was an important element in battle and Bainbridge had effectively trained the men to fire and reload in one and one-half minutes or less. The training also got the men use to the smoke and noise of the cannons. When they in a battle the smoke would be so thick that only practice with firing the gun could provide the men with the capability to shoot and reload without seeing and hearing.

The fifteenth gun was in the captain's cabin and the captain's clerk was in charge of that gun with his crew. The Captain's cabin had to be prepared for battle. All of Bainbridge's belongings were removed. Susan would not have been pleased with the handling of the floor covering and curtains.

Cannon Shot Types

Round shot, bar & chain shot, Bundle shot, grape & canister shot, Sangrenel, (basically a bag of jagged scrap iron, and nails) explosive shells & hot iron shot Shrapnel.

The projectiles which were used through the early 19th century varied depending upon the target. Solid cast-iron balls were used in attacking the hulls of other ships. Chain shot, consisting of two shot secured to each other with a length of chain, and bar shot, consisting of two solid hemispheres secured by a bar, were effective at short range against sails and rigging but were very inaccurate in their flight.

Canister and grape shot were used against the crews. Canister was a tin cylinder fitting the bore of the gun and packed with musket balls. Grape shot consisted larger balls held in a cylindrical frame. Both types broke up on leaving the muzzle, with the clustered balls dispersing. These were especially effective when fired from carronades in short-range engagements, such as before sending fighting men to board the enemy vessel.

Grape and canister were replaced after Henry Shrapnel in 1784 devised a thin-cased shell containing musket balls and a powder bursting charge. A burning fuse ignited the powder while the shell was in flight and liberated showers of small missiles. Hot shot also came into use against wooden hulls. It was fired with just sufficient velocity to splinter the wooden sides and render them favorable for burning when ignited by the red-hot cannonball.

The gun crew first unfastened the lashings which held the gun secure at sea. This had to be done with care. Gun carriages were not fixed to the deck; if one should break loose in a seaway, the consequences could be dangerous to the ship and fatal to the men who had to bring the massive rolling weight under control. To this day, a dangerously-irresponsible individual is sometimes called a "loose cannon."

The crew now removed the covers that kept dampness out of the bore, and took various gunnery implements from their racks. Guns of this period were equipped with firing locks, but lengths of lighted slow match-cord soaked in an inflammable solution; it burned down slowly, as a lighted cigarette does; they were put in safe places along the gun deck for use in case a lock should fail. Down below the frigate's waterline, the gunner and his assistants opened the forward and aft magazines and began to break out sausage-shaped flannel powder cartridges for the guns and carronades. Other men took stations along the lower decks to pass cartridges up to the gun crews.

The *HMS Java* was windward, north west of the *Constitution*. The day remained pleasant, the seas were flat but there was still a light wind from the northwest. The *Java* was off shore and headed in a direction towards the *Constitution* and evidently wanted to engage the American vessel.

FORTY-SIX

Constitution/Java
10:45 a.m. December 29, 1812

The *William* continued to head for port. The USS *William's* was a recent prize taken by the British war-ship the *HMS Java*. The *William's* had failed to realize the *Hornet* was closer to shore. The *Hornet* had the advantage and attacked the *William* and recaptured her.

Lieutenant Parker made sure that there were midshipmen from the *USS Hornet* assigned as assistant division officers. There were a number of midshipmen posted on the quarterdeck to relay the captain's orders. In the din of battle it was important that orders from the captain were heard.

11 a.m., December 29, 1812

Bainbridge was convinced that the vessel was a ship of the line. Bainbridge ordered the *Constitution* to tack to the southeast and eastward. He ordered the mainsail to be full and that the royals to be taken in.

"Captain the ship is taking in all her studding-sails and appeared to be preparing for action," Lieutenant Parker reported.

The *Constitution* was under 'easy' sail. Bainbridge ordered the ship to tack to the southeast to avoid being maneuvered into pro-British Portuguese waters. The *Constitution* was sailing as close to the wind as possible with all sails set to the royals.

"Lieutenant Morris, do we have all the sails in place?" Captain Bainbridge was concerned the *Java* was moving faster than they were.

"Aye, we do sir."

"Keep the men alert, we don't have long before we will be in range for a broad side."

"We want to engage the *Java* without any interference from another vessel."

11:30 a.m. December 29, 1812

At 11:30 a.m., Captain Bainbridge had midshipman, James Delaney, attempt to signal the *Java*.

"Sir, I am not getting any response," He was using flags that could be seen with the naked eye.

"Keep trying for another five minutes and then give it up."

The *Java* was not about to answered any communication from the *Constitution*.

"Lieutenant, make sure to set the mainsail and royals to draw the strange sail off from the neutral coast, and separate her from the sail in company."

Bainbridge was much the superior sea captain even though the captain of the *Java* felt he could just toy with this inferior American.

From the Journal of Captain Bainbridge:

"Wednesday, the thirtieth of December, (nautical time,) latitude 13° 6' south longitude 31° west, ten leagues from the coast of Brazil, commenced with clear weather and moderate breezes from the E. N. E.; hoisted our ensign and independent. At fifteen minutes past meridian, the ship hoisted her colours, an English ensign, having a signal flying at the main. At twenty-six minutes past one p. m., being sufficiently from the land, and finding the ship to be an English frigate, took in the mainsail and royals, tacked ship, and stood for the enemy."

WB

FORTY-SEVEN

Noon: Continue to close
12:00 p.m. December 29, 1812

"Lieutenant, show our colors."

"Midshipman Ward, see that we show our colors."

"Captain, they have set a British red ensign," Parker voice was becoming excited.

"They are also showing a bunch of recognition signals, I have no idea what they are."

At 12:15 p.m., fifteen minutes past meridian, the ship hoisted her colors, an English ensign, having a signal flying at the Main, red yellow-red. The English frigate then hauled down her colors but left a jack flying.

Both ships ran upon the same tack (zigzag pattern), about four miles apart. Midshipman Delaney was again attempting to signal the *Java* and after ten minutes Bainbridge told him to stop.

Bainbridge then tacked away from the *Java* under all plain sails.

The *Java* was unable to raise their Royals but with the breeze they were going at least ten knots and they were gaining on the *Constitution*.

"Here, let me look," Bainbridge, took the telescope. "They look like signals appropriate to British, Spanish, and Portuguese warships. I am sorry I cannot read them."

Captain Lambert gauged that the *Java* was less than four miles from the *Constitution* when she made a signal and immediately tacked and made all sail away upon the wind.

From the *Java*: "Lieutenant, I believe we a gaining on her and we have the advantage of her in sailing, we are coming up on her fast," Captain Lambert commented.

"Captain she has just hoisted her American Colors," the Lieutenant remarked back to Captain Lambert.

"Lieutenant Parker, prepare for battle. Make sure all the gun crews captains have their gun loaded and ready to fire. Have the crew sand the decks and remove all loose items," Captain Bainbridge announced the orders.

"Bring the ship around through the wind and head towards the enemy. We want to keep the vessel off the coast. We also don't need to draw the other ship that is well inshore to the party."

Captain Lambert on the *Java* was like most English Captain's in their attitude towards American vessels; they were full of self confidence and ego. The English felt the Americans were amateur seamen, and that there vessels were all easy prizes.

"You will see Lieutenant that in two hours or less we should have a prize. By sundown we should have that vessel under our control," Captain Lambert proudly announced.

"Yes sir, we will certainly make a good accounting of ourselves and demonstrate the superiority of the Her Majesties Service."

"It would appear that the American vessel is attempting to escape us, Lieutenant."

Captain Bainbridge was drawing the English ship out further from shore.

"Shorten sail, Mr. Parker," said Bainbridge quietly.

"Shorten sail," was heard by those on the rigging.

"Lieutenant Parker in about ten minutes we are going to tack ship. I want the decks cleared for action immediately."

The day was bright, the sky had a few wispy clouds but other than that the sky was blue.

The two frigates were approaching each other with their sails full and moving rapidly through the water.

"Lieutenant Ludlow, instruct the officer of the third division to fire one gun ahead of the enemy. We need to make him show his colors; then have the starboard guns fire a broadside."

The *Constitution's* colors shone brightly in the breeze as to advertise their gallantry as they cut through the water.

Most of the men on the *Constitution* had stripped to the waist.

"Damn if I am going to have anybody sticking something in my body looking for pieces of my shirt," midshipman William Gordon said to his friend John Wish.

The gun crews were alert and ready, the decks were sanded. The grim tables were laid out below in the cockpit to take care of the wounded. The men were mostly silent as they anxiously await the command to take action.

"Midshipman Packett called down from his lookout on mizzen mast platform that the ship had hoisted an English Ensign at the Peak, and another in his weather Main Rigging, besides his Pendant.

"Thank you Mr. Packett, keep your eyes peeled."

The oncoming vessel was now flying at her peak on the mizzenmast the British flags. They were coming directly at the *Constitution*.

The *Java* intention was to rake the *Constitution* with their starboard guns as they passed. Bainbridge was well aware of what the *Java* had in mind. Much to the surprise of the Java's Captain Bainbridge changed the ships' course turning her stern windward rather than tack. Bainbridge was very clever in this maneuver to avoid the *Java* being able to fire on them. He was going to make his own tactical move to get into position to use the *Constitution's* larboard guns to rake the *Java*.

"Well that's a strange thing!" remarked Lieutenant Aylwin who had been a midshipman on board the *Constitution* in her fight with the *Guerrière*. "See, she has lowered all her flags except the jack at the mizzenmast-head!"

Lieutenant Aylwin glanced aloft at the spars of his own ship; from every masthead, from the peak, and from two places in the shrouds, fluttered the Stars and Stripes.

Nearer the two frigates approached in dead silence except for the sound of breaking water that was being displaced as the ships cut through it. It was generally customary for vessels of the American and English service to go into action cheering; but no one seemed disposed to lead off on the *Constitution,* it was too early in the game and the tensions were high.

FORTY-EIGHT

Constitution/Java Battle
1:26 p.m.to 7 p.m., December 29, 1812

At 1:26 p.m. Bainbridge felt the *Constitution* was sufficiently away from the coast so they didn't need to worry about shallow waters and interference from other ships.

"It is defiantly an English frigate the *Java*," Bainbridge commented.

"Look they are taking in the mainsail and royals," Lieutenant Parker responded.

"Lieutenant, tacked the ship, and stand for the enemy."

Captain Bainbridge ordered the mainsails and royals to be taken in, to tack the ship and stand for the enemy.

The *Java* was headed for the *Constitution* again. Bainbridge could see that the guns on the starboard side of the frigate were all run out. Bainbridge was drawing them in and he knew their intension was to attack with a full broadside.

Bainbridge ordered that the American colors be hoisted.

The *Java* had closed to less than two miles.

"Shortened sails," meaning he wanted his top-gallant-sails, jib, and spanker shortened; the sails luffed up to the wind. Bainbridge wanted to slow the *Constitution* to 30-40% of its speed calculating that the Java's speed was greater than his.

The *Java* hoisted their colors and put their ship under the same sail. The *Java* was going to mirror the *Constitution's* movements.

By about 1:35 p.m., it was certain that the enemy was closing on the *Constitution*, something no ship of the line could do, and so Bainbridge tacked (turned through the wind) toward an opponent he now recognized as another frigate, taking in his mainsail and royals and clearing for action.

1:50 p.m. December 29, 1812

From the Journal of Captain Bainbridge:

"At fifty minutes past one p.m., the enemy bore down with an intention of raking us, which we avoided by wearing.

At two p.m., the enemy being within half a mile of us, and to windward, and having hauled down his colours, except the union Jack, at the mizenmast bead, induced me to give orders to the officer of the. third division, to fire a gun ahead of the enemy, to make him show his colours, which being done, brought on a fire from us of the whole broadside, on which the enemy hoisted his colours, and immediately returned our fire. A general action, with round and grape then commenced; the enemy keeping at a' much greater distance than I wished; but could not bring him to a closer action. Considerable maneuvers were made by both vessels to rake and avoid being raked."

WB

At 1:50 p. m. the enemy shortened sail upon which she bore down with an intention of raking the *Constitution*, which Bainbridge avoided by wearing. The winds were shifting to the east-northeast. They could see the sailors tightening the rigging in one area, and loosening it in other. This can create the most stress on the stays but it gave them more speed.

The enemy attempted to cross Bainbridge's bow and rake him, this maneuver was prevented by the Constitution wearing around (turning away from the wind) on a southeasterly heading, placing the Britishers to windward on his larboard quarter and closing. Clearly, the enemy had a speed advantage over the *Constitution* and they were aware of it.

The *Constitution* had made 180 degree turn leaving the *Java* to their stern.

"Bring the bow around and fire at will when you feel you may do damage to the ship."

"Lieutenant, let us see if we can destroy their rigging."

"Captain, I think they are closing on us."

2:00 p.m. December 29, 1812

By two, p.m. the *HMS Java* was within half a mile of the *Constitution*, and windward.

Lieutenant Aylwin reported the *Java* had hauled down his colors, except the union jack at the mizenmast head.

The *Java* returned fire. They were in range for grape and canister shot.

The men on the rigging had hoisted on board the *Constitution* an American Union Jack at the mizzen top-gallant and a Broad Pendant at Main, and another lashed to the main-rigging of the mast head and at the end of the spanker's gaff.

The *Java* was accurate in their firing using their lee or starboard battery and the *Constitution's* jib halyards were shot away. They would have lost the sail but the quick thinking of Seaman Asa Curtis slid down the foretopgallant stay to reattach it. He was fortunate that with the raining of iron and splinters penetrating the air that he was not injured.

The *Java* was maintaining greater speed then the *Constitution* and appeared to be drawing ahead.

"Lieutenant, have all the guns angle their port side guns and let loose with a broad side before they do."

The broadside was successful in tremendous damage to the stern and starboard side of the *Java*.

The *Constitution* was fortunate to have avoided a raking broadside from the *Java*. The smoke from the *Constitution's* broadside was thick and Bainbridge wisely wore around in the smoke.

Captain Lambert directed the *Java* to follow the *Constitution*. The *Constitution* was now ahead of the *Java* with the *Constitution* on the port side.

"Lieutenant ordered the starboard gun crews to fire into the bow of the *Java*."

"As soon as the guns fire, turn 45 degrees."

"Yes sir."

"Captain, the *Java* is moving up on us again."

All at once iron and splinters were raking the main deck and doing a great deal of damage to the *Constitution* stern. The mizzen mast was damaged but it held. The mizzen topgallant staysail was slack from the stays being cut. Many of the crew on the *Constitution* were wounded from the spraying on splinters, some much worst then others with a few dead lying on the deck.

Lieutenant Parker was encouraging his gun crews to load and fire as rapidly as possible. Parker figured the men were getting shots off every one and one-half minutes. The smoke was blinding and the roar of the cannons had temporally left the crews on deck deaf.

They were using round and grape shot though the *Java* was keeping her distance making the round shot the better choice.

The cannons on the *Java* were also raining cannon balls towards the *Constitution*.

"Lieutenant Aylwin, we need to draw the enemy closer to us," Bainbridge was concerned that he could not inflict the damage he wanted too. "I do not want the ship to be able to rake us."

Bainbridge had the *Constitution* on a south-easterly course and then as the *Java* mimicked their maneuvers Bainbridge turned to the south west.

The English warship returned the *Constitutions* fire with both round and grape shot.

The entire crew of the *Constitution* was involved. Lines of men were delivering powder and shot to the guns crews. Others were repairing and moving debris from the destruction cause from the enemy fire. Men were being wounded and others needed to step into their places on the operating of the guns. Patrick Conner was swabbing gun nine when he was decapitated by the chain between two balls hitting him directly under his chin. The eruption of blood from the artery in Conner's neck sprayed the rest of the gun crew. His head was carried through the air and plastered on the main mast.

Captain Bainbridge had to relay all orders through his officers up close since the noise was thunderous.

Raking fire was particularly devastating. The bow and the stern of a ship was generally the weakest part of the hull and the most desirable to take aim on. A round ball bursting through the timbers resulted in a storm of splinters through the deck. An ideal maneuver would be to cross the enemies bow or stern and fire all gun.

Bainbridge ordered the fore and main sails to be set, and luffed up close to the enemy in such a manner that his jib-boom got foul of the Englishman's mizzen-rigging.

2:10 p.m. December 29, 1812

The *Java* was approaching the *Constitution* from the south-east. The *Constitution* was waiting for the *Java* just to the north-east.

From the Journal of Captain Bainbridge:
The following minutes were taken during the action."*At ten minutes past two, p.m. commenced the action within good grape or canister distance, the enemy to windward, but much further than I wished.*"
WB
At 2:10 p.m. when about half a mile distant she opened her fire giving us her larboard broad-side which was not returned till we were close on her weather bow; both Ships now maneuvered to obtain advantageous positions.

The *Java* engaged the *Constitution* with their larboard guns. They were range for grape and canister shot.

The *Java* was sending continuous cannon fire but avoiding closing the gap between the two ships. The cannon fire was coming high indicating their effort to do damage to the *Constitution's* masts.

"Captain, our bowsprit has been hit."

"Get a damage report Lieutenant."

The head of the bowsprit had been hit with a round shot and the jib staysail was banging the severed portion of the bowsprit against the bow of the ship.

"Captain, the jib staysail is useless and the jib boom and other running rigging are severely cut. I am afraid we are not able to preserve the weather gauge," Lieutenant Parker reported.

"Carry on Lieutenant, and let's do some damage to them."

"Commence action when we are within effective distance for shooting grape and canister shots," Bainbridge directed.

"We need to get closer Sir."

The enemy was delivering relentless fire. The *Constitution's* jib halyards were shot away.

Bainbridge on the quarter using his mouth trumped to bark orders to the crew when a sharp sting of a musket-ball lodged in his hip. "Damn, somebody got lucky." The musket ball only slightly wounded him and he all but forgot about it in a few minutes. The heat of battle was no time to take your attention away from anticipating what your next move might be.

The *Java* now had the speed advantage so Bainbridge let the ship draw ahead. *Java's* intension was to turn across the bow of the *Constitution* and deliver a devastating raking shot. Bainbridge ordered the broadside loosened, and then masterfully wore around in the smoke.

The *Java* watched the maneuver and followed, but once again was in a position somewhat astern, this time to starboard, and having to catch up. The *Java* for a second time moved up and somewhat ahead of the *Constitution*. Bainbridge repeated his broadside and turned in the smoke in a graceful maneuver.

Mark Snow on the number four gun was killed instantly when a ball hit the rail of the ship and a large splinted was driven through his chest. Snow was thrown to the deck by the force of the impact. The last thing he remembered was looking at the large splinter sticking straight up out of his chest.

2:27 p.m. December 29, 1812

Both vessels tacked to the east. The *Java* again began with the *Constitution* north of the *Java*. The *Java* began moving up, but this time, he suddenly turned downwind and unleashed a murderous raking broadside at the American's stern. The mizzen mast was damaged but not dropped. A number of the shrouds were cut and no longer attached to the chain plates. The crews were out immediately to reattach them. The men that were killed or wounded remained on her quarterdeck waiting to be carried below. John had been attending to everyone, primarily attempting to stop the bleeding or making the sailor's last minutes on earth as comfortable as possible.

John Cheeves had both legs nearly shot off at the knees. John Ridgely got to him within minutes. He was bleeding profusely but he was able to stop the blood loss using belts to act as tourniquets.

The fighting was fierce though he was able to get two seamen from the starboard side to carry the seamen to the safety of the cockpit below.

Nicholas Hanwood was busy working on William Cooper. A round shot had hit him in his right thigh destroying most of it. He was also removed from the battle. There was little hope that either man would survive much longer.

Lieutenant Morris was directing fire on cannon number nine when a cannon ball hit Seaman Jonas Ongrain in his head removing it. Blood was cascading all over the deck like a fountain before Seaman Ongrain fell over and sprayed Lieutenant Morris with his blood.

Surgeon Mate Jonathan Cowdery attended to Peter Woodbury. His left knee was shattered by a cannon shot. Cowdery bandaged the knee the best he could and had him removed to the cock pit. He would have to have his leg amputate when the fighting stopped. Cowdery would have to endure excruciating pain until then.

Many of the men were wounded but they tended to their wounds the best they could so they could continue fighting. John Ridgely and his two mates were dealing with the carnage as best they could. They were more concern with stopping the bleeding and then dealing with the wound.

When a gun crew member fell in battle he was quickly replaced by whoever was nearby. The crew knew the importance of keeping the cannons firing and the urgency to have the fire as rapid as possible; their very lives depended on it.

2:30 p.m. December 29, 1812

From the Journal of Captain Bainbridge:
"At thirty minutes past two, our wheel was shot entirely away."
WB

At 2:30 p.m., the *Java* got lucky and destroyed the *Constitution's* wheel.

"Damn!" said Captain Bainbridge as he was hurdled to the deck. The 24-pound round ball made a direct hit on the ships wheel, destroying it entirely. Bainbridge was standing near the wheel when the ball hit and drove a small copper bolt into his thigh. This was a dangerous wound that laid him out on the deck.

"Sir, you have been wounded, I'll get Mr. Ridgely

Bainbridge instructed Lieutenant Aylwin to take two able bodied men to take charge of the rudder lines and to act on his instructions that were hollered through three other midshipmen to the men on the rudder lines.

"There's more than one way to steer a ship!" Bainbridge exclaimed. "Order eight men down into the after hold, and station three midshipmen on the after companion ladders to pass the word."

During the rest of the engagement the *Constitution* was handled by means of steering tackles from below.

"Mr. Waldo, are you hit?" Bainbridge shouted over to him.

Charles Waldo was at the wheel when the cannon made a direct hit.

"I'll be all right Captain, mostly splinters."

Bainbridge managed to get up with the assistance of two sailors that had been summons to assist him.

Bainbridge saw that he needed to bring his ship so she was first in coming to the wind on the other tack.

"Hold her steady and be prepared to fire on her decks," Bainbridge was weak from the shock of the thigh wound.

John came to Bainbridge's side as soon as he heard that he had been wounded.

The port side cannons all roared sending devastating raking fire on to the *Java*. The *Constitution* was running free with the wind on their quarter and the *Java* was windward of the *Constitution*.

"Captain, let me look at that wound," John had a furrow on his forehead.

"Thanks John, I haven't got time to deal with it right now."

John was down on one knee looking at the wound.

"Well as bad as the wound looks Captain I believe the bone has not been compromised and fortunately no arteries were severed."

John removed the copper bolt and tied up the wound with his shirt. With all the carnage on the deck he was out of bandages and would have to go below to the cockpit to get more.

"The rifle ball that hit you earlier is can still feel in the wound. I will have to take you to the cockpit to remove it."

"Not now John, let's get our prize first."

"Here' take a swig of this it will help with the pain."

Bainbridge did and said, "What was that?"

It is Laudanum and it should abate your pain for a while at least. When you need more Laudanum, have a seaman find me."

The Captain of the *Java* was surprised that the *Constitution* did not maneuver immediately after they had fired on them. Then he could see that the *Constitution* had lost it wheel.

"Now is our chance men, the *Constitution* has lost her wheel, we can come around and rack them into oblivion," shouted Lambert.

The *Java* re-crossed Bainbridge's wake, the *Java* fired another raking broadside at long range before resuming his windward position to the *Constitution*. Bainbridge was concerned that he needed to reduce the *Java's* speed so he could gain the advantage.

William was glad that the challenge of the battle was occupying his present consciences. He was suffering signs of shock and the pain was excruciating. He sent Seaman Curtis to find John.

2:40 p.m. December 29, 1812

From the Journal of Captain Bainbridge:
"At forty minutes past two, determined to close with the enemy, not withstanding his raking. Set the fore and main sail, and luffed up close to him."
WB

The *Java* was surprised when the *Constitution* was all of sudden able to tack to the north-west. The *Java* also tacked the same course and the two vessels exchanged fire.

The *Java* crossed the bow of the *Constitution* firing another raking broadside. They were shooting from a far distance and the results were minimal. The *Java* continued on their windward heading.

"Lieutenant Parker, we need to reduce the speed of the enemy's forward progress. They have the advantage of speed and that is not to our benefit."

Bainbridge was determined to stay close with the enemy, notwithstanding his raking. Set the fore and mainsail, and luffed up close to him.

The two vessels came in range of each other. The *Java* was to the port side of the *Constitution* exposing their bow and starboard side.

Bainbridge timing was accurate. "Fire, he called out and all four lieutenants were making sure the gunners were delivering all the smashing power of the cannons. The 32 pounder carronades were doing their job of destroying masts and rigging of the *Java* before suffering any further damage. Bainbridge was correct and the gunfire shattered the enemy's flying jib and jib booms. The *Java* turned into the wind, becoming temporarily taken back.

The *Java* continued ahead and the *Constitution* wore again and was able to get in a stern rake before the *Java* regained control. The *Java* was having difficulty maneuvering.

Barney Hart was on cannon nine when a ball made a large wound in his left thigh fracturing and splintering the bone. The back part of the right thigh was carried off. He could not be moved without incurring more damage but he had to move out of the active firing of the cannon. He was bleeding profusely. He lost consciousness and died within five minutes.

Mr. Gascoine was a passenger on the *Java* in route to India. He was among the dignitaries the *Java* was perhaps showing off too. Unfortunately what was Captain's Lambert's idea of providing a show for his distinguish passengers was tuning deadly. Mr. Gascoine was hit with a round shot in his right thigh.

The combatants now ran free with the wind on their quarter. The *Java* was to the windward on the *Constitution*.

The medical team was going from man to man treating wounds. Gun shots to the arms and legs could also prove fatal due to infection. The bullets would pull strands of filthy cloth into the body. The bullets were made of lead and often contained impurities. Many of the men on the main deck would that their clothes off so being hit by a bullet, splinters, grape would have a better change of not having an infection from cloth being buried in their bodies.

2:50 p.m. December 29, 1812

From the Journal of Captain Bainbridge:
"At fifty minutes past two, the enemy's jib boom got foul of our mizzen rigging. At three, the head of the enemy's bowsprit and jib-boom were shot away by us."
WB

The *Java* crossed over the *Constitution's* bow and the *Constitution* was able to use it port guns to rake the *Java*.

"Continue firing," Bainbridge thought he was screaming but Lieutenant Ludlow could barely hear him.

The port guns were being fired as they were made ready with fresh powder and shot. The accuracy of the cannon fire was devastating. The decks of the *Java* were running in blood and body parts. More sand was thrown down on the deck to prevent slipping. The previous sanding of the deck was being washed off by the flow of blood.

The *Java's* gun crews were taking much longer to operate because of fallen comrades, and the slipping in the brains and guts of their fallen friends and ship mates.

The *Constitution* delivered a heavy raking broadside into the stern of the *Java*. The two vessels were about two cables' length distant.

The *Java* fired grape shot over the *Constitutions* deck. Seaman Mark

Snow was hit in the lower part of the abdomen ripping open this abdominal area exposing his intestines. He looked down at his wound and with both hands trying to prevent his guts spilling out. He collapsed on the deck but he did not die right away. He lay on the deck holding his intestines for about one hour before dying.

2:55 p.m. December 29, 1812

At 2.55 p.m. the two warships were in pistol-shot range. The master on the *Java* was wounded and taken below.

Those unlucky enough to be hit with a gunshot had to wait until the more severely wounded were attended to. The medical team would probe for the bullet using their fingers. The person doing the probing had not washed his hands so infection was almost guaranteed. Once the bullet was located a bullet extractor or knife was used to cut the bullet out. The wound would be allowed to bleed in order to wash out any cloth and hopes of preventing infection. The wound would be sewn up all without benefit of any pain killer.

The cries of the wounded were eerie and a constant reminder of the carnage that was taking place on the ship. Cries of help were going unnoticed; many were not heard because the roar of the cannons had deafened most of the ship mates.

3:00 p.m. December 29, 1812

The *Java* was losing control of the ship and had to tack to the south before swing around to the north. The *Constitution* continued it aggression on the *Java* so they could continue to pound the *Java* with gun fire.

The *Constitution* cannon fire destroyed the head of the *Java's* bowsprit and jib-boom. The *Java* attempted to close by running down on the *Constitution's* quarter. A few minutes later the *Constitution* poured a heavy raking broadside into the stern of the *Java*. Continuous gun fire was being directed on to the *Java*. The fore-mast of the English frigate went by the board, cashing through the forecastle and main deck in its passage. More *Java* seaman were injured or killed as the fore-mast tumbled down. Many of the wounded on the deck were crushed.

The men on the *Java* were receiving the worst of the battle. The impact of the cannon balls shot through the wooden Bulwarks was causing projectiles of every kind to be imbedded into human flesh; the slaughter was appalling!

Bainbridge was experiencing the rush of adrenalin flowing through his body. The pain from his wound was intense but his mind was into anticipating the enemy's next move. Bainbridge was not about to allow his damaged body to interfere with conducting the battle. Bainbridge knew he was at the critical point in the battle that what he directed would either win or lose the prize. There was no time for dealing with personal thoughts when men were suffering and dying obeying his commands.

3:05 p.m. December 29, 1812

From the Journal of Captain Bainbridge:
"At five minutes past three, shot away the enemy's foremast by the board. At fifteen minutes past three, shot away his main top-mast just above the cap."
WB

Both vessels were now going to the north-west and the *Constitution* was raking the *Java*.

The rigging of the *Java* was cut to pieces and their fore and main-masts were badly wounded.

Captain Lambert felt his only hope was to board the *Constitution* and beat them in hand to hand combat. The *Java* was being beaten by the *Constitution* and the Captain felt the first panic of pending defeat.

The *Java* bore up to the port stern of the *Constitution* a-breast of their main-chains. Captain Lambert had not counted on his bow-sprit passing over the *Constitutions* stern and catching his mizzen-rigging and prevented the *Java* from raking the *Constitution*.

The men on the *Java* were somewhat confused when they could not see many men on the *Constitutions* top deck. They were feeling good about the prospect of boarding the *Constitution* and taking possession of her. Captain Lambert was feeling good that the prospects of success were taking over the fear of defeat.

3:15 p.m. December 29, 1812

At 3:15 p.m. All of Captains' Lambert hopes for victory were dashed. His thought of success was sort lived and their maneuver failed.

Captain Bainbridge took advantage of the *Java's* miscalculation by wearing across the *Java's* bow and raking them and taking down their

294

main-top mast. The foremast was severed by a double-headed shot, just below the fighting top (above the cap) and plunged downward through two decks of the *Java*. The mast came down so suddenly that the men in its path were unable to seek safety. Large splinters were lodging in flesh of those nearby while the falling timbers were crushing others. The cries of agony could be heard above the sounds of battle. The crews on both frigates were experiencing the worst of war, the human toll. Only the very hardened warriors could dismiss the sounds of the dying while the majority of the others were experiencing a living Hell.

The *Constitution* again was wearing and came around to the *Java's* stern. Captain Bainbridge was changing the ship's course by turning her stern windward. The two ships were again close to each other.

3:30 p.m. December 29, 1812

At 3:30 p.m. Sergeant Adrian Peterson, a Marine sniper was on the platform just above the lowest sail and took aim on Captain Lambert. He fired and the ball from his musket mortally wounded Captain Lambert.

"Captain, the *Java's* Captain has just fallen to the deck and it seems he has blood on him."

Captain Lambert had been shot in his left side and the ball had lodged in his spine. Moving him was not a smart idea but then with all the carnage on the deck and the promise for more it did not make any sense to leave him exposed to more gun fire. The moving of Captain Lambert did not come quickly; he had to endure the pain and suffering on the deck for almost forty-five minutes before being carried below.

The *Constitution* continued firing full broadside taking down the *Java's* main top and topgallant masts, shot through just above the cap. The massive rigging and broken spar's tumbled down on the gun crews disrupting their ability to fire their gun.

Bainbridge was only now thinking that he had to continue raking the rigging of the *Java* and they would become helpless. The loss of their captain also meant there was confusion on board the *Java* even if the Lieutenants were capable of continuing the fight. Bainbridge knew he could not leave his post.

3:40 p.m. December 29, 1812

From the Journal of Captain Bainbridge:

"At forty minutes past three, shot away the gaff and spanker-boom."
WB

The *Java* was becoming unable to adjust their direction of travel and continued on the north-west course. Only the sails on the mizzen mast were providing any propulsion at all for the *Java*. The *Java* had lost all speed hampering their ability to maneuver the ship.

3:55 p.m. December 29, 1812

From the Journal of Captain Bainbridge:
"At fifty-five minutes past three, shot away his mizzen-mast, nearly by the board."
WB

The *Constitution* had tacked across the *Java's* bow while continuing to rake the *Java* into submission. After firing on the *Java's* stern the *Constitution* made another loop to the south-east and then back on the north-west course. The bow and the stern are the two most vulnerable spots on a frigate.

The *Constitution* shot away the *Java's* mizzen mast nearly by the board. The two vessels lay broadside to broadside, engaged in deadly conflict, yard-arm to yard-arm. The crew on the *Constitution* was firing their guns with smoothness and rapidity inflicting devastating damage to the enemy. It was only to be minutes before the *Java* recognized defeat.

4:00 p.m. December 29, 1812

From the Journal of Captain Bainbridge:
"At five minutes past four, having silenced the fire of the enemy completely, and his colours in the main rigging being down, we supposed he had struck; we then hauled down courses and shot ahead, to repair our rigging which was extremely cut, leaving the enemy a complete wreck: soon afterwards discovered the enemy's flag was still flying. Hove to, to repair some of our damage."
WB

At 4:00 p.m.: The *Constitution's* guns destroyed the *Java's* gaff and spanker boom. The *Constitution* had come around to the *Java'* stern and was able to bring all the force of his heavy guns from their blind spot.

The *Constitution* then slid forward to a position abeam of the *Java*. The *Java* was now dealing with fires that were popping up each time they fired a cannon. The cannons were causing fires in the ruined rigging shrouding the ship.

"Captain, I believe the guns on the *Java* have gone quite.

"Parker do you see any colors flying," Bainbridge inquired while in grimacing pain.

"I don't see any colors flying, I believe they have surrendered."

The *Constitution* continued to the north-west sailing past the *Java*. Lieutenant Parker had been given orders from Bainbridge travel a short distant from the *Java* so they could make some repairs to their rigging which was extremely cut.

They thought it to be prudent to make the repairs before claiming their prize. Bainbridge ordered all the able bodied men to repair what damage they could. For the next hour repairs to the *Constitution* were made. The decks were cleared of debris and the wounded were attended too. Temporary sails were hoisted in place while securing his masts so they would support the sails. Bainbridge thought they had left the *Java* a complete wreck.

"Captain, they have raised their colors."

"Prepare to attack," Bainbridge ordered.

Lieutenant's Nerringham and Buchanan on the *Java* were determined to engage the *Constitution* again.

"Captain, it would appear the *Java* has attached a spare spar to the stump of the foremast and a staysail rigged between it and the remains of the bowsprit to try and regain some maneuverability," Lieutenant Parker observed.

While the *Java* was attempting major repairs their luck failed when the remains of the main mast tottered and fell wounding a half dozen more men.

4:20 p.m. December 29, 1812

From the Journal of Captain Bainbridge:

"At twenty minutes past four, wore ship and stood for the enemy. At twenty-five minutes past five, got very close to the enemy in a very effectual raking position, athwart his bows, and when about to fire, he most prudently struck his flag ; for had be suffered the broadside to have raked him, his additional loss must have been extremely great, as he laid an unmanageable wreck upon the water."

"After the enemy had struck, wore ship and reefed the topsails, then

hoisted one of the only two remaining boats we had left out of eight, and sent Lieutenant Parker, first of the Constitution, to take possession of the enemy, which proved to be his Britannic Majesty's frigate Java, rated thirty-eight, but carried forty-nine guns, and manned with upwards of four hundred men, commanded by Captain Lambert, a very distinguished officer, who was mortally wounded."

"The force of the enemy at the commencement of the action was, no doubt, considerably greater than we had been able to ascertain. The officers were extremely cautious in discovering the number. By her quarter bill, she had one man stationed at each gun more than we had. The Constitution was very much cut in her sails and rigging, and many of her spars injured."

WB

The action continued from the commencement to the end of the fire, one hour and fifty-five minutes.

The enemy had ceased firing and it was assumed that the *Java* had struck her colors. The crew was repairing the rigging that had been extremely cut.

"Look Captain, their flag is flying!"

4:50 p.m. December 29, 1812

Bainbridge ordered the *Constitution* to wear round and renew the conflict.

"Be ready to fire and continue to fire until they strike," Bainbridge was amazed at the *Java's* stupidity.

"Captain, the *Java* is like a stationary target, we will destroy the vessel," Lieutenant Parker commented.

5:10 p.m. December 29, 1812

The *Constitution* began to close in again on the *Java*. An ensign had been re-hoisted at what was left of the *Java's* mizzen mast. They were also making efforts to set more sail.

5:25 p.m. to 7:00 p.m. December 29, 1812

The *Constitution* was now in control of it sails and came around to the north-east and Bainbridge brought the *Constitution's* starboard side to be blocking the *Java* from any forward motion. The *Constitution* had the dominating position across her bow.

"Lieutenant Parker advised the gunners to prepare to fire," Bainbridge was going to end this fight. The *Constitution* got very close to the enemy in a very effectual raking position, athwart his bows, and was at the very instant of raking him, when the *Java* most prudently struck their flag.

If the *Constitution* had inflicted a broadside raking the *Java* one final time the loss of life would have been unthinkable. After the British frigate struck at 5:50, the *Constitution* wore, and reefed topsails.

"Let go the anchor," Lieutenant Parker instructed.

Midshipman, Alexander Belches was there to receive the orders and proceeded to make sure they were acted on.

"Lower the longboats and prepare to board the enemy ship," Bainbridge directed his orders to Lieutenant Morris in a firm voice.

"Sir, I think we have a problem, most of the boats were destroyed in the battle."

One of the only two remaining boats out of eight was then hoisted out, and Lieutenant Parker of the *Constitution* was sent to take possession of the frigate *Java*. The *Java* was rated as a 38-guns but it had been retrofitted to carry 49-guns. She was manned by upwards of four hundred men, and was commanded by Captain Lambert, a very distinguished naval officer. He had been taken to his cabin and laid in his bunk mortally wounded from the sniper shot.

John Cheever, seaman from Marblehead, was laying on the deck in the agonies of death, by the side of a dead brother, Tolin, who had been killed in the early part of the action. Cheeves was still conscience and was able to hear the word passed that the enemy had struck. This animating intelligence giving a momentary reflux to his fast ebbing spirit, he raised himself on his left hand, pronounced three cheers with loud and joyous vehemence, and then fell back and expired with a smile of content and satisfaction playing upon his facial expression.

The nine dead *Constitution* sailors were laid out on the deck. Killed in the afternoon's battle were Seaman Jonas Ongrain, Do's Tobin Cheeves, Patrick Conner, Barney Hart, John Cheeves, Mark Snow, John D. Allen, William Cooper, and Private Marine Thomas Hanson.

The wounded were many, so many that it was not possible to count the number until later. Some of the wounded were making every effort to assist with the rigging, clearing the deck and attending to those with serious life threatening wounds.

The sailors were going about their work of repairing the ship. They didn't need to be told what needed to be done. They were handy at all kinds of work, they were true Jack-of-all-trades.

First Lieutenant George Parker's orders were to board the *Java* and to see to the safety of those men who were still alive. His next duty was to inquire as to her name and to take possession of her as a prize.

When Lieutenant Parker boarded the *Java* he was speechless. The deck of the warship was a disaster. The cannon shot from the *Constitution* had smashed the *Java* so bad it was not salvageable. He could only think that the *Java* was a wreck and should be left for the sea to claim.

The deck was strewn with body parts, blood and debris from the devastation cause from the intense cannon fire. I was not easy to determine who was dead and who was wounded. Some of the bodies were on top of each other. Lieutenant Parker saw arms and legs sticking out of debris only to discover they were not attached to a body. The stench of death was already over whelming. Lieutenant Parker had a bandana tied over his face attempting to obscure some of the stench.

The *Java* had been one of the finest frigates in the British navy but now it was in ruin beyond salvage.

"There is no saving her," Lieutenant Parker hollowed over to Captain Bainbridge.

"Lieutenant Morris, instruct Lieutenant Parker to order all the *Java* survivors to get all their personal belongings and get off the hulk," Bainbridge was beginning to feel the intensity of the pain caused by his thigh wounds. The adrenalin of doing battle had worn off and the reality of his being wounded beginning to take its toll. He was hoping that John would bring him more Laudanum.

Transporting the wounded and survivors to the *Constitution* was no easy task. The Java had lost all her boats, and the *Constitution* had only two of their eight boats still serviceable.

The hull of the *Java* was so badly shattered by round shot that there was no patching her. The Java was taking on water and fires were burning out of control in multiple locations.

The *Constitution* was also very much cut in her sails and rigging, and many of her spars injured. The crew was busy at making repairs as the transfer of men from the *Java* to the *Constitution* was being made.

The *Java's* main mast had gone overboard. Tier mizzen-mast was shot out of the ship close by the deck, and the foremast was carried away about twenty-five feet above it.

The *Java* was on fire and taking on water; nothing could save her or the souls on board if the *Constitution* had also been disabled.

. The *Constitution* had nine men killed and twenty-five wounded. The *Java* had sixty men killed and 101 wounded. A letter was found later that indicated 170 wounded on the *Java*. The men did not have any time for counting wounded crew as they were being placed on the *Constitution*

"Gentlemen I want all the crew of the *Constitution* to treat the captives of the *Java* with respect and kindness. Do you understand me?" Bainbridge was concerned the *Java* crew would not be treated well.

The *Java* had been on an important mission. They were carrying Lieutenant-General Hislop and his staff, Captain Marshall and Lieutenant Saunders of the Royal navy, to Bombay, which place he had been appointed governor. They had also been carrying several naval officers for different vessels in the East Indies. Also more than one hundred other officers and men destined for service in the East Indies. She had dispatches for St. Helena, the Cape of Good Hope, and for every British establishment in the Indian and Chinese seas. She had in her hold copper for a 74-gun vessel and for two brigs. The vessels were being constructed in Bombay and the officers going there were to supervise their progress.

The *Java* officers while on board the *Constitution* mentioned that the frigate *Java* was formerly the French ship the *La Renommee*. The English had captured the *La Renommee* near Madagascar on May 20, 1811 in company with the *La Jveriede* after severe action by the *Phoebe, Astrea, and Galatea*. The *La Renommee* had 44 guns and the British retrofitted the frigate and added five guns.

7:00 p.m. December 29, 1812

From the Journal of Captain Bainbridge:

"At seven p.m., the boat returned with Lieutenant Chads, the first lieutenant of the enemy's frigate, and Lieutenant General Hislop, governor of Bombay, Major Walker, and Captain Wood of his staff Captain Lambert of the Java, was too dangerously wounded to be removed immediately."

"The cutter returned on board the prize for the prisoners, and brought Captain Marshall, master and commander in the British navy, who was a passenger on board, and several other naval officers destined for ships in the East Indies."

"The Java was an important ship, fitted out in the complete manner to

convey Lieutenant-General Hislop and staff to Bombay, several naval officers, and a number of seamen for ships in the East Indies."

"As I watch the transfer of the officers from the Java to Constitution the recollection of my dream was revived. I said to Lieutenant Parker that is the identical officer I saw in my dream."

WB

7:00 p.m. the boat returned with *Java's* First Lieutenant Chad's. Also with them was Lieutenant General Hislop (the newly appointed Governor of Bombay) and his immediate staff, Major Walker, and Captain Wood, and Captain Marshall, master and commander in the British Navy. They were all being transported to the East Indies to take command if a sloop of war there.

"She had also dispatches for St. Helena, Cape of Good Hope, and every British establishment in the India, and China seas."

"There was copper for a seventy-four gun vessel, and two brigs being built in Bombay, and a great many other valuables, but everything was blown up in her, except the officers' baggage," Lieutenant Parker reported.

Commodore Bainbridge remained on deck in spite that he was severely wounded. The musket ball, in the hip was not as pain full as the piece of langrage he had taken in the thigh. Though these wounds were severe and extremely painful, he only let John pour some whiskey on the damaged flesh and wrap his wounds. Bainbridge was not about to turn his duties over to his Lieutenants even though they were more than capable of attending to them.

Bainbridge was concerned foremost of having the wounded attended too. The dead were piled on the poop deck to get them out of the way. Many of the wounded were being attended to where they fell. Those that John determined needed a limb removed were carried to the Cockpit; the surgery was done in the order that men were delivered to him.

Bainbridge was concerned that the officers and guests on the *Java* were treated with respect and brought over to the *Constitution.*

Bainbridge stayed on the deck until after eleven o'clock that evening. His left leg soaked in blood he made quite a sight and inspiration for the others who were also suffering.

He was carried to his cabin and placed on a blanket on the floor. Captain Lambert had been placed in Bainbridge's bunk as per his orders.

"William I need to get that ball out of you," John was beyond tired and looked it.

"Go to bed John, I need to have you fresh in the morning to take care of all you new patients; but before you go give me another slug of your Laudanum."

"I am concerned William that you wound may become infected. At least let me pour more whiskey on it to flush it out and rewrap it with a clean cloth. I'll leave the bottle of Laudanum with you so you can take more when you need it."

Bainbridge did not have the bullet extracted for two days after the wound had been inflicted. John had whiskey applied regularly to the wound that kept it clean and also helped in numbing the area afflicted. Bainbridge demanded he be on deck during the day. Bainbridge was aware of the constant irritation produced by the metal lodged his muscles. The irritation of the ball gave rise to symptoms of tetanus.

"William, that ball has to come out and now," John had his medical tools with him.

Bainbridge was feeling weak and he was in no condition to argue with John's medical advice.

"Let's get you down to my surgery."

Bainbridge was able to lie down on the clean surgeon's table in the center of the very small room with a low ceiling. The room had been washed down with vinegar so the smell of death was not apparent.

John took William trousers off and washed the area around the two wounds. John probed the wound in search of the ball. The ball had imbedded in the muscle on the lateral thigh and was to the femur.

John was not as confident as he was making out to be. John's experience was that most gunshot wounds not including the wound from the bolt were potentially fatal.

"Let's get to it John, I have work to do."

"Here bite on this leather strap, there is going to be some pain."

John needed to make a small cut through the subcutaneous tissue to the level of the muscle. John was aware of the greater saphenous vein and the major vessels of the leg lie on the medial side of the femur.

John poured some whiskey on his hands before probing with his index finger for the ball.

"I feel it, we are in luck."

"That is easy for you to say, that hurts like hell."

"Put the leather back in your mouth and lie still!"

With a bullet forceps and one finger John was able to extract the musket ball.

"Got it! I don't believe there are any pieces of fabric in the wound."

John closed the flap over the wound and with a silk suture sewed the wound closed. He then poured more whiskey on the wound area and took a clean cotton piece of bedding and wrapped the wound area.

"Thank you John, I think you attempting to kill me but I'll forgive you."

Though the mighty war ship *Constitution*, received damaged, the crew was able to salvage the *HMS Java's* steering wheel and replace *Old Ironsides* wheel that was destroyed when the ball hit it. Once the wheel was on board the *Constitution* the ship's carpenter, William Godley, and his two mates set to work installing it.

"Thank you gentlemen, that will make things easier," Bainbridge managed a smile.

"Captain, where do you want us to take the fifty cases of French wine we removed from the *Java*?"

"Put them in my cabin and we will deal with them later."

"What is the wine they had on board the *Java*?" John asked.

"The wine is a lovely red from Chateauneuf-Du-Pape area. The wine has a dense bluish/purple color and a big, sweet nose of blueberries, damp earth, and spring flowers. I believe from tasting the wine on previous sailing that you will enjoy the full-bodied impeccable tasting wine."

"May I join you for a glass this evening?"

"You may certainly do that. After what you have been through we may empty countless bottles."

Since the *Java* was carrying dignitaries the ship was well supplied with fine French wines and he made sure his officers offered some to them.

Bainbridge was in glory since he did not have the money to stock the *Constitution* with wine of any notoriety not that he was in any condition to celebrate now.

"Well done men, thank you for taking care of the officer and crew of the *Java*.

The *Java* had also been carrying a sizeable treasury. Some of the money was for Lieutenant General Hislop for the Bombay operation. The money would sweeten the purse each man would receive when they returned home.

Bainbridge liked General Hislop and they had some long discussions in their short acquaintance over a glass of wine taken from the *Java*. They would remain friends and correspond with each other for many years to come.

"Lieutenant Parker and Lieutenant Morris, take the boat and make one last trip to the *Java*. Search it once more to make sure we have not missed somebody. When you are satisfied all those who survived are off the *Java* set charges to blow the ship up." Bainbridge was in relentless pain but he was still in charge of his ships duties.

HMS Java was beyond repair at sea. There was no way to make repairs to keep the frigate afloat until they got back to port. Lieutenants Parker and Morris took four midshipmen with him for one last trip to the *Java*. Many of the *Java's* crew were on the rail of the *Constitution* to see what was going to happen to their ship.

Lieutenant Parker went to the *Java's* gun room and using a large piece of sail material he made a fuse. He placed black powder on the sail cloth and rolled it like a cigarette. He placed the end of the fuse in gun powder left in the gun room. He then dragged up the ladder to the upper deck and lit the powder.

"Come on men let's get off this frigate before it blows and sinks."

The rubber Necker's on the *Constitution* were waiting to see what was going to happen to their dead friends and ship mates.

Lieutenant Parker and the four midshipmen arrived at the *Constitution* just about the time the gun room exploded opening a large hole in the hull where the water rushed in. The ship slowly sank with its crew of dead sailors who had given their lives in the fierce battle.

Bainbridge had two sailors assist him to the rail so he could say a pray for the dead. Others on the deck of the *Constitution* could not help notice that the Captain of the *Constitution* was offering a prayer for those on the *Java*. The crew also removed their hats and bowed their heads in silence.

The *Constitution* had boarded 337 people from the *Java*: lieutenant-general, one major, one captain, one post-captain, one master and commander, five lieutenants, three lieutenants of the marines, one surgeon, two assistant surgeons, one purser, fifteen midshipmen, one gunner, one boatswain, one master, one carpenter, two Captain's clerks, 297 petty officers, seamen, and marines making altogether 337 men. There were also nine Portuguese seamen, eight passengers, private characters.

The *Constitution* was housing almost double the capacity of the frigate. There were almost two hundred and thirty wounded to attend to and there accommodations were wretched. The healthy sailors were formed into groups to take watches looking out for the care of the wounded and removing those that died from the group. They were taking lemonade and tamarind water to the wounded and making sure they drank it.

The accommodations on the *Constitution* were filled with wall to wall humanity. The kitchen was in twenty-four hour production. The surgeon's from both ships were going non-stop to see to the wounded.

Lieutenant Aylwin of the *Constitution* was severely wounded during the action. Bainbridge felt the young officer had great promise as a future naval captain. He had received a ball through his shoulder. Lieutenant Aylwin was in uniform when he was shot exacerbating the chance of infection. Most of the men choose to fight with the least amount of clothing on as possible.

Lieutenant Aylwin died of his wounds. He had been in the previous action between the *Constitution* and *Guerrière*, and for his gallantry and good conduct on that occasion he was promoted to a lieutenancy.

They had all seen too many of the men struck down in battle but not killed, to then see them died from infection. If you were wearing clothing the garment fabric would be introduced into the body and infection was going to happen. Where as if the sailor was not wearing clothes and was wounded the object causing the wound could be removed and rum poured on the wound to lessen the chance of infection.

FORTY-NINE

After the battle
December 29, 1812

NO ROSES
There are no roses on sailor's graves,
Nor wreaths upon the storm tossed waves,
No last post from the Royals band,
So far away from their native land,
No heartbroken words carved on stone,
Just shipmates bodies there alone,
The only tributes are the seagull's sweeps,
And the teardrop when a loved one weeps.

Quoted from: Royal National Lifeboat Institution.

Captain Lambert was too dangerously wounded to be removed immediately, the cutter returned on board the prize for the balance of the prisoners. Finally Captain Lambert was transported to the *Constitution* and placed in Captain Bainbridge's cabin in his bunk.

John Ridgely was extremely busy but he made sure he did all that was possible to alleviate Captain Lambert's sufferings.

Captain Bainbridge was in much pain from his wounds. John had treated him and he would check on him also.

"You must know that you should be lying down, William," John was adamant as to what Bainbridge should do.

"Perhaps so, but I need to see that the ship is put into order and that the men are all attended too."

Captain Lambert was brought up on deck on a cot just before the *Constitution* was to drop anchor. The officer's and crew were going to be dropped off under the care of the Island officials.

Bainbridge was also on deck with the aid of Surgeon Evans and Lieutenant Shubrick. Bainbridge was not in good shape, his wound was still seeping and he looked gaunt.

When Captain Lambert's cot was on the deck being prepared for transferring to the smaller boat Captain Bainbridge went to his side. Bainbridge had the sword that Captain Lambert had surrendered to him. William laid the sword next to the dying man and said, "I return your sword, my dear sir, with my sincerest wish that you will recover and wear it, as you have hitherto done, with honor to yourself and to your country."

Captain Lambert was in a state on mild delirium but was coherent enough to murmur his thanks, "Your kindness is appreciated." Captain Lambert grasped Bainbridge's hand with his feeble fingers.

General Hislop presented to Bainbridge a handsome sword, not in surrender, but in token of gratitude for his conduct and treatment of those unfortunates whom the fate of war had placed in their keeping.

The cordial relations established between Bainbridge and the Governor General was of a lasting character, and the latter was always proud to speak of the American captain as his friend.

FIFTY

USS Constitution
December 31, 1812

From the Journal of Captain Bainbridge:
"The Constitution lay by the Java for two days until so that all the wounded and prisoners, with their baggage could all be transferred to the Constitution. They also took all the gun power, cannon balls, and weapons to the gun room."
WB
January 1, 1813
St. Salvador, Brazils
"My dear sir:
I am sorry to inform you of the unpleasant news of Mr. Gascoine's death. Mr. Gascoine and myself were shipmates in the Mary borough, and first came to seen together. He was shot early in the action by a round shot in his right thigh, and died in a few minutes afterwards. Four others of his messmates shared the same fate, together with sixty men killed and 170 wounded. The official account you will no doubt have read before this reaches you. I beg you will let all his friends and relations know of his untimely fate.
We were on board the Java for a passage to India when we fell in with

this frigate. Two parcels I have sent you under good care, and I hope this will reach you safely.
Yours truly,
Lieutenant P.V. Wood
22nd reg. Isle of France.

The fallowing correspondence exhibits the character of Captain Bainbridge in a light so honorable, and so well calculated to exalt the national character, that we are happy in the opportunity of giving' it publicity.

Source: National Archives, Record Group 45, Captain's Letters, 1813, Vol.1, No.8 1/2.

FIFTY-ONE

Prisoners
January 3, 1813

Bainbridge sailed the *Constitution* into the harbour at San Salvador on January 4th. He found the *Hornet* was still maintaining the blockade of the port exactly where he had left her.

Commodore Bainbridge requested Captain Lawrence to pilot his frigate into the harbour, as he had some previous knowledge of the channel. As his vessel was entering it, a boat came alongside with information that the *Bonne Citoyenne* had hove short, loosed her sails, and that Captain Greene had expressed his determination to go to sea that night.

Bainbridge was hoping to find the *Essex*, but no such luck. The *Essex* for some reason had failed to make her rendezvous.

Captain Bainbridge made sure the crew of the *Java* was placed on shore and that all the men were going to be taken care. Bainbridge landed all his prisoners on parole of honour, not to serve again during the war, or until regularly exchanged by their respective governments.

Captain Lambert was dying when they were unloading the *Java* crew. The two wounded commanders grasped hands in mutual respect and admiration. Lambert lingered through the night and died the following morning on January 4th.

Bainbridge presided over the funeral. William felt like it was necessary for him to conduct the funeral service and oversee the burial. The crew's of the two vessels attended the funeral that was held at the base of the harbour. He was buried at St. Salvador with military honors.

Commodore Bainbridge earned the great respect from the crew of the *Java* and made a deep and lasting impression on the officer's. His kindness to the *Java* officers and enlisted men inspired them with great admiration of the American character.

United States' frigate Constitution,
St. Salvador, Jan. 3, 1813.

Sir, — I have the honor to inform you that on the 29th ult. at 2 p.m., in south lat. 13 6, and west long. 38, about 10 leagues distance from the coast of Brazil, I fell in with and captured his B. M. frigate Java, of 49 guns and upwards of 400 men, commanded by Captain Lambert a very distinguished officer. The action lasted 1 hour 55 minutes, in which time the enemy was completely dismasted, not having a spar of any kind standing. The loss on the Constitution^ was 9 killed and 25 wounded, as per enclosed list. The enemy had 60 killed and 101 wounded certainly, (among the latter Captain Lambert, mortally) but by the enclosed letter, written on board this ship, by one of the officers of the Java and accidently found, it is evident that the enemy's wounded must have been much greater than as above stated, and who must have died of their wounds previously to their being removed. The letter states 60 killed and 170 wounded.

For further details of the action I beg leave to refer you to the enclosed extracts from my Journal. The Java had, in addition to her own crew, upwards of one hundred supernumerary officers and seamen to join the British ships of war in the East Indies: also lieutenant general Hislop, appointed to the command of Bombay; major

Walker and captain Wood of his staff, and captain Marshall, master and commander in the British Navy, going to the East Indies to take command of a sloop of war there.

Should I attempt to do justice by representation to the brave and good conduct of all my officers and crew during the action, I should fail in the attempt— therefore suffice it to say, that the whole of their conduct was such as to merit my highest encomiums. I bet leave to recommend the officers particularly to the notice of the government, as also tile unfortunate seamen who were wounded, and the families of those brave men who fell in the action.

The great distance from our own coast and the perfect wreck we made the enemy's frigate, forbade every idea of attempting to take her to the United States — I had therefore no alternative but burning her, which I did on the 31st ult. after receiving all the prisoners and their baggage, which was very hard work, only having one boat left out of eight, and not one left on board the Java.

On fallowing up the frigate Java I proceeded to this place, where I have landed: all the prisoners on their parole to return to England, and there remain until regularly exchanged, and not to serve in their processional capacities in any place, or in any manner whatsoever against the United States of America, until their exchange shall be effected. I have the honor to be, 8cc.

(Signed) W. BAINBRIDGE. ,
January 6, 1813

GENERAL HISLOP TO COMMODORE 3AINBRIDGE.
Salvador, January 3, 1813.

Dear Sir — I am justly penetrated with the fullest sense of your very handsome and kind treatment, ever since the fate of war placed me in your power, and I beg once more to renew to you my sincerest acknowledgments for the same.

Your acquiescence with my request in granting me my parole, with the officers of my staff, added to the obligations I had previously experienced, claims from me this additional tribute of my thanks. Not that I now finally flatter myself, that in the further extension of your generous and humane feelings, in the alleviations of the misfortunes of war, that you will have the goodness to fulfill the only wish and request I am now most anxious to see completed, by enlarging on their parole (did the same conditions you have acceded to with respect to myself) all the officers of the Java still on board your ship a favour I shall never cease duly to appreciate by your acquiescence thereto. 1 have the honour to subscribe myself, dear sir, your most obliged and very humble servant.

(Signed) T. HISLOP.
Commodore Bainbridge.

ANSWER OF COMMODORE BAINBRIDGE.
United Statics frigate Constitution, St. Salvador, 3d January, 1813.

Dear Sir — I have received your letter of this date, conveying sentiments *of your feelings for my treatment towards you since the fate of war placed you in.*

The Java is rated in steel's List a- 38 gun frigate. Her real force was 28 eighteen pounders on the main deck — 14 thirty-two pounders on the quarter deck — 4 thirty-two pounders, and 2 large twelve pounders on the forecastle — and one shifting gun, a twenty-four pounder.

The British rate their ships from the number of guns on a particular deck; and a frigate carrying 28 eighteen pounders on her main deck, is regularly called by them a 38, which rate has frequently fifty-two mounted.

There are on board the Constitution some of the Java's shot, from which it has been ascertained, that there is scarcely three pounds difference between her eighteens and the American twenty-fours, so claimed my power. The kind expressions which you have been pleased to use, are justly appreciated by me, and far overbalance those common civilities shown by me, and which are always due to prisoners. I regret that the lumbered state of my ship prevented me from making you as comfortable on board as I sincerely wished to have done. I have complied with your last request, respecting paroling all the officers of the Java. In doing so, your desire, in addition to my disposition to ameliorate as much as possible the situation of those officers, considerably influenced me.

Permit me to tender you (notwithstanding our respective countries are at war) assurances of sincere esteem and high respect, and to assure you that I shall feel at all times highly gratified in hearing of or from you. With fervent wishes for the recover} - of the gallant captain Lambert, I have the honour to subscribe myself, very respectfully, &c.

(Signed) Wm. BAINBRIDGE.

January 4, 1813

GENERAL HISLOP TO COMMODORE BAINBRIDGE.

St. Salvador, 4th January, 1813.

Dear Sir — Allow me once more to express my sincerest acknowledgments for this last instance of your kind attention to my wishes, by having complied with my request in behalf of the officers of the Java. Lieutenant Chad's delivered to me your very polite and obliging letter, and be assured that I still feel no less gratification at all times to hear of and from you than that which you are so good as to express you will derive in receiving information respecting myself.

May I request now that you will be so good as to cause to be looked for a small chest, containing articles of plate, more valuable to me on account of having been presented to me by the colony of Demarara, where I commanded for several years. I have the honour to be, &c.

314

(Signed) T. HISLOP.

On January 28th Lieutenant John Cushing Aylwin died from his wounds. He had been standing with his two comrades, Morris and Hush when the two vessels came in contact. John was shot in the left shoulder by a musket ball when one of the crew of the *Java attempted to board* the *Constitution*. Aylwin was also firing his pistol at the enemy when he received another ball through the same shoulder. The ball went deep and shattered the bone knocking Aylwin to the deck.

FIFTY-TWO

Home
February 15, 1813

On January 6th the breezes were strong and the *Constitution* was displaying all her sails and on their way for the United States.

The *Constitution* had good weather allowing the ship to reach Boston on February 15, 1813.

"Lieutenant Ludlow, please deliver this letter with great hast to the Secretary of the Navy before we get mobbed."

"Yes sir."

There were thousands of people lined on the docks, crowded on Balconies and windows cheering loudly to wish the *Constitution* and its crew a hardy welcome. There was artillery fire, bands playing Yankee Doodle and much cheering and waving. Ladies were waving their handkerchiefs.

Susan was part of the celebrating well wishers standing in the snow on that cold cloudy day. She had a serious look of concern on her face. She could see that William was not all right. Two midshipmen were assisting Bainbridge off the *Constitution*, one under each arm.

Susan went running to him. "Oh William what has happen?"

William gave her a hug and the Midshipmen made sure their captain didn't fall down.

"I am okay, we were engaged in a bloody battle and I am sorry to say there was a lot of death and many wounded some that might not make it."

"Are you sure you that you should not be taken directly home and put to bed?"

"Later my love, these men are determined to take us to the Exchange Coffee-house."

"Tell me, where did you get hurt, and is it all better?"

"I am getting better every day. I was wounded in the left hip, but I was lucky. John took good care of me and patched me up. I'll be healed before you know it."

Captain Bainbridge was greeted by Commodores Rodgers and Hull. The two men escorted Bainbridge in a procession to the Exchange Coffee-house. The streets were strung with banners and streamers.

Rogers and Hull were also willing to except the exuberance of the crowd.

Bainbridge had left Lieutenant Parker in charge of making sure the wounded were transported to the hospital and the rest of the men secured the ship before taking liberty.

At nine o'clock they had assembled at the theatre where Captain Bainbridge was the guest of honor. The victory of the Captain was expounded on by Commodore Rogers and the crowded theatre responded with wild enthusiasm. The Bainbridge's stayed for what seemed like an eternity, trying to smile and thank those there for their congratulations.

"Let's go home William," Susan was more concerned about William not being a well as he pretended.

Two of the ship's midshipmen assisted Susan in getting Captain Bainbridge to their home. William was very weak and feeling feverous.

"Thank you gentlemen, I don't believe I could have made it without your kind assistance."

"Yes, thank you for helping my husband. One more favor would see that he gets to our bedroom?"

"Yes madam, it is our pleasure, we owe the Captain a great deal and are more than happy to assist in whatever manner we can."

"I need to wash before retiring, Susan," William tried to sound strong.

"Can I help you undress?"

"Do I have a choice?"

"No you don't, now unbutton those clothes."

Susan got William undressed and saw the thigh; it was a large ugly purple area with a large red circle around the perimeter.

"Oh my God, William! You go wash and I am going down stairs and bring some whiskey up to dab on that."

William had a fever. The wound was leaking. Susan got William into bed and began the nursing her husband back to health.

"Susan there is a package in my case that is wrapped in flowery paper; would you get it for me?"

"I don't....Oh I see it now."

"Bring it to me please."

"This is for you."

"May I open it," Susan was getting excited about what it might be.

"Oh my God William, they are the most gorgeous string of pearls I have even seen," Susan's eye lit up.

"They tell me they are Australian South Seas white pearls, and the best in the world. See how the pearls are smaller at the top and graduates perfectly to the exceptional centerpiece."

"They have such a high luster and each pearl looks perfect."

"I was told each pearl is carefully picked to ensure the highest quality of white pearl."

"I can hardly wait to wear these at the next formal event."

The United States House of Representatives at the second session of the Twelfth Congress: "Resolution requesting the President of the United States to present medals to Captain William Bainbridge, and the officers of the frigate *Constitution*;"

The joint resolution from the Senate, "requesting the President of the United States to present medals to Captain Bainbridge and the officers of the frigate *Constitution*," was read the first time; and, on motion, the said resolution was read for the second time and ordered to be read the third time. The said resolution was read the third time and passed unanimously. March 1, 1813.

Mr. Speaker; The Senate have passed "A resolution requesting the President of the United States to present medals to Captain Bainbridge and the officers of the frigate *Constitution*."

FIFTY-THREE

Celebration
February 18, 1813

> "Come, lads, draw near, and you shall hear,
> In truth as chaste as Dian, O!
> How Bainbridge true, and his bold crew,
> Again have tamed the lion, O!
> 'Twas off Brazil he got the pill
> Which made him cry peccavi, O!
> But hours two, the Java new,
> Maintained the battle bravely, O!
> "But our gallant tars, as soon as they were piped to quarters, gave three cheers, and boldly swore, by the blood of the heroes of Tripoli, that, sooner, than strike, they'd go the bottom singing,
> Tid re I, Tid re id re I do."

The following day the Legislature of Massachusetts was still in regular session passed a resolution of thanks to Captain Bainbridge, his officers and crew.

The Common Council of New York presented to Bainbridge the

freedom of the city in a gold box, and ordered his portrait painted for the picture-gallery in the City Hall.

The city of Philadelphia presented him with an elegant service of silver plate, the most costly piece of which was a massive urn, elegantly wrought. The "United States Gazette," wrote a very flattering article of the event.

LEGISLATURE OF MASSACHUSETTS.

On motion of the Hon. Mr. Otis, it was voted, unanimously, that the answer be entered on the Journal of the Senate.

In the House of Representatives, February 13.

Whereas every event which reflects inspire upon the American name, and contributes to elevate the national character in the view of foreign powers, ought to be distinguished and mourned by the people of the United States: And whereas the brilliant victories achieved by our gallant navy since the commencement of the present war with Great Britain, are highly calculated to produce that effect, and while they demonstrate to the nation, the wisdom and patriotism of that policy Vanish projected and created a navy, they strongly urge upon the national government, the importance of encouraging and increasing that species of defense. It becomes the representatives of the people of Massachusetts (whatever may be their opinions in relation to the present war) to testify their high approbation of the gallant and able conduct of those officers and crews of the navy, to whom. The fortunate opportunities have occurred of giving reputation to the American arms, and of signalizing their own velour, enterprise, and nautical skill. Therefore,

Resolved as the opinion of this house. That commodore Bainbridge and Decatur captains Hid and Jones of the United States Navy, their officers and crews, in the splendid victories by them recently obtained over the British ships of war the Java-, Macedonian. Guerrière, and Frolic y and in their generous conduct to their captured enemies, have acquired for themselves a distinguished title to that consideration and applause of their fellow citizens, which is due to a heroic and able discharge of duty, and which is the legitimate reward of the brave man who devotes his life to the service of his country.

Ordered that the Speaker be requested to communicate the above resolve with its preamble to the respective naval officers to which it has reference.

Attest, B POLLARD, Clerk.

February 19, 1813

Senate, February 19.

The Senate President offered up the following resolution: "The Commonwealth of Massachusetts Senate extends it up most thanks to Commodore William Bainbridge, and the officers and crew of the frigate *Constitution* under his command, for their brilliant achievement, in capturing and destroying his Britannic Majesty's frigate *Java*. The Commonwealth of Massachusetts Senate requests that Commodore Bainbridge be requested to communicate the same to his officers and crew, with an assurance from this branch of the legislature that they will hold in grateful remembrance those who fell in fighting for the essential and violated rights of their country."

Resolved, that the President of the Senate cause an attested copy of this resolution to be transmitted to Commodore Bainbridge.

Samuel Dana, President.

The following neat and dignified answer was returned by Commodore Bainbridge.

United States frigate *Constitution*,

Harbour of Boston, February 20, 1813.

Dear Sir, I have had the honour, through you, to receive the vote of thanks from the Senate of the Commonwealth of Massachusetts to myself, officers, and crew, for capturing and destroying the British frigate Java.

" To merit and receive the approbation of our country, ever has, and ever will be our highest ambition. I am sir, very respectfully, your obedient servant,"

Wm. Bainbridge.

The Hon. Samuel Dana.

February 22, 1813

HOUSE OF REPRESENTATIVES OF THE UNITED STATES.
Monday, February 22.
To the Senate and House of Representatives of the United States.

"I lay before Congress a letter with accompanying documents from Captain Bainbridge now commanding the United States frigate "the Constitution" reporting his capture and destruction of the British frigate, Java." The circumstances and the issue of this combat afford another example of the professional skill and heroic spirit which prevail in our naval service. The signal display of both by Captain Bainbridge his officers and crew, command

the highest praise. This being the second instance in which the condition of the captured ship, by rendering it impossible to get her into port, has barred a contemplated reward for successful valor. I recommend to the consideration of congress the equity and propriety of a general provision allowing in such cases, both past and future, a fair proportion of the value which would accrue to the captors on the safe arrival and sale of the prize."

JAMES MADISON President of the United States of America

The event over the next weeks caused great exultation throughout the United States. The *Constitution* was now popularly called *"Old Ironsides."* Orators and rhymers, the pulpit and the press, made the gallant exploits of Bainbridge the theme of many words and verse and prose.

The Congress voted to pay him and his crew $50,000. The Congress also ordered that a gold medal be struck of Bainbridge and silver medals for each of his officers.

FIFTY-FOUR

Constitution/Boston
March 3, 1813

Dinner in honour of Commodore Bainbridge.

A splendid banquet was given at the Exchange Coffee-house for Bainbridge and the officers of the United States Frigate the *Constitution*. They were recognized for the brilliant naval victory in taking of the prize *Java*. A British man-of-war had not ever been taken as an American prize. The British were becoming more humble in how the perceived American capabilities.

Commodores Rogers, Captain's Hull and Smith, and the officers of the squadron now in our port were invited. The procession was formed in Faiuiel Hall, by Major Tilden, and was escorted amidst the applauses of the townsmen, to the Exchange Coffee House. There was a battalion composed of the Boston Light Infantry and the Winslow Blues, commanded by Coronel Sergeant. The Hall was completely filled. The Honorable Christopher Gore presided. The Honorable Harrison G. Otis, Honorable Israel Thorndike, Arnold Welles Esq. Thomas L. Winthrop Esq. Hon. Peter C. Brooks, and Wm. Sullivan Esq. assisted as Vice Presidents.

Mr. Jones provided the excellent entertainment. Before everyone was instructed to sit down at a table the blessing of Almighty God was asked in a most impressive manner by the Rev. Mr. Holley.

After thanks were returned, the Honorable Mr. Gore addressed the gentlemen present on the occasion. In a very elegant and impressive manner he displayed the high honor and distinguished benefits resulting from the brilliant achievements of our gallant heroes, and tendering to Commodore Bainbridge and his officers the granulation of the company. He proposed as a toast the health of their distinguished guest, which was drank amid plaudits that made the welkin ring.

Commodore Bainbridge replied in a very interesting manner; after which the following toasts were received with the highest demonstrations of pleasure and gratification.

Captain Bainbridge struck his glass with his table knife and spoke loudly. "I would like to offer up a toast to our country, its honor is our pride, the support of its honor is our Navy."

Here, here…

"I would like to follow that with a toast to the President of the United States of America. The Governor of the Commonwealth his name indicates his character; strong in intellect; strong in principle and strong in the affection of the people," First Lieutenant Parker stood and raised his glass.

Third Lieutenant Ludlow was not about to be left out, he stood and loudly announced, "too the Battle of the 29th of December. The sun of American glory then first beamed in the southern hemisphere. May its luster increase through the successive periods of time, and in all the divisions of the globe."

Lieutenant Morris took his turn, "The Memory of Lieutenant Aylwin and his companions in arms, which fell in the action with the *Java*. "When fall the brave, their brilliant doom. Age after age shall memory keep, and chase the darkness from the tomb."

The drinking was heavy and the more they drank the louder the participants became. The toasting went on and on.

"Opportunity to the brave; may the frigates *President* and *Congress* be soon rated in England as "Seventy-fours in disguise."

"To the gallant spirit of our Naval Chiefs in battle, fearless in victory, modest and humane."

"The Memory of Washington, his spirit approves us from the skies — we will never forget that his valor and his wisdom have prepared our triumphs."

"The American flag protected by true American blood — it will protect all who sail under it."

"The defenseless coasts of New-England — May those whom it concerns remember, that it is treason to give harbors to our enemies."

"Massachusetts, firm and honest — tenacious of her rights mindful of her obligations though not disgraced — assailed, but not dismayed—-.disquieted, but not in despair."

"Independent America — she wants no instruction in the Freedom of the seas from the Tyrant of the land — her gallant TARS can vindicate alone the honor of her flag — they need no insidious aid from a despot."

"The Crew of the *Constitution* — May our country never be reluctant to spend money for those who spend their lives for us."

"Our National Rulers— May they learn from our victories on the ocean, that the path to honorable peace, is not through the wilderness, but over the Atlantic."

John Ridgely also entered into the spirit of the event, "Here is to the glory that our Hull, Jones, Decatur and Bainbridge, have brought from the Ocean, shall beam with brighter luster, when the brave who have sought, shall share their fame."

"That Skill and Valor which deserve victory — that Magnanimij Mch commands the gratitude of the conquered."

By Commodore Bainbridge, "The Town of Boston, the Cradle of American Independence."

By Commodore Rodgers — "The Citizens of the State of Massachusetts May their patriotic spirit and hospitable feeling find a suitable return in the breasts of their countrymen."

By Captain Hull — "The Enemy — should he attempt to enter our harbor, may he be taught that we have a Bunker Hill, and Bostonians to defend it."

After the umpteenth toast, the President of the day announced in an affecting and eloquent address, that the money arising from the subscription which was usually appropriated to decorations, had been on this occasion reserved for the benefit of the widow Cheeves, who had lost in the battle with the *Java*, her only two sons, her stay and support; and he offered this to the Commodore as an apology for an omission of decorations of the hall, as had been usual, and doubted not it would be acceptable. The Commodore expressed his grateful sense of the compliment implied in the apology; and all present felt that the compliment was justly due.

'Honour to the Brave.'

An attested copy of this resolve was communicated to each of the Naval Officers mentioned, in an appropriate letter from the hon. Timothy Bigelow, Speaker of the House.

In Common Council (New York), March 1, 1813. The following resolution was proposed by Mr. Bracket, and unanimously adopted.

In testimony of the high sense entertained by the Common Council, of the gallantry and skill of Commodore William Bainbridge, and his officers and crew, on board the United States frigate Constitution, in the late capture and destruction of his Britannic majesty's frigate, the Java; whereby new laurels have been acquired by our gallant navy; and a new instance afforded of the practical utility of that kind of defense, for the protection and encouragement of the important commercial interests of our country.

Therefore Resolved, That the freedom of the city be presented to Commodore Bainbridge, in a golden box; and that his Portrait be obtained, and set up in the gallery of portraits, belonging to this city; and that the thanks of the Common Council be presented to his officers and crew, who were engaged in this achievement, so honorable to themselves and the nation.

"I transmitted your letter to me of yesterday to Captain P. B. Greene, to whom the substance is directed; and having his reply, I herewith insert it, verbatim."

"I hasten to acknowledge the favour of your communication made to me, this day, from Mr. Hill, consul of the United States of America, on the subject of a challenge stated to have been offered through Mr. Hill, by Captain Lawrence, of the United States sloop of war, the Hornet, to myself as commander of his en Britannic Majesty's ship; the Bonne Citoyenne, anchored in this port, pledging his honour, as well as that of Commodore Bainbridge, that no advantage shall be taken by the Constitution, or any other American vessel whatever, on the occasion."

"I am convinced, sir, if such a recapture were to take place, the result could not remain long dubious, and would terminate favorably to the ship which I have the honour to command; but I am equally convinced, that Commodore Bainbridge, could not reserve so much from the paramount duty which he owes to his country, as to become all inactive spectator, and side a ship belonging to the very squadron under his orders fall into the hands of an enemy: this reason operates powerfully on my mind, for exposing the Bonne Citoyenne to a risk upon terms so manifestly disadvantageous, as those proposed by Commodore Bainbridge; indeed, nothing could give me a greater satisfaction than complying with the wishes of Captain Lawrence; and I earnestly hope, that chance will afford him an opportunity of meeting the Bonne Citoyenne

under different circumstances, to enable him to distinguish himself in the manner he is so desirous of doing. I further assure you, that my ship will, at all times, be prepared, wherever she may be, to repel any- attack; made against her, and I shall also act offensively whenever I judge it proper to do so."

"I am,

P.B. Greene

The commodore forwarded this correspondence to the secretary of the navy, accompanied by the following animadversions.

"Captain Greene's excuse, I have no doubt, will be viewed by those who see it in its proper light He certainly was not warranted in questioning the sacred pledge I made to him. The confidence which I had in the gallant commander, brave officers and crew of the Hornet, all of whom exhibited the most ardent desire for the conflict, induced me to take the responsibility, from which I never would have swerved. The strongest proof, indeed, which I could give of that, was leaving the Hornet for days together, off the harbour in which the Bonne Citoyenne laid, and from which might be discovered that the Constitution was not within forty miles; therefore, at any period. Captain Greene could have been certain of contending with her alone. Finally, to prevent his having the least possible excuse, I went into the harbour of St. Salvador, and remained at anchor there for three days, where he could have detained me twenty-four hours, on application to the governor. These three days, the Hornet remained off the harbour, and the Bonne Citoyenne continued in it, safely riding at her anchor."

February 22, 1814

It seemed like the United States was always in conflict with other countries.

The United States had made great efforts and sacrifices to move the Capital of the United States to Washington D.C. The British felt it was their desire to inflict and much misery on the new independent nation as possible.

In the summer of 1814 the British invaded Washington D.C. with only the one thing on their mind, destruction.

The Secretary of the Navy not wanting the ships and supplies to fall into the hands of the British ordered the Ships yards burned. The British had taken control of the city.

God was looking after the Americans. A hurricane with intermittent tornado's past through less than a day after the initial invasion. It was reported the storms killed more British then American guns. The British ships that had transported the troops were badly damaged by the storm. The actual occupation of Washington lasted about twenty-six hours.

President Madison and the rest of the government quickly returned to the city.

Following the War of 1812 Bainbridge was given command of an anti-piracy squadron, but through force and diplomacy, Captain Stephen Decatur brought the Barbary Corsairs to terms before he could sail.

Commodore Bainbridge was a naval hero while his friend Decatur was a pirate-fighting hero.

William was finally at home most of 1814. He was home to witness the birth of their daughter on November 19, 1814, Lucy Anne Bainbridge was born.

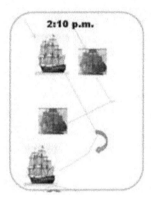

FIFTY-FIVE

Navy Yard
July-December 1815

Bainbridge next duty was in command of the Navy Yard,
Charlestown, Massachusetts.

While Bainbridge was in command at Charles-town the British
blockaded Boston harbor. Bainbridge was concerned about the blockade
but he also felt that he could escape it whenever he wanted too.

The people of Boston were concerned that the British would fire on the
city and some want to build better defenses. Bainbridge was not in favor of
more land defenses he felt that might endanger the city more.

Politics elevated the tensions among the citizens. Some of the politicians
were indifferent to what happened to public property being that it belonged
to the administration. Bainbridge insisted that it belonged to the nation
and should be protected at all hazards.

Bainbridge was at odds with the governor and council of Massachusetts
as to how the harbors along the coast should be defended.

Boston was making overtures that they would act alone. Bainbridge
conveyed that there could be terrible consequence on acting independently.
Bainbridge was the better person displaying his diplomacy and conveying
the high level of duty, honor, and patriotism to the community.

Boston did develop a proper system of defense and danger was adverted. Since Bainbridge was the only qualified person with extensive military experience it was to Boston's continual survival that they allowed Bainbridge to lead and not those with political motivation.

While Bainbridge was stationed in Boston he established the first United States Naval School in 1815. The Secretary of the Navy was hoping Bainbridge would agree to teaching young midshipmen that showed promise as officer material how to get there. The United States was desperate for naval officers with experience.

Bainbridge proved to be an excellent teacher just like he was when taking over a new crew on a new ship. His class room was on ship board; this was hands on training, and the students learned or they were requested to leave.

Shortly after the beginning of the war with Great Britain, war was declared again against the United States by Algiers. Finally on the conclusion of peace with Great Britain, Congress declared war against the regency of Algiers. The United States was no longer going to be subservient to North Africa. The Congress ordered the Secretary of the Navy to assemble a large squadron under the command of William Bainbridge, in 1815, to protect American commerce in the Mediterranean.

Bainbridge was back to dealing with the Bashaw of Tripoli and the Dey of Algiers. Bainbridge felt the only way to get the Bashaw and Dey to make peace was to demonstrate the resources of force of the United States in the Algerian port. The only way in which peace could be maintained with these people, so faithless in regard to political obligations, was by operating on their fears. Bainbridge was concerned about making the necessary arrangements for the protection of American commerce in the Mediterranean; force against North Africa needed to be demonstrated.

FIFTY-SIX

Second Barbary War
May 20, 1815

The Second Barbary War had broken out. The United States was again fighting the Ottoman Empire's North African regencies of Algiers, Tripoli, and Tunis. The United States had support from the United Kingdom of Great Britain and Ireland and also the United Kingdom of the Netherlands.

Commodore Bainbridge welcomed this opportunity in his career to command the Mediterranean Squadron against the renewed threat Barbary pirates in the Second Barbary War (1815-1816). Bainbridge had a score to settle, and he was finally given the free hand to do what he had wanted to do for over a decade, negotiate with his cannons.

Commodore William Bainbridge was on the new *USS Independence* Commodore of the squadron. Bainbridge had requested Stephen Decatur, Jr. to join him on the *USS Guerrière*. The squadron was made up of ten United States war-ships. The squadron left from New York on May 20, 1815 and was heading for Gibraltar. In Gibraltar they would regroup before sailing to Algiers. Bainbridge had traveled these waters many times. He was returning to end the attacks on American merchant vessels in the Mediterranean and the practice of holding their crews and officers for ransom. He finally felt that he was not being ordered into battle with his hands tied behind his back. Bainbridge was order to make sure the war practice against American shipping was ended.

Commodore Bainbridge was in command of the new *Independence* 90-guns, (30-pounders). There were 790 officers and enlisted men. The ship was new having only been launched June 22, 1814. William felt delighted that he was able to sail with many of the crew that had been with him a few years earlier on this state of the art war-ship.

Commodore Decatur, Jr. was in command of the *USS Guerrière* a 1508 long ton frigate with thirty-three 24-pounders and twenty 42-pounders and a complement of 400 officers and enlisted men.

Bainbridge reached Gibraltar on June 15, 1815. William was always humbled going through the narrow channel separating the Atlantic Ocean from the Mediterranean and seeing the towering rock of Gibraltar. The squadron regrouped at Gibraltar before departing on June 17, 1815 en route to Algiers. The plan was to make sure the squadron was all assembled and that everyone was prepared to do combat if the need arose along the way.

"Sails off the starboard bow," the call was yelled down from one of the Able Seamen on look out duty.

"Lieutenant, all sails raised, we are going to give chase," Bainbridge could feel the adrenalin pumping through his body. Bainbridge was feeling the acceleration of adrenalin reminding him how much he missed being back in action.

"Lieutenant, make sure the other ships are aware of the enemy and have them give chase also.

"It is one of theirs, Sir," one of the officers commented.

"Algerian?"

"I believe so Sir. It appears to be a flagship of the Algerian Navy."

Bainbridge recognized the ship as the *Meshuda* of 44-guns.

Bainbridge idea was to make the *Meshuda* go back towards the *Guerrière* and sandwich the Algerian ship.

They were just off Cape Gata when the *Guerrière* opened fire on the *Meshuda* with two broadsides. Bainbridge also crossed the stern on the *Meshuda* and fired ten of the ships carronades loaded with grape shot. The desk of the *Meshuda* was bloody site of red visible with the naked eye from the deck of the *Independence*.

The *Meshuda* struck her colors and the crew of the *Guerrière* took control of the Algerian flagship. They had captured four hundred and six

Algerians. The wounded were numerous and the thirty died. The *Guerrière* had four dead and ten wounded. The four that died were not from the enemy's fire but from one of the cannons blowing up.

They spotted the Algerian brig the *Estedio*, 22-guns and drove the ship to shore and captured it.

The squadron proceeded to Algiers arriving on June 28, 1815.

Going back to Algiers brought back bad memories for William and many of the crew. He did feel good that the arrival of the ten war-ships in their squadron could concentrate enough cannon fire on the city to totally destroy it.

The Dey was not being going to make any demanding threats on Bainbridge this time. Bainbridge was going to make sure the Dey was fearful for his life.

As in the pass, the Dey sent a boat out to the squadron to demand what the intensions of the ships being there. The boat was directed to the *Independence* to address their inquiries with Commodore Bainbridge.

Bainbridge received the messenger and demanded an audience with the Dey. The messenger took the request back to the Dey that Commodore Bainbridge was demanding a meeting with him. The Dey reluctantly granted an audience for the following morning at his palace.

"I never thought I would see you again," Bainbridge greeted the Dey of Algeria.

"You Christian dogs, do you think I am afraid of you."

"You should since we are prepared to get what we want or wipe your dirty filthy scum you call Muslims and those hill side defenses off the face of this earth," Bainbridge was staring directly at the Dey.

"You dare to threaten me you Christian dog?"

"I am not only threatening you but I am going to follow through unless you release all the prisoners and cease prying on American merchant vessels. I have a list of demands we have drafted into a treaty."

I will never agree to anything with a Christian dog."

Bainbridge turned to his First Lieutenant. "Go outside and give the signal to the ships to take out the harbor cannons and whatever portion of the town they can."

Bainbridge turned to the Dey and explained what was about to happen. Before the Dey could insult Bainbridge once again the cannon fire commenced to rack the harbor defenses.

Ten ships of the squadron were anchored so they could all deliver a broadside. The noise was deafening and the smoke was so dense that the ships were no longer visible.

The Dey was on his feet and rushed outside to see the unbelievable damage that 125 cannons could cause. The harbor defenses were destroyed and well as all the surrounding dwellings.

"This is the deal," Bainbridge addressed the Dey. "Tomorrow morning at ten a.m. a group of my officers will be here to escort you to the *USS Guerrière* where will fully expect you to enter into a treaty granting the United States full shipping rights, the guarantee that no further tributes will be necessary. You are also going to pay the United States $10,000 for payment of seized shipping. We will exchange captives and to sweeten the deal we will return the *Meshuda* and *Estedio*.

The Dey met with the senior officers in the squadron on Decatur's ship the *Guerrière* on July 3, 1815. The Dey did not argue about the treaty not after the damaged inflicted on his own defenses.

Bainbridge had the signed treaty in his hands.

"I offer you this advice, if you slip one time and inflict injury or demands upon any American vessel or American citizen we will be back. When we come back it will be with all guns firing until all we can see of your city is smoke."

The officers felt they needed to go first to Tunis and then to Tripoli to display their show of force.

The squadron arrived in Tunis and achieved a peace settlement on July 13, 1815 and on to Tripoli on August 9th. The incident in Algiers had preceded the arrival of the squadron.

The Squadron returned to Gibraltar and anchored in the harbor area. Bainbridge hosted a gathering of all the ships officer's on the deck of the *Independence.*

The *Independence* was the first ship-of-the-line commissioned in the United States Navy. The *Independence* had been launched on June 2, 1814 in the Boston Navy Yard. The first orders for the new ship were to be with the *Constitution* in the protection of Boston Harbor. The *Independence* wore the broad pennant of Commodore William Bainbridge and was under the command of William Bainbridge.

"Gentlemen, my congratulations to all of you; we have accomplished in six weeks what a few years ago we failed to do in five years," Bainbridge hoisted his glass in a toast the men.

I would also like to brief all of you on the new Mediterranean Squadron. Today we have here the largest assembly of American warships ever collected under the American flag; we are eighteen warships strong. We have five frigates, two sloops-of-war, seven brigs, and three schooners and of course the ship we are on, the *Independence.*

"We are going to part of a permanent naval fleet in the Mediterranean," Bainbridge announced proudly.

The fleet was successful in protecting American interests in the Mediterranean and evolved into the present day as the '6th Fleet.' One of the new destroyers in the 6th fleet was named *USS Bainbridge.*

The war was the final war with the pirate states and for the most part ended piracy in that region but not entirely.

Bainbridge returned to the United States on 15 November 1815.

Bainbridge was saying good-by to the crew after they had docked at Boston Station he was given document from one of the officers and contained the signatures of eighteen officers.

"The undersigned, cockpit and steerage' officers of the United States ship Independence, beg leave to express their unfeigned regret at the prospect of your departure from the ship which you have commanded for so long a period, and with so much dignity. Be pleased to accept their sincere thanks for the many indulgences and the kind treatment received from you, while serving under your command. With regret for the bereavement which they are about to experience in the loss of your paternal care, receive their congratulations on your transfer to a command of equal or superior importance, convinced as they are, that there is no situation in which you would not confer honour on the naval character of our country. Anxious to rejoin you shortly, they remain with sentiments of the highest respect and esteem."

You're most obedient servants.

The weather had turned cold and according to Susan they had two heavy snow falls which was unusual this early in the year.

William was happy to be home and spend the holidays with his family. This was the first time he had arranged to be home for both Thanksgiving and Christmas.

"We are so happy to have you home. I never cease to worry when you are gone," Susan's face reflected her happiness.

"My but haven't we all grown while I was gone! No let me see if I remember, Lucy is going to have her first birthday on the 19th, young William you must be six years old and how you have grown, Mary your getting to be quite the young lady of four and Susan, gosh, I hardly can believe my eyes, you are a tall as your mother."

"I am twelve papa and I been helping mother take care of my brother and sisters," Susan gave her dad a peck on the face.

FIFTY-SEVEN

USS Constitution
1816-1819

Commodore Bainbridge was again on land. He was no longer needed on a war-ship. Peace was being preserved by the French, English, and the North coast of Africa was not causing problems or at least there were few reports of problems.

The Secretary of the Navy, Benjamin Crowninshield, requested Bainbridge to serve shore duty at various stations. Crowninshield was dependant on Bainbridge's knowledge and expertise in keeping the navy together and ready.

On February 3, 1817, Benjamin Crowninshield ordered William Bainbridge from Boston to Washington. He had appointed Bainbridge as one of the board members of the Washington Naval yard.

The Washington Naval Yard was the largest employer in the District of Colombia. There were over 300 men employed and they were paid a per diem wage. The wages were adequate, a mechanic would make between $1 and $2 per day.

The Washington Naval Yard was burned in 1814 as was most of Washington. The yard was just beginning to come back as was the reconstruction of the offices of government. Money was tight, the new county was struggling, and the dedication of men like Bainbridge was making the comeback possible.

The Congress had been busy passing contracts for new war-ships; on December 16, 1814 a 74-gun ship-of-the-line to be named the USS *Chippewa.*

In 1816 Samuel Brown's 2 1/4 inch iron stud link chains were installed on the *U.S.S. Constitution* and the *U.S.S. Guerrière* and were considered a great success. In the same year the Royal Navy standardized on iron chain instead of hemp for all new vessels of war. Also in 1816 Walker, of Philadelphia, wrought the first American-made stud link anchor chains for the U.S. Navy.

The United States Navy organized a chain making plant in the Washington Navy Yard in 1817. In five months sufficient 2 1/8 inch and 2 3/8 inch un-studded and twisted chain was welded to equip two vessels.

In November of 1817 Bainbridge was ordered to the command of the new line-of-battle-ship *USS Columbus,* and appointed to command the Mediterranean squadron.

The *USS Columbus* was a 92-gun frigate. The 2,480 ton ship had 68 32-poundes and 24 42-pounders (carronades), 780 officers and enlisted men.

The *Columbus* was a ship of the line meaning it was a powerful enough war ship to take a place in a battle line. The ship was referred to a 'line of battle ship' which eventually became known as 'battleship' much later in time.

Bainbridge set sail from Hampton Roads on April 28th for the Mediterranean arriving at Gibraltar on June 4, 1820. Commodore Bainbridge was the Commander of the United States Naval forces.

The governor of the garrison of Gibraltar was General Don. General Don was at odds with the Americans and he had issued an order that Americans were not to have any intercourse with either the town or garrison.

"Lieutenant, Governor of Gibraltar has imposed a harsh stand that I find unreasonable and I need to go immediately to the garrison and see if I can have it rescinded."

"The men would certainly be appreciative if you could, Sir."

"The men deserve the right to be allowed on shore and release some of their pent up energies and hormonal tensions."

"Why has this General Don been so hard on Americans?"

"Well, what I have been told, his animosity has grown out of the repeated quarrels and duels which have taken place between Americans and British officers."

"I see Captain, but we have not been a part of that."

"Well perhaps I have over the years, that is, my not taking lightly to the arrogance the English have shown against Americans on the seas. We are now faced with dealing with this national prejudice and it is time we faced it and got over it."

It was late in the morning when Bainbridge finally was able to free himself from his ship's duties and pay an obligatory visit to General Don. The visit was expected from all sea captains when docking at a foreign port. Bainbridge's other motive was to propose an adjustment to the dispute between the officers under their respective commands.

"General Don, thank you for seeing me, I always looked forward to my visits with you."

"Cut the crap Bainbridge, you could care less about seeing me."

"Do I hear some animosity in for voice General? Of course I always enjoy our visits."

"Okay we had our visit, now I must get back to work."

"One thing General I would like to request from you before I go. I would like it if you would grant an immediate end to the dispute between the officers under our commands. We have no wish not to get along with the English and my men would take it as a tremendous jester of cooperation between our countries if your order could be rescinded."

"What is in it for me?"

"My orders are to protect the Mediterranean on continual bases and put an end to the piracy enabling merchant vessels free passage."

"So go about you business."

"There is where the rub comes in, in order for my squadron to protect you town we need to enter into an agreement," Bainbridge was not going to leave the matter up in the air.

"Well let's get to it, we certainly will cooperate with you on matters of security of our ports and harbors," the General was aware of the large presents the Americans were displaying in his harbor.

"That is the problem General; there will be no negotiations for your protection until you lift the ban on Americans coming ashore and being allowed to circulate."

"You think you have me don't you Captain!"

"It is up to General, I will wait on your response to reach me by

341

morning. If you continue your vendetta than I will sail out of here and let the pirates pry on merchant vessels attempting to do commerce with you."

"You will have my response. Now good day to you," the General was agitated that an American was getting the best of him.

Bainbridge went back to the ship feeling that he had made his case but he was not sure what the General might do. He always had the feeling the English considered themselves superior over Americans. Americans to the English were second class beings to be treated with distain.

"Welcome back Captain. Do I dare inquire how the meeting with the Governor went?"

"Thank you for asking Lieutenant. I believe the meeting went as expected. The Governor has until morning to get back to us with his answer as to cancelling his foolish interdiction," Bainbridge smiled as if he was sure as to his eventual success. "Tell the crew we should have our answer by morning or we will be leaving the port."

"Aye, aye, Sir."

Bainbridge did not have to wait until morning for his answer. A messenger approached the ship late in the afternoon requesting he deliver an important document from General Don.

Dear Captain Bainbridge. Your persuasive appeal to the interdiction prohibiting American officers from visiting Gibraltar has been be rescinded effective immediately. The appropriate authorities have been notified to expect your men to leave their respective ships for visiting our town. Please call on me at your earliest convenience to further discuss the matter of American protection on the Mediterranean.

General Don, Governor of Gibraltar.

"Lieutenant, please prepare the men for shore leave."

USS Columbus served as flagship for Commodore William Bainbridge in the Mediterranean until returning to Boston July 23, 1821.

Bainbridge enjoyed duty in the Mediterranean Sea and the ports he visited. He always felt comfortable sailing the enclosed sea, the waters were deep, not the depth of the Atlantic but he felt you only need so much water under you and the rest meant nothing. The water circulation in the Mediterranean is dominated by salinity and temperature differences rather than winds in the Atlantic and so sailing was more predictable.

FIFTY-EIGHT

Correspondence
July 9, 1818

The Secretary of the Navy, Benjamin Crowninshield, ordered Bainbridge to go from Boston to Washington D.C.

"Boston, July 9, 1818
Mr. Dear General,

"Having this moment heard, that an officer of the British army is about to sail from this port to join your command in the East Indies, I eagerly avail myself of the opportunity to revive our acquaintance, and to tender to you the assurance of my sincere regard. In whatever situation you may be placed, you will always have the esteem of one who will ever feel a lively interest in your welfare. Though I was indebted to the fortune of war for my first knowledge of you, yet the gallantry and firmness which you displayed on that occasion, and your subsequent conciliatory deportment, have made an impression upon me which can never be eradicated."

"Should the events connected with either peace or war brings us again together, I am certain that after our duty to our country is performed, we will meet as friends. — How delighted I should be to see you in the United States, in order that I might offer you proof of my great respect for your character; and

at the same time to thank you for the handsome and liberal manner in which you have represented my conduct after your return to England."

"This I feel the more sensibly from the circumstance of your making them during the period of war, when the feelings and passions are often too much excited, to allow us to do strict justice to an enemy."

"Since the termination of the war I have observed, with great satisfaction, that our respective governments entertain a higher respect for each other than they did previously to the occurrence of that event. It is the true interest of each to cherish such sentiments, and that they may continue to do so, is my ardent wish."

"I should be greatly gratified to hear from you, and be assured, you have no friend who would be more pleased to learn of your welfare, I pray you to rest assured of the unfeigned friendship and esteem of, William Bainbridge."

The following letter from General Hislop sent to William Bainbridge.

Madras, March 14, 1819.

My Dear Sir,

"I have been highly gratified by the receipt of your very kind and friendly letter of the 9th of July last, which came to hand about a week ago, having been forwarded from Calcutta. Accept in consequence, my dear sir, of my most sincere and grateful thanks for your friendly remembrance of me, and be always assured, that the recollection on my part of the liberal and generous treatment, together with the personal kind attention which I and every other officer with me, who by the fortune of war became your prisoners, (after the hard fought action which terminated in the capture of the Java, by the frigate Constitution under your command) has made an impression of gratitude which no time or circumstances can erase those sentiments arising out of those feelings, which impelled me to take every occasion after my arrival in England from the Brazils to render you that justice by the unreserved acknowledgments for your very great kindness and liberality to which you were so justly entitled, and which I could not have concealed, consistent with what was due to my own feelings as an honorable man, "It Would, indeed, afford me very sincere pleasure, could 1 indulge in the probability of a prospect of again meeting with you, (though not exactly in the same way as that which brought me to your acquaintance,) tut were it possible that such a recurrence could take place, in whatever way the contest might terminate, our personal friendship would not, 1 am convinced, suffer any diminution by the result. I most earnestly hope, however, that the blessings of peace may long continue to subsist between our respective countries, certain as I am that it will be for the advantage of both."

"Through the channel of the public papers, you will possibly have become acquainted with the war which broke out towards the end of the year 1817, in this quarter of the globe, between our government and the confederated Mahratta princes, which a few months after the opening of the campaign sufficed to deprive them of their thrones and their power."

"It was my good fortune to give the death blow to their machinations, on the 20th of December of that year, on which day, I attacked the army of Holcar, one of the most powerful of these princes, and by the power of the Almighty, totally defeated him, capturing all his artillery, treasure, &c. In a few days after the action, he sued for peace, and we got it upon our own terms. After an absence of ten months service in the field, I returned to Madras on the 24th of June last, since which, I have been enjoying repose, accompanied by a great share of good health, which continues to reconcile me to the climate."

"How long I shall remain in it is yet uncertain, but I expect it will be at least a couple of years longer. Should you, therefore, oblige me, by doing me the favour of another letter, after this reaches you, I request you to send it by the way of London and under cover to Messrs. Greenwood and Co., Craig's court, Charring Cross, from whence they will forward it to me by the packet."

"I will conclude by complying with Captain Wood's request, who is with me, and who desires me to make his kindest remembrances to you. — Major Walker, if alive, is in the West Indies; but he was very ill when I last heard from him. With every good wish for your enjoyment of health, and every earthly happiness, I remain, my dear sir,

"Yours most sincerely " and faithfully,

T. Hislop.

In Common Council, City of Albany, July 19, 1819.

"Whereas the board has received the gratifying intelligence of the arrival in this city of Commodore William Bainbridge, the heroic commander of the frigate Philadelphia, off Tripoli in 1803, of the frigate Constitution, off the coast of Brazil in December, 1812: and, whereas, this common council entertain a high sense of the distinguished services of the gallant naval hero, and a high respect and veneration for his exalted character; Therefore, Resolved^

That the freedom of this city, in a gold box, be presented to

Commodore Bainbridge, with a suitable address by his honour the mayor."

This resolution was accordingly conveyed to the commodore, enclosed in the annexed letter from the chief magistrate of the city.

To Commodore William Bainbridge of the Navy of the United States.

Sir,

"*In conformity with a resolution of the common council, I have the honour to present to you the freedom of this city, as a testimony of the sense which we entertain of your naval services and reputation.*

"*Permit me to add the assurance of my personal esteem and respect, accompanied with my sincere wishes for the prolongation of your valuable life to support your country's flag, and advance her naval glory.*

I have the honour to be,

Yours, &C.

P. S. VAN RENSALAER.

FIFTY-NINE

USS Constitution
July 9, 1818

William. Bainbridge, Esq.
        United States navy

On October 29, 1819, Bainbridge was selected to preside over the first board ever convened for the examination of young officers for promotion in the United States Navy. This was the first examination of midshipmen instituted by the government. This was a total success in its being advantageous to the navy. The exam for promotion to lieutenant was rigid, examining all aspects of seamanship. The midshipmen were also required to demonstrate satisfactory testimonials of moral conduct and gentlemen like deportment. The exam eliminated the ignorant and profligate from the service and they were asked to leave immediately.

Bainbridge as President of the astute assembly of captains thanked the successful midshipmen for diligence.

"Gentlemen and I mean that sincerely, you have worked hard to earn the right to be called Lieutenant in the United States Navy. You are all important in the building of the United States Navy and in the protection of this great county. You leadership will be needed now and in the future to teach and train other midshipmen to take over the positions you have now earned. The future of safety at sea is in your hands, we know we can count on you to do your upmost to defend it with honor."

Bainbridge was ordered from Boston on November 9, 1821 to command the Philadelphia station, and then back to the Boston Station on January 7, 1822. The Navy wanted to take advantage of Bainbridge's professional abilities in fitting out the ship-of-the-line, *North Carolina*.

On February 12, 1821 an unfortunate event took place that was between Commodore James Barron and Commodore Stephen Decatur. Commodore Bainbridge was in Washington conferring with the Board of Commission along with Decatur.

Barron got wind that Decatur was going to be in Washington and made a special trip to be there also. Barron was bound and determined to confront Decatur over his being block from any further Naval assignments.

James Barron was certainly not the quality of leader that William Bainbridge was. Barron's sloppiness caught up to him when his flagship, the *Chesapeake*, was stopped by the British warship the *Leopard* on June 22, 1807. The Chesapeake was not prepared to protect itself and the British boarded her.

The Secretary of the Navy, Robert Smith, was beside himself over the incident and he had Barron court-martialed. The court-martial was conducted and Barron was found guilty of "Neglecting, on the probability of an engagement, to clear his ship for action." The results of the court-martial were Barron's suspension from duty for five years.

James Barron was pissed over the matter and that is where Stephen Decatur comes into the picture. Barron was convinced that he was being barred from returning to duty in the Navy by Decatur.

Barron accelerated the situation by confronting Stephen Decatur to his face and challenged him to a duel on March 22, 1821. Decatur was tired of Barron's acquisitions and agreed to the duel.

The duel took place in Bladensburg, Maryland. Commodore William Bainbridge was Decatur's second and Captain Jesse D. Elliot was Barron's second.

Neither of the men aimed to kill the other. Both men were hit in the thigh but the ball that struck Decatur ricochet up into his groin. It took Decatur twelve hours of extreme agony to die.

In a letter that Samuel Chandler Crafts wrote to Coronal Joseph Scott on March 23, 1821 he made mentions of the duel. This is an excerpt from that letter.

"A circumstance happened yesterday which has created a very great situation here. Commodore Decatur & Commodore Barron have fought a duel in which they both fell. Decatur was shot through the body and is now dead. Barron was shot near the top of his hip and the ball is still in him, it is thought however that he will recover. Decatur has been the pride of the Navy and has done more to raise it to its present high standing than any other, he was one of the navy commissioners and his life is as much regretted here, as the life of any other man could be.

Mr. Rudolph made a motion in congress this morning that congress adjourn until after the funeral, which will take place tomorrow, and remain closed during the remainder of the secession out of respect to his memory but the motion was appeased, on account of the manner of his death, and was afterward withdrawn."

(Signed) *Samuel C. Crafts*

Commodore Bainbridge was the first to advocate a Board of commissioners for the Navy. Both he and Decatur had seats on it.

Bainbridge long experience in naval concerns satisfied him that the administration of the navy could never be wisely conducted without a preponderance of professional men in connection and working in accord with the civil element.

Stephen Decatur was a popular American hero. William Bainbridge was also a popular hero but he made a mistake in being a second for Decatur. The irony of the matter was Bainbridge had actually harbored a long-standing jealousy for Decatur.

The public did not ever forgive him for not stopping the duel. Congress was aware of the outcry and so as to not offend voters Bainbridge never made another navy voyage after 1821.

On February 5, 1823 Bainbridge was permitted to go to Washington.

The Secretary of the Navy ordered Bainbridge to the Charleston Navy Yard on August 1, 1823.

The Charleston Ship Yard in Boston was one of the oldest ship yards in the United States having been established in 1801. The ship yard existed back to the American Revolutionary War but as a private ship year.

The war-ship that had been built there or were going to be built there were by the United States Navy were:

Independence	74-Gun Ship	*June 22, 1814*
Alligator	Schooner	March 26, 1821
Vermont	74-Gun Ship	1825
Virginia	74-Gun Ship	1825
Boston	18-Gun Sloop	Oct. 15, 1825
Warren	18-Gun Sloop	Sold 1/1/1863
Falmouth	18-Gun Sloop	Jan 19, 1828

Commodore Bainbridge was in New York in 1824 presiding over a court marshal. He then went back to Philadelphia to be with his family. The Secretary of the Navy was constantly directing Bainbridge to travel to the various ship yards to assess their progress and report back to him.

LS dated 26 May 1827, Washington City. Vis-a-vis plans for British dock yards.

May 26, 1827
My dear Sir
I have recently been appointed one of three officers to survey the Navy Yards in this country & to report a systematic plan for their permanent improvement. You will oblige me personally & may under a public service, by processing & forwarding as early as practicable, a plan, (no matter how rough) of the Dock yards at Plymouth, Portsmouth & Diptford; any expense you may incur will be cheerfully paid on demand by;
Your friend & obedient servant,
Wm Bainbridge

Bainbridge was appointed a Board Member of the Naval Commission on December 23, 1825. He was later Commandant of the Boston Navy Yard, and then he was Commandant of the Philadelphia Navy Yard in 1828.

Bainbridge was in command of the Philadelphia Station until March 11, 1831. When he left he took a two plus months leave until June 27, 1831. He was assigned back at the Charlestown Naval Yard. He stayed there until November 19, 1832.

That was his last effort for the Department of the United States Navy. He was not well. His hip was very bothersome and it was difficult to walk on the foot that had been crushed.

SIXTY

Death
July 27, 1833

William Bainbridge's health began to fail early in 1833. His robust constitution was worn out at the early age of 59. He had just turned 59 on May 7th. The years at sea had taken a toll on him reinforcing Susan's nagging complaints that he was neglectful of his health while in command of his assigned vessels.

William had a restless night, coughing and generally feeling achy all over. It was July 22nd and the windows were all open so the summer breeze could circulate in the bedroom.

"God Susan, I don't feel well!" William was still lying in bed coughing.

Susan reached over and placed her hand on William's forehead. "You are burning up William!"

"I feel cold like I might need another blanket," William could not remember when he felt as bad as he did.

Susan got up and located a rag she could dip in the water in the bathing room and brought it to William to place on his forehead.

"You just stay in bed. I am going to fetch some warm water and give you an enema. We have to get your fever down and get you well. I also bring you some cool water to drink."

After Susan administrated the enema she went to the kitchen to make a remedy for clearing out the lungs. She took one-half ounce of Boneset and one ounce of Mallow leaves and put them in pint and a half of boiling water. She then infused one ounce of Pleurisy Root in the same quantity of boiling water. She mixed both infusions. When the water had cooled she placed the liquid mixture in a pitcher and took it upstairs to their bedroom.

William had finished in the bathing room and he was back in bed.

"Can you sit up? I want you to drink a wine glass full of this every fifteen to twenty minutes."

"What is it? It tastes awful."

"Never mind, just do as I say."

Susan also made up a liniment to rub on William's back. She took two drachms of laudanum, mixed with two tablespoonfuls of olive oil.

William did as Susan instructed and spent the entire day in bed. He was coughing more and was coughing up rusty tenacious sputum.

The following morning the fever was still the same and William was complaining about the pleurisy pain in the upper center of his back. The pain was great enough that he had to get out of bed to see if he could find some relief.

"William, get back in bed and get those covers over you!" Susan was getting very concerned about how sick William really was. William face was flushed and she could see he was not getting better. She was giving him fluids, though William was not particularly interested in drinking them. She gave him another warm water enema with one grain of powdered opium in the water hoping to ease William's pain. She also kept cool cloths on his neck and forehead.

William dozed off and on during the day; that night manifest in sleeplessness and delirium. Susan was up most of the night attending to him.

On the third day his respiration had become rapid and shallow. She could hear the congestion in his chest. He was coughing up some blood in the mucus. His head hurt and the stabbing pain in his upper back was unbearable.

Susan gave William two enemas that day in hopes of lowering the fever. She stayed by his side and made him drink honey and lemon juice.

They talked some but for the most part William was worn out from the exertion it took to breath and the pain that made it impossible to get comfortable.

The next three days Susan followed the same routine. She was attempting to get him to eat but William was not responding to eating anything; liquids he would take but he was having a difficult time rising up in bed to drink them.

Susan had a live in house keeper, Martha, helping her get William out of bed to use the commode after they gave him enemas and to bath him. He was looking gaunt and you could tell he had lost weight. His lips were almost purple and his color had drained from his face.

"Martha, I need to ask you to go tell the children that I think their father is dying; they need to come immediately to the house."

"Will you be okay while I am gone?"

"I believe so; I'll be up in the bed room doing what I can to make him rest easier."

Martha took the buggy and went to find children. Susan was now thirty, William twenty-three, Mary twenty-two and Lucy was eighteen. It took Martha most of the day to locate them. They were all concerned and promised to come to the house as soon as possible.

Martha went back to the house and after she had taken care of the horse she hurried to the bedroom.

"How is he doing, Mrs. Bainbridge?"

"Not so good Martha, his breathing is very shallow and he is very congested. His fever is high so I am keeping cool rags on his head and neck."

The children began drifting in and finding their way upstairs to see their father.

Martha went to the kitchen to prepare dinner for the family. The girls also pitched in assisting with the dinner preparation, setting the dining room table and taking glasses of juice and water to their father.

William was in and out of consciousness. He appeared to recognize his children and thanked them for coming.

After dinner they sat in the bedroom with William until it was time for everyone to get some sleep. Susan didn't bother getting into bed she just pulled a chair up next to the bed and held William's hand.

Susan dozed off and when she woke up William hand was limp. He was still warm but he was dead. She laid her head on the edge of the bed and cried.

William Phillip Bainbridge had died on July 28, 1833 of pneumonia.

His remains were interred in Christ Church burying-ground, in Philadelphia.

The Philadelphia Gazette and the Philadelphia Inquirer newspapers both ran a tribute to Commodore William Phillip Bainbridge.

Commodore Bainbridge was a model of a naval officer, he was six feet in height, and had a finely molded and muscular frame, which enabled him to endure any amount of fatigue. His complexion was rather fair, his beard dark and strong, and his eyes black, animated, and expressive. His deportment was commanding, his dress always neat; his temperament was ardent and somewhat impetuous, though he could qualify it with the greatest courtesy and the most attractive amenity.

William Bainbridge had trained many young officers so they could advance in rank. He was the perfect example of what an officer in the United States Navy should convey. Bainbridge knew what the proper meaning of patriotism was and he lived that belief.

Susanna Hyleger Bainbridge lived in Philadelphia until her death in 1857.

William Phillip Bainbridge's name has been carried on and honored in various ways. The United States Navy has named several ships in honor of his memory, USS Bainbridge.

He has an island named for him, Bainbridge Island, Washington across from Seattle, Washington. Commodore Bainbridge has two cities names after him, Bainbridge, Ohio, near Chillicothe, Ohio, and Bainbridge, Georgia. There is a major highway in Tallahassee, Florida, Old Bainbridge Road.

Remembrance
July, 1833
Street Names of Old Montgomery
182 years later, most of us know that the town of Montgomery was formed in 1819 by the merger of John Scott's East Alabama Town and Andrew Dexter's New Philadelphia. We know that Dexter had named New Philadelphia's five east-west streets for the first five presidents of the United States and its six north-south streets for six naval heroes of the War of 1812, but how much do we know about these leaders?

The presidents were George Washington (Washington Avenue), John Adams (Adams Avenue), Thomas Jefferson (Jefferson Street), James Monroe

354

(Monroe Street), and James Madison (Madison Avenue). The naval heroes were Oliver Hazard Perry (Perry Street) James Lawrence (Lawrence Street), Isaac Hull (Hull Street), Thomas McDonough (McDonough Street), William Bainbridge (Bainbridge Street), and Stephen Decatur (Decatur Street).

SIXTY-ONE

USS Bainbridge
April 8, 2009

After nearly two hundred years since William Bainbridge defended American rights against pirates the world still has pirates attaching merchant shipping. We still have our heads buried in the sand hoping pirates will go away by some magical wave of a wane.

It is interesting that the pirate activity in April of 2009 evolved the destroyer name after William Bainbridge, the *USS Bainbridge*.

According to news reports, "pirates attacked the *Maersk Alabama*, and seized the ship early Wednesday, April 8th off the Horn of Africa."

"All twenty of its remaining crew members were in good physical shape," said Ken Quinn, second officer of the ship, in a satellite call placed by CNN. "There's four Somali pirates, and they've got our captain," Quinn said.

Maersk spokesman Kevin Speers said the guided-missile destroyer *USS Bainbridge* was near the *Maersk Alabama* and that its crew was talking to the Navy.

"When the Navy comes in, they're in charge," Speers told CNN.

The hijackers boarded the *Maersk Alabama* early Wednesday, when it was about 350 miles off the coast of Somalia, a haven for pirates attacking shipping through the Gulf of Aden. Capt. Richard Phillips was being held in the lifeboat after the pirates reneged on their agreement to exchange him for one of their own, who himself had been captured by the crew members, Quinn said.

"We returned him, but they didn't return the captain," said Quinn, who added that the crew members were in radio contact with Phillips.

Quinn describes the hijacking to CNN:

By 8 p.m., the *USS Bainbridge*, part of the allied fleet that patrols the waterway, had reached the *Maersk Alabama* to assist, a senior Defense Department official said. A Navy plane had reached the area an hour before.

B.J. Talley, a spokesman for the *Maersk* line, said the ship was about 215 nautical miles off the Somali coast at 7 p.m. ET when it was boarded.

"The 780-foot (237-meter) *Maersk Alabama* is the first U.S. ship to be seized in the latest wave of piracy off largely lawless Somalia. Joe Murphy, whose son Shane is the ship's first officer, called the hijacking "a wake-up call for America."

"They're making more money in piracy than the gross national product of Somalia, so it's not going to go away any time soon until there's international concern and international law enforcement," said Murphy, an instructor at the Massachusetts Maritime Academy.

The Gulf of Aden, at the southern mouth of the Red Sea, is a key transit point for ships moving into or out of the Suez Canal. In 2008, Somalia-based pirates attacked more than 100 ships in the gulf or off the Horn of Africa, capturing about forty of them. The ships and their crews typically are held for ransom that is paid before they are freed.

Since 2006, the United States has had an agreement with Kenya to try captured pirates with American assistance. Tom Fuentes, a former FBI official who worked with Kenyan authorities to prosecute pirates, said a 1988 treaty gives every nation the authority to pursue, capture and try pirates, regardless of the nationality of the victims -- but the United States can't tell shipping companies how to deal with hijackings, he said.

"Every shipping company so far has paid the ransom, and every victim has been released unharmed up until this point," he said.

After a lull early this year, attacks surged again in March, with fifteen attacks reported to the Malaysia-based International Maritime Bureau, which tracks piracy. An international task force under U.S. command was set up in January to crack down on the problem, and the European Union, India, China and Russia have ships deployed to the area as well.

U.S. Secretary of State Hillary Clinton called Wednesday for more international cooperation during an appearance with Moroccan Foreign Minister Taib Fassi-Fihri.

"I think Morocco was the very first country that recognized us, going back a long time," Clinton said. "We worked to end piracy off the coast of Morocco all those years ago, and we are going to work together to end that kind of criminal activity anywhere on the high seas."

William Bainbridge believed that negotiations from the barrel of a cannon was the only way to negotiate with pirates.

The *Maersk Alabama* was carrying relief supplies for USAID, the U.N. World Food Program and the Christian charities World Vision and Catholic Relief Services. The U.N. agency said its portion of the cargo included nearly 4,100 metric tons of corn-soya blend bound for Somalia and Uganda, and another 990 metric tons of vegetable oil for refugees in Kenya.

"There are starving people in Africa who need this food," Reinhart said.

Maersk Alabama was seized about 7:30 a.m. (12:30 a.m. ET), the ship's owner said. There were twenty-one American crew members on board at the time.

Quinn said the pirates were armed with AK-47 assault rifles, while the freighter's crew carried no weapons. The crew -- apparently minus the captain -- locked themselves in the compartment that contains the ship's steering gear, where they remained for about 12 hours with their captive, whom Quinn said they had tied up. The three other pirates "got frustrated because they couldn't find us," he said.

The pirates had scuttled the small boat they used once they climbed aboard the freighter, Quinn said, so Phillips offered them the Alabama's 28-foot lifeboat and some money.

John Reinhart, CEO and president of Norfolk, Virginia-based Maersk Line Ltd., said the crew can try to outrun the pirate boats or turn fire hoses on anyone trying to board the ship, "but we do not carry arms."

The waters off the coast of Somalia has been a lawless land for years and these pirate attacks have become more frequent in recent months. It seems apparent that any ship traveling through that area is going to have to be willing to fight off these Somali pirates by whatever means necessary before the attacks will stop.

The Second Mate of the merchant ship, Ken Quinn, reported that the crew had a lengthy battle with the pirates. After they secured their ship, they attempted to negotiate a deal with the pirates for the release of their captain. They released one of the attackers in exchange for the release of Captain Phillips. However, after the deal was made and the pirate was released, they refused to release Captain Phillips.

At this time the U.S. Navy has dispatched the American warship, USS Bainbridge and other vessels to the scene.

Barack Obama has yet to make a statement about the attack on an American ship. Even though there have been numerous attacks on merchant ships off the coast of Somalia, this is the first time in modern history that the pirates have dared to attack an American ship and crew.

It seems apparent that the perception is that the United States is greatly weakened with this President and therefore predators around the world are pushing the envelope to see how he will respond to their aggressions towards the United States. We now have an attack on an American ship and a hostage situation on our hands. But Obama is still trying to charm Europe and put American interest under the control of the United Nations.

The destroyer, *USS Bainbridge*, shadowed and later encircled the Somali pirates during the standoff, at which time the pirates and *Bainbridge* began negotiating for the safe release of the captive captain. On April 12, 2009 Captain Phillips was freed—reportedly in good condition—during a US Navy SEAL team assault. Three of the Somali pirates were killed by US Navy SEAL sharpshooters aboard *Bainbridge*, and one was captured

The last time the United States had pirate problems our forefathers built the *USS Constitution* to deal with them and end their terrorist attacks on our young nation. That was the end of our problems with the Barbary pirates.

The *USS Bainbridge* was launched on November 13, 2003 at the Bath Iron Works in Bath, Maine. She is sponsored by Susan Bainbridge Hay who is the great-great-great granddaughter of Commodore William Bainbridge, the ships namesake. The *USS Bainbridge* was commissioned on November 12, 2005 under the command of Commander John M. Dorey. Her homeport is Norfolk, Virginia.

Book Four

Navy regulations, Crews, Supplies, & Ships

Crew of gun number twelve on the Gun Deck.

SIXTY-TWO

Crew of Constitution
1812

The Crew of the Constitution:		Per Year:
Commander:	William Bainbridge	$2,017.60
First Lieutenant:	Parker, George	$ 786.60
Second Lieutenant:	Morgan, Charles W.	
Third Lieutenant:	Hoffman. Beekman V.	
Lieutenant-Marines:	William Osbourne	$ 564.40
2nd Lieutenant:	John Contee	
Sailing Master:*	John Cushing Aylwin	$ 684.40
Master's Mate: Nichols, John		

MIDSHIPMEN:		$ 432.40
Purser:	Robert C. Ludlow	$ 684.40
Surgeon:	John Ridgely	$1,804.40
Surgeon Mate:	Jonathan Cowdery	$ 564.40
Surgeon Mate:	Nicholas Hanwood	$ 564.40

Clerk 1:   William Adams
Carpenter: William Godley
Carpenter's Mate:
Carpenter's Mate:
**Boatswain: (Bosun)   George Hadger $ 444.40
Boatswain's Mate:
Yeoman of gun-room
Gunner: Richard Stevenson $ 444.40
Quarter-Gunners (11)
Coxswain: (Ranking petty officer)
Sailmaker: Joseph Douglass $ 444.40
Cooper:
Steward 1:
Armorer 1:
Master-at-arms1:
Cook 1:
Chaplain 1:   John Carleton $ 684.40
SEAMAN: (Topman, forecastle hand, waistman or after guard)
Able Seamen (120) $ 228.00
Ordinary Seamen (150) $ 96.00
Boys (30)
Marines, including sergeants
And corporals (50)

*Sailing master was the officer charged with navigation of the ship
**Bosun was responsible for inspecting the ship's sails and rigging every morning.
Midshipmen & Seaman: All hands are called 1} to assigned stations; or 2} action stations.

Adams, Joseph, killed
Adams, Peter, boatswain
Allen, John D., killed
Bamy, Frederick
Bateman, Enos, wounded
Baury, Frederick, midshipman
Beatty, Thomas A., midshipman
Belcher, John A.
Belches, Alexander, midshipman

Biddle, James
Brimblecon, William, wounded
Brown, Samuel (w). ordinary seaman
Cheeves, John, killed
Cheeves, Tolin (killed).
Clements, John (w).
Conner, Patrick, killed
Cook, Phillip
Cooper, William, killed
Cross, Joseph, midshipman
Cummings, John C., acting midshipman.
Curtis, Asa, seaman
Cutbush, William Cutbush
Cutbush, William.
Darling, Ezekiel, gunner.
Delaney, James W., midshipman
Eddy, Abijah, wounded
Eskridge, Alexander, midshipman
Etwell, John, wounded
Evans, Pet. (w). seaman
Fields, Ambrose L., midshipman
Forrest, Dulaney, midshipman.
Gamble, Robert .
Germain, Lewis, midshipman.
Gibbon, James.
Gilliam, Henry, midshipman
Gordon, William L., midshipman.
Greenleaf, James, midshipman, Killed
Grerman, Lewis
Hammond, Jas. P., wounded
Hanson, Thomas, private marine
Hart, Barney, killed
Henry, Bernard.
Hogan, Daniel, wounded
Jones, Richard R.
Leverett, George, midshipman
Long, John C., midshipman.
Long, William, wounded
M'Carty, William D., midshipman.

Nixon, Z. M., midshipman
Ongrain, Jonas (killed) seaman.
Packett, John, midshipman
Patterson, D.T.
Reader, Anthony, private marine, wounded
Reed, B. F.
Renshaw, James.
Sanders, Reuben, wounded
Shepherd, Steven, wounded
Smith, Simon Smith.
Snow, Mark, killed
Taylor, William Y., midshipman
Voyle, John, wounded
Waldo, Charles F., master's mate, wounded
Ward, Henry, midshipman
Ward, Joseph, wounded
Weaden, William, wounded
Webb, Stephen, wounded
Williams, Thomas (3rd seaman) (w).
Winter, Richard, midshipman
Wish, John A., midshipman
Woodbury, Peter, wounded
Wormly, Wallace.

SIXTY-THREE

Decks on Constitution
1812

Deck and space on the *USS Constitution*:
(The decks were the Orlop, berth, gun and spar.)
    1. Orlop Deck
        a. Midshipmen's berth
        b. Surgeon Cockpit
        c. Spirit room
    2. Lower Deck:
        a. Men's primary mess
        b. Lieutenants wardroom, abaft
        c. The galley
        d. Manager (livestock accommodations forward by the hawse holes for the anchor cables.
    3. Gun Deck:
        a. 30-24 pound cannons.
    4. Top Deck:
        a. Poop deck (the highest deck)

b. Quarterdeck (the wheel and binnacle close to the entrance of the Captain's cabin)

c. Forecastle

d. Sick bay

e. Heads on the break heads.

(See letter of Captain Bainbridge, Oct. 16, 1814; it is letter No. 51, in the fortieth volume of " Captains Letters," in the clerk s office of the Secretary of the Navy.)

The ship carried eight boats and landing craft consisting of: 1x36 foot longboat; 2-30 foot cutters; 2-28 foot whaleboats; 1x28 foot gig; and 1x22 foot jolly boat; 1x14 punt.

In the United States Navy, the diet was not unwholesome, but it was fearfully monotonous at sea, where all provisions were dried or salted. The ration fixed by Congress in 1801 for each man is given in the following table:

Sunday: 1 Ib. beef, 14 oz. bread, J Ib. flour, Ib. suet, 1- pint spirits.

Monday: 1 Ib. pork, 14 oz. bread, J pint peas, pint spirits.

Tuesday: 1 Ib. beef, 14 oz. bread, 2 oz. cheese, 1- pint spirits.

Wednesday: 1 Ib. pork, 14 oz. bread, J pint rice, 1-pint spirits.

Thursday: 1 Ib. beef, 14 oz. bread, 1 Ib. flour, Ib. suet, pint spirits.

Friday: 14 oz. bread, pint rice, 4 oz. cheese, 2 oz. butter, pint molasses, 1-pint spirits.

Saturday: 1 Ib. pork, 14 oz. bread, J pint peas, pint vinegar, one-pint spirits

Clothing worn on Constitution, 1812

Clothing worn on the Constitution:

Slops for first year per man:

Pea jacket (to serve for two years)	1
Blue cloth jackets for winter.	2
Blue cloth trousers for winter	2
White flannel shirts	2
White flannel drawers	2
White yarn stockings	2 pairs
Black handkerchiefs	2

Duck frocks for summer	2
Duck trousers for summer	2
Shoes	4 pairs
Mattress	1
Blankets	2
Hammock	1
Red cloth vest	1
Hats-black	2

Each man was also allowed to purchase from the purser each year: 25 pounds of soap, 3 tin pots, 3 spoons, 2 bottles of mustard, ½ pound of pepper, 4 knives, 4 combs, 3 brushes, 3 yards of ribbon, needles and thread in reasonable quantities.

SIXTY-FOUR

Crew of *USS Philadelphia*
1803

Complete list of the officers on the Philadelphia:

David Porter
Jacob Jones
Theodore Hunt
Benjamin Smith
John Ridgely, Surgeon.
Wm. Osboume, Lt. Marines,
Keith Spence, Purser.
Jonathan Cowdery,) Surgeon's mate
Nicholas Hanwood,) Surgeon's mate
William Knight, Master.
William Godley, Carpenter.
George Hadger, Boatswain.
Richard Stevenson, Gunner.
Joseph Douglass, Sail-maker.

Midshipmen:

Robert Gamble,
Bernard Henry,
B. F. Reed,
James Gibbon,
D. T. Patterson,
James Biddle,
James Renshaw,
Wallace Wormly,
Wm. Cutbush,
Richard R. Jones,
Simon Smith,
Wm. Adams, Captain's clerk.
Minor Fountaine, Master's
mate.*

SIXTY-FIVE

Naval Regulations
1812

Rules and Regulations of the United States Navy, 1812
Captain or Commander.

1. When a captain or commander is appointed to command one of the Unites States' ships, he is immediately to repair on board, and visit her throughout.

2. To give his constant attendance on board, and quicken the dispatch of the work; and to send to the navy department weekly accounts, or oftener, if necessary, of the condition and circumstances she is in, and the progress made in fitting her out.

3. To take inventories of all the stores committed to the charge of his officers respectively, and to require from his boatswain, gunner, Sailmaker, carpenter and purser, counter parts of their respective indents.

4. To cause his clerk to be present, and to take an account of all the stores and provisions that come on board, and when; which account he is to compare with the indents, in order to prevent any fraud or neglect.

5. To keep counter-books of the expense of the ship's stores and provisions, whereby to know the state and condition of the same; and to

audit the accounts of the officers entrusted therewith, once a week, in order to be a check upon them.

6. When ordered to recruit, he is to use his best endeavors to get the ship manned, and not to enter any but men of able bodies, and fit for service: he is to keep the established number of men complete, and not to exceed his complement.

7. When the ship's company is completed, they shall be divided into messes and guards; and he shall order, without delay, the partition of the people for an engagement, to the end that, before they sail, every one may know his post.

8. He may grant to private ships of the nation the succors he lawfully may, taking from their captains or patrons a correspondent security that the owners may satisfy the amount or value of the things supplied.

9. at all times, whether sailing alone or in a squadron, he shall have his ship ready for an immediate engagement: to which purpose, he shall not permit anything to be on deck that may embarrass the management of the guns, and not be readily cleared away.

10. As, from the beginning of the cruise the plan of the combat ought to be formed, he shall have his directions given, and his people so placed, as not to be unprovoked against any accident which may happen.

11. If it is determined to board the enemy, the captain is not, under any pretext, to quit his ship, whose preservation must be the chief object of his care; but he may appoint his second in command, or any other officer he thinks proper for that duty, without attending to rank.

12. He shall observe, during his cruise, the capacity, application, and behavior of his officers; and to improve them, he shall employ them in works and commissions that may manifest their intelligence.

13. He is to cause all new-raised men and other, not skilled in seamanship, daily to lash up their hammocks, and carry them to the proper places for barricading the ship, whenever the weather will permit; and also to have them practiced in going frequently every day up and down the shrouds, and employed on all kinds of work, to be created purposely to keep them in action, and to teach them the duty of seamen.

14. To keep a regular muster-book, setting down there in the names of all persons entered to serve on board, with all circumstances relating to them.

15. Himself to muster the ship's company at least once a week, in port or at sea, and to be very exact in this duty; and if any person shall absent

himself from duty, without leave, for three successive musters, he is to be marked as a run-away, on the ship's books.

16. To send, every month, one muster-book complete, to the navy office, signed by himself and purser.

17. To make a list of seamen run away, inserting the same at the end of the muster-books, and to distinguish the time, manner, and by what opportunity they made their escape: if the desertion happens in any port of the United States, he is to send to the navy department their names, place of abode, and all the circumstances of their escape.

18. The captain of the ship shall be responsible for his crew, whose desertion shall be laid to his charge, whenever it proceeds from a want of necessary care; but if it proceeds from the neglect of an officer who shall have the charge of a watering party, or any other duty on shore, and, from his negligence, any part of the crew entrusted to him shall desert, that officer shall be responsible for the same.

19. He is to make out tickets for all such seamen as shall be discharged from his books, signed by himself and purser, and to deliver them to none but the party; and if the party be dead or absent, he is to send the ticket forthwith to the navy-office.

20. He is not to suffer the ship's stores to be misapplied or wasted; and if such loss happens by the negligence or willfulness of any of the ship's company, he is to charge the value thereof against the wages of the offender, on the muster and pay-books.

21. He shall make no alteration in any part of the ship.

22. He is to keep sentinels posted at the scuttle, leading into all the store-rooms, and no person is to pass down but by leave from the captain or commanding officer of the watch, which leave must be signified to the sentinel from the quarter-deck.

23. He is to observe seasonable times in setting up his shrouds and other rigging, especially when they are new and apt to stretch; and also to favor his masts as much as possible.

24. He is to cause such stores as require it, to be frequently surveyed and aired, and their defects repaired; and the store-rooms to be kept airy and in good condition, and secured against rats.

25. He is not to make use of ship's sails for covering boats, or for awnings.

26. The decks or gratings are not to be scraped oftener than is necessary, but are to be washed and swabbed once a day, and air let into the hold as often as may be.

27. He is to permit every officer to possess his proper cabin, and not to make any variation therein.

28. No person is to lie upon the orlop but by leave from the captain, nor to go amongst the cables with candles, but when service requires it.

29. Such as smoke tobacco are to take it in the fore-castle, and in no other place, without the captain's permission, which is never to be given to smoke below the upper gun-deck.

30. Care is to be taken every night, on setting the watch, that all fire and candles be extinguished in the cook-room, hold, steward-room, cock-pit, and every where between decks; nor are candles to be used in any other part of the ship but in lanthorns, and that not without the captain's leave; and the lanthorns must always be whole and unbroken.

31. He is not to suffer any person to suttle or sell any sorts of liquors to the ship's company, nor any debts for the same to be inserted in the slop-book, on any pretence whatsoever.

32. Before the ship proceeds to sea, he is, without any partiality or favor, to examine and rate the ship's company, according to their abilities, and to take care that every person in the ship, without distinction, do actually perform the duty for which he is rated.

33. Before the ship sails, he is to make a regulation for quartering the officers and men, and distributing them to the great guns, small-arms, rigging, &c.; and a list of such order and distribution is to be fixed up in the most public place of the ship. He is also frequently to exercise the ship's company in the use of the great guns and small-arms; and to set down in his journal the times he exercises them.

34. The following number of men at least, (exclusive of marines) are to be exercised and trained up to the use of small- arms, under the particular care of a lieutenant or master at arms.

35. If any officers are absent from their duty when the ship is under sailing orders, he is to send their names to the navy- office, with the cause of their absence.

36. He is to take care of his boats and secure them before blowing weather; also, the colors are not to be kept abroad in windy weather, but due care taken of them.

37. He is not to carry any woman to sea, without orders from the navy-office, *or the commander of the squadron.*

38. When he is to sail from port to port in time of war, or appearance thereof, he is to give notice to merchantmen bound his way, and take

them under his care, if they are ready; but not to make unnecessary stay, or deviate from his orders on that account.

39. He is to keep a regular journal, and at the expiration of the voyage, to give in a general copy to the navy-office.

40. He is, by all opportunities, to send an account of his proceedings to the navy-office, with the condition of the ship, men, &c.; he is likewise to keep a punctual correspondence with every of the public officers, in whatsoever respectively concerns them.

41. He is not to go into any port, but such as are directed by his orders, unless necessitously obliged, and then not to make any unnecessary stay; if employed in cruising, he is to keep the sea the time required by his orders, or give reasons for acting to the contrary.

42. Upon all occasions of anchoring, he is to take great care in the choice of a good birth, and examine the quality of the ground for anchoring, where he is a stranger, sounding at least three cables lengths round the ship.

43. In foreign ports he is to use the utmost good husbandry in careening the ship, and not to do it but under an absolute necessity; none are to be employed in careening and refitting the ship but the ship's company, where it can be avoided; and for the encouragement of his own men, they are entitled to an extraordinary allowance per day; and to prevent any abuse herein, each ship has the number of operative men limited as follows:

To master carpenters, carpenter's mates, shipwrights and caulkers, for working on board the ship they belong to, in caulking and fitting her for careen, and graving or tallowing her, fifty cents per day. For working on board any other of the United States' ships, 75 cents per day.

And there shall be allowed no more for caulking a ship, fitting her for careen, graving or tallowing her, or other necessary works for each careening or cleaning, than what amounts to the labor of the following number of men for one day, viz.

For a 44-- 180 men for one day.
For a 36-- 160 do. do.
For a 32-- 140 do. do.
For a 24-- 90 do. do.
For an 18-- 70 do. do.
All under-- 30 do. do.

44. If he is obliged to take up money abroad, for the use of the ship, he is to negotiate it at the best exchange.

45. He is to advise the proper officer of what bills he draws, with the reasons thereof, and with the said bills send duplicates of his accounts, and vouchers for his disbursements, signed by himself and purser.

46. He is to take care that all stores brought on board, be delivered to the proper officers; and to take their receipts for the same.

47. Upon the death of any officer, he is to take care that an inventory be taken of all his goods and papers, and that the same be sealed up, and reserved for the use of such as have a legal right to demand them.

48. When any officer who has the custody of stores or provisions shall die, be removed or suspended, he is to cause an exact survey and inventory to be taken forthwith of the remains of such stores, which is to be signed by the successor, who is to keep a duplicate thereof, and also by the surveying officers.

49. Upon his own removal into another ship, he is to show the originals of all such orders as have been sent to him, and remain unexecuted, to his successor, and leave with him attested copies of the same.

50. He is to leave with his successor a complete muster- book, and send up all other books and accounts under his charge, to the officers they respectively relate to.

51. In case of shipwreck, or other disaster, whereby the ship may perish, the officers and men are to stay with the wreck as long as possible, and save all they can.

52. When any men borne for wages are discharged from one ship to another, the captain of the ship from which they are so discharged, is to send immediately pay-lists for such men to the navy-office, and the purser of the ship from which they are so discharged, is also to supply the purser of the ship to which they are transferred, a pay-list, stating the balances respectively due them.

53. To promote cleanliness and health, the following rules are to be attended to. 1. All men on board are to keep themselves in every respect as clean as possible. 2. That the ship be aired between decks as much as may be, and that she be always kept thoroughly clean. 3. That all necessary precautions be used, by placing sentinels or otherwise, to prevent people easing themselves in the hold, or throwing anything there that may occasion nastiness. 4. That no fruit or strong liquors be sold on board the ship; *except in the judgment of the commander of the squadron, a*

limited quantity of fruit be necessary for the health of the crew, in which case he will issue an order.

54. He is responsible for the whole conduct and good government of the ship, and for the due execution of all regulations which concern the several duties of the officers and company of the ship, who are to obey him in all things which he shall direct them for the service of the United States.

55. He is answerable for the faults of his clerk; nor can he receive his wages without the proper certificates, and must make good all damages sustained by his neglect or irregularity.

56. The quarter-deck must never be left without one commissioned officer, at least, *and the other necessary officers which the captain may deem proper* to attend to the duty of the ship.

57. Commanding officers are to discourage seamen from selling their wages; and not to attest letters of attorney, if the same appear granted in consideration of money given for the purchase of wages.

Lieutenant.

1. He shall promptly, faithfully, and diligently execute all such orders as he shall receive from his commander, for the public service, nor absent himself from the ship without leave, on any pretence.

2. He is to keep a list of the officers and men on his watch, muster them, and report the names of the absentees. He is to see that good order be kept in his watch, that no fire or candle be burning, and that no tobacco be smoked between decks.

3. He is not to change the course of the ship at sea without the captain's directions, unless to prevent an immediate danger.

4. No boats are to come on board or go off without the lieutenant of the watch being acquainted with it.

5. He is to inform the captain of all irregularities, and to be upon deck in his watch, and prevent noise or confusion.

6. He is to see that the men be in their proper quarters in time of action; and that they perform all their duty.

7. The youngest lieutenant is frequently to exercise the seamen in the use of small-arms; and in the time of action he is to be chiefly with them.

8. He is to take great care of the small-arms, and see that they be

kept clean, and in good condition for service, and that they be not lost or embezzled.

9. The first lieutenant is to make out a general alphabetical book of the ship's company, and proper watch, quarter and station bills, in case of fire, manning of ship, loosing and furling of sails, reefing of topsails at sea, working of ship, mooring and unmooring, &c. leaving room for unavoidable alterations. This is to be hung in some public part of the ship, for the inspection of every person concerned.

10. No lieutenant, or other officer, belonging to a ship of the United States, to go on shore, or on board another vessel, without first obtaining permission from the captain or commanding officer, on his peril; and in the absence of the captain, the commanding officer to grant no permission of this sort, without authority from the captain, previous to the captain's leaving the ship.

Sailing Master.

1. He is to inspect the provisions and stores sent on board, and of what appears not good, he is to acquaint the captain.

2. He is to take care of the ballast, and see that it be clean and wholesome, and sign for the quantity delivered; and, in returning ballast, to see that vessels carry away their full lading.

3. He is to give his directions in stowing the hold, for the mast-room, trimming the ship, and for preservation of the provisions; and the oldest provisions to be stowed, so as to be first expended.

4. He is to take special care that the rigging and stores be duly preserved; and to sign the carpenter's and boatswain's expense-book, taking care not to sign undue allowances.

5. He is to navigate the ship under the direction of his superior officer, and see that the log and log book be duly kept, and to keep a good look-out.

6. He is duly to observe the appearances of coasts; and if he discovers any new shoals, or rocks under water, to note them down in his journal, with their bearing and depth of water.

7. He is to keep the hawser clear when the ship is at anchor, and see that she is not girt with her cables.

8. He is to provide himself with proper instruments, and books of navigation.

9. He is to be very careful not to sign any accounts, books, lists, or

tickets, before he has thoroughly informed himself of the truth of every particular contained in the same.

10. He is to keep the ship in constant trim, and frequently to note her draught of water in the log-book. He is to observe that alterations made by taking in stores, water or ballast; and when the ship is in chase, or trying her sailing with another, he is to make memorandums of the draughts of water, the rake of the masts, state of the rigging, and to note every possible observation, that may lead to the knowledge of the ship's best point of sailing.

Surgeon.

1. To inspect and take care of the necessaries sent on board for the use of the sick men; if not good, he must acquaint the captain; and he must see that they are duly served out for the relief of the sick.

2. To visit the men under his care twice a day, or oftener, if circumstances require it: he must see that his mates do their duty, so that none want due attendance and relief.

3. In cases that are difficult, he is to advise with the surgeons of the squadron.

4. To inform the captain daily of the state of his patients.

5. When the sick are ordered to the hospitals, he is to send with them to the surgeon, an account of the time and manner of their being taken ill, and how they have been treated.

6. But none are to be sent to sick-quarters, unless their distempers, or the number of the sick on board, are such that they cannot be taken due care of; and this the surgeon is to certify under his hand, before removal.

7. To be ready with his mates and assistants in an engagement, having all things at hand necessary for stopping of blood and dressing of wounds.

8. To keep a day-book of his practice, containing the names of his patients, their hurts, distempers, when taken ill, when recovered, removal, death, prescriptions, and method of treatment, while under cure.

9. From the last book he is to form two journals, one containing his physical, and the other his chirurgical practice.

10. Stores for the medical department are to be furnished upon his requisition; and he will be held responsible for the expenditure thereof.

11. He will keep a regular account of his receipts and expenditures of such stores, and transmit an account thereof to the accountant of the navy, at the end of every cruise.

Chaplain.

1. He is to read prayers at stated periods; perform all funeral ceremonies over such persons as may die in the service, in the vessel in which he belongs: or, if directed by the commanding officer, over any person that may die in any other public vessel.

2. He shall perform the duty of a schoolmaster; and to that end, he shall instruct the midshipmen and volunteers in writing, arithmetic and navigation, and in whatsoever may contribute to render them proficient's. He is likewise to teach the other youths of the ship, according to such orders as he shall receive from the captain. He is to be diligent in his office.

Boatswain and Master Sail Maker.

1. The boatswain is to receive into his charge the rigging, cables, cordage, anchors, sails, boats, &c.

2. He is not to cut up any cordage or canvass without an order in writing from the captain, and under the inspection of the master; and always to have by him a good quantity of small plats for security of the cables.

3. He and his mates are to assist and relieve the watch, see that the men attend upon deck, and that the working of the ship be performed with as little confusion as may be.

4. His accounts are to be audited and vouched by the captain and master, and transmitted to the navy-office.

5. If he has cause of complaint against any of the officers of the ship, with relation to the disposition of the stores under his charge, he is to represent the same to the navy-office, before the pay of the ship. He is not to receive his own wages until his accounts are passed.

6. He is not to sign any accounts, books, lists, or tickets, before he has thoroughly informed himself of the truth of every particular therein contained.

7. *Master Sail-Maker.* He is, with his mate and crew, to examine all sails that are brought on board, and to attend all surveys and conversions of sails.

8. He is always, and in due time, to repair and keep the sails in order, fit for service.

9. He is to see that they are dry when put into the store- room, or very soon to have them taken up and aired, and see that they are secured from drips, damps and vermin, as much as possible.

10. When any sails are to be returned into store, he is to attend the delivery of them for their greater safety.

Armorer, and Gunsmith.

1. The gunner is to receive, by indenture, the ordnance, ammunition, small-arms, and other stores allowed for the voyage; and if any part thereof be not good, he is to represent the same to the captain in order to its being surveyed and returned.

2. He is to see that the powder-room be well secured, and in right order, before the powder is brought into the ship.

3. Powder in the copper-hooped barrels to be lodged in the ground tier; to see that the doors of the powder-room be fast locked, the skuttle well shut and covered, and to deliver the keys to the captain.

4. He is timely to advise the captain when any powder comes on board, nor is he to remove it, prepare furzes, &c. without the captain's directions, so that the fire and candles may be extinguished, sentinels posted, and all care used to prevent accidents.

5. He is not to go or send any one into the powder-rooms, but by leave of the captain, and to take care that they have nothing about them that will strike fire in falling.

6. No more than three rounds of parchment cartridges are to be filled at a time.

7. Perishing stores are to be surveyed and condemned; but if near any port in the United States, and they can conveniently be returned into store, they must be, otherwise may be thrown overboard.

8. Empty powder-barrels are not to be staved, but preserved, to shift such as may be decayed.

9. *The Armorer and Gunsmith* are to assist the gunner in the survey and receipt of small-arms, and to keep them clean and in good order; but not to take them too often to pieces, which is detrimental to locks, &c.

10. Their station is in the gun-room, or such other place as the commanding officer may direct, where they are to observe the gunner's orders.

11. *The Gunner* is to receive the armorer's tools, and to account for them at the end of the voyage, in the same manner as for the other stores under his charge.

12. In foreign parts, if the small-arms want such repairs as cannot be done on board, the captain must cause a survey, and the defectives may be sent ashore to be repaired; but the armorer or gunsmith must attend to

see the reparations well executed. They must return the small-arms into store, clean and in good order.

13. The quantities of powder for exercise, and on occasions of service and scaling, must be regulated] by the captain or commanding officer. In time of action the allowance of powder must be reduced by degrees, until the same be lessened to one fourth the weight of the shot. He is not to swab a gun when it grows hot, for fear of splitting.

14. He is to take care that the guns be placed upon their proper carriages; for by this means they will fit, and stand a proper height for the sill of the ports.

15. He is not to scale the guns oftener than the ship is refitted, unless upon extraordinary occasions, and with the captain's orders; and when they are loaded for service, he is to see them well tompioned, and the vents filled with oakum.

16. He is to use great caution in order to prevent damage to such guns as are struck into the hold, by paying them all over, with a coat of warm tar and tallow mixt, &c.

17. He is to take care of the stores committed to him; for no waste that is not perishable, will be allowed him, only reasonable wear; and if any accident, it must be vouched by the captain.

18. He is to keep the boxes of grape-shot and hand-grenades in a dry place.

19. He is not to load the guns with unfit mixtures, which greatly endanger their splitting.

20. If he has cause of complaint against any of the officers of the ship, with relation to the disposition of the stores under his charge, he is to represent the same to the navy-office, before the pay of the ship.

Carpenter.

1. To take upon him the care and preservation of the ship's hull, masts, &c.; and also the stores committed to him by indenture.

2. To visit and inspect all parts of the ship daily; to see that all things are well secured and caulked; order the pumps, and make report to the captain.

3. In an engagement, he is to be watchful, and have all materials ready to repair damages; and frequently to pass up and down the hold with his crew, to be ready to plug up shot-holes.

Master-at-arms and Corporal.

1. Daily, by turns, (as the captain shall appoint) to exercise the ship's company.

2. He is to place and relieve sentinels, to mount with the guard, and to see that the arms be kept in order.

3. He is to see that the fire and candles be put out in season, and according to the captain's order.

4. He is to visit all vessels coming to the ship, and prevent the seamen going from the ship, without leave.

5. He is to acquaint the officer of the watch with all irregularities in the ship, which shall come to his knowledge.

6. *The Corporals*, are to act in subordination [to] the master-at-arms, and to perform the same duty under him, and to perform the duty themselves where a master-at-arms is not allowed.

Midshipmen.

1. No particular duties can be assigned to this class of officers.

2. They are promptly and faithfully to execute all the orders for the public service, of their commanding officers.

3. The commanding officers will consider the midshipmen as a class of officers meriting, in an especial degree, their fostering care. They will see, therefore, that the schoolmasters perform their duty towards them, by diligently and faithfully instructing them in those sciences appertaining to their department; that they use their utmost care to render them proficient therein.

4. Midshipmen are to keep regular journals, and deliver them to the commanding officer at the stated periods, in due form.

5. They are to consider it as the duty they owe to their country, to employ a due portion of their time in the study of naval tactics, and in acquiring a thorough and extensive knowledge of all the various duties to be performed on board of a ship of war.

Cook.

1. He is to have charge of the steep-tub, and is answerable for the meat put therein.

2. He is to see the meat duly watered, and the provisions carefully and cleanly boiled, and delivered to the men, according to the practice of the navy.

3. In stormy weather he is to secure the steep-tub, that it may not be washed overboard; but if it should be inevitably lost, the captain must

certify it, and he is to make oath to the number of pieces so lost, that it may be allowed in the purser's account.

There shall be a distinct apartment appropriated on board of each vessel, for the surgeon, purser, boatswain, gunner, sailmaker, and carpenter, that they may keep the public goods committed respectively to their care.

Provisions.
1. Provisions and slops are to be furnished upon the requisitions of the commanding officer, founded upon the purser's indents.

2. The purser being held responsible for the expenditure, shall, as far as may be practicable, examine and inspect all provisions offered to the vessel; and none shall be received that are objected to by him, unless they are examined and approved of, by at least two commissioned officers of the vessels.

3. In all cases where it may appear to the purser that provisions are damaged or spoiling, it will be his duty to apply to the commanding officer, who will direct a survey, by three officers, one of whom, at least, to be commissioned.

4. If upon a settlement of the purser's provision account, there shall appear a loss or deficiency of more than seven and a half per cent upon the amount of provisions received, he will be charged with, and held responsible for, such loss or deficiency, exceeding the seven and a half per cent, unless he shows, by regular surveys, that the loss has been unavoidably sustained by damage or otherwise.

5. Captains may shorten the daily allowance of provisions when necessity shall require it, taking due care that each man has credit for his deficiency, that he may be paid for the same.

6. No officer is to have whole allowance while the company is at short.

7. Beef for the use of the navy is to be cut into ten pound pieces, pork into eight pound; and every cask to have the contents thereof marked on the head, and the person's name by whom the same was furnished.

8. If there be a want of pork, the captain may order beef in the proportion established, to be given out in lieu thereof, and *vice versa*.

9. One half gallon of water at least shall be allowed every man in foreign voyages, and such further quantity as shall be thought necessary on the home station; but on particular occasions the captain may shorten this allowance.

10. To prevent the buying of casks abroad, no casks are to be shipped which will want to be replaced by new ones, before the vessel's return to the United States.

11. If any provisions slip out of the slings, or are damaged through carelessness, the captain is to charge the value against the wages of the offender.

12. Every ship to be provided with a seine, and the crew supplied with fresh provisions as it can conveniently be done.

Slops.

1. Slop-clothing is to be charged to the purser at the cost and charges; and he is to be held accountable for the expenditure.

2. And in no case will the purser be credited, even for any alleged loss by damage in slops, unless he shows, by regular surveys signed by three officers, one of whom at least to be commissioned, that the loss has been unavoidably sustained by *damage*, and not by any neglect or inattention on his part.

3. And, as a compensation for the risqué and responsibility, the purser shall be authorized to dispose of the slops to the crew at a profit of five per cent; but he must, at the end of every cruise, render a regular and particular slop-account, showing by appropriate columns the quantities of each several kind of articles received or purchased, and the prices and amounts, and from whom, when and where; and he shall show the quantities disposed of, and to whom, and at what prices; so that his slop-account will show the articles, prices, and amount, received and disposed of.

4. On the death or removal of a purser, the commanding officer will cause a regular survey to be made on the slops remaining on hand, and an inventory thereof to be made out and signed by at least two commissioned officers.

5. Seamen, destitute of necessaries, may be supplied with slops by an order from the captain, after the vessel has commenced her voyage.

6. None are to receive a second supply until they have served two full months, and then not exceeding half their pay, and in the same proportion for every two months, if they shall be in want.

7. Slops are to be issued out publicly and in the presence of an officer, who is to be appointed by the captain, to see the articles delivered to the seamen and others, and the receipts given for the same, which he is also to certify.

8. The captain is to oblige those who are ragged, or want bedding, to receive such necessaries as they stand in need of.

9. The captain is to sign the slop-book before the ship is paid off; or, on his removal from the ship at any time, the purser is to send the same to the proper accounting officer, duly signed.

10. On the discharge of a man by ticket, the value of the clothes he has been supplied with, must be noted on the same in words at length.

11. If necessity requires the buying of clothes in foreign parts, the captain must cause them to be procured of the kinds prescribed for the navy, and as moderate as possible: he must also, by the first opportunity, cause an invoice of the same to be forwarded to the navy department.

Courts Martial.

All courts martial are to be held, offences tried, sentences pronounced, and execution of such sentences done, agreeably to the articles and orders contained in an act of Congress, made on the 23d of April, in the year 1800, entitled, "An act for the better government of the navy of the United States."

Courts martial may be convened as often as the President of the United States, the secretary of the navy, or commander in chief of a fleet, or commander of a squadron, while acting out of the United States, shall deem it necessary.

3. All complaints are to be made in writing, in which are to be set forth the facts, time, place, and the manner how they were committed.

4. The judge advocate is to examine witnesses upon oath, and by order of the commander in chief, or, in his absence, of the president of the court, to send an attested copy of the charge to the party accused, in time to admit his preparing his defense.

5. In all cases, the youngest member must vote first, and so proceed up to the president.

Convoys.

1. A commander of a squadron, or commander of a ship appointed to convoy the trade of the United States, must give necessary and proper instructions in writing, and signed by himself, to all the masters of merchant ships and vessels under his protection.

2. He is to take an exact list, in proper form, containing the names of

all the ships and vessels under his convoy, and send a copy thereof to the navy department before he sails.

3. He is not, in time of actual war, to chase out of sight of his convoy, but be watchful to defend them from attack or surprise; and if distressed, to afford them all necessary assistance. He is to extend the same protection to his convoy when the United States are not engaged in war.

4. If the master of a ship shall misbehave, by delaying the convoy, abandoning, or disobeying the established instructions, the commander is to report him, with a narrative of the facts, to the secretary of the navy, by the first opportunity.

5. The commander is to carry a top-light in the night, to prevent separation, unless, on particular occasions, he may deem it improper.

6. He may order his signals to be repeated by as many ships of war under his command, as he may think fit.

7. When different convoys set sail at the same time, or join at sea, they are to keep together so long as their courses lie together: when it thus happens, the eldest commander of a convoy shall command in the first post; the next eldest, in the second; and so on according to seniority.

8. Commanders of different convoys are to wear the lights of their respective posts, and repeat the signals, in order, as is usual to flag-officers.

9. Convoys are to sail like divisions, and proper signals to be made at separation.

The President of the United States of America, ordains and directs the commanders of squadrons, and all captains and other officers in the navy of the United States to execute, and cause to be executed, the aforesaid regulations.

By command, Secretary of the Navy.
Source: *Naval Regulations Issued by Command of the President of the United States of America* (Washington, D.C.: Printed for the Navy Office, 1814).

BIBLIOGRAPHY

Alison, Sir A. History of Europe Ninth edition. 20 volumes. London, 1852.

Barnes, James. *Commodore Bainbridge.* (New York, N.Y.; D. Appleton and Company, 1908)

Barnes, James. *Naval Actions of The War of 1812.* New York: D. Appleton and Company, 1897.

Bobby-Evans, Alistor. "The Tripolitan War 1801-1805," 2001.

Boot, Max. *The Savage Wars of Peace.* New York: Basic Books. 2003.

Brown, Richard D., *Knowledge is Power.* New York: Oxford University Press, Inc., 1989.

Burnett, John S., *Dangerous Waters.,* New York: Plume, a member of Penguin Group (USA) Inc., 2003

Butler, Adjutant-General Robert. Official Report for the Morning of Jan. 8, 1815.

Castor, Henry. The Tripolitan War 1801-1805. Franklin Watts, In. New York, 1971.

Channing, Edward. The Jeffersonian System 1801-1811. Cooper Square Publishers, Inc. New York, 1968.

Chidsey, Donald Barr. *The Wars in Barbary: Arab Piracy and the Birth of the United States Navy.* New York: Crown, 1971.

Codrington, Admiral Sir Edward. Memoir of, by Lady Bourchier. London, 1873.

Cole, John William. Memoirs of British Generals Distinguished during the Peninsular War. London, 1856.

Cornell, Jimmy., *World Cruising Routes.,* Camden, Maine: International Marine., 1987.

Dearborn, H. A. S. *The Life of William Bainbridge, Esq..* (Princeton, N.J.; Princeton University Press, 1931)

Dearborn, H. A. S. *The Life of William Bainbridge, Esq..* (Princeton, N.J.; Princeton University Press, 1931)

Dinnerstein, Leonard and Kenneth T. Jackson., *American Vistas.* New York: Oxford University Press, Inc., 1971.

Dooley, Patricia., *The Early Republic.*, Westport, CT: Greenwood Publishing Group., 2004.

Garraty, John A. and Mark C. Carnes, editors., *American National Biography.*, New York: Oxford University Press, 1999.

Gleig, Ensign H. R. Narrative of the Campaigns of the British Army at Washington, Baltimore, and New Orleans. Philadelphia, 1821.

Harris, Thomas M.D. *William Bainbridge, United States Navy.* Philadelphia: Carey Lea & Blanchard, 1837.

Harris, Thomas, M.D. *The Life and Services of Commodore William Bainbridge.* (Philadelphia, Penn.; Carey Lea & Blanchard, 1837)

Hunt, Gaillard., *Life in America One Hundred Years Ago.*, New York: Harper & Brothers., 1914.

Irwin, Ray W. (1970). The Diplomatic Relations of the United States With the Barbary Powers 1776-1816. Russel & Russel. New York.

Jackson, Andrew. As a Public Man. A sketch by W. G. Sumner. Boston, 1882.

James, William. Military Occurrences of the Late War. 2 vols. London, 1818.

James, William. *Naval Occurrences of the Late War.* T. Egerton, Whitehall., 1817.

Keane, Major-General John. Letter, December 26, 1814.

Ketchum, Richard M., *Divided Loyalties.* New York: Henry Holt and Company, LLC., 2002.

Kitzen, Michael L. S. *Tripoli and the United States at War: A History of American Relations with the Barbary States: 1785–1805.*

Lake, Thomas T. *Early American Manual Therapy, Version 5.0:* Compiled, 1946.

Lambert, General. Letters, January 10 and 28, 1815.

Latour, Major A. Lacarriex. Historical Memoir of the War in West Florida and Louisiana. Translated from the French by H. P. Nugent. Philadelphia, 1816.

London, Joshua E. *Victory in Tripoli: How America's War with the Barbary Pirates Established the U.S. Navy and Shaped a Nation* New Jersey: John Wiley & Sons, Inc., 2005.

Long, David F. *Ready to Hazard: A Biography of Commodore William Bainbridge, 1774-1833*. (Hanover, N.H.: University Press of New England, 1981)

Lossing, Benson J. Field-Book of the War of 1812. New

Lossing, Benson J., *Pictorial Field-Book of the War of 1912*. New York: Harper & Brothers., 1896

Malone, Dumas. Jefferson and the Rights of Man. Little, Brown and Company. Boston, 1951.

Malone, Dumas. Jefferson the President First Term 1801-1805. Little, Brown and Company. Boston,1970.

Nash, Howard Pervear. *The Forgotten Wars: The Role of the U.S. Navy in the Quasi War with and the Barbary Wars 1798–1805*. South Brunswick, N.J.: A. S. Barnes, 1968.

Patterson, Com. Daniel G. Letters, December, 1814, and

Peninsula. 5 vols. New York, 1882.

Philbrick, Nathaniel., *Sea of Glory*. New York: Viking Penguin a member of Penguin Group (USA) Inc., 2003.

Pike, John. "Barbary Wars". http://www.fas.org/man/dod-101/ops/barbary.htm. York, 1859.

Preston, Wheeler., *American Biographies.*, New York: Harper & Brothers Publishers, 1940.

Rohbrough, Malcolm., *The Land Office Business*. New York: Oxford University Press, Inc., 1968.

Scott, Lieut. -Gen. W. Memoirs, by himself. 2 volumes New

Thornton, Col. W. Letter, Jan. 8, 1815.

Toll, Ian W., *Six Frigates.*, New York: W.W. Norton., 2006.

Tucker, Glenn. *Dawn Like Thunder: The Barbary Wars and the Birth of the U.S. Navy*. Indianapolis, Ind.: Bobbs-Merrill, 1963.

Williams, Thomas, *America's First Flag Officer*. Bloomington, IN: AuthorHouse, 2008.

Wilson, James Grant, Jon Fiske editors. *Appleton's Cyclopaedia of American Biography.*, New York: D. Appleton & Co., 1888-1889.

CPSIA information can be obtained
at www.ICGtesting.com
Printed in the USA
BVHW031038050223
657905BV00005B/33